DESPERATE GAMBLE

"Comrade Trey!" ordered Comrade Vanov. "I want a bridge crew to replace these mercenaries as soon as they can board." Lily did not move, except to turn her head enough to see the Mule. It sat quite still at the nav console, one hand covering the other.

Vanov, too, glanced that way. "Turn the nav console off," he ordered. The soldier stationed by navigation reached out and flipped the auto nav to manual.

"Comrade Vanov!" called a soldier. "They're still running nav!"

"That's impossible," broke in Comrade Trey. "You can't run vectors on manual."

In two strides Vanov closed the distance between himself and Lily, and wrenched her arm up behind her back. She began to twist away.

Vanov pressed the muzzle of his pistol against Lily's ear. "Take this ship off nav!" he snapped.

Lily caught Hawk's gaze with hers and blinked twice, deliberately. The pistol against her head smelled of cold, unfeeling steel.

"Five seventy-two," hissed the Mule. *"Break!"*

They went through the void just as Vanov pulled the trigger.

Ask your bookseller for the Bantam Spectra titles you have missed:

THE HIGHROAD TRILOGY

Volume Three:

The Price of Ransom

******

by Alis A. Rasmussen

BANTAM BOOKS
NEW YORK · TORONTO · LONDON · SYDNEY · AUCKLAND

THE PRICE OF RANSOM
A Bantam Spectra Book / October 1990

ISBN 0-553-28788-5

Published simultaneously in the United States and Canada

Bantam Books are published by Bantam Books, a division of Bantam Doubleday
Dell Publishing Group, Inc. Its trademark, consisting of the words "Bantam
Books" and the portrayal of a rooster, is Registered in U.S. Patent and
Trademark Office and in other countries. Marca Registrada. Bantam Books,
666 Fifth Avenue, New York, New York 10103.

PRINTED IN THE UNITED STATES OF AMERICA

OPM   0 9 8 7 6 5 4 3 2 1

*This book is affectionately dedicated to
Rhiannon,
for being patient as well as inspiring,
and to
Alexander and David,
who were the reason that writing it was so interesting.*

Acknowledgments

I could not have completed this book without the support of many people, some of whom are listed below. Many many thanks are due them.

To Betsy Mitchell and Team Spectra, for their patience and their belief that I would actually finish book three:

To my parents, Gerald and Sigrid Rasmussen, for all the hours they invested, and to my siblings, for entertaining me on the phone and remaining positive:

To my in-laws, Ruth and Milt Silverstein, for like reasons:

To Brandon and Dianne, and Kit and Howard, for bringing us dinner:

To Dr. Karen Urbani, for taking such good care of the boys:

To Carol Wolf, for comments and typing and all-around egging me on:

To Raven Gildea, Katharine Kerr, Jane Butler, Judith Tarr, and the Whensday People—Teresa, Ellen, Dani, Joy, Kevin, Mike, Bob, Kim, Dean, Delores, and Beth—for valuable feedback, without which it would not have been nearly so coherent:

And finally, to my husband, Jay, who bore up pretty well, infant twins, two-year-old, and all.

Will ye gang tae the Hielands, my bonnie, bonnie lass?
Will ye gang tae the Hielands wi' Geordie?
And I'll tak' the high road, and ye'll tak' the low,
And I'll be in the Hielands afore ye.

—Traditional

The Price of
Ransom

1 In Another Part of the Forest

****

The poisoned atmosphere swirled past Korey's clear face mask. As he topped the rise, stumbling on loose rocks, he saw through a gap in the mist the writhing form of the alien.

No way to sneak up on it. The bastard had chosen this terrain for its lack of cover—if it could even think tactically. And without Fred and Stanford—but he couldn't bear thinking about what had happened to them. Just kill it, before it killed him and consummated its horrible rite, and be done. Revenge could come later.

The woman, tied to a stake well within reach of the alien's lashing tentacles, had lost most of her clothing, and the tatters left revealed the rich curves of her pale flesh. Seeing him emerge out of the fog, she began to fight frantically against the cord binding her to the stake, trying to free herself. Her struggling caused the last remnants of her clothes to rip and, shredding, be torn off of her in the rough wind, leaving her naked. The alien slithered closer.

He drew his knife and charged.

The first tentacle he dodged, but the second whipped across his chest, throwing him down. He stabbed at it, gouging a rent across the putrid skin. Gouts of acidic fluid spattered his face. It burned, eating into his skin, slowing him. A second tentacle wrapped around his leg. He slashed at it, but another grabbed him, and another, until at last even his knife arm was pinned to his side. All he could hear were the woman's cries as the alien's maw, rimmed with red, gaping suckers, lowered toward him and attached itself with viscous strength to his blistering face.

"I lost again!" Korey screamed, but the shudder that ran through him as he woke from the dream was not part of his nightmare.

A blow cracked the door to his hostel unit. Before he could even swing his legs off of the liquor-stained couch, the plasboard splintered and separated and two constables broke through the opening. Both had their power-spiked batons out and at the ready.

"Korrigan Tel Windsor?" An electronic shield masked the man's real voice.

Still muzzy from the aftereffects of the dream, Korey could only press the heel of one palm to his forehead and grunt an affirmative. His other hand reached to grope under the pillows of the couch.

"Both hands where we can see them," snapped the second constable, a woman.

Both constables tensed and crouched as Korey pulled out a cylindrical vessel, but he merely flipped off the top and took a deep draught of whiskey from a grimy glass bottle.

"That's disgusting," muttered the woman.

"Korrigan Tel Windsor," began the man again, ignoring his colleague's comment, "you are under arrest for illegal possession of the drug Asperia chronofoam. Dream crystal. You have the right to remain silent—"

"I would suggest," broke in a low, gravelly—and distinctly nonhuman—voice from the third door, "that you switch off those enhanced batons of yours and we discuss this like civilized beings."

"Oh, piss it, Berto," swore the woman, turning to see a squat, simianlike creature appear in the doorway. "Xiao swore top to bottom that the Pongos were gone. I'll have his ass for this."

Berto swung slowly around.

"Drop the rods." This was a second voice, lower and rougher than the first.

Faced with a primitive, but clearly operative, double-barreled shotgun held in the powerful hands of the second simian, both constables carefully set down their batons, the only weapons they were armed with.

Hands shaking, Korey took another slug of whiskey. "Fred," he said after a moment to the one holding the shotgun. His voice was still hoarse from dream crystal. "Let's not have any trouble. I can't afford to lose my license."

Fred hesitated, regarding the constables with deep suspicion.

"Really, Frederick," said the first simian. He was as alike in build as a twin, but leaner in his hairy face. "I cannot understand why you continue to prefer that outmoded piece of hardware when we have sufficiently modern weapons available."

"Yeah, Stan," agreed Fred, "but they ain't got the kick this one's got." He set down the shotgun and shoved it away with a hairy three-toed, one-thumbed foot.

The constables retrieved their batons.

"According to our warrant," said Berto, unclipping a thin computer slate from his vest, "your bounty license is suspended until such time as you appear before the tribunal at League headquarters on Concord."

"Son of a bitch." Korey took another drink from the bottle.

"Frederick," interposed Stanford as Fred reached for the shotgun. "Korrigan, I will call your advocate."

"Sure, sure," mumbled Korey, but Stanford had already disappeared into the back room. He glanced up at the masks that disguised the features of the two constables. "So what's the real charge, or are you chumps just the errand kids?"

At a nod from Berto, the woman picked up the shotgun and followed Stanford into the back room. Fred lingered, undecided and a little confused, on the threshold.

Berto peeled aside the mask to reveal dark features and unexpectedly cheerful eyes. "Buddy," he said, his voice abruptly normal now that it was removed from the electronic overlay, "some people hold it against you for what you did in the war, but I say we couldn't have won without your kind."

"Thank you."

"Anyway," Berto continued, evidently missing Korey's sarcasm, "I just bring in the warrants, and I've got six constables outside in case you give us any trouble. But I will tell you this. There's a one-way ticket for you and the Pongos down at precinct, and it's for Concord, so I guess that's where you're going, whether you want to or not."

"Don't call them 'Pongos,'" said Korey wearily. He ran a hand through his brown hair. It looked like it needed to be washed.

"Yeah," agreed Fred belligerently. "It ain't nice, calling us names."

"Which reminds me," added Berto, unfazed by this rejoinder, "their visas *are* up to date, aren't they?"

Korey lifted the whiskey to his lips, hesitated, and with a sigh lowered the bottle and capped it. He rose. He was not a particularly tall man, but he was compact with a strength that

the seediness of his surroundings and the general air of
dissipation and odor of alcohol and drugs could not completely
mask. The constable kept his baton raised.

"Just going to pack a carry," said Korey, mocking the man's
caution. Fred pulled back his lips in a parody of a human
grin. "Get on, Fred. Get your stuff together."

Berto pulled his mask back over his face, hiding his features.

Stanford emerged from the back room, followed by the
other constable. "Unfortunately, Korrigan, your advocate has
already been contacted by Concord Intelligence about the
matter. She says her hands are tied."

"Am I surprised," murmured Korey cynically, without making it a question. "Hustle up. Let's get it over with."

It was the matter of a few minutes to pack three carrys, and
then the two constables ushered them outside. With the
other six officers added on, they made a procession that
enlivened the interest of all the residents of the rundown
hostel. When the party paused in the lobby for Berto to clear
Korey's bill with the manager, a small crowd of disreputable-
looking folk gathered to stare and comment.

"Izzat the bountyman?"

"Yeh. Pretty brave of them connies to bring him in."

"Who do ya s'pose he were hunting?"

"Dunno."

"Clean's the place up, though, don't it? Getting rid of him,
and those Pongos. I don't like bounty men."

"What, you afraid one's looking for you, Ferni?"

A general swell of raucous laughter greeted this sally, made
bolder by Korey's lack of response.

"Nah. Ferni ain't dangerous enough to be passed over to
the bounty list by the connies."

"Am so."

"Shut up," snapped Berto as he stepped back from the
desk. "Or we'll do a proper raid here one of these days. I can
smell dream crystal on every one of you. Now piss off."

The crowd dissipated abruptly. "Thanks," murmured Korey
laconically. Looking disgusted, Berto motioned, and the constables led their charges down the entry stairs.

"I dislike this," said Stanford, subvocalizing to Fred as they
marched down and then were settled in the back compartment of the secure wagon that would ferry them to the
precinct office. Korey sat at the opposite end of the compart-

ment, eyes shut, face pale under several days' growth of
beard.

"Yeah," agreed Fred, tapping his stubby foot claws against
the floor. "It sucks."

"No, Frederick. I mean that I am deeply disturbed by
Korrigan's meekness. It is simply too much at odds with his
character. I fear that this current binge of drug taking masks
some severe form of depression that has overtaken him
recently. I advised him before that bounty work was not
suited to his talents."

They both turned to gaze at their companion, concern clear
on their apelike features. Fred wrinkled up his nose, taking
in the unpleasant antiseptic stench of the compartment, their
own pleasant and familiar scent, and the stronger smell—to
him, at least—of Korey's unwashed clothing and skin.

"Yeah." Fred shrugged his powerful shoulders, his equivalent of a nod.

Korey opened his eyes, looking directly at them, and with
the barest grin, he winked.

It took a ship's week to reach Concord, the web of interlinked
stations in orbit around a nondescript star whose only claim
to importance was its position in the approximate center of
League space.

Stanford and Fred hogged the bubble viewport in the
transport bringing them into docking with Intelligence's hub.
Behind them Korey slept, snoring softly. If he looked better
than the day he was arrested it was probably because the
drugs and whiskey he had tried to smuggle along in his carry
had been confiscated at the precinct office.

Fred simply gaped at the view: a complex net of stations
and connecting tubes and solar arrays and ships in various
stages of repair, manufacture, or loading that, in the reflected
light of its sun, presented an astonishingly intricate and
beautiful pattern against the deep night of space.

Stanford had his computer slate out and was busy calculating stresses, area to volume, and mass while on a second
window he sketched out as complete a diagram of the web as
possible, labeling it as he went.

The light chime warned them just as the door to their cell
slipped aside. Fred whirled into an aggressive stance: hind
legs bent, he leaned heavily on his thick, long arms, ready to

propel himself forward. Because he was just about as thick as he was tall, the effect was intimidating.

Korey opened his eyes, although he did not move from his pallet, and glanced at the two guards who had just taken three steps back from the threshold.

"Fred," he said quietly. "Lighten up."

Fred rocked back onto his haunches, grinning again; Stanford had already taken the opportunity to surreptitiously tuck his slate back into the sling on his chest in which he usually carried his weapons.

"Get up, Windsor," snapped the foremost guard. "We're taking you off the ship in a flyer. The two Pongos stay on board."

Korey laughed, short, and settled his hands behind his head, looking comfortable. "Someone afraid we'll go on a rampage if we set foot in the happy zones?"

"You must be aware," replied the guard stiffly, "that your record of the past fifty years does not give the common run of humanity any reason to trust you."

Korey rolled smoothly up to his feet. "Listen, I didn't come here for a morality lecture. I'm ready to go." As he spoke he made a few quick gestures with one hand, sign language to his two companions. Fred rubbed vigorously at one shoulder, cursed abruptly, and with surprising delicacy removed a tiny insect from his long, dark hair and popped it in his mouth, smacking his lips.

"Move it," said the guard, unable to hide his disgust.

Korey grinned and followed him.

The ride to the station was uneventful.

Several elevators took him, escorted by a shifting company of eight to ten guards, to some undetermined level of the Intelligence complex. He was shown into a small, square room and left alone.

He paced it quickly, measuring, and then sprawled himself untidily in its single uncomfortable chair and waited. As he had expected, the lights dimmed around him, leaving him isolated in a spotlight of brightness, and the closest wall took on a translucent sheen to reveal three persons sitting at a console behind it.

"Korrigan Tel Windsor?" A man's voice, even and very deep.

He did not bother to answer.

"Are you aware that you have been arrested under League provision—"

"Let's dispense with the formalities," broke in a second voice, a woman. "I scarcely think we need bother to waste time on such as him."

"If we do not 'waste' time on such as him, my dear," replied the first man calmly, "then we cannot claim to be a free and equal society." He paused.

Her lack of reply was eloquence enough.

"You know I'm Windsor," said Korey, getting impatient with this. "I know what the charges are and if you can even make them stick the most they'll pull me is a fine. I want to know what monkey has suspended my bounty license and how the hell you expect to uphold that suspension in a court of law. That is," he added with a sardonic smile, "if people like me and what's left of 'my kind' are allowed access to the courts of law anymore."

"You see what I mean," muttered the woman. The second man, beside her, murmured something Korey could not make out, although its tone sounded like assent.

"I see no reason to continue fencing in this manner," said the first man, maintaining his calm. "The fact is that you possess that license on sufferance, not from any intrinsic right to hold it. You know as well as I that it can be revoked at any time."

Korey straightened in the chair, focusing his gaze on the man's shadowy form. "Maybe I didn't think it would come to this. I've been good. As good as I can be, I guess *you'd* say," he added, directing the comment to the woman, who sat in the center. "So maybe this isn't about me personally. Maybe the old man has been dead just long enough now that you figure his memory can't protect us anymore."

"Surely," interposed the second man—an impatient and slightly nervous voice, "surely you can't expect us to condone the life you and the other saboteurs that Soerensen—bless his memory—established, the life you led, the actions you took. Even Soerensen had to disavow some of the things you did."

"That's a lie," growled Korey. "He knew the stakes we were running. I don't claim we were angels, or even *civilized* like you folks—"

"And none of you," interrupted the woman sharply, "*None* of you *ever* did anything excessive?"

Korey was silent.

"My dear," said the first man reprovingly.

"We saved your asses from the Kapellans, and now all you intellectual types have gotten squeamish about the methods we had to use to do it. Why am I not surprised?"

No one answered him.

"So what do you want me for?" he asked finally, resigned.

"A simple trade," said the first man, still temperate. "You bring us in a few people, and we restore your license—*without* the revocation clause."

"What?" Korey retorted, disbelieving. "You want me to bring in the queen of the highroad, or something? It can't be done."

The first man chuckled. "We do not interfere with the privateers. No. Here is a display—some likenesses."

To the right of the three shadowed forms a console lit up, and eight faces appeared on a screen.

Korey stood up. "No!" He strode straight forward to the wall and slammed it with a closed fist. "I won't hunt my own down, you bastards."

"On the record," said the woman smugly, "it states that when you were first granted your license you agreed that if any saboteurs had broken codified law they would be an acceptable bounty. And you did bring in one ex-saboteur named Trueblood. Seventeen years ago."

"Trueblood deserved what he got. He went sour after the war ended, and no matter what you think, there weren't any of 'us' who condoned rape. We killed a guy once—a nice, respectable stationmaster—who we caught trying to do some poor underage Kapellan female who was a refugee from Betaos. Actually," he grinned, a predator's look, "*we* didn't kill him. We just got him drunk and convinced him to sleep with a sweet je'jiri girl, and let her clan do the rest."

So close to the glass, he could see their bodies react, if not their faces. The second man shuddered, obvious. The woman stiffened, tense and disapproving.

Only the first man remained unruffled. "I am relieved to hear that there is still honor, of a kind, among thieves. Shall we return to the screen? The alternative, you realize, is that you will be arrested under inter-League law as adopted at the Second Concordance Postwar Convention and immediately sentenced to life in the prison station here at Concord, from which, I might remind you, there have been no—and I mean zero—escapes since its installation."

"That's it, huh? What about my partners?"

"Their visas will be revoked, and they will, of course, be allowed passage to the nearest Ardakian embassy so that they can return to their home planet."

"And I'll bet you know damned well that they're not welcome there." Korey opened his fist, tapped his index finger twice on the shielding wall, and moved to get a better look at the screen.

Eight faces. He examined them one by one.

"Apple? He's dead. You're Intelligence. I thought you would know that." He chuckled, low. "Though it makes me feel better to know you didn't. Jewel. Can't help you there. She signed on with Yi about six years back and I'm not going to tangle with him."

"Ah," said the first man. The first two pictures flicked off into blackness.

"Eboi. I don't know what happened to him. He was as decent as they come, by any standard, and he must be going on old by now. If anyone deserves some peace, he does." He glanced back at them, scornful. "But I guess you just can't chance that he might have some latent savagery in him, can you? And you certainly won't trust my word." This said with mockery. "And who's this? Katajarenta?" He laughed, frankly amused. "You'll never find her." Dismissed her by moving on to the next photo. "Wing." He grinned again. "Serve you right to bring her in. She'd cut you to pieces just with her tongue." He shook his head briefly. "She disappeared a good twenty years ago."

"But," interrupted the woman, "she's always been closely linked with—"

"Gwyn?" exclaimed Korey, disbelieving. "You expect *me* to bring in *Gwyn*? You're crazy. Even if I could *find* him—"

"We have a less than two-year-old location on him," said the woman sharply. "He was last going under the name of Heredes."

"You're crazy," Korey repeated. "I'm not qualified. Nobody is. He's the best."

"If I may," interposed the first man smoothly. "I understood there was reason to believe that Gwyn was dead."

"Dead? Right, and I have four arms."

"I want it substantiated," said the woman in a voice made more cold by its implacability. "And everyone associated with him tracked down."

Korey glanced through the glass again, wishing he could make out her face. A tone in her voice caught at him, and he felt it important that he identify her. He shrugged and looked at the last two pictures. "Hawk? What's he doing here? He's in prison."

"Not anymore." Fury underlay the words. The woman turned her head to look at the screen, revealing in that movement the careful, traditional coiffure of her hair: it took him a moment, but then he identified it: Indian subcontinent, neo-Hindi. "He was last seen with Gwyn."

"Well, good for Hawk," muttered Korey under his breath. Louder, he said, "I don't recognize this last one. Never seen her before."

"She was also seen with Gwyn," explained the first man. "We suspect her to be a new recruit."

"Well, I never thought of Gwyn as a recruiter." He hesitated examining the six photos left and then his three inquisitors. "What's her name?"

"We believe it to be Heredes also. Lily Heredes."

"All right," said Korey, stepping back from the wall. "I'll bring her in. In trade for my license back."

"That wasn't the deal." The woman dismissed the suggestion with a brusque wave of her hand.

"Listen. I bring her in, she's got current information on Gwyn, and maybe on Hawk. You make a deal with her, and you won't be asking me to break old loyalties."

"He's got a point," said the second man.

"Anjahar!" snapped the woman. "Are you suggesting that we bargain with—with *this*?"

"My dear—"

"No," broke in Korey. "He seems to be suggesting that revolutionary notion that we saboteurs might yet have some semblance of human loyalty. I know you're ready to lock what's left of us in the zoo and let the kids come down on the holidays to get a gaze at the old throwbacks to the days when we'd just as soon rip each other's throats out as rip out the throat of the local rabbits for food, but hell, even back then before fire was invented we ran in packs. So don't push me."

The woman rose from behind the console. "You've got no ground on which to threaten me."

"My dear." The first man's voice had not lost its evenness, but it was firm. She did not sit down, but she stopped speaking. "Agreed," he said, looking back at Korey. "Bring in Lily Heredes, and we'll restore your license."

"Without the revocation clause?"

"Agreed as well. You're a good bounty man, Windsor. We'd hate to lose you."

"I'll just bet you would," muttered Korey. "You don't find many people these days willing to track out into The Pale. So where do I find her?"

"You'll start by going to Diomede."

"It is The Pale, then."

It might have been his imagination, but through the shadowy glass he thought he saw the man smile. "No. It's a little farther out than that."

After the guards had removed the prisoner, the three agents sat in silence for only a few moments before the woman turned, abruptly and with anger, on the first man.

"I can't *believe* you bargained with *him* like that."

"Maria, my dear, we *are* civilized human beings. I hope. And he is, I think, also human." His tone was gently reproving.

"Yevgeny, that we approved cruelty, violence, and aberrant behavior in our long and frequently sordid history does not mean we should continue to tolerate those in our midst who are—as Windsor himself quite rightly put it—throwbacks to the very worst in human nature."

"I think you exaggerate, Maria." Yevgeny tapped his vest slate, reading the time display, and rose. "I have an appointment. We'll meet again next week?"

She nodded, curt, but respectful. But as the door slipped closed behind him, she turned to her other companion. "Just think, Anjahar, the eight saboteurs on that screen are known to be collectively responsible for five thousand deaths. Officially recorded ones, that is."

"Maria," protested Anjahar, "you know I dislike them as much as you do, but after all, all but seven of those deaths were during the war. And most were Kapellan casualties."

"The war," she repeated sarcastically. "That excuses everything, doesn't it? And maybe, just maybe—although I'm still not convinced—that was the only way to free the League from the Empire. Or at least the most expedient one. But they're inured to killing now, to destruction, to that entire mind-set of using violence as a way to solve conflict. We might as well reinstate human sacrifice. I won't let that happen. I'll use every means I have to see that every last one of Soerensen's terrorists is put in prison."

"You're not going to get them *all* in prison," he replied, standing and going to the door. It slipped open. "Are you coming? I'm going to get something to eat."

Maria remained fixed in her place, staring at the chamber in which Korrigan Windsor, bounty hunter, hell-raiser, and former terrorist, had so recently walked. "Then they're better off dead."

"You really hate them, don't you?" He sounded surprised. "I dislike what they did as much as the next person, and I certainly want to make sure that their way of thinking is never again fostered in our children, but—you do seem rather vehement."

She did not reply immediately, as if she was considering whether or not to confide in him. After a bit he came back into the room and the motion of the doorway sliding shut behind him triggered something in her. She spoke in a low voice. "The saboteurs killed my sister."

"*Killed* her? I'm—I'm sorry, Maria. Was it at Chaldee? That's the only place I know of that civilians died."

"Besides nonhuman civilians? Who don't count? No. She was seduced into joining them. *She* was a saboteur. She disgraced our family. And now she's dead."

"I'm sorry," he repeated helplessly. "I didn't know."

"No one does. My family disowned her, and we never spoke of her again. But I loved her. I'll never forgive them for her death." Then, as if this admission ended the conversation, she rose and went to the door, waiting as it opened. "Dinner sounds good," she said in an entirely different voice, casual and pleasant. "How about Stripe's cousin's place, over at Benthic Nexus? She does those great Ridani pastries, dappling tarts."

The door, unbidden, sighed shut behind them as they left. On the screen, the remaining pictures flicked off, one by one, into blackness.

2 Forsaken

****

The corridors of the *Forlorn Hope* held a luminescence that fascinated Gregori. Dimmed down, the lights revealed intricate, textured shadings on the walls that seemed endlessly interesting to him. He could follow them for hours, aimlessly, or hide in the shadows to listen to the impassioned conversations that brightened the half-lit mess hall or the high banks of Engineering. The only place he never went was the Green Room—that impenetrable mass of growing things—because it scared him.

Sometimes he even managed to slip unseen onto the bridge, dimmed now like every place else. He would stand in the darkest, most obscure corner and stare at the captain where she sat brooding at the captain's console, ensconced in a deep-backed chair, the miraculous Bach hovering at her side. It seemed she spent most of her time here the past few days, while they had been drifting in some forgotten tag-end of space; just sitting, staring at the screen of space and stars and one distant sun, a suggestion of brilliance at the edge of the screen.

The dimness lent her pale skin a luminescence that reminded him of the corridors of the ship, as if she were slowly taking in the essence and reflecting it back. As if she were becoming part of the ship in the same way he often felt he was: knowing it too well, so that eventually one's own self could no longer be separated from the self, the *substance*, of the *Forlorn Hope*.

He knew that she knew that he was there, hiding in the shadows. The others—most of them—often forgot he existed, or ignored him, but she was always aware of him, at least when he was on the bridge. That she allowed him to stay, or at least did not care if he did, when others might have chased him off, had long since become one of the reasons he admired her with the kind of fierce, proud admiration that only the very solitary can develop.

But this time there was someone else on the bridge, one of the technicians, busy at a console and oblivious to his silent presence, but the tech's very shuffling and breathing obliterated the mood of communion he felt had grown in those quiet times he shared with the captain on the bridge: she brooding over their troubles, he absorbing the force of her concentration.

So he turned and slipped out again and padded by back ways and circuitous routes through the darkened corridors to the mess hall. With power shut down to one-third, it had become the central meeting place and general living area for the crew, and it was here that he found his mother.

She drew a seat in beside her so that he could sit down, and he did, not wishing to offend her. As usual, the table was too crowded for his tastes—he long since having learned to prefer an empty cubicle or the secret interstices that others passed by. There were six people, and all of them talking, loudly and without any order whatsoever. When the captain presided over a discussion, people never spoke loudly or out of turn.

"But we've been drifting on the edge of this system for three days now, on cut power, cut rations—not to mention the casualties still in Medical who as far as I know are on cut drugs and bandages."

This was Finch, whose voice, in Gregori's opinion, always got a little grating when he was agitated.

"The casualties in Medical are the least of *my* worries," countered Yehoshua. Somehow he always remained calm when emotions rose to their highest. "Whatever other problems or reservations we might have about Hawk, he's the best doctor I've seen work. But we have twelve people on this ship—not counting the casualties who couldn't be moved, of course—who stayed with us after the mutiny, and their loyalty is not ultimately to the captain but to whatever opportunity she represents, and eventually they're going to get tired of being refugees and want some tangible proof of that opportunity."

"And how are they going to get it," Finch demanded, "when we're stuck in this system because we don't have enough power and basic supplies to leave?"

"Enough to leave," interposed the Mule fluidly, "but certainly not enough to assay this fabled 'way' to the old worlds, where presumably opportunity lies."

The Mule's comment brought silence. Gregori squirmed

restlessly in his chair. Past the tables, he could see the
opening through which food was served from galley to mess.
In the half-darkness of the galley itself he made out Aliasing's
insubstantial form busy at some task. Normally she would
have been out here, sitting beside his mother, contributing
now and again to the conversation. But lately, ever since the
mutiny, she had kept to herself, as if she were avoiding his
mother, even Gregori himself. Some other concern seemed
to be preoccupying her, and while it hurt him that she now
had little more than an absentminded pat for him when he
wandered in to the galley to beg a scrap of sweet between
meals, he had long-since developed an ability to hide his
feelings, even from his mother.

He sighed, swinging his legs in the gap between the seat of
his chair and the floor.

"I still don't see that we have any choice but to sell our
services," said Pinto, breaking the silence. He sounded a
little defensive, which to Gregori at least lent his statement
interest. "We can transport cargo—"

"Without permits?" asked Yehoshua.

Pinto dismissed the caveat with a negatory sweep of one
hand. "What permits? Central's authority is gone. I doubt the
new government has had time to institute their policies in
such detail, and certainly not out this far on the fringe. I'm
sure these systems need some quick and reliable transports."

"Hold on." Jenny shook her head. "That's all very well, and
probably true, but the incoming comm-traffic we've picked
up indicates that Forsaken is still under the authority of
Central's troops."

"Or what's left of them out there," added Yehoshua. "Jehane's
people will be out eventually to mop them up."

"And we'd better be out of here before they get here,"
Finch snapped. "We can't hare off doing merchant's work. It
locks us onto roads that will leave us vulnerable to Jehane's
fleet. We've got to reprovision, refuel, dump the casualties
who don't want to stay with the ship on the nearest Station
hospital, and run. That's our only chance."

"Which brings us back around to the original question,"
added Yehoshua drily. "How do we resupply without any
means to pay for it?"

Another pause. Finch shifted restlessly in his seat, lancing
a brief, resentful glare at the two Ridanis—Pinto and Paisley—
who sat opposite him. Gregori looked up at his mother, but

her attention had drifted toward the galley. He could only see her profile, but her expression as she watched the obscure shape of Lia moving along a shadowed counter disturbed him with feelings he had no name for.

"Sell the Hierakas Formula," muttered Finch with a multinous glance at Paisley. "For supplies."

Paisley responded by pushing up instantaneously to her feet. "Never! Min Ransome shan't *never* sell ya Formula. It be ya wrong, min Finch, never you mind what you think, and it would be ya sore kinnas to insult ya memory of ya man as died to see it made free for all to have."

"Then can you suggest what else we have to trade?" Finch shot back, undaunted by her fierce gaze. "Or perhaps you and min Pinto would volunteer to sell your—ah—services to the curious planetside."

Pinto jumped up.

"Finch!" Jenny snapped, rising as well at the same time as she reached out to forestall Pinto from punching Finch in the face. "That remark was totally uncalled for. Pinto, sit down."

Pinto did not sit down. Gaze still fixed on Finch, he answered Jenny. "You can't expect me to just let that go."

"Yes, I can," demurred Jenny. "And I do. We have more serious problems to consider." She applied a slight, but firm pressure on his arm and he sat, much unwilling. Letting go of him, she turned to smile coldly at Finch. "And perhaps an apology would be in order?"

Finch glowered at the tabletop, looking not quite as sullen as Pinto.

Paisley laughed. "Hurts, don't it?" she said, but not in any triumphant way. "But it be sure I were already volunteered to sell my services, on Harsh, and it weren't no happy time for me, that be ya truth."

Finch glanced up at her, looking at last a little shamefaced. "I forgot about that," he mumbled. "I'm sorry." And looked down again.

Paisley sat.

"Thank you," said Jenny with a sigh. She and Yehoshua exchanged a glance fraught with long-suffering complicity.

"But it still doesn't answer," Finch muttered, unrepentant, "what we're going to use to pay for supplies. We've only got two shuttles left, since we sent Machiko and his people off in the other one, so we can't afford to lose one of those. And certainly none of us has any legitimate credit anymore, with or without clips to link into the bank net. I just don't see what choice we have but to sell the Hierakas Formula. And I *know,*" he added with a swift glance to mollify Paisley, "how Lily—how the captain—feels about it being accessible to every citizen of Reft space."

"I don't suppose that it's occurred to any of you," said Jenny softly, "that with a warship of this class, and a decent contingent of mercenaries, which we have, we don't *have* to pay. We can just take what we need."

Yehoshua smiled slightly. Gregori stopped fidgeting. For once, Finch looked as righteously shocked as Paisley, and they began to protest vocally at the same moment, halting in confusion at the other's words.

The Mule hissed, long and sharp. "That would be immoral," it said. "And perfectly human of you. I will have no part in such an enterprise."

"And in any case," Pinto pointed out, "the people on Forsaken have never done anything to us."

Jenny grinned, glancing at Yehoshua again. "But if they had, it would be all right to take what we need by force?"

"B'ain't *never* right," exclaimed Paisley.

"Do you expect me to believe," asked Finch, "that you, or any other tattoos—Ridanis—never stole from the people who weren't Ridanis while you lived on Station? It's common knowledge that it's all right for Ridanis to steal from people who aren't tattooed, just not from each other."

"Sure it be ya common knowledge," replied Paisley scornfully, "cause it be ya easier to believe ya worst o' us than ya truth. That way it be less burdensome to treat us so bad."

Finch blushed. It was a little hard to see, because of the duskiness of his skin, but the tightening of his mouth added to his expression of discomfiture.

Yehoshua chuckled. "Hoisted you with that one, comrade."

Finch shoved back his chair and without a word stood up and stalked out of the mess.

Paisley rose as well, looking abruptly worried, but Jenny caught her eye and shook her head. "Let him go, Paisley," she said. "It won't hurt him to dwell a little on his sufferings."

"But I didna' mean—" began Paisley.

"Paisley," interrupted Pinto. "I can't *begin* to understand how you can have any sympathy for that little bastard, considering how many times he's made it quite clear how he feels about us filthy tattoos."

"Because he's min Ransome's friend," said Paisley with
dignity, "and because it be ya wrong o' us to return prejudice
with hatred." She sat down, looking fierce and a little haughty.

Yehoshua applauded softly. Jenny smiled. The Mule said
nothing.

"That's fine," said Pinto, looking disgusted, "for people like
that writer, Pero, but look where he is now."

"Pinto! It be sore wrong o' you to speak such o' ya dead—"

Gregori slipped out from under his mother's careless touch
and off his chair and padded out of the room, leaving behind
what bid fair to develop into one of Paisley's full-blown
polemics. That she was the merest slip of a girl, scarcely
twice Gregori's age, seemed to amuse the others, but it
depressed him. It was one of the reasons he so rarely spoke
up. If they found her opinions, as passionate and generous as
they were, more delightful than provoking, and she so old as
sixteen, what then would they think of him, a thin sprite of
some seven ship's years, expressing the deep and private
thoughts that moved him to wander this ship? Paisley might
be oblivious, or immune, to their amusement, but he could
never be.

So he went to find the one person who always took him
quite seriously, and who never treated him like a child. He
went to Medical.

He checked the lab first, but the counters and console bays
where Hawk could often be found working were silent and
dark. Slipping past the Ridani guard who was always left as a
precaution at the Medical door, he padded into the main
ward.

Hawk's blue hair was harder to distinguish in the half light,
but still his figure was the first and most obvious one in the
large space. The broad flats of beds lay awash in light that,
although dimmed even here, seemed brilliant compared to
the severe rationing imposed on the rest of the ship. Hawk
moved with quiet grace from couch to couch, checking stats
and speaking briefly with each couch's occupant—those who
could speak.

Hawk's assistant trailed after him, a young Ridani woman
who had gotten medical technologist training when she had
joined Jehane's forces some four years back. To Gregori, it
seemed that Flower lived and walked in perpetual amazement that someone of Hawk's skill and experience would
treat her, tattoos and all, with respect. Pausing to watch her

as she bent over a patient, Hawk observing but not interfering, Gregori was not surprised that she and the other Ridanis had so readily defected to the mutiny.

"His signs look ya better," the assistant murmured. "But with ya trauma to ya head I just don't know if he'll ever regain consciousness."

Hawk laid a hand on the man's brow, a gesture that to Gregori's eye looked more like a benediction than one bearing any resemblance to the rude temperature-taking his mother caressed him with on those few occasions he had caught some illness.

Hawk removed his hand and shook his head. "This one has gone deep," he said softly. "I still can't predict if we'll be able to bring him back."

Flower stared raptly at him, admiring. He gave her a brief, if absentminded, smile and began to turn to the next couch.

Stopped. Paused, as if some unseen information had just come to him, and turned abruptly to gaze right at Gregori.

Gregori began to step forward.

And realized that someone else had come in behind, and that Hawk's attention had focused on this new arrival.

"Hollo, Gregori," said the captain casually as she walked past him.

Hawk moved obliviously past his assistant's admiration and went to meet her. He did not touch her, but the force of his attention was almost tactile, it was so strong.

"How are the casualties?" she asked, not so casually.

"Six are still in a coma, eight are at least partially conscious but seriously disabled, and the other nine you've seen in the convalescent ward. None of them are going to be active any time soon."

"Otherwise we would have shipped them off with Machiko. I know." She looked troubled. "Hoy. Good thing there were fourteen well enough to be moved."

"Seven of the convalescents could have gone but asked to stay," Hawk reminded her.

"Mostly because of you," she replied absently. The crease in her forehead that marked her brooding appeared as she spoke. Her eyes took in each still or restless patient in the ward, a concise survey, and she acknowledged Flower with a terse nod. "But too high a percentage of the power we're using is routed into Medical to sustain these people. We have to go in to Forsaken, and except for those who specifically asked to stay with us, I want the rest transferred to planetside hospitals."

"No," said Hawk. He paused to flick a glance at the Ridani woman. She coughed self-consciously and, picking up her com-clip, walked out into the convalescent's ward.

Gregori slunk into the shadows of a far corner.

"No," Hawk repeated. "Maybe some of these people won't recover, but none of them, even the ones who are recovering, will have anywhere near as good a chance for a normal recovery in Reft hospitals as on this ship."

"In your care," she echoed, sounding a little irritated. "Damn it, Kyosti. How much mercy can you expect this ship to extend to people who may never be able to give service in return?"

"Infinite mercy," he said sharply. "And infinite compassion. That's my business. You ought to understand why."

To Gregori's surprise, she did not argue but instead sighed and drifted across to gaze at the occupants of the couches, her expression a mask behind which Gregori could not discern her true feelings. Hawk did not follow her, except with his eyes.

"In any case," Hawk added after she had visited most of the couches, "the care these people will receive once we get back to League space will as far exceed what I can provide in this unit as this units exceeds Forsaken's hospitals."

"Kyosti, we don't have enough power to find our way by trial and error and what sketchy charts this boat has to League space."

"I'm not giving up my patients, Lily."

She turned and walked briskly to the door, her face still a mask. "I'll consider it," she said brusquely as the door sighed aside to reveal the corridor and the Ridani guard, "but I may have no choice."

And she was gone.

"Lily," Hawk began, sounding annoyed and imploring at the same time. He lifted a hand to his hair, pulling his fingers through the coarse strands with a movement more troubled than angry. After a moment he dropped his hand and abruptly swiveled to look directly at Gregori, who was still huddled in the corner.

Gregori emerged cautiously from the shadows.

Hawk smiled, a little wryly. "You don't need to look so apprehensive."

Gregori moved forward now to peer at the shifting stats at the base of one of the couches. "I'm not scared of you."

"Thank you," murmured Hawk with an irony that Gregori did not understand and so ignored.

"I just don't want you to think I'm a sneak."

"You're not a sneak, Gregori. You're just a solitary child."

And Gregori felt that with those words, their understanding was complete.

"Can we go run the topo...topograph program in the geography folder?"

"I'll bring it up for you," said Hawk, beginning to sound distracted again, "but I can't stay with you today."

Gregori sighed ostentatiously.

Hawk smiled and reached out to ruffle the boy's golden hair with surprising tenderness. "It's a hard and lonely way to grow up, Gregori. Just remember to be true to yourself."

Gregori looked up at him. "Can I try the advanced program again?"

Hawk chuckled. "Don't push your luck. Yes, you can. Come on."

Hawk followed her trail to the mess, but by the time he got there she had already left.

As had most of the others: Jenny lingered at a table, turning a ceramic mug slowly round and round with one hand as she waited for Lia to finish up in the galley.

She looked up as Hawk came over to her. "Eight-hour rest shift, and then we're going in."

"Going in?" He was distracted by the slow dissolution of Lily's scent on the air. The monotone whirring of the ventilation system hung like the merest whisper over the sounds of Lia busy at the counter.

"To Forsaken," answered Jenny.

The com chimed, and Finch's voice came over it, repeating what Jenny had just said.

"Ah," said Hawk. He nodded at her, still preoccupied, and moved away, continuing his hunt.

He ran her to ground in the captain's suite on gold deck. The outer room was empty but easily accessible; the door to the inner had a special lock that could only be keyed in to a single person, so he had to wait, and identify himself, before it slid aside to reveal the captain's most private sanctum.

For some reason the designers, or the original captain, had

chosen to make the room circular. The walls shone a burnished, deep gold, somehow inobtrusive, hiding closets, a terminal, and other arcana he did not know of. Two chairs, a dark wooden table—looking strangely primitive and yet complementing the tone of the walls—and a large bed completed the room.

Lily was lying on the bed, ankles crossed, head resting on her linked hands. Her black hair spilled out across the pale coverlet that draped the bed's surface. She was staring at the ceiling, and did not speak as Hawk entered and the door whispered shut behind him.

He prowled the room a moment, touching a closet pad so that the wall slipped aside to reveal empty cupboards and two plain white tunics hanging from a bar. Lily's scent had not yet permeated the chamber, but after three weeks it was beginning to. Machiko had not used this suite; perhaps he had found it too imposing, but in any case the only lingering aroma was of a woman, long dead, who smelled of a dry wit, deep cynicism, and unshakable courage. They lingered all over the ship, faint but unmistakable: the fragrance of the *Forlorn Hope*'s original crew, slowly being overlaid by its new inhabitants.

Hawk turned from the closet and went to the bed. He lay down on it, next to her, on his side, propping his head up on one hand. "Where is Bach?"

"On the bridge." She continued to stare at the ceiling.

He waited out her silence.

"Did you know," she began finally, "that the sta assigned to the ship with Machiko wouldn't let the Mule into navigation? Of course, they left with Machiko, but I suppose it's as well. I couldn't keep the Mule down on the lowest deck just to please their prejudices. And despite Jehane's"—her voice choked on the name momentarily—"avowed emancipation of the Ridanis, none of them were treated equally. It's no wonder they all sided with us when it came to mutiny. I was told that Jenny had to stop Rainbow from slugging some guy who had spit on her once. I'm amazed the *Hope* made it to Arcadia intact in the first place."

Because she seemed in the mood to talk, he kept silent.

"I've settled on a command structure," she continued. "I'm going to leave Jenny as Commander for the military unit, and move Yehoshua to First Officer, but there's no one on board who has the breadth of experience to be Second. And we've

got to start intensive training utilizing Bach's knowledge so
we have a complete set of shifts on the bridge and in
Engineering, at the least. With the seven convalescents
added to the able-bodied, we can *just* cover it. *If* we can get
them trained."

"What are we going to do when we get to Forsaken?"

"Distribute the Formula." She frowned and, finally, shifted
her head to look at him. "I'm going to invite what's left of
Central's forces to run with us."

"Are you really?" He grinned, quick and delighted with the
audacity of it.

"Short of force, it's the only way I can figure to get
supplied for that long trip given that we've got no credit to
buy with."

"Get in trade for a better future," he murmured. "I
wonder if it will work."

She shifted her legs on the bed, crossing her ankles in the
opposite direction. "Do you want to go back?" she asked,
softly.

"Lily, my heart," he said, as slow as it was deliberate. "I
don't care where I go, as long as—" He stopped and thought
better of revealing his hopes, and fears, too plainly to her.

But her gaze, on him, was clear and suddenly acutely
comprehensive. And without judgment against everything
that she knew he was. "No, I don't suppose you do." She
looked at him a moment longer before she sighed and turned
her head once more to stare up at the ceiling. "I'm not sure I
like this job," she muttered, sounding cross.

For a moment he was taken aback. Then he understood
that she meant, not him, but the job of being captain of the
Forlorn Hope.

She did not seem to need an answer, so he did not give her
one. He just lay, enjoying the intimacy of their mutual
silence. And in the slow seep of air through the vents, the
measured rise and fall of her respiration, and the complex
bouquet of her that he took in with each breath, he realized
that he was content. It was a feeling he had not known since
his childhood, before his mother and her clan had been
forced by every good reason—none of which he could blame
them for—to exile him to his father's kin.

She knew the truth, and she had not rejected him or used
it to control him.

He smiled. He thought of leaning across to kiss her, but

there was time enough for that. Patients who needed and benefited by his care awaited him in Medical. Next to him lay a woman who was perfectly happy and perfectly comfortable— and perfectly passionate, at the proper time—when she was with him.

He could not imagine any greater happiness.

3 Fount of Blood

****

They took their time, circling in, and broadcast their arrival across a wide band so as not to startle the undoubtedly nervous inhabitants of Forsaken and its twin orbiting Stations.

"I've got a go-ahead from Station Alpha for docking," said Finch at comm as they entered orbit.

"Start docking countdown," replied the captain, expressionless in her chair.

"Hold on." This from Yehoshua, on scan. "I thought there were only two military ships here. I've caught a third in Station Omega's shadow."

"Can you get readings?" Lily asked sharply. "Give me what you've got."

A pause while Yehoshua transferred coordinates.

"And we've got movement," he added suddenly. "I don't like this."

Lily cursed, hard and abrupt. "Weapons bank up," she snapped. "Full alert. That's the *Boukephalos*. Why didn't we pick up any comm-traffic from them?"

"They weren't broadcasting!" Finch protested. He paled, but quickly regained his color when it became apparent that the captain accepted his explanation.

"Weapons bank at full," said Nguyen from his console. "But I'm registering considerable power drain on our reserve power."

"We try to bluff," said Lily. "Open channels, Finch. I want a standard query to the *Boukephalos*."

"Hold on." Finch punched his channel focus and made adjustments. "I've got comm coming in. Switching to speaker."

"This is Comrade Vanov commanding the *Boukephalos*." The voice came loud and brassy. Finch hastily adjusted the volume. "We are in control of this system. You are in illegal possession of a government vessel. Surrender into our custody immediately."

"Vanov?" muttered Yehoshua. "I don't remember any Vanov."

It took Lily a moment, but as the silence lengthened—the *Boukephalos* waiting for a reply—she suddenly recalled a short, heavyset man with too-small eyes. "Hoy," she said in an undertone. "He's the one who killed Senator Isaiah and threw Robbie's body in the ocean."

"Killed who?" asked Pinto sharply, startling her because she had not thought he could hear so well, strapped into the pilot's console. Mercifully, Finch did not repeat her comment to him.

"We're down forty percent on weapons," said Nguyen from the bank. "At this rate we'll lose either our engines or the power to do any damage."

"Cut weapons to minimum coverage. Finch, tell Jenny to get her troops in gear for possible boarding."

"Another incoming," replied Finch.

"*Forlorn Hope*. If you do not reply to this broadcast, we will be forced to fire on you. Who is in charge?"

"Pinto, give us a course that will allow us to drift right under them without their being able to catch us. Mule, we need the nearest window. We're going to bluff and run. Finch, relay the message to the *Boukephalos* saying that we are prepared to surrender and asking for terms. Make it as long-winded as possible." She tapped the com for Engineering. "Blue. We're leaving the system. How much power do we have?"

"But Captain"—Blue's voice came back sounding nervous as well as tinny—"by my calculations we can only accommodate two vectors safely. And a third—I wouldn't risk it."

"Get us one now, Blue." She tapped off. "Pinto, Mule. Can you get us a vector that tight and unexpected? If it comes to a real chase, we can't outrun them." She fingered the com again, reaching her cabin. "Bach, I need you on the bridge." Flicked it over even before hearing the robot's whistled assent.

"I've got their conditions," said Finch. "Surrender of the vessel. The following persons to be taken into custody by Comrade Vanov: Lily Heredes, the physician Hawk, Eugenie Keos Amharat and her biological son Gregori, and Quincina Aliasing Feng. All other mutineers to be judged on a case-by-case basis. *Eugenie?* Is that Jenny? And Feng? Isn't Senator Feng the praetor of the Senate?"

"Finch."

He stopped talking.

"Any other condition?"

"Weren't those enough?" he asked testily.

"Captain," broke in Yehoshua, "I have a detach from the *Boukephalos*. A large shuttle, I believe."

"Course?"

"Looks like it's headed this way. I can't estimate intercept time yet. It's broadcasting on a scrambled code in our direction."

"If they fire on us, it'll be from the *Boukephalos*. And I don't believe they'd risk losing the *Hope* by breaching it. Keep monitoring them, Yehoshua." Lily studied the screen on her console arm. "Do we have a vector yet?"

"Two hours to the closest window," hissed the Mule, "but Station Omega is refusing us coordinates."

The bridge door swept aside and Bach floated in, singing a three-note query.

"Can you make do with Bach?"

The Mule glanced at her. Its crest raised, just enough that she thought it found the challenge amusing. "I can guarantee nothing."

"*I* can guarantee that Comrade Vanov is not a man we want to surrender to." Lily whistled a quick command to Bach, and the robot sped over to plug into the navigation console.

"Without Forsaken Station's coordinates, the risk to vector is great. Surrender is sometimes preferable to death."

"In this case," replied Lily, grim, "for most of us, I suspect surrender *is* death. I'll take the vector."

"Ah." The exclamation slipped smoothly from the Mule. It turned back to the console and began to calculate, Bach singing softly next to it.

Gregori had found a corner in Engineering where Blue would not stumble across him. Paisley knew he was there, of course, but Paisley understood him. And the technician who had stayed on after the mutiny was a quiet and dutiful worker, not one to question the movements of the ranking mercenary Commander's only son.

So the boy watched them at the great consoles that controlled the *Hope*'s engines. He didn't like Blue much, but he respected Blue's ability to understand engines. It seemed to

him little short of miraculous, considering Blue was so young
and so ill-tempered and touchy. He especially disliked the
way Blue treated Paisley: with a contempt tempered only by
the fact that he had no one with which to replace her.
Outside of Engineering, of course, Blue merely ignored her,
being smart enough to realize that more public derision
would not be well received by the captain. As far as Gregori
knew, Paisley had never complained. Her ability to brush off
Blue's scorn he found more miraculous than Blue's genius for
engines.

"What are you doing here?" Blue's harsh voice startled the
boy out of his reverie. "We've got an emergency. Now *get
out!*"

Gregori got. Paisley cast him a brief, taut smile as he
scuttled past her toward the door, but it was all she had time
for before Blue appeared, scolding her as well.

The door sighed shut behind Gregori, cutting off Blue's
words, and left him in the hush of iron deck corridors. It was
especially silent down here, because virtually no one except
the Engineering techs, and the occasional mercenary patrol-
ling the shuttle bays, ever came down this far. Even the
ghosts, who seemed to Gregori to haunt the ship's corridors,
were scarce here, finding more to occupy, and recall, higher
up.

When he saw a figure slip hurriedly past a far intersection
of corridor, he thought at first it might be one of the ghosts.
After all, Hawk knew about them as well, so it could not be
entirely his imagination. They were like faint presences, not
seen so much as felt, and a few of the stronger ones he had
given names to: Happy, who lived mostly in Medical; Fearful,
whose path disappeared frequently into the Green Room,
where Gregori was not inclined to follow; and Grumpy, who
Gregori quite liked because he seemed to leave a trail of
laughter behind him.

But he had never actually *seen* one before, so he padded
quietly after it, careful to stay unobtrusive.

It led him to the bay left empty by the forced departure of
Machiko and crew on one of the shuttles. It wasn't until the
figure paused outside the door to the control overlook, looking
almost comically furtive before it opened the door and vanished
inside, that Gregori realized who he was following.

Under any other circumstances, he would have been more
cautious, but he simply walked boldly in behind her.

"Lia," he asked as he came through the door, "what are you doing?"

She gasped and spun around, but by then it was obvious: the great hold doors were parting to reveal the airless black of space and one shuttle, brilliant in the sun's reflected light, poised to enter. The light on com began to blink a furious red, but Lia ignored it.

"But who's that?" Gregori asked. "Blue said we had an emergency. Have they come to help us?"

Lia did not answer. Instead, she began madly tapping override commands into the console, and even manually locked the overlook door that led into the corridor. Then she extended the hatchway that would attach to the shuttle, which had angled precisely in and settled on the hangar pad.

Intrigued, Gregori reached out and tapped the ship's com.

"—who the hell is down there?" came the captain's voice, tight and angry.

"We have all entrances covered, and have manually locked all cargo doors from the outside. But the overlook is sealed. I am concentrating my people there."

"But Lia," said Gregori, "that's Momma out there. Shouldn't we let her in?"

"*No.*" It was all she would say, and delivered in such a cold voice, so uncharacteristic of Lia, that he did not care to argue. The set, frightened, and yet resolute look on her face scared him. He retreated to a corner to wait her out. She could not possibly remain so utterly changed forever.

She shut off the com and linked up the hatchway. Within moments troops emerged, too many even to all stand in the overlook. One stripped off his face gear. He had tiny eyes in a round face, and his expression terrified Gregori.

"Is this your way of betraying us?" he snapped at Aliasing.

She shrank before him, looking even more unsure of herself and yet still determined.

"No, Comrade Vanov," she said, so quiet Gregori could barely make out her voice. "I would never betray Jehane."

The way she said the name had a flavor, a passion, that confused the boy, because he had never heard her speak so ardently about, or to, anyone, not even his mother.

"Well, we've been monitoring ship's com," replied Comrade Vanov, mocking her, "and there's a tidy selection of mercenaries outside that door, nicely set up, I'm sure, to rip us to pieces as we come through."

"Who's this?" asked one of the other soldiers, a woman with a mild face.

Both Vanov and Lia swung to stare at Gregori.

"Who is it?" barked Vanov. His interest petrified Gregori.

Lia began to speak, stopped, wrung her hands and turned away. "It's Jenny's boy," she whispered.

"Good work," said Vanov, not making it much of a compli-ment. With abrupt speed, he reached out and grabbed Gregori and yanked him in tight against his uniform. Drawing his pistol, he pressed the muzzle against the boy's temple.

"Let's go," he said. "They won't fire on us if we have hostages. Trey." He nodded at the woman who had first noticed Gregori. "Take the woman."

"Vanov," protested Trey. "You can't put a child at risk like that. What if they shoot him?"

"Are you disputing my command?" His tone was harsh and challenging.

"No, comrade. Of course not."

"You *said* he wouldn't be hurt!" exclaimed Lia.

"I think it unlikely anyone will fire on him," replied Vanov. "I'm only doing this to make sure there's as little bloodshed as possible. Surely you understand?"

Lia looked uncertain. Comrade Trey looked skeptical.

"Very well," snapped Vanov, impatient with this delay. "Form in order. We're going out. Disarm and detain their mercenaries, sweep for crew, kill if you have to, and merge on the bridge. Is that clear?"

Everyone nodded. Vanov waited an extra moment, eyes tight on Comrade Trey.

"Yes, comrade," she replied, expressionless.

Gregori was too shocked, and too horrified by Lia's betray-al and the hard circle of the pistol pressed against his hair, to fight or even to ask why.

Hawk understood that things had gone quite bad when Jenny came over com to say that she would retreat without firing because the boarding party had somehow managed to get Aliasing and Gregori as hostages. Her normally imper-turbable voice held a definite tremor.

Hawk wondered for a moment if Lily was going to order

Jenny to fire anyway, but the captain only made the cryptic reply: "Lock coordinates to Engineering."

Securing all patients, he then went into the lab and locked away his supplies of the Hierakas Formula. And because he always, at any place he spent more than an hour's time in, identified a bolt hole, he hid himself there and waited. Touched briefly each of the weapons he had stored there. All were operational.

He scented Jenny's mercenaries first. They smelled scared and confused as they retreated higher and higher up. Jenny he did not detect.

Then the first wave of Jehane's troops, herding those few of the crew who had been left unarmed: Blue and the tech from Engineering, and UnaDia Wei from the Main Computer banks. Soon enough they passed through Medical and collected Flower.

It was easy enough to wait them out and then follow after they'd left, thus giving Lily the backup she'd need. Except that they held a wild card that he did not expect. Eight came in, Lia with them.

"Then he must be here still," she was saying to a stocky man whom Hawk quickly identified as Kuan-yin's crony from the *Boukephalos*. "If he wasn't in the captain's cabin. I don't want anyone to get hurt. Gregori once said he had a hiding place here."

"Spread out and give yourselves cover," ordered Vanov to his soldiers. "We'll just wait him out."

Hawk did not bother to dwell over how Gregori had come to discover the bolt hole. The boy knew the ship very well. He did calculate the amount of damage he could do, but Vanov's soldiers were well trained enough to cover each other as well as the room, and Vanov left with Aliasing before he could make a choice.

So he stowed the weapons farther back and surrendered himself. As they marched him up to gold deck, and the bridge, he wondered what Gwyn would have done in the same situation. But Gwyn had been the best, and whatever Hawk's skills as a saboteur and terrorist, which were not inconsiderable, his real expertise had always lain in healing.

It was no relief to discover, on reaching gold deck, that they could have used Gwyn. Whether through the shock of Lia's betrayal, or the use of hostages, or because of his sheer ruthless efficiency, Comrade Vanov had taken control of the bridge. As Hawk was herded in, he was disposing of the prisoners.

"All the tattoos in one detention block. Just seal them in for now. But leave the ones in Engineering and in Computer until we get replacement crew. The two Engineering techs, the computer tech—we'll need them later."

Hawk smelled blood, but he had to look around to find Jenny prostrate on the floor by the nav console. She had blood on her face, and one of her arms was lying at a bad angle. She stirred, but did not moan; she was still conscious. On the opposite side of the bridge, Aliasing stared in horror. Gregori, held by a rough-looking trooper, looked paralyzed by his mother's injury.

The bridge cleared somewhat as the people named by Vanov and their guards left, revealing Lily standing isolated by the captain's console, a soldier on either side of her. She looked unhurt. Her expression, when she saw Hawk, did not change: it was emotionless now.

"I am a doctor," said Hawk easily into the silence left by the departure of the others. "May I see to the wounded woman?"

"No," said Vanov. "I don't waste medical help on people whom I have orders to kill."

Lia gasped, audibly, and went white. She staggered slightly, catching herself on the back of the chair Yehoshua was sitting in. A soldier moved to grab her arm.

"But you said"—she began, her voice as much breath as vibration—"No one was to be hurt. *He* promised me." By the tone of her voice, there could be no doubt that *he* was Alexanu · Jehane.

Vanov seemed not to have heard her. He looked over the bridge crew—Yehoshua, Nguyen, Finch, Pinto, the Mule, and Bach—with a precise eye, as if measuring what to do with them.

"Comrade Trey," he ordered. "Get on comm and call the *Boukephalos* in. I want a bridge crew waiting to replace these as soon as they can board."

Comrade Trey moved to comm. Finch, glancing up at her set face and then at the score or so of soldiers still crowding the bridge, moved aside to let her at the controls.

Lily had not moved, except to turn her head enough to see the Mule. It sat quite still at the nav console, one hand covering the other; Bach hovered beside it just below the level of the counter, his curve pressed up against the siding.

It seemed to Hawk some message passed between the two that he could not read. The Mule hissed slightly. Pinto, hidden by the stillstrap, stared straight ahead. If he was watching the numbers click across the chin harness of the strap, it was not apparent.

Vanov, too, glanced that way. "Turn the nav console off," he ordered. The soldier stationed by navigation reached out and flipped the auto nav to manual.

Lily was still looking at the Mule. Her expression did not change. The Mule's crest rose and fell, like a rustling, and it removed its hands from the console and rested them as if resigned on Bach's keypad.

Jenny stirred again. Her breathing was ragged but even. Vanov, secure now, glared at the mercenary.

"Kill her first, then the boy," he ordered, cool now that he was totally in control.

On Pinto's chin strap, red numbers still clicked across the tiny screen.

"Comrade!" protested Trey, standing up from the comm-station. "I wasn't informed of these orders. Killing children is *not* what I became a Jehanist for."

"Are you challenging me, comrade?" Vanov demanded, his voice as hard as his eyes. "You know the punishment for insubordination."

"That child is not old enough to have been party to this mutiny. He can't be held accountable."

Lia broke free of the soldier who had been grasping her arm. "But you *said* no one would be hurt!" she cried, flinging herself at Vanov. "You lied to me!"

Vanov slapped her full in the face. She staggered, and Vanov regarded her with cool disdain. "Kill her as well," he said calmly.

"But you can't—" The extent of his betrayal shocked her into silence for a moment. She held one hand against the reddening patch where he had hit her. "You *must* know I got a message from Jehane—that he would send someone to bring me to him. You can't defy Jehane's orders."

Vanov shrugged, unconcerned. "It might be true that he did mean to send someone for you. You're pretty enough. But my orders didn't come from Jehane." It was said so impassively that it clearly was true.

Lia slumped forward, defeated by his dispassion, and began to cry. "Jenny," she sobbed. "I'm sorry. I'm sorry."

"Who did your orders come from?" Lily asked. The self-possession of her voice seemed uncanny on the tense bridge.

Vanov smiled. He made it an ugly expression. "Comrade Kuan-yin sent us."

"Of course," Lily echoed. Her head was still canted to keep the Mule in her peripheral vision. "With orders to kill the five of us and deal with the rest as you see fit."

"Exactly. I'm glad we understand each other, Comrade Heredes."

"Ransome," said Lily. "My name is Ransome."

"Comrade Vanov!" said the soldier by nav, surprised. He was staring at Pinto in his stillstrap. "They're still running nav."

"I told you to turn the console off," snapped Vanov.

"But Comrade, I *did*," insisted the soldier.

"Then it's impossible," broke in Comrade Trey. "You can't run vectors on manual."

In two strides Vanov closed the distance between himself and Lily and wrenched her arm up behind her back. She began to twist away.

"Kill the other four," he ordered. Lily froze. The soldiers hesitated.

"Wait—" began Comrade Trey.

Vanov pressed the muzzle of his pistol against Lily's ear. "Take this ship off nav."

In the instant of indecision before anyone could act, the air rank with the scent of confusion and fear, stained with the salt of Lia's tears and the heavy aroma of Jenny's blood and the unexpected pungency of Vanov's rabid hatred, Hawk could not smell any emotion in Lily at all. It was as if she was already dead, her essence fled, gone, torn from him forever.

The horror of losing her paralyzed him. He did not even act when two soldiers put their hands on him, when he felt the shift of their bodies as they slowly—or slowly it seemed to him, caught in this moment, strung out beyond ordinary time—raised their weapons. The ghosts of the *Forlorn Hope*'s lost crew crowded the bridge, their fragrance overwhelming him, tenuous and yet stronger now than it had ever been before.

Lily caught Hawk's gaze with hers and blinked twice, deliberately. The pistol against her head smelled of cold, unfeeling steel. Her hair hid its muzzle where Vanov held it thrust against her ear.

"Five seven two," hissed the Mule. *"Break."*

"You bitch!"

They went through just as Vanov pulled the trigger.

4 Old Secrets

****

blood blood blood agony howl pain blackness blood blood

And came out.

"Perfect," hissed the Mule.

There was silence on the bridge. No answer at all.

Pinto unclipped his chin harness and twisted to look at the same time as the Mule turned in its chair.

It was hard to make sense of what was on the bridge. The first movement that had form was that of Lily slowly rising to her feet. Her face was pale with shock. Blood spattered her clothing. She saw first Pinto, then the Mule, and last Bach, and as if they gave her stability, she took one step forward and stared around the bridge.

The step brought her foot into a heavy obstacle. As one, she and the Mule and Pinto looked down. Bach sang something muted.

It was Comrade Vanov's body. Scarlet stained his Jehanist whites. His throat had been ripped open. Blood still flowed, pooling in the crook of one bent arm.

Behind, someone began to retch violently. Jenny moaned, and stirred. A tiny voice said, "Momma," and began to cry.

Lily eased her boot away from Vanov's corpse and turned slowly to survey what lay about her: Lia standing in blank-faced shock, Gregori sobbing beside her; Yehoshua gripping his chair back so hard his knuckles were mottled white; Jenny crumpled under one console, trying to lift her head. Nguyen had fainted. Finch was throwing up.

Bodies littered the floor like so much dross. The marbled deck was awash in blood. It was hard to imagine that fifteen bodies could produce so much of it.

All the soldiers were dead. Their throats had been ripped out.

Not all: by Finch, Hawk stood, holding the woman Trey by

a portion of her tunic. Her face had the sheen of terror. She was too paralyzed by fright and shock to move. Her eyes were locked on Hawk's face like any helpless being stares at the monster that has entrapped it.

Hawk's expression was too blank to be human. It had an alien cast, as if some other creature possessed him. He looked horrifying. His clothes bore huge spatters of blood. His hands were red. As she watched, a single drop coalesced off one palm and fell to shatter on the floor. More red spattered his blue hair, like some cosmetic pattern in a new fashion. But worst of all, his face was streaked with it, fresh blood, and most of it around his lips.

"She smells of Robbie," he said, as if explaining something, his voice both hoarsely his own, and yet entirely foreign. He opened his hand off her jacket and without a sound collapsed unconscious to the floor.

Comrade Trey began to shake, and cough, and then to cry uncontrollably. But she remained standing, because to sink down would bring her closer to Hawk, and she had not the ability to move any farther away from him.

The Mule hissed, a long, sibilant sound expressing sheer disbelief and revulsion.

Lily took another step, back to the captain's chair and the ship's com.

"To those soldiers under Comrade Vanov's command still remaining on this ship. This is Captain Ransome speaking. Your commander is dead. Put down your weapons and return to your shuttle. If you do so without harming any of this crew, or any part of this ship, we will let you leave unharmed. If you do not, at whatever cost to us, we'll kill you all."

A pause, snap, and reply. "Min Ransome? Be it truly you? This is Paisley. I be still in Engineering. I hid."

"Paisley?" Lily glanced at Pinto. "Did you run the vector coordinates through Engineering?"

"Yes, min."

Lily did not reply for a moment. Pinto smiled slightly. The Mule hissed, sta-ish laughter.

"Damn my eyes," Lily murmured. "Stay at your station, Paisley. Well done." She flipped com to all-channels and waited for what was left of the Jehanist troopers to reply. "Yehoshua, collect their guns. Starting with *her*." She made an economical gesture toward Comrade Trey.

Looking grim and not a little queasy, Yehoshua began to pick his way through the corpses.

"Finch."

He looked up at the sound of Lily's voice, wiping his mouth on his sleeve. His eyes looked glazed.

"See to Jenny."

"But—"

"Finch."

Keeping his gaze averted from Hawk's unconscious form, he complied.

"Mule. Carry Hawk into my cabin. Clean him up as well as you can." As the Mule stood up, showing no expression whatsoever at the command, she reconsidered. "And take Pinto and Yehoshua as guards. Armed. Bach, monitor all systems."

Ship's com snapped to life.

"Captain? This be Rainbow. Be you there?"

"Yes. What's your status?"

"Ya comrades gave theyselves up, Captain. We got ya weapons. There be twelve here. Shall we kill them?"

"No. Detail a group to escort those twelve to their shuttle and seal them in. I want you and the others to first make sure the rest of our crew is safe and returned to their stations. I need Flower up here, and you, and as many as you can spare from guarding the shuttle. We'll have two prisoners for detention, and I'm afraid some rather ugly"—she hesitated, and refrained from glancing around the bridge—"cleanup to do."

"Sure, Captain," Rainbow responded. Her voice sounded incongruously cheerful over com. "We got ya bastards, didna we?"

"Get moving," snapped Lily, because to reply to Rainbow's question was too painful. "And Yehoshua," she added, just as he was about to leave, escorting the Mule with its terrible burden, "take Aliasing and Comrade Trey to detention. I'll want to speak with them later."

Lia began to cry again, but she did not resist as Yehoshua took her arm—none too gently—to lead her away. Comrade Trey followed dully, looking if anything relieved to be escaping the carnage.

Gregori gave Lia a long, piercing stare as she left. She would not look at him—at anyone. But once the bridge doors sighed together, concealing her, he sidled carefully around the bodies and knelt by Finch. Didn't say anything, just crouched there, face pale and frightened.

Finch had turned his back on the careless litter of death behind him as he checked over Jenny's injuries, but he essayed a glance at Gregori—risking a glimpse of the dead soldiers—and patted the boy with tentative solicitude on one arm. "She'll be all right," he murmured. "Just a couple days' rest, and this arm will have to heal."

"But all the blood—" Gregori whispered.

Finch winced, and then realized the boy meant on his mother's head and face. "Head wounds always bleed a lot," he explained, and winced again, thinking of their throats. Unconsciously, he lifted a hand to brush at his own neck, and he shuddered.

"I need to get her down to Medical," he snapped, desperately wanting to get out of the bridge. "We'll have to observe for concussion."

Gregori wiped away tears with the back of one hand.

"Holy Void." Nguyen was finally getting his first unadulterated look at the bridge. "What happened?"

"Nguyen." Lily's voice was taut. "Help Finch get Jenny down to Medical. Take Gregori with you."

In his haste to get out as quickly as possible, Nguyen did not even bother to reply.

But when they left, she was alone with Bach and fifteen mutilated, bloody bodies. The bridge reeked of death. She was almost afraid to move from her haven in the center of the bridge.

"I can't believe he had *this* in him," she whispered. "What kind of creatures are they?"

Bach began to sing softly.

> *Blute nur, du lieber Herze!*
> *Ach, ein Kind, das du erzogen*
> *Das an deiner Brust gesogen*
> *Droht den Pfleger zu ermorden,*
> *Denn es ist zur Schlange worden.*

> "Bleed on, dear heart!
> Ah, the child that you raised,
> That sucked at your breast,
> Threatens to murder its guardian
> For it has become a serpent."

On his final note the doors shunted aside to reveal Rainbow and six Ridanis in full mercenary gear. Rainbow took a step in, then halted, staring. The others crowded up behind her.

"What happened?" she asked, awed by the savagery of the scene.

"I underestimated him," Lily said, thinking of her signal to Kyosti—she had meant: disable them while we're in the window. "I never meant this to happen."

Rainbow shook her head. "I seen it in his eyes, min," she said sagely. "He were ya hard type, that one. It be what he meant to do to us, b'ain't it? I say they deserved it, ya square."

Behind her, the other Ridanis murmured agreement. Lily realized belatedly that Rainbow was talking about Vanov, not Hawk, and found she could not frame a reply.

"Sure, Captain," Rainbow continued, a little solicitously. "Be it sure you got ya other arrangements to work out. We can clean this up. Sure, and we hae seen as bad, most of us, in our time. Ya Immortals done as bad to us tattoos at Roanoak and Bistro Station."

"You couldn't have been there," Lily protested, remembering Roanoak. Remembering Kyosti at the clinic, healing with the same sure touch with which he killed.

Rainbow shrugged. "We hear."

The Ridanis stood aside to let her pass. It took her a moment to realize that they meant her to leave, to spare her the sight of their cleaning up. With great effort, she picked a careful path around the corpses. Paused by Rainbow, giving her a brief nod. Rainbow nodded back, and Lily left.

She went straight to the captain's suite, not wanting to see how the Ridanis chose to dispose of the remains. Inside, she found Yehoshua and Pinto, both armed, and the Mule, sitting uncomfortably in the couch and chair that furnished the outer room.

"Where is he?" she asked.

"Unconscious," replied the Mule, drawing the word out into a long, sibilant flowering on the s. "I cleaned him up as best I could and discarded his clothing and left him on your bed. Was that well?"

"Well enough," interrupted Yehoshua in a sharp voice. "I knew he was a psychopath. Void bless us, I've never seen anything so horrible. He ought to be committed to an institution."

"Just remember," said Pinto, drawling slightly, "that we would have all been dead. Between you and me, I'll take that trade any day."

"If he indeed does have some strange ability that allows him to"—Yehoshua paused, struggling for a word to embody a concept none of them truly believed in—"*exist* inside a window, then he damn well could have disarmed them, couldn't he?"

"I'm *glad* he killed them," Pinto replied with unexpected fierceness. "Vanov's the one who killed my father, isn't he?" He looked at Lily for confirmation, but Yehoshua replied instead, harsh words that provoked an equally heated response from Pinto. Lily heard only the tone, not their words, because a sudden flood of memory, of the last moments before they had gone through the window, choked her. Vanov had killed her.

Pinto stopped talking. They all stopped talking, seeing her face.

Yehoshua stood up. "Do you need to sit down?"

She let him guide her to the chair and sit her down. "He killed me," she said, dazed by the discovery. "He fired the pistol. I should have been dead."

"Who killed you?" Pinto asked.

"Vanov," said Yehoshua slowly, trying himself to recall the sequence of events. "I knew he had the gun against your head."

"Ah." The flow of the exclamation gave it a sagacious flavor. "You have overlooked the obvious conclusion," the Mule continued, having gained their attention. "Hawk *also* thought you were dead. It would explain the—severity of his reaction. He is not particularly stable, and his attachment to you is deeper than most. And he is not in any case fully human."

Pinto just blinked, looking confused. Lily did not reply.

"What do you mean?" Yehoshua demanded. "He's not 'fully human.'"

The Mule smiled, a peculiarly out-of-place expression on his half-sta face. "Like recognizes like," he replied. "I knew the moment I met Hawk that he is, as I am, a half-breed." He turned his gaze from Yehoshua's disbelieving face to Lily's quiet one. "But to more than that, I cannot answer."

Lily sat, remembering the bridge of La Belle Dame's *Sans*

Merci, where the aliens—what had La Belle called them? Where the je'jiri had run their prey to ground.

The other three waited. Eventually it became clear to her that they expected an explanation. And even, perhaps, in the face of the circumstances, that they deserved one.

"I just found out myself," she began softly. "After Blessings. His father is human. His mother is one of an alien species called je'jiri. They're hunters. I saw them—" She halted, unwilling to share the memory of what had happened on La Belle's bridge. "I saw them," she repeated, ending the sentence there. "They're not like us."

"Enough like us," said Yehoshua, "that mating could produce a child."

"I don't know how that works, or how usual it is in League space to find half-breeds. But not very usual, I don't think. The je'jiri don't approve of it." The comment seemed even to her ears ridiculous, a gross understatement of the bloody aftermath of their hunt. The man who had been killed on the *Sans Merci* had not looked so different from Comrade Vanov and his compatriots.

"Is that why Hawk is so unstable?" Yehoshua asked, continuing to press the issue.

Lily looked directly at him. "Yes. That's why. His—attachment to me isn't"—she hesitated—"It isn't a *human* attachment. That's why I can't abandon him."

"So you expect us to continue serving on this ship with him running loose?" Yehoshua's voice was rough. "After what we've seen he can do?"

"It's true," said Pinto, finding his voice. "I'm not sure he shouldn't be locked up. It almost gives me sympathy for Finch."

The Mule hissed slightly, laughing.

Lily stood up. "All right. I agree to keep him quarantined in my cabin until we get to League space, where I'll hope we can find a doctor, someone who knows more about this than we do. The lock is manually coded to my imprint alone in any case. Whatever else he can do, I don't think he can walk through walls." She walked across the room to the door that led into the inner chamber.

"You're not going in there?" Yehoshua asked, amazed and horrified at once. "*Alone?*"

"He won't hurt me. It's the one thing I *am* sure of." She paused before touching the panel that would shunt the door aside. "Yehoshua. Escort Lia up here. I'm going to want to talk to her after I've checked on Hawk."

"Do you wish company?" the Mule asked unexpectedly.

She considered the offer, but at last shook her head. "No. Thank you. This is best done alone." She touched the panel and stepped inside the other room.

The door sighed shut behind her. Kyosti lay on the bed. At first she thought he was asleep, but as she watched him he shifted, muttering words in too low a voice for her to make out their sense.

She approached the foot of the bed cautiously. His eyes were shut. His head turned on the coverlet. Muted red still tipped his hair and his fingers. A slight stain streaked his jaw just below his mouth. The Mule had put him in a clean white tunic and trousers. He seemed unhealthily pale against the stark fabric. He had never seemed so pale before.

She was about to speak his name, softly, when he abruptly sat up, so sudden and violent a movement that she jumped back, bracing herself.

"Lily!" he cried.

A pause, and she realized he did not see her, but was looking at something, some sight he alone could see. He was not aware of her at all.

"I saw him and he said to me, Hypsiphrone, although you dwell outside me, follow me—"

Lily had no idea who Kyosti thought he was talking to. His eyes had opened, and they focused on a spot halfway between the bed and the wall. His voice was low, but it had an edge on it, as if he was just clinging to the last vestiges of calm.

"—and I will tell you about them. So I followed him, for I was in great fear. And he told me about a fount of blood that is revealed by setting afire . . ."

"Kyosti?" she whispered. She took a step toward him.

"There was no water on Betaos. It was only sand. But it got sticky when her blood leaked into it. It gave off a sweet smell, that combination. No one could ever explain to me why that was."

"Kyosti."

He continued to rave, on and on, describing incidental details about a place called Betaos. And then another place, called Helsinki, and a room, and the texture of a chair and the smell of spring flowers opening in the cool morning air. Mixed with the scent of death.

Lily knelt on the bed and reached out and cupped his face in her hands.

"Kyosti." She was more frightened of his complete nonrecognition of her than by anything that had happened before. Violence, or accusations, or pleas, she could have dealt with. But now she was afraid that he had lost his mind.

He did not respond to her touch, not even when she put her arms around him. He only continued to talk, gesturing with his hands as he described more precise details, mostly of scents, to his unseen audience.

She let go of him finally because it was too painful to her to think that he no longer knew her—that she could be obliterated so easily from his world. It hurt. Worse than any physical wound, because still, after all this time, she had not brought herself to the conscious point of admitting how much he meant to her. Because it was too late for the admission to make any difference: that she had sheltered him all this time, shielded him from the consequences of his attacks on Finch, from his murder of the asteroid miner who had once been her lover, for the most shameful reason: that she loved him. She would have cried, but she no longer had the luxury of such a display. At Roanoak clinic her tears—unplanned, surprising even her—had made him come with her. He had said she would be better off without him. Maybe it was true. But maybe *he* would have been better off to have stayed there, to continue his work unconstrained by attachments. And yet—

"Kyosti," she said, trying one last time.

He continued talking as if he had not heard her. His speech was deteriorating into a language she could not understand, sprinkled with words she did. She stepped back to the door, laid her hand on the panel.

He broke off in midsentence and looked straight at her. She took her hand off the panel, feeling a sudden thrill of relief.

"Don't lock me up." He spoke to her as he would speak to any unsympathetic stranger. "Please. Don't lock me up." It was almost as if he was begging her. He sounded very young and frightened.

"It's only for a little while." She moved toward him. "I'll be here with you as often as I can, Kyosti, but you have to understand—"

"Don't lock me up. Please." Like a broken recording or the decayed loop of the *Forlorn Hope*'s distress beacon, he was simply repeating some phrase from his past that her movement to the door had triggered. He was not talking to her at all, really. "Don't lock me up."

She had to look away. It was too agonizing to watch him deteriorate into someone confused, reduced to this kind of abject pleading. It was as if Kyosti was not even in the room with her anymore.

"Don't lock me up. Please."

And in any case, she had no choice.

"I'm sorry," she said, and she pressed the panel and left the room, coding it to lock behind her.

In the outer room, the Mule still sat, waiting. Mercifully, it said nothing. Pinto had left. Before she had even had a chance to recover, the door slipped aside to admit Yehoshua and Aliasing.

Lia's eyes were red, puffed from tears. She had huddled in against herself. Small to begin with, she seemed on the verge of collapsing into nothing. She did not sit until Lily motioned her to the chair, where she sat gripping her knees, shoulders hunched, head down.

At a nod from Lily, Yehoshua and the Mule left. Lily remained standing.

"They won't tell me how Jenny is," said Lia at last, her voice so faint it almost dissolved into the hush of the cabin.

"Do you think you deserve to know?" Lily demanded.

For a moment she regretted the harshness of her words. Lia trembled, shrank, and put a hand up to cover her eyes. But lowered it again, although she still stared at the floor.

"No," she murmured. "I don't deserve to know."

She stopped, but there was such a palpable air of her being about to go on, given enough resolve, that Lily kept silent.

"They said they just meant to impound the ship and take everyone back to Arcadia to appear before a court. That's the way it worked before, in military matters. My mother often dealt with the military arm, and any soldier of whatever rank was always given an appearance before a fair court."

Lia paused, catching her breath after this first effusion, and looked up at Lily as if hoping that the matter was now explained.

"I don't understand." Lily paced to the door and back. "If you didn't agree with the mutiny in the first place, why didn't you ask to go with Machiko and the others when we put them off the ship? Fair court or not, I think you know that mutiny is comparable to treason and the penalty is death."

Lia did not reply immediately. She seemed to shrink farther into the couch, looking so insubstantial as to be almost nonexistent. Her cloud of dark hair fairly screened her face.

"They said—" she began, and faltered. Her voice was so faint that Lily had to approach the edge of the couch to hear her. "They said Jehane had sent them, to bring me back to them. He sent me a private message, while we were still in orbit around Arcadia. Before your accident. Before Central fell. He said he would send for me, when he controlled the planet. He wanted me to be his—" Her voice caught, but she mastered the impulse to cry. "To be his consort." The words, or some memory of Jehane or his message, seemed to give her strength. "But I didn't hear anything else from him. And then Pinto and Paisley brought you back, and you were hurt so badly. They said Jehane tried to kill you, but . . ."

"But you didn't believe them," Lily said, feeling tired. She wondered if Lia's obvious, and long-repressed, love for Jehane had blinded her as thoroughly as Robbie's idealism had blinded him.

"No," Lia admitted, sounding strangely matter-of-fact. "That someone else, one of his lieutenants, might have tried—I could believe that. But not Jehane."

Lily smiled wryly. "Well, I'll say this for him, he was sincerely sorry to have to do it."

Lia glanced up. A surge of anger sparked in her expression, as if she was about to argue with this assertion, and then she thought better of it and lowered her gaze to stare at the floor again.

"Then the mutiny came," Lia continued. "I couldn't stop it, not by myself. And Jenny"—for a moment she looked as stubborn as Paisley—"I *do* love Jenny, for everything she's done for me." She stopped, waiting for Lily to dispute the fact. But Lily could only turn away, glad that Jenny was not here to discover that Lia's love for her sprang out of gratitude, not sentiment.

"I wanted Jenny to have a home," Lia insisted. "I wouldn't have left her without a place that belonged to her. Even when I found out who Jehane was, that he was Mendi, I could have gotten a message to him. But I wouldn't have left her without the stability of a home, of a family. But she has that now. There's no reason I can't go back to Jehane."

Lily turned sharply back. It was not even that Lia had betrayed Jenny and Gregori, and the entire crew. But the thought that Lia's action had precipitated the events that had led to Kyosti being locked in the next room, the possibility that his perhaps inevitable reaction to that moment when he believed Lily dead had driven him insane . . . that Aliasing could calmly sit there and so blithely forget what she had seen on the bridge—

An abrupt surge of physical anger ripped through Lily. She had to resist the urge to raise a hand against Aliasing. Until, turning, she saw Lia's face. The animation, all unconscious, that lit Lia's face as the young woman contemplated her return to Jehane tempered Lily's anger. She herself had acted impulsively, going into a riot at Roanoak to find Kyosti. It was no excuse, and yet she recognized that there are times when emotion overwhelms rationality. Sometimes it led to great victories. Sometimes it led to disaster. And she remembered the look she had seen on Alexander Jehane's face when he had met Lia again on Blessings. Sweetness was not a trait she would ever have identified in Jehane, but that one time—that one time, the way he had commented on Lia's beauty, she would even have called him tender. The full force of what might be the only authentic emotion Alexander Jehane had ever allowed himself to feel would be hard to resist. She could not bring herself to vent her fury on Aliasing.

"If you did go back to Jehane, what makes you think that his lieutenant Kuan-yin—who, according to Comrade Vanov is the same person who arranged for our deaths, and *yours* and Gregori's, here—won't try to kill you again? And succeed next time."

There was a slight chime at the door, and it slipped open to reveal Jenny. The mercenary had one arm in a sling, bound to her chest. Her face, though clean, was bruised and swollen.

Lia's back was to the door. "Jehane will protect me,"

she said firmly. She turned her head. "Jenny!" And stood up.

Jenny's expression, beneath the bruises, was a mask, taut and controlled. "You're leaving with the survivors," she said at last, as if she had just that moment realized it. "Back to the *Boukephalos*." Behind her, in the corridor, Gregori loitered; behind him stood Yehoshua, still armed.

"Sit down," Lily said, gesturing to the chair.

"I'd rather not," Jenny replied.

"Jenny," Lia began, pleading, "I never meant—"

"I don't want to hear it," Jenny snapped, losing her temper. "You made it pretty damn obvious when you let Vanov on board. You almost killed my son."

"I couldn't have known," Lia exclaimed, defending herself with anger. Behind Yehoshua, two Ridanis passed carrying a stretcher. A thin plastine sheet covered the body that lay on it. *"You don't understand."*

"You're wrong." Jenny's voice was calm again. She shifted and winced, some pain in her body aggravated by her new stance. "I might have done the same thing, for you."

Lia began to cry. Silent, and with dignity, but tears coursed down her face, slipping off her jaw to wet the collar of her tunic. Jenny's lack of reaction was more distressing to Lily than her previous anger.

"You'd better go," Lily said to Aliasing. "Yehoshua will escort you. You can collect your belongings, and then he'll take you to the shuttle."

Lia seemed not to have heard her. "Don't hate me, Jenny," she said, soft.

Jenny turned her face away. "I don't hate you, Lia," she replied, softer.

Without looking at anyone else, Lia walked out of the room. Gregori backed away from her. Lia's shoulders shook, as if that tiny, final rejection had finally broken her composure.

Yehoshua, face painfully blank, led her away. The veil of her black hair was the last sight Lily had of her.

"Jenny." She said the name tentatively.

"Not now." Jenny's voice was drawn tight with anguish. She stood, not moving, not speaking, for a long space of time. The angle of her head highlighted a fresh cut, running from the corner of one eye to the cheek beneath, one more legacy of Vanov's short stay. Finally she turned and without a word

went out into the corridor, took Gregori's hand, and walked
away.

Rainbow appeared in the doorway, hesitating. She held a
pistol in one hand, by the barrel.

Lily motioned her in. "What's that? I thought Yehoshua
collected all their guns."

"We found ya one, Captain," Rainbow explained, holding
the pistol out. "It were in the back corner by ya life support
console. Some person flung it so hard it dented ya console.
Can't have come there any other way, we reckoned by seeing
where it lay." She shrugged. "I thought you might wish to see
it."

"No." Lily took a step back, realizing with sudden revulsion that this dull, inert thing must be Vanov's pistol, flung
so far and so hard away from her in that infinity of time
given Kyosti inside the window. "No," she echoed. "Take it
away."

With a brisk nod, Rainbow retreated. The door sighed shut
behind her, leaving Lily alone in the captain's suite.

The silence was for the moment too oppressive. She
returned to the other room to check on Kyosti. He did not
respond to her entrance. He lay still on the bed, eyes open
and dilated. His breathing seemed regular, but it was
shallow. Frightened, she tried to find his pulse, but it was
faint and slow. His skin seemed uncomfortably cool to her
touch.

She jumped up and slapped the com. Within minutes
Hawk's assistant Flower arrived. Her look of concern, incon-
gruous against the wild cheerfulness of the tattoos decorating
her face and hands, deepened as she examined him. At last
she looked up at Lily.

"I think he be gone catatonic, min Ransome. There be
nothing I can do, but watch him and keep him in fluids."

"What have I done?" whispered Lily.

"B'ain't nothing you done, Captain," Flower answered,
puzzled. "It be ya shock, likely. It be up to him to come out
when his mind can face up to what he done, back there. You
just mun be ya patient."

"My best virtue," muttered Lily, but Flower did not get
the joke. And the only thing that came to Lily's mind, staring
at Kyosti's inert form, was an old chorale that Bach sang on
occasion.

Ich bin's, ich sollte büssen,
An Händen und an Füssen
Gebunden in der Höll'!
Die Geisseln und die Banden,
Und was due ausgestanden,
Das hat verdienet meine Seel'.

"It is I. I should atone,
My hands and feet
bound, in hell.
The scourges, and the fetters,
and all that Thou didst endure,
that has my soul earned."

5 Belly Down Day

****

Yehoshua felt some sympathy for Aliasing. He had met Alexander Jehane about five years back, and he still remembered vividly the impact of that meeting. Its main result had been to send his cousin Alsayid into a frenzy of revolutionary fervor. Born two years apart to sisters in a large House, the two boys had naturally grown close, with Yehoshua's practicality tempering Alsayid's enthusiasms. Jehane had impressed Yehoshua, but Alsayid had drawn him into Jehane's revolution and eventually into Jehane's army. It still seemed ironic to Yehoshua that he, not Alsayid, had been given more responsibility and what was in essence—despite Jehane's official stance against 'rank'—a higher position within the Provisional Armed Forces. And doubly ironic that Alsayid, the real convert, had died for the cause.

And yet not ironic at all. But Alsayid's death had destroyed Yehoshua's faith in Jehane. He knew it was irrational, to assign blame for what had been a tactical failure—the disastrous attempt on Landfall—but his belief in the revolution had clouded over and slowly atrophied over the course of the following months. Lily seemed a more immediate, and involved, leader to him than Jehane; she had been the one to salvage the Landfall expedition and destroy the ship that he considered the cause of Alsayid's death. Over that time, the *Forlorn Hope* had become his home. He had discovered, slowly and with surprise, that he had no great desire to return to a life of mining at Filistia House. The revolution had changed him enough to make such a return difficult.

So whatever sympathy he felt for Aliasing was tempered by his anger at her for jeopardizing the one future he felt he could look forward to, and by his anger at what her betrayal had done to Jenny. Truth to be told, he was quite happy to see Aliasing go.

She did not speak to him, gathering up her few possessions. A few tears dappled her cheeks, but that was all. She kept her expression tautly controlled. Followed him meekly to the shuttle bay and boarded without incident.

He watched the dark fall of her hair and the loose swirl of her skirts disappear around a corner of the pressurized tube that led to the shuttle, and then he sealed the hatch and left the four Ridani guards to keep an eye on the bay. He even whistled a little, returning to the upper decks.

He found the captain in the outer room of her suite. She waved him in, and he sat down beside Flower on the couch. Lily was standing. Her face had a drawn cast to it, as if she had sustained a shock but was trying to conceal, or overcome it.

"We were discussing the casualties," she said to Yehoshua. "Flower says that she doesn't have enough knowledge to help them improve, but that she can maintain their current condition and continue to rehabilitate those who are recovering. The question is whether we should transfer them to Station Hospital on Forsaken or ask the *Boukephalos* to take them. After all, these are heroes of the engagement at Blessings."

"What about Hawk—" Yehoshua began, and stopped, seeing the expression that shuttered the captain's face. She looked at Flower, as if she could not bring herself to answer the question.

Flower regarded Yehoshua gravely. "He be gone ya catatonic, min. No telling how or when he might come clear o' that."

"I see," Yehoshua murmured, not sure he did see. He felt mildly guilty that he had called Hawk a psychopath, and yet vindicated at the same time.

"There's no guarantee," the captain went on, "that they'll recover in any case."

"I'm not sure what other choice we have," said Yehoshua. "Take them with us to League space. Find medical care there. Flower can monitor them so far."

"And if they recover in League space, how many will thank us for taking them so far from home?"

Flower grinned. "Being ya dead be furthest from home I can think on, min. Min Hawk wanted them to go."

"Min Hawk," said the captain tonelessly, "had his own ghosts"—she caught on the word as if she had not meant to say it—"to atone for."

The comment left an uncomfortable silence in the room. Yehoshua broke in briskly, more out of compassion for Lily's pain than to cover his own discomfort.

"This all presupposes that we can convince the *Boukephalos* to retreat without engaging us, get supplies at Forsaken, and get across uncharted vector space to your League. On the other hand, Pinto and the Mule ran that last damn vector on *manual.*" He ran a hand through his silvering hair. "I'm getting too old for this." Then laughed, exchanging looks with Flower. "Unless this Formula is true, in which case I won't be getting *older* for a while yet."

"You don't believe it?" Lily asked, a little defensive, perhaps. "Do you? Really?"

For the first time, he had the relief of seeing the barest smile crack her grim facade. "No, not really," she admitted. "But I expect we'll get used to the idea eventually." She turned and strode with abrupt energy to the door. Yehoshua and Flower both rose. "I want bridge and Engineering back on as soon as Rainbow is—finished. We don't have any time to waste." She paused. "Then meet me in detention. I want to ask Comrade Trey one question before we put her on the shuttle. Flower, return to Medical."

"Yes, min."

"What question?" Yehoshua asked.

"I want to know what Kyosti meant when he said that she smelled of Robbie."

She left, and he followed Flower out behind her. Got a verbal estimate from Rainbow of the time until the bridge was usable again—he did not care to check for himself. Put all personnel on ready and, curious now, made his way down to detention.

The captain was waiting for him outside the cell that held Comrade Trey. They observed her through the one-way for a few minutes. She sat on the edge of the bunk, shoulders slumped, hands covering her face. She breathed; otherwise, she did not move.

Her head jerked up as the door opened. Her eyes had the white edge of fear, and she caught at the thin blanket as if to shield herself with it. Then, registering her two visitors, her face relaxed slightly, but she remained tense.

"I just have one question to ask you," said Lily quietly. "Then you'll be escorted to the shuttle and transferred back to the *Boukephalos* with the others."

"You're just going to let us go?" asked Trey, not believing it. She had a broad face, slightly flat with dusky skin; handsome in its own way partly because of the mildness that even now showed through her agitation. "The *Boukephalos* has orders to bring you in."

"Your Commander is dead. What will your First Officer do?"

"I don't know," Trey admitted. "I'm nominal First. This expedition was put together very hastily, and people from several different ships were pulled in to cover it."

"You didn't know Comrade Vanov before?"

"No," Trey seemed about to say something more, perhaps about Vanov, and then thought better of it.

"Is Dr. Prachenduriyang still on board?" Lily asked.

"Prachen...? The only doctor on board I know of is Tzu."

Lily glanced at Yehoshua, as if the look shared information that he ought to know. "I suppose that settles it. The casualties will stay with us."

"If I may," said Yehoshua. Lily nodded. "I'd like to know why Comrade Trey is being so very forthcoming. Under the circumstances."

"Comrade Trey," said that woman with a mild hint of irony, "is appalled at the actions of her former Commander and is not entirely sure she wants to return to the *Boukephalos*. If this is what Jehane's revolution has come to—killing children—I want no part of it."

"Did you know Robert Malcolm?" Lily asked abruptly.

Trey's face changed. Yehoshua recognized her expression. It wasn't hard. A memory mixed of sorrow and joy: she had loved him, once, or loved him still. How the sorrow fit in he could not guess.

"You're Maitreyi, aren't you?" said Lily, and she unexpectedly took two steps forward and knelt before Trey. "He loved you."

Trey stared at Lily as if Lily's soul had just been illuminated before her. "You knew him," she breathed. She put out her hands and Lily took them in hers, an act of such unconscious sisterhood that it made Yehoshua feel awkward and intrusive.

"Who are you talking about?" he asked, and was embarrassed to hear his own voice sound so grating.

"Robert Malcolm," Lily said, not looking at him. "Robbie." When he still did not react, she finished, "Pero."

"Oh." It was all he could manage to say, knowing that it was Pero's death—his murder—that had brought them this far.

"After the Finegal Revolt on Veritas," said Trey, oblivious to anything but Lily's regard, "when I had to turn him in, when he tried to escape from the hospital, after that they shipped my unit off to the next assignment, I couldn't forget him. Or the things he had said. And I couldn't forgive myself for stopping his escape."

"He forgave you," Lily murmured. "No, there was no forgiveness in it. He simply never blamed you for doing your duty. He admired you for it."

Trey shook her head slightly, either not believing or believing too much. "I finally deserted. I joined Jehane and learned ships, because that was where they needed people then. When we came to Arcadia at last I thought, I'll find him again. I knew he had taken the name Pero. I thought it wouldn't be hard to find him, to show him that I finally understood, about the Finegal Revolt, about Jehane's revolution. And then he was dead." Clearly she was not a person who cried easily. Pain invested her expression, her entire body, but she only hesitated a moment before she went on. "I volunteered to come out on the *Boukephalos*. Vanov as good as said that the people they were going after were the ones responsible for Robbie's death. But I began to distrust Vanov. And after this"—she had not ceased looking at Lily—"I think he must have been lying, wasn't he?"

The line of Lily's mouth quirked up into a rueful smile. "Not entirely. I was responsible for his death, because of something I told him. But it was Jehane who had him killed."

This revelation proved too much for Trey. She broke her hold on Lily's hands and covered her face again. "Jehane," she murmured. "After everything Pero had done for him. How can I believe that?"

Lily looked up at Yehoshua. Understanding the signal quite well, he nodded to her and left the two women alone. Waited outside for perhaps five minutes, watching Lily's lips move as she began her explanation, Trey's muted responses, and the shivering of her shoulders as each piece of Jehane's betrayal of Pero fell into place. But he began to feel like a voyeur, so he left.

He checked in with Rainbow again. Cleanup was progressing. Bach was taking systems through their paces, and evidently both the Mule and Pinto had already reported to the bridge and were beginning their calculations. Yehoshua still did not feel like making a personal inspection.

Instead, he wandered to the mess. Its lights were dimmed down so far that one could scarcely make out the two occupants, one seated on the lap of the other at the table in the farthest, dimmest corner.

He entered cautiously.

Jenny sat in a posture so utterly uncharacteristic of her—so despondent, so drained of life—that for a moment he wondered if he had mistaken her. But the child huddled on her lap could be no one but Gregori. The boy had disposed himself both carefully, not touching his mother's broken arm, and with the absolute urgency of a child needing comfort. His face was pressed against Jenny's breast, his legs curled up completely on her lap. She had her good arm clasped tight around him. But her gaze was focused on the wall, seeing, and not seeing.

She heard his footsteps and turned her head just enough to see him. A flare of hope—but it died abruptly as she recognized who it was.

He approached and halted at the other end of the table.

"Is there anything I can get you?" he asked, feeling like an idiot as he said it.

"She went," Jenny said, not a question.

He bowed his head. "Yes." Hesitated. "I'm sorry." Wished immediately that he hadn't said it.

She did not reply.

A soft footfall sounded at the mess entrance. Both Jenny and Yehoshua looked up, she with awful hope, he with fear that turned to guilty relief when he saw the captain walk across to them.

Lily's face was grave. She nodded first at Yehoshua. "Trey is joining our crew. As acting Second Officer, for the time being. Can you show her around?"

"Are you sure—?" he began, shocked at this sudden change of sides.

"Quite sure."

"But we aren't free of the *Boukephalos* yet. This could be a ploy on her part."

"Yehoshua. I know the risks. She isn't one anymore. We both loved Robbie, in different ways. She'll stand by us."

He bowed his head again, although this time it was a gesture of acquiescence, and tactfully retreated to the entrance. But he paused to look back.

Lily was just standing, watching Jenny. He could not make out her expression in the dimness, but he heard her say, low: "Jenny."

Just that, and Jenny raised her head and shifted in her chair.

"What am I going to do?" she asked. A simple enough question, but her voice caught and choked on the words and to Yehoshua's horror Jenny—brave, mercenary Jenny—began to cry. He took two involuntary steps toward them, but Lily had already knelt to hug both Jenny and the silent Gregori, enclosing them as well as she could, comforting them with what comfort she had to give.

And Yehoshua knew that he was not only unneeded, but out of place. Yet still, the thought that came into his mind as he left, quiet as he could, was both bitter and ironic: what quality did men like Hawk and Pero and Jehane have, to instill such love and loyalty in women? It was no wonder he and Alsayid had made such a good team, because clearly his problem was not that he was getting old—he was not even forty yet, after all—but that he was dull.

No one chased Gregori off the bridge when they came into Forsaken system a second time, so he sat quietly on the floor next to the elevator. His mother had armed up again, preparing for battle, but Gregori preferred to stay away from the lowest deck, the too-recent scene of Lia's betrayal. The others had seemed reluctant to step back onto the bridge, but after a first, nervous glance, the place seemed to Gregori to look exactly as it always had. Maybe some of the consoles gleamed more than usual. The other memory was already fading, like a nightmare.

Finch hailed the *Boukephalos*. The captain, in the tersest voice Gregori had ever heard her use, outlined the situation to the *Boukephalos*'s nervous Second Officer in words satisfying for their brevity and coolness: something on the lines of, "Leave quietly, or we'll blow you up." The invading shuttle was released from the *Hope*'s hold, taking Aliasing with it, and the *Boukephalos*—its new Commander evidently unwilling to take on the ship that had vanished so abruptly and unexpectedly and then returned having disposed of a soldier as rabid as Vanov—left. Quietly.

Comm flooded with signals from Stations Alpha and Omega, and from the remains of Forsaken's old Central military command from planetside. The two military ships had been hulled by the *Boukephalos* on her arrival. Those of their crew who had escaped had shuttled down to the old command base near Forsaken's largest city. The *Forlorn Hope* had saved them: Did her captain mean to lead the fight to restore Central against the upstart Jehane?

The captain's announcement of her twin goals—to distribute the Hierakas Formula and then leave to attempt to cross the old road back—brought silence to comm. Then a brief message apologizing for the delay. And finally, after some fifteen minutes, an offer to provide whatever the honorable captain needed so that she could leave as soon as she saw fit.

"In other words," said Yehoshua from scan, grinning, "they think we're crazy, and they want us out of here before we can change our minds about just what crazy thing it is we're going to do next."

"But after all," hissed the Mule with surprising sympathy, "there are only two charted vectors out from Forsaken, so they live on the edge of known space every moment. Of all people, they would be most superstitious."

The captain relayed the ship's needs to Station Alpha and also a distribution schedule for the Formula. Fifteen of the seventeen conscious patients in Medical asked to remain at Forsaken and were duly ferried across with the shipment of the Formula base. None of the active crew left.

It took two days to resupply. The captain supervised, from shipboard, the equitable distribution of the Formula on Forsaken and its Stations, as well as the portion set aside to be passed on to the other nearby systems and stations.

Every four hours she took Flower with her to check on Hawk's condition. Gregori asked politely if he could go, too, and because he was underfoot anywhere else, especially because his mother worked long hours stowing the influx of goods, he was allowed to tag along. Hawk's catatonia fascinated him. Hawk did not seem quite alive to Gregori, lying there so motionless and pale, and yet the tiny swell and fall of chest as he breathed marked him as not dead.

The bustle of resupply ended abruptly. The bay released the last of Forsaken's supply shuttles. Grappling lines from the bulk tanker receded. Stationmaster bid them a relieved farewell.

The *Forlorn Hope* vectored twice on charted jumps, and after each window the captain went immediately to check again on Hawk. No one asked why. His condition did not change.

Have Mercy Station welcomed them with surprise. Its population of pygmies and stranded Ridanis and a handful of contract personnel obviously saw little traffic at this hinder-most shore on the edge of the ocean of uncharted space. The captain sent them a vial of Formula—enough to cover their population with some to spare—as a final gift.

And then the *Forlorn Hope* left the last outpost of Reft space and nosed out into the unknown, onto Paisley's Haunt-ed Way. Wandering the corridors of the *Forlorn Hope*, Gregori caught snatches of song from the Ridanis. They all seemed to be singing from the same work, holding on to it as if it was some kind of shield, or talisman. Its chorus whispered through the corridors in a muted undertone:

> Lost we are, belly down day
> Through ya mountains winds ya way.

Everyone seemed too busy to pay any attention to the child left solitary by their business. And yet they journeyed slowly, and with great caution. Each window was preceded and followed by intense periods of discussion, arguments over what constituted landmarks and which old and half-forgotten traditions about the way back were to be trusted. The ship drifted in orbit in each new system—all empty of beacons or stations or any sign of previous traffic—for long slack periods while new courses were charted, discarded, and recalculated.

The time strung itself out until Gregori felt that they would wander the road forever. Still, his mother went about her duties as if there was not enough time to do all she had to do, or as if she made sure there was not. Paisley rarely emerged out of Engineering. Two convalescing patients, relatively mobile, took over Aliasing's domain in the galley, making it a different place. People still gathered there, for breaks, but not people Gregori was comfortable with. Now and then Yehoshua attempted to entertain him, but Yehoshua did not understand children, much less Gregori, and Gregori felt obliged to be polite but not to endure his company for long. He did not dislike Yehoshua, just found him dull.

Only two things made the journey bearable. The first was his visits, four times a ship's day, to the captain's suite with Flower to look in on Hawk. As days turned into a week, and then two, the captain's attendance slacked off until she only actually entered the suite twice a day, although she had to be there to open the door each time. She still slept in the outer room, on the couch.

The second was the slow expansion of the awareness of the ghosts on the ship. He wondered if Paisley was right, if they *were* on the Haunted Way, but he did not have the nerve to ask her. Happy, Fearful, and Grumpy still strode their phantom paths, and now others, too faint to identify as more than presences before, came clearer to him. Spoiled, who hogged one particular chair in mess; Old, who walked very slowly, and seemed confused; and the Other Captain.

Gregori was not sure how there could be another captain, but there was no doubt who she was. She haunted the captain's suite, and the bridge, and one lab in particular on silver deck. Gregori could not decide whether he liked her or not, because he felt that if she knew he was following her she would, unlike Lily, chase him off. But she didn't notice because she was, of course, only a ghost.

But she did inadvertently show him something else. He took to trailing her eidolon, because she knew the ship best and because, despite the fact he suspected she would have no tolerance for children tagging after her, he admired the feelings of competence and courage that he caught off of her.

The more he concentrated on her, the clearer and stronger her presence seemed to him. And he discovered that she had a different code than the one Lily used to unlock the inner suite.

When he tried it, it worked. He went in, cautious, but he was only alone with the still form of Hawk. He talked to him for a while. Nothing happened, except that the deadening, uncomfortable silence that seemed to him to permeate the room was lessened, muted by his voice.

Later he asked Flower if Hawk could hear them.

"I don't know," she admitted. "Could be he can. There be no way of telling. I talk to ya patients as be in ya coma. I think it does ya good, for them to hear ya voice, though they may not understand ya words or even that I be talking to them."

So Gregori took to bringing in his com-screen and reading his lessons out loud to Hawk. Sneaking in, really. Flower's visits were precisely timed, and the captain was too busy running an uncharted road, backtracking here and there, soothing her nervous crew and the superstitious Ridanis, to be a likely danger. Once he overstayed his time and had to hide in the closet while Flower did her usual check of vital signs and refilled the fluid bags.

Gregori began to enjoy himself. He knew better than to tell anyone about his discovery. Weeks lengthened into a month, one month into two. He made great progress with his lessons. Flower observed once that Hawk seemed somehow less taut. And concentrated on his secret, Gregori let his awareness of the ship's ghosts dwindle a bit, although it never faded entirely. Tight in this little cocoon that he and Hawk shared, he grew isolated from the rest of the ship.

So it took him quite by surprise when abruptly, one day, com chimed and the captain's voice came across the shipwide channel.

"All hands. We have come into hailing distance of the beacon for a station calling itself Diomede. We have reached inhabited space. We are now bearing in-system. Full alert."

Gregori was so astonished that he jumped to his feet, letting his screen fall onto the bed next to Hawk's feet, and ran out the door, heading for the bridge. He did not wait to make sure the door shut behind him.

It took only moments to reach the bridge. The atmosphere was hushed but expectant.

"Comm incoming," said Finch as Gregori slipped inside, stationing himself by the door.

"This is Diomede Center." The man's voice was cheerful but strangely accented, so that it was hard to understand him. "We receive you, *Forlorn Hope*. We have five berths open. I suggest you dock at List Seven. Can you please give me your registry number so that I can log you in?" The request was made without any hint of threat or impatience.

Finch looked at Lily.

"Give me a channel," she said. He nodded, and she went on. "Diomede Center, this is Captain Ransome on the *Forlorn Hope*. We are new to League space. We have no registry number. Can you suggest another form of identification that we can give you?"

"Captain Ransome, can you wait a moment while I get my shift manager? And we'll run your specs"—his voice broke off abruptly and then, as if he had forgotten to flip off his comm, they heard him say, quite distinctly—"My God."

"Captain." A new voice, this one just as accented, but crisper. "I'm min Provoniya, shift manager here. Are you aware that the ship's designation 'Forlorn Hope' is interdicted under League Law? Has been since the disappearance of fully half of the hard-luck fleet some two centuries ago?"

"*What* is the hard-luck fleet?" Yehoshua asked.

The term nagged at Lily, until she remembered Heredes using it: the exploratory fleet sent out before his birth; the same ships—or at least five of whose ships—Central had impounded to serve as the basis of their military fleet.

"Comrade Provoniya," Lily replied, not knowing what honorific to use, "this *is* the *Forlorn Hope*."

"My God," said someone again.

"Captain," Provoniya's voice had a certain edge, even awe, in it. "Let me notify Diomede's Coordinator. I feel he would be eager to know of your arrival. Please dock in any case at List Seven. Under the circumstances, we may have to hold you in quarantine for a short time. I hope you understand."

"I understand," replied Lily.

"And by the way, *min* Provoniya is fine. 'Comrade' is rather an old-fashioned term for someone of my ancestry." She sounded amused.

"Certainly, min Provoniya. We are happy to comply." Flicking off her channel, she nodded to Finch to continue docking procedures.

"Captain," said Yehoshua. "One of the ships docked here picks up identical specs to a ship in our files."

"Let me see that." She brought it up on her console. "Damn my eyes," she murmured. "That has to be La Belle Dame."

"Who is—?"

Ship's com interrupted Yehoshua's question.

"Captain? This be Flower, in Medical." Her voice sounded flushed with consternation. "I swear I saw min Hawk in here. It were just ya flash, in ya corner o' my vision, but when I went to go look, I found one o' ya medical kits—one o' ya portable bags—be missing."

Lily stiffened. "Meet me in my suite," she ordered, and rose and swept past Gregori without noticing.

He followed her, sudden guilt staining his expression. The door to the inner room stood open. No one lay on the bed. A faint impression showed the imprint of a body, but even as they stared, the depression filled and leveled, adjusting to the lack of weight.

Lily muttered something Gregori did not catch, except that it sounded like a swear word.

"I didn't mean—" he began in a very small voice.

Com chimed on again.

"Captain!" Jenny's voice. "We've got a detach. Someone just stole the two-person recce boat and left the ship."

The captain simply stared at the empty bed. Gregori sensed that she was engaged in some sort of inner struggle, but he could not imagine its provenance or her course of thought.

Then she slapped the com. "Finch. Get me Provoniya—*min* Provoniya. Hawk ran. We have to warn them."

"But Lily—"

"And then get me a line to La Belle Dame's ship."

"But Captain. I have Stationmaster—*Center Coordinator*—waiting to talk to you."

"Oh Hells," said Lily, so low Gregori scarcely caught it. She turned, glancing at him as she moved to the door. "You'd better go to Medical, Gregori," she said absently as the door slipped aside to let her onto gold deck corridor. "Stick with Flower for now. We're going to be busy for a while."

She paused, polite enough to let him reply.

He just nodded. He felt a horrible, horrible feeling, as if, like Lia, he had betrayed her. But he didn't have the courage to tell her that it was his fault that Hawk had escaped.

6   Diomede

****

Lily surveyed Jenny, who stood before her outfitted in her full mercenary rig. "I'm not sure it's appropriate," she said slowly.

"But it's standard procedure," insisted Yehoshua. "Any ship's captain is always escorted by military personnel, unless you're an in-system boat. And even then, sometimes—" He shrugged.

Lily checked her own pistol, clipped next to her comscreen on her belt. "All right. Jenny. Pinto. Trey. Rainbow. Let's go. Yehoshua, she's all yours."

He nodded, grave. Lily led her party out into the link bubble and then into the short tunnel that connected the *Hope* to Diomede Center. The far door, octagonal in shape, soundlessly rotated open. They came out into the gleaming curve of bright walls and a high, broad, cavernous corridor lined with stark columns.

Three people awaited them: a woman, a man, and a Ridani man. They were smiling. The Ridani man had a baby in a sling on his hip.

The woman stepped forward, extending one hand. Stopped. Her eyes widened as she took in Jenny's rig. She seemed at a loss for what to say. Neither her nor her companions wore anything that looked like a weapon.

Lily halted her party five steps from them. As if sensing her confusion, the Ridani man came forward unerringly to her. He also put out his hand. "Captain Ransome?" She nodded and, a bit surprised, shook hands with him. The baby cooed and squealed. "My name is Ska-morian-isfacat, although," a glance here for Pinto, "you might prefer to call me Scallop. I'm conservative enough that my family still takes on the pattern names. I'm Diomede Coordinator. With me are min Provoniya and her assistant, min Hoshea. And my daughter, Mori. It is my pleasure to welcome you here. If our records are showing the correct information, you must have quite a story to tell us."

For a moment Lily could only stare at him, until she became aware of what it was about him that bothered her. Clearly a Ridani—the facial structure confirmed it as well as the tattoos covering his face and neck and left arm. Except his right arm was bare. His skin was a pleasant brown, much like Finch's, but it was as bare, as unmarked, as her own. And the baby had no visible tattoos at all, except for one elaborate snowflake on her left cheek. Lily became aware that she was staring, and that the rest of her party was as well.

"Thank you," she murmured.

His smile turned apologetic. "I'm not sure where you have come from. Diomede is on the border of The Pale." She did not recognize the word and wondered if it was just his thick accent that made it incomprehensible. "But I ought to tell you now that one doesn't really carry weapons in inhabited zones." He seemed slightly embarrassed at having to point this out to her. "I don't mean to offend you, of course."

"Of course not. We didn't know there were laws against it."

He glanced at his two companions. They all looked surprised. "Why would we need laws for something like that? If you can show me your privateer or bounty license we can certainly—ah—see that you might feel more comfortable—although usually they respect the custom—"

Lily grinned suddenly, liking him because he seemed for the moment just as confused as she was. "*Min* Scallop." The Ridani honorific came strangely to her lips. "This *is* League space. Am I correct?"

He blinked. "Yes." But now he waited, aware that she meant to tell him more.

"I'd better try to make this succinct. And I'm not sure how to. We're not from League space. Several centuries ago lowroad colonization ships were sent out from League space."

"My God," murmured the other man. "The cryo boats. I thought they'd all vanished."

"We're the descendants of those people. They did find landfall, some of them. Colonized an area of space we now call the Reft. And *we* found—myself and the people with me—this ship, and decided to look for the League."

"But how did you—" began Scallop. He stopped. "Perhaps we'd better go to my office. I can see this is going to be a very long story, and that we'd better record it for the Concord representative here. This has incredible ramifications." He looked both ecstatic and bemused.

"Would you like us to disarm?" Lily asked. She had noticed that people passing were giving them strange looks.

"Lily—" hissed Jenny, warning. Lily shook her head, and Jenny subsided, looking disapproving.

"I, for one," offered Provoniya, stepping forward, "feel rather like a Soviet might feel confronted by a party of Mongols. *I* would feel more comfortable."

"Mongols?" asked Jenny in a low voice.

"Please excuse min Provoniya," interposed Scallop. "She's a fanatic for history. If you wouldn't mind—"

At Lily's nod, they disarmed, and Rainbow took the weapons back inside the ship. Scallop smiled, looking as relieved as Provoniya. Reflexively, he patted the baby's bottom. "Then, if you'll come this way."

There was too much to see to register what was similar and what totally different. Once they arrived in the spacious Coordinator's office and seated themselves in delicate-looking but wholly comfortable chairs, Lily introduced her party. No one even blinked when she introduced Pinto as her pilot. Scallop's only comment, addressed to Pinto, was that he must be from an orthodox sect.

A moment later the Concord representative came in and introductions were done again. The representative, a very black, very tall woman named Thaelisha, sat down beside Scallop, got the baby to smile at her, and then turned to regard Lily expectantly.

"Captain." Her voice was smooth, her accent more tone than pronunciation, making her at once easier to understand and yet, for some phrases, far more difficult. "You and the people with you present a unique case. Not just because you have returned in possession of a famous ship believed lost about two hundred years ago. But imagine *our* interest, and delight,' in discovering that there is, as one might call it, a lost colony out there. What we record here today will be transmitted immediately to Concord."

"What *is* Concord?" Lily asked.

Thaelisha chuckled. "There. Proof positive, apart from

your accents, and your style of clothing. Concord is the administrative center for the various autonomous systems which together make up League space. We can show you a map if that would help you to get your bearings. Otherwise, please go on."

Lily chose to go on. "Our computers can supply you with more information about the location and size of Reft space than I can. My navigator can better describe the various physical anomalies existing between League space and Reft space that made navigation with the vector drive, and a set path, difficult to find and maintain, which is the reason as far as I know that the Reft stayed isolated this long. It took us almost four months to run a fairly straight course that once properly charted with a full crew would probably take about one month to cover, according to our pilot and our navigator."

"You only had one of each?" Provoniya broke in, astonished. "For that kind of trip?"

"Yes, but they're good." Lily smiled as Pinto scowled at her.

"They must be," agreed Provoniya. She turned to look directly at Pinto. "My respects."

His scowl turned quickly to embarrassment.

"We also," Lily went on, to spare him, "have the usual ship's library, with the usual historical, geographical, economic and literary files. When we found the *Forlorn Hope* its entire log and library had been wiped, except for the ship's operating system."

"What happened to her?" asked Thaelisha.

"We don't know. We didn't find any bodies, either. The crew simply vanished. There's no trace of them at all. The *Hope* itself was an old legendary ghost ship, haunting ya— *the*—way back. You know the kind of story. She must have been drifting for decades and was finally caught by a small planet. We found her quite by accident."

"And brought her here," mused Scallop. "What made you decide to attempt to find League space, Captain? I'm just curious."

Lily sighed. She did not care at this time to bring in the whole story of Jehane and his successful revolution against Central, and his betrayal of Pero. At the same time, she was not sure how much she should say about Master Heredes and her acquaintance with Wingtuck Honor Jones or the saboteurs in general. If everything Heredes and Wingtuck, and Kyosti, had said about their current status in League space was true, she certainly would not give any clue to Wingtuck's whereabouts. The problem, of course, was what to do about Hawk.

"Two reasons," she began, finally deciding what tack to take. "At least one League ship has been in Reft space. Perhaps someone from Concord."

"My God," muttered the assistant Hoshea from the back corner.

"It would make sense," agreed Thaelisha, not looking very surprised. "But again, go on."

"I—ah—ran into them accidentally," continued Lily, deciding not to explain the circumstances of their meeting any further—specifically the fact that they had believed *her* to be involved with the saboteurs.

"Of course it makes sense, Thae," said Scallop abruptly. "Excuse me for breaking in. I know it's not supposed to be common knowledge, but I've heard rumors that Concord Intelligence is searching for all the old Soerensen network, those left alive, that is. It makes sense that if one ship could find its way across, others might have, years ago, ferrying saboteurs to safety in anonymity. Fair enough, if you ask me. I always thought they were persecuted through no fault of their own."

"I didn't think one could persecute psychopathic criminals," interrupted Provoniya. "If you ask me, I think the lot of them ought to be locked up—"

"—and the lock code erased," finished Scallop, as if he'd heard this argument many times before.

"It's certainly possible," said Thaelisha calmly. She smiled ruefully at Lily. "Excuse us for hanging out our dirty laundry. We don't mean to interrupt you. You said there were two reasons."

"I also accidentally ran across the *Sans Merci*. I believe she's docked here now."

Provoniya laughed. "The queen of the highroad. So that's where she came from. We don't usually see her here. She usually stays within The Pale. I feel a little sorry for Reft space, for where La Belle Dame goes, the rest of the privateers will soon follow. And your government has none of the covenants Concord has set up to control them."

Lily smiled back. She rather liked Provoniya, despite what

she had called the saboteurs. "I'm not sure Reft space is rich enough to interest them. I also met a privateer who called himself Yi."

Provoniya and Scallop looked blank. This time Thaelisha smiled. "That must have been interesting. You've had an eventful time, Captain."

She left a deliberate pause after her words and Lily knew that she was leaving unspoken her real question: Why you? So Lily chose the best method to deflect it—by asking a question in her turn. One she had to ask.

"These saboteurs you mentioned. Who—or what—are they?"

All three began to speak at once, stopped, chuckling a little, and then Thaelisha began unopposed.

"If my history is correct, the cryo ships that colonized your Reft space would have left here before we met the alien culture known as the Kapellan Empire. They—the Kapellans— gave us the vector drive, we put out the exploratory ships, known ever afterward as the 'hard-luck fleet' because so few returned, and soon after that the Empire decided to annex League space. We had no choice but to accept annexation into their Empire. Many decades later a man of Terran birth named Charles Soerensen led a revolt against them that almost succeeded. For some reason—and you'd have to get a xenologist who had studied them to explain it to you—the Kapellans ennobled him rather than executing him. Thereby putting him in a difficult position, you see. After many years, Soerensen put together a network of saboteurs, based on information—well, let me make this as short as I can—"

Scallop shifted and began to stand. "If you'll excuse me a moment. My daughter—"

Hoshea stood up and came swiftly over. "I'll change her. You stay here."

"Thank you." They transferred the child smoothly, and Hoshea disappeared out the door.

"In any case," Thaelisha continued, "they began to disable by sabotage the industry and communications and transport web, and so on, of the Empire, especially within old League space and the regions bordering it. So that in time, when Soerensen launched a second revolt with a number of other leaders, the saboteurs had undermined enough of the Kapellan superstructure, and continued to do so throughout the revolt, that the League was able to sue for peace and gain autonomy and a large neutral zone which we call The Pale. Privateers are given a free rein within it, but must accord to strict covenants without, which is why we are surprised to see the *Sans Merci* here. But that's another story."

"I don't understand." Jenny, moved by this tale, spoke up unexpectedly. "Why would you want to lock these people, these saboteurs, in prison? I'd think they would be heroes."

Thaelisha folded her hands in her lap, a quiet gesture. "You must understand that the methods these people used were often ones that normal people find repugnant." She paused. "Quite repugnant."

"Disgusting," said Provoniya decisively. "They had—still have, one supposes—the ability to kill without remorse or even a second thought."

"You mean they *enjoyed* it?" Jenny asked, unable to comprehend their revulsion.

"Some might have, I suppose. When one has already crossed the line it scarcely makes much difference. At least the mentally ill ones are treatable. The others"—Provoniya shuddered and glanced at Scallop and Thaelisha as if for confirmation—"are simply sociopaths."

"I see," murmured Jenny. It was clear to Lily that she did not see at all. Lily herself could only guess at the assumptions that grounded their statements from things Kyosti and Heredes had said to her.

"That isn't entirely fair." Scallop addressed himself to Jenny. "It is true that without the saboteurs we could not have extricated ourselves from the Empire. We may deplore their methods, their willingness to use violence to solve what is better solved by negotiation—"

"You know, Ska-morian," put in Thaelisha to Scallop, "some still say that at that time we had no ground on which to negotiate with the Empire."

"How hard did we try?" demanded Provoniya. "To find civilized solutions and not opt out once again for the easy solution of violence?"

"There *was* no widespread fighting," said Thaelisha gently. "We were spared that much."

Scallop chuckled. "I'm afraid we're confusing our visitors. What I *meant* to say, min Seria, is that a certain undercurrent of, shall we say, admiration—"

"Morbid fascination," muttered Provoniya, unrepentant.

"—for the saboteurs has always existed. Stories still circulate, more legends, really, by now. The engagement at Betaos led by a handful—no more than five—saboteurs, who held off an entire Kapellan battalion."

"Massacred one, you mean. They *are* life just as we are, and deserve the same respect. Common soldiers."

"That woman Motley who actually snuck into the Imperial capital and wreaked havoc on their main intelligence computers before they caught her. Incredible."

"What happened to her?" Jenny asked.

"Killed her, of course. I don't try to excuse *their* conduct."

Provoniya grinned. "Still, what a way to go. Can you imagine getting through that security? Some say the only reason they caught her is that she couldn't resist trying to steal the Imperial slippers off of the Emperor's feet while he slept."

"And the master," continued Scallop, "who had twin sons— one of whom went good and one of whom went—quite bad. They still talk about his masterpiece: rerouting an entire imperial fleet through the wrong vectors. Manually, from Boots Seven."

"What happened to him?" asked Lily carefully, recognizing the story her half-brother Adam—the "good" twin son had told her once, long ago, about Heredes.

Scallop shrugged. "No one knows."

"What about that woman Katajarenta?" asked Thaelisha. "She was half-Sirin, you know, so we heard all kinds of tales about her at my circle's crèche. And that hell-raiser—what was his name? He saved two Ardakians in some engagement and went on working with them after that."

"Do you really think that's true?" protested Provoniya. "Everyone knows Pongos won't work closely with humans because we smell so bad to them."

Thaelisha shrugged, with a brief smile.

"Or that physician," Scallop said, still indulging his fascination. "The one who affected blue hair like a je'jiri—" He stopped.

There was no mistaking the expressions on Jenny and Pinto's faces. Lily, not as surprised, had managed to keep hers neutral.

"Have the stories spread *that* far?" asked Scallop. "It's hard to imagine how they could. It's only been thirty-four years since emancipation."

Jenny and Pinto looked at Lily, expectant. Trey looked doubly confused. Lily sighed, heartfelt, hating herself for what she was about to do and yet in such strange and unknown surroundings she was not sure she had any choice. She only hoped that Kyosti could forgive her.

"He's a member of the *Hope*'s crew," Lily said quietly, and she went on while her audience was still too startled to react. "But there's been a slight—problem. Hawk had no reason to love the League, but even he assured me that the League dealt fairly with its citizens. I don't know your laws. I don't know League space at all. But because of—circumstances—I have no choice but to trust you now." She paused. If Provoniya and Scallop were still looking puzzled, Thaelisha at least had some measure of comprehension in her face. "A *valued* member of the *Hope*'s crew, I should add. But I'm afraid that as we came into the system he—he ran. Took one of our two-man boats and escaped. He hasn't been well lately—" The sentence sounded terribly weak to her ears.

"Do you mean"—Trey had a look of outraged shock on her face—"that man—the one who—on the bridge"—the memory made her shudder—"That man's a psychopath!"

"He is *not*—" Lily began hotly, and then controlled herself.

"But Lily," said Pinto suddenly, "you said yourself that he's only half—"

"*Pinto.*"

Pinto shut up. For once, he did not look sullen, but rather thoughtful.

"I'm not sure I understand what exactly happened," said Thaelisha, watching this interplay with an eye that Lily feared was too acute.

Lily said nothing for a moment, because she could not decide what to say. Trey looked angry. Jenny and Pinto waited patiently. The door opened and Hoshea returned. "I'll take her," Provoniya offered, and she settled the infant on her lap. The baby stared with wide, intent eyes at all the faces in the room.

"It's very important," Lily began slowly, "that he not be arrested or put in a cell or put in prison or—it's *very* important that I—that *we*—get him back. That's what I need your help for."

"Are you saying he's physically ill?" asked Scallop.

Lily hesitated.

"No," said Thaelisha softly. "I feel somehow that what Captain Ransome is *not* saying is that she fears he is mentally ill. If that is the case, I am curious as to why you're protecting him, or feel that he needs protection. We don't throw our insane into institutions anymore, you know. All citizens have equal access to humane psychiatric care."

"Maybe I'm afraid he won't get equal treatment because of his background. As one of the saboteurs."

"I hope we're not such savages!" exclaimed Provoniya, looking righteously shocked.

"I sense there is something else," murmured Thaelisha. "Why *you* want him back so badly."

Lily looked at Jenny, feeling suddenly helpless. It was hard to admit even to herself the sick worry she felt in her gut at the thought of Kyosti running loose in who knew what frame of mind.

Surprisingly, it was Pinto who spoke up. "You might as well tell them the truth, Lily. It was the only understandable reason anyone would keep him around after what he tried to do to Finch. I know he's a fine doctor, but"—His smile had a touch of unkind glee in it—"Poor Finch. I could never decide if he was more afraid of Hawk, or jealous of him."

"*Jealous* of him?"

Pinto's smile remained unsympathetic. "Since he wouldn't stoop to sleeping with any filthy tattoos, that didn't leave many available women, did it? And he *did* know you from before, as he forever kept reminding us."

"Poor Finch," echoed Jenny, but with rather more charity, as if she understood quite well what Finch had been suffering.

"All right," conceded Lily, aware that her other audience had grown quite bemused. She met Thaelisha's gaze. "He's my lover."

"Your *lover*!" Trey jumped up to her feet. "You could—with someone who could do what he did to Vanov and the others? That's *sick*."

"Trey. Sit down." The sudden, chill snap of Lily's voice sat Trey down. "You have no idea. None. I'm not excusing what he did, but until you know *all* the facts I suggest you not question my judgment."

Trey's expression went blankly neutral. Pinto coughed nervously into his hand.

"What did he do?" asked Provoniya, eyes bright. From her lap, the infant's gaze fixed unnervingly on Lily.

"In League space he hasn't done anything," replied Lily a little testily, "except run from the *Forlorn Hope*."

"If you'd like, Captain," said Thaelisha, smoothing over the chill in the air, "you can help me prepare a report for my superior at Turfan Link. Under the circumstances, a report will have to go out in any case, but certainly we can include your comments." She tapped her fingers thoughtfully on Scallop's desk. "There's also the matter of the *Forlorn Hope* itself. I have no idea if salvage rights apply to a vessel invested under the League Exploratory Guild, although like the other ships it was declared lost. But I can give you no guarantees, except that citizenship in the League is open and your livelihood would certainly not be taken away from you without proper and legal recompense."

"Frankly," said Lily, grateful to Thaelisha for allowing her to regain her composure during this speech, "I have no idea how your economy works, and we have nothing to use for credit anyhow."

Thaelisha smiled. "Given the unexpected avenue of your arrival, and the momentous news you bring, I think it would be possible to arrange a, shall we say, open letter of credit, to be presented to any Concord official wherever you stop. Now that you're here, what do you intend to do, Captain? You and your people?"

"Find Hawk," said Lily immediately. Stopped, looking at Jenny and Pinto and Trey. Trey's mouth was tight. Pinto looked astonishingly relaxed. Jenny looked—like Jenny had looked ever since Lia's departure: bitterly unhappy and determined not to show it, but right now, it was mixed with a real spark of interest as she gazed back at Lily. And Lily wondered if Jenny had ever put aside completely her dreams of bootlegging and smuggling. If the League even had such people—other than, she supposed, what appeared to be the strange, shadowy legality of privateers such as La Belle and Yi.

"I don't know," said Lily, as she realized that it was true. "I never really thought beyond just getting here."

"We'll put out an all points," Scallop said, sounding reassuring. "For the physician. We'll need a description. But there should be no problem alerting all ships to let us know if he tries to get passage. Diomede is a small Center, after all. He won't be hard to track down."

"Well," replied Thaelisha briskly. "Then I expect, once

that's settled, that you may as well take yourselves to Concord in person. The Mother knows they'll be interested in your story, and eager to reestablish ties with Reft space. I'm sure min Provoniya can provide someone to discuss the various routes available with your navigator."

Provoniya nodded.

"Can we meet again later?" Lily asked. "I'd like to return to the *Hope* and discuss this with the rest of the crew."

"Of course. One can only make such a decision with full input. Perhaps meet here again in"—Thaelisha glanced at Scallop—"Will four hours be enough?"

It was agreed on. Thaelisha and Lily rose at the same time, they all shook hands, and departed.

"Oh, Jenny," Lily said softly as they walked along the brilliant hub of Diomede Center toward their berth. "Did I do the right thing? Or did I just condemn him, by asking for their help? I feel like I've thrown him—" She shook her head.

"What is that old phrase?" Jenny asked. "Thrown to the hounds?" Lily shuddered. Not noticing it, Jenny went on. "Or—wolves? Some kind of animal. I read it on some story tapes once. But what else could you do, Lily? In Reft space, we could hunt him ourselves, but here—"

Her gaze swept their surroundings comprehensively. Pinto walked in front of them. Before him, Scallop, who in an excess of hospitality had delegated himself to show them back to their ship, walked beside the still unforgiving Trey, his daughter back in the sling. The baby had fallen asleep. That was all that was familiar. Everything else . . .

Humans, of course; they looked the same, except for the exotic way they dressed, a veritable cascade of brilliant colors and bizarre styles. And their age, or better their lack of it; they saw a fair number of children, one single woman who showed signs of aging, but the rest seemed suspended in that eerie limbo of mature adulthood when chronological age can scarcely be guessed.

And twice, they saw totally unknown alien beings so unremarked by the rest of the population that they clearly were not remarkable.

As for the surroundings themselves, they were not so much unrecognizable as just familiar enough to be doubly strange. The berth connections were octagonal and dilating, rather than square. They strolled along a shopping district. Its mottled white walls bore fantastic scenes carved in relief in long, two-meter-high strips, stories told to the eye as one walked: a woman passed through a series of gates, encountering peculiar beasts and sinuously complicated gatherings of people on her way to some unseen goal. Storefronts broke the tale at intervals. Clusters of tables marking busy cafés obstructed it. It was altogether unlike the cobbled-together utilitarian lines of Reft stations, where function superseded any attempts at decoration.

"Oh, wait," said Pinto. Scallop and Trey halted to look at him. He gave Lily a pleading look. "Look at that *fabric*." He motioned toward a shop. Material lay spread out on tables under a bright striped awning. "Paisley would love it. Can't we just look for a second?"

"For a second, Pinto," Lily agreed, aware that she was humoring him because he so rarely showed any sentimental emotions.

Trey, evidently not immune to such riches, followed him. Scallop, with a smile, followed her.

"There," said Jenny. "Another one. Or maybe it's the same one I saw before."

"Another what?" Lily asked, turning to look. Foot traffic eddied around them. Several small driverless carts loaded with packages sped by, deftly avoiding pedestrians.

"That alien. I've seen pictures in the story tapes of something like it. Shaped like us, but hairy. What were they called? Except I think they weren't supposed to be as intelligent as humans. And this one doesn't look quite right either. *Apes*, that's it."

"I don't see—Oh." It was half-hidden by a stand of some peculiar green globes that she thought might be fruit. For an instant the creature stared disconcertingly straight back at her with eyes that were just slightly too large to be in proportion to its head. Then it was gone.

"And did you notice the Stationmaster—what is it they call him?—Coordinator? Scallop. One of his arms isn't tattooed." Jenny was more animated than Lily had seen her in months. "What do you suppose he meant when he asked Pinto if he was *orthodox?*"

As Lily turned back to answer, someone collided with her. Hard. Instinctively she let her knees absorb the impact, bending slightly, and she spun to face—him.

"Lily!" he exclaimed. "What a surprise to meet you here!"

She had never seen him before. Not much taller than she, he had a rough, unshaven face and a broad chest. He moved to hug her. The gesture was so unexpected that his arms were around her before she reacted.

She dropped, broke his grip, and shoved him away. Jenny went for her gun.

Did not have one, of course. But as her hand brushed her belt in its instinctive draw, another hand grasped hers. Hair tickled her wrist. A strong, musty scent assailed her, and she sneezed.

"Excuse me. This will just take a moment," said a very, very low, peculiarly gruff voice in her ear.

Lily had dropped to a fighting crouch.

The man facing her sighed. "Make this easy for us both, will you?" he asked, sounding weary. He reached and unclipped a thin slate from his front pocket, held it out to her.

Peripherally, Lily could see that Trey had turned and that her hand too had gone to her belt. Scallop, watching intently, put a staying hand on Trey's arm. Pinto had disappeared into the shop.

"Legal and signed," said the man. "Take a look."

"What is it?" demanded Lily.

"Bounty papers," he explained, putting on a patient tone as if he did this every day to people far more cooperative than her. "I have legal right from Concord to take you in."

A single glance to Jenny was signal enough. They both acted at the same time, Jenny to sweep and take down her opponent, Lily to break back and circle.

But one step back took her flat into another body. She did not break the flow of her movement but dipped and spun and punched to its midriff.

Met what felt like steel. Caught a gasp, and went for the sweep.

It was over in moments. She found herself facing Jenny, who was also clasped in the viselike grip of two long, hairy arms, hard against a very broad chest. Hot breath, strong like garlic but not unpleasant, hissed in and out beside her ear.

"Sorry," said the man. He glanced over at Trey, still standing held back by Scallop. Pinto, startled and alarmed, came running out of the store and halted stock-still, staring at

the unfamiliar sight of Lily and Jenny completely subdued.
The man grinned, just a little. "Don't take it bad. You just
don't know their weak points. Can't take 'em out like you
would a human. Hey!" This to Scallop. "You Center personnel?"

Scallop nodded and came briskly forward. Trey followed
him, using his body as a shield from behind which she might,
perhaps, launch her own attack.

"I don't want any trouble," said the bounty hunter. He
handed over the slate.

Scallop had only to glance at it briefly. He sighed, heartfelt, and turned to Lily. "I'm sorry, Captain. This is quite
legal. My hands are tied. If you have an advocate you wish
me to call—" Her expression betrayed her incomprehension
of this remark. "No, I don't suppose you do. I can't understand how Concord could have—unless your story isn't true..."
He trailed off, clearly at a loss what to believe.

"Come on, boys," said the bounty hunter. "Pick 'em up
and let's go."

"But, boss," said the one holding Lily. "I thought we was
only taking in this one."

The man jerked his head to indicate Jenny. "You want her
at our backs? No thanks. Hoist them."

The two aliens simply picked up Lily and Jenny bodily, as
if they were no more than light sacks of food.

"Wait a minute!" began Lily, looking at Scallop. "This is
outrageous. What about—"

"Hold on," said Scallop. "Min—Windsor, is it?" He regarded
the bounty hunter with obvious distaste. "You only have
license for this woman. I suggest you leave the other with
me."

Windsor hesitated, taking in Scallop's authority as well as
the stiff politeness with which he was being treated. "All
right. Fred, move it. Stanford, you wait here. Give us enough
time and then release her and follow." He began to walk
quickly, Fred in front of him.

Lily attempted to struggle, but she might as well have
tried to bend steel, so she gave it up.

"Captain!" called Scallop after her rapidly receding figure.
"I'll notify Thaelisha." Foot traffic had ceased, people from all
around turning to stare at the scene. "I'll make sure that..."

But Fred's smooth, loping gait took her out of earshot
before she could hear what Scallop would make sure of.

It did not take long to reach a berth, to enter the ship

docked there, and to dump her into a tiny cabin where Windsor efficiently cuffed her hands and feet in some metal tubing.

The hairy Fred sat back on his haunches, resting his long arms on his knuckles, and grinned at her. "You all right?" he asked, friendly. "Sometimes I squeeze too hard."

"Don't know your own strength," muttered Windsor. He finished securing Lily and stepped back to regard her, his mouth a thin, tight line.

"Who the Hells are you?" Lily demanded, glaring at him from her undignified seat on the cabin's only bunk. She tried to shift to give herself more authority.

"Korrigan Tel Windsor, at your service," he replied, bowing in a way that suddenly, and bitterly, reminded her of Kyosti. "Bounty hunter, to the polite. I won't bore you with the other names I've been called. This is Fred."

Fred grinned.

"I have no idea what I could possibly have to do with you—" began Lily, still furious, mostly at the ease with which they had captured her.

"That's what they all say," murmured Windsor. "Say." A spark of interest lit his otherwise jaded eye. "Do you know Gwyn?"

"Gwyn? Who the Hells is—" An unexpected memory of Kyosti back when she first met him, calling Heredes "Gwyn," struck her with such force that she ceased speaking. Suddenly, surely, convinced that it *was* Heredes he meant.

"Yup," said Fred succinctly. "The lips always give it away."

"Wait a minute," said Windsor, speculative now. "That might explain—I suppose you knew Hawk, too." His gaze was piercing, touched with suspicion.

"What makes you mention them now?" she asked carefully.

He shrugged, but the gesture was brimful of some other emotion. "I found Hawk hours ago, half out of his mind. I'm not sure he even recognized me. But I paid what I could for short passage on the *Sans Merci*. She was scheduled to break dock about"—he checked a thin band clasped around his wrist—"forty minutes ago. So even if you were after him, he'll be well clear of Diomede by now."

"If I were *after* him?" Lily cried. "What have you done?"

"Don't scold *me*," Windsor snapped. "Fred, search her."

Fred's touch was remarkably light, rather prim, but efficient. He handed Windsor her com-screen, which Windsor took without a word, and finished his search. "Nothing but this, boss," he said, and flipped out the chain that hung around Lily's neck, revealing the medallion Heredes had given her.

Windsor stared at it. "Oh fucking hell," he exclaimed. He whirled and flung himself out of the cabin, leaving Lily and Fred to regard the closed door in silence.

7 Hard Luck

****

"I'm sorry," Thaelisha paused to examine the conference room on the *Forlorn Hope*'s gold deck—the room itself more than its six other occupants. "Teak," she murmured mysteriously, running one hand along the grain of the table's frame. "Quite remarkable."

"I don't understand," demanded Yehoshua, impatient with her distraction, "how there could be nothing you could do. If you are indeed the local representative of this—what is it called?"

"Concord," said Pinto.

"Surely you have some authority to override this man's license."

"Let me attempt to explain." She surveyed her audience. Her gaze rested longest on the Mule. Its presence alone, Yehoshua felt sure, had gone far to convince her that their story was true. Much against his own instinct to caution, Yehoshua had given her access to their navigation log, which he did not suppose anyone had yet learned to fake over such a complicated journey.

"Yes, Concord is the administrative center of League space, but each system is autonomous, with its own local government. Concord resolves intersystem disputes only when such things arise. Its usual task is as an overseer and, again, as an administrative center. Just as Diomede sends a representative to League Council, which meets at Concord, Concord sends a representative—in this case, myself—to be available to Diomede should they need advice or a negotiator."

She smiled apologetically around the table. "*That* is the short explanation. I'll see if I can get you an abbreviated library of League history and law, which ought to help. As it stands, bounty hunters are licensed from Concord as an intersystem covenant to deal with that small element of society which has been declared dangerous Leaguewide. The man's license and bounty were quite legal. *And* they issued from Concord itself. Now do you see why there was nothing I could do?"

Yehoshua glanced at Jenny. Her face was tight, desperate in a way that it had not been since the days just after Lia's departure. "But what were the charges?" he asked.

Now Thaelisha looked uncomfortable. "Aiding and abetting a dangerous fugitive. Felony accessory to intersystem flight. The physical description was accurate, but they had part of her name wrong." She met Yehoshua's gaze. "It listed her as 'Heredes,' not Ransome."

Yehoshua looked at each person at the table in turn: Jenny next to him; then Pinto and the Mule, both quiet and sober looking; Finch sitting tight-lipped beside the Concord representative, and finally Paisley, who had insisted so loudly on attending the meeting that he had thought it easier to give in than to try to keep her out. Bach, out of a sense of prudence, he had kept hidden. Currently, the robot was in the adjoining tac room recording the conversation.

"Ransome is the captain's real name," he said carefully. "I believe Heredes is a name she used for expedience during the war."

"The *war*?" Thaelisha could not hide her surprise. "You had a *war*?"

Yehoshua exchanged startled glances with Jenny. Jenny shrugged. "We called it a revolution," he said, even more carefully. "The old Central government was quite corrupt."

"I *must* get you to Concord. When they hear about this they'll certainly send an expedition with all haste. A *war*."

"But what about—" Jenny began hotly.

Yehoshua, daring much, laid a hand over her clenched fist, and she broke off and, her lips thin with anger, glared down at the smooth sheen of the tabletop.

"You must understand that we can't go anywhere without our captain," Yehoshua said, quiet but firm. Then he realized he was still touching Jenny and, a little embarrassed, he removed his hand. She did not seem to notice.

Thaelisha frowned. "I understand your concern. But in any case, you will be going to Concord as well. Although there are a number of routes you could potentially take to get there, one is most direct. I can only assume the bounty hunter will choose that one. When min Provoniya comes aboard to go over this with your"—here another glance for the Mule—"navigator, it would be an easy enough question to ask. Whatever ship the bounty hunter has commissioned is listed on the public register by berth. Of course, I can give you no help officially, except the open credit." She reached into the pocket of her shirt and removed a thin, hand-size slate and pushed it across the table to Yehoshua.

He fingered its slim casing but left it resting on the table. "So you suggest we follow the bounty hunter's ship?"

"I don't suggest anything," Thaelisha countered. "Although I will tell you frankly that I have always disliked the Intelligence Bureau's use of bounty hunters. It seems to me that most bounty men are no better than the criminals they're sent after."

"Yes. Well," Yehoshua murmured. "We have bounty hunters in Reft space, too." For a moment, he felt that he and Thaelisha shared an unspoken concordance on this subject, at least.

"There is one more thing." Thaelisha's gaze took in Jenny again, that taut tension that informs the body of a soldier at alert, before she encompassed the whole group with her attention. "A warning. Once at Concord you'll want to tell them about the—troubles in Reft space. But until you get there, I wouldn't talk about it. You'll find that people"—she hesitated—"will treat you differently. We don't—have wars anymore. We don't—" hesitating again, she seemed at a loss for what to say.

"Well, we don't commonly have wars either," said Jenny tartly. "But you have to stay prepared."

"I'm not sure what to say," replied Thaelisha. "Some people will judge you for coming from a society that is prepared to have wars. Others will work so hard *not* to judge you that they'll act"—she smiled ruefully—"rather like I am now. I only mean to advise you to be cautious in what you say."

Yehoshua nodded. "I think I understand," he said, although he was not altogether sure that he did.

She sighed, as if a burden had been lifted from her, and pushed back from the table and stood up. Yehoshua stood as well. "Now. Min Provoniya should be arriving soon, to discuss navigation. I don't doubt you'll want to leave as soon as possible."

The sudden movement of Paisley jumping to her feet startled everyone. "What about min Hawk?" she demanded.

"We can't just leave him here. Captain wouldna' like it. You know it be so," she finished, staring fiercely at Yehoshua.

"Min Hawk?" asked Thaelisha, regarding Paisley with a slight frown. "Ah. The former saboteur. We *are* looking for him, min—Paisley, was it?"

Paisley nodded, only just civil.

"We can't afford to wait," said Yehoshua, brusque because he knew that he would just as soon leave Hawk behind whatever the circumstances, and he could not help but wonder if that prejudice was affecting his judgment.

The look on Paisley's face changed. Around the table, people braced themselves, because it was clear a tirade was coming.

"I must go," said Thaelisha calmly into the encroaching storm. "If anything further has come to light about min Hawk, I'll let you know."

"I'll show you out," said Pinto quickly, with uncharacteristic politeness, and he escaped just behind the representative. The door hissed shut.

"You *can't* just abandon min Hawk!" Paisley cried. "It be *wrong* o' us to do it, just cause we feel ya cool at what he done before. But Captain will feel ya more hurt and sore if we show up without him. What do you think—"

"Paisley," said Yehoshua, "the captain has to be our first priority."

"You just say that cause you be scared o' him."

"I think—" began Finch.

"*You* think?" Paisley rounded on Finch without mercy. "You be ya worst o' all. B'ain't none o' us here got ya right to judge min Hawk. We all killed, for min Jehane, so what be so different in us? And he never treated people different just cause they be *tattoos*. Bain't no one else you would leave if—"

"Paisley," said Jenny in a deceptively quiet voice. "*Shut it up*."

Paisley, mouth still open, stopped talking.

"Maybe you'd like to volunteer to stay and look for him," muttered Finch. "Since you feel so strongly. What, were you sleeping with him, too?" His mouth curled down with scorn.

"I asked," said Paisley with dignity. "And he refused me ya proper way, showing respect for ya offer."

"You *asked* him!" Finch stood up. "That's *disgusting*! How could you even want to *touch* him? How could you—"

"He be attractive. He never treat me like there be something ya wrong with me just cause I got ya tattoos," she retorted.

"You little *slut*—"

"Finch! That's enough!" Yehoshua moved swiftly around the table to put himself between the two. "Mule," he said in a softer voice. "Is there anything you wanted to say before I—disband—this meeting?"

"Yes," hissed the Mule, standing up. "I shall go await this min Provoniya in quieter quarters. As for min Hawk, while I have sympathy for his predicament, I also see the need to follow the captain while we still have a chance to keep track of her." Its hiss was fluid with sta-ish laughter as it glanced at Paisley. "I leave the decision up to you." It left.

"Thanks," said Yehoshua. "Finch?"

"I guess I'm too prejudiced to have a vote," he said bitterly, and he left before anyone could answer.

"Well, it be true," muttered Paisley, unrepentant. She glanced at Jenny and did not attempt to say anything more.

"Jenny," said Yehoshua, sitting down as if he was too weary to stand. "What should we do?"

But Jenny was still staring at the table. "I can't believe I let them take her," she said in a low voice. "I can't believe, with all my training—I feel like I"—her voice caught—"betrayed her."

"Don't be an idiot!" snapped Yehoshua with real anger, hating the look of self-reproach on her face. "Trey *and* Pinto said there was nothing you could have done. I don't doubt their word."

"You didn't ask Trey to this meeting, did you?"

"Someone had to stay on the bridge," he replied, but the excuse sounded lame.

"Min Seria." Paisley set her hands on her hips, a remarkably prim, old-fashioned gesture in her. "She be gone now, so it be no use casting blame. We mun get her back."

Jenny let the barest touch of a smile curve her lips. "I suppose you're right, Paisley. And damn my eyes, but that thing—that alien—was strong. I wouldn't have believed it if it hadn't happened to me."

"Then," said Yehoshua, sounding relieved, "that's settled. Flower wants to talk to the Stationmaster about the patients we have in Medical. As for Hawk, there's a simple enough solution. We have an open line of credit. Once Hawk is

found, we ask Representative Thaelisha to send him—guarded,
I suppose, since he's not quite all there—on to Concord after
us. Then we'll all end up in the same place."

Paisley sighed ostentatiously, but was forced to be content.
Jenny, however, remained seated until Paisley left the room.

"Is something wrong?" Yehoshua asked, aware of a foolish
hope that perhaps she had stayed behind just to be alone
with him.

"A saboteur. And we know he came from League space
originally, before he got to the Reft. But I never found out
how he got to traveling with Lily. Yehoshua, what if he's the
dangerous fugitive? If he is, then Lily as good as admitted to
those charges at the meeting, however unwittingly."

"But that's impossible. How could they have known she
was traveling with him in Reft space? That road has been lost
for generations."

"How did Hawk get over, then? And what about that
privateer, La Belle Dame?"

"Or the one," Yehoshua mused, "who gave me this arm."

They regarded the arm together, with misgiving. "Maybe
there's something Lily hasn't told us," Jenny said finally.

"I hope not," Yehoshua replied, but he looked skeptical.

When Lily woke, she merely lay still, breathing for a
moment. One of the Ardakians was with her—one always
was. She could tell by its scent: she wondered if this was how
Kyosti always sensed the world, with such strong smells, or if
his sense of smell was tuned to subtler differences. Sighed,
thinking of him, and turned over, hoping it was Fred with her
now.

Seeing her open her eyes, the Ardakian grinned.

"Hello, Fred," she said with relief. Stanford never grinned,
aping human mannerisms in that way; she supposed he
thought it beneath his large and imposing dignity. "Can you
unbuckle me so I can use the washroom?"

"Sure." Fred undid her leg bindings and loosened the ones
around her wrists. Finishing, he glanced around the tiny
cabin and then leaned closer to her. "Most humans ain't so
clean."

His head provided a tempting target, but Lily had tried
once at shift change to break out. The attempt had been a
dismal failure, although, in fairness, neither of the Ardakians

seemed to hold the attempt against her. Windsor she had not
seen since they left Diomede some five days since.

"It's the only recreation I've got," she said instead, sighing
as he scooted back to his guard post beside the door.

"What is?"

"*Washing.*"

"Oh, that. Yeah." He grinned again and appeared to be
thinking quite hard. "Could get you another disk for your
slate if you got done with the text Stan got for you yesterday."

"No, I'm not done with them yet. But thanks." She swung
her legs off the bunk and did some leg warm-ups and then
more strenuous exercise, what she could in the cramped
space.

Fred watched with his usual keen interest in anything
physical. "Can't bend my knees like that," he said; he always
said it. His voice was pitched so low it sounded as much like
a growl as words, but he was easy enough to understand once
you got used to it, Lily reflected as she began to do kata,
adapted to her current state. Stanford, of course, spoke in a
deep but clear voice. "Nice kicks." Stanford, of course,
usually offered criticism of her form. To be fair, some of it was
useful.

"Oops." Fred's eye ridges lifted, a sign she now recognized
as his receipt of an order from some unseen communication
hidden on his person. "Siddown. Boss is coming."

Lily sat. Fred tied up her ankles. The door opened and
Windsor slouched in. He looked tired and unkempt. Lily
suspected that *he* was the one who did not wash often
enough. In the corridor, Stanford sat at ease on his haunches.
One long arm balanced his body weight over the floor, the
other held one of the tiny, thin ubiquitous slates that were
the League's more advanced equivalent of the Reft's com-
screens.

"Siddown," said Windsor, rubbing a hand over his eyes as
if the light hurt them. He blinked several times, making a
sour face, and looked at her, squinting. "Can you turn that
damned lighting down?"

"Maybe you should drink less," suggested Lily, having seen
the same signs in her Ridani crewmen.

"I didn't ask your opinion. We got a little problem, Heredes."

"Ransome."

"Ransome. Heredes. What the hell do I care? We still got
the problem."

"My heart goes out to you."

"She always this smart?" Windsor asked.

"Nope," said Fred.

"Yes," said Stanford. "Although I must agree with the esteemed captain that your consumption of alcohol and other illegal and mind-altering substances is currently out of proportion to your body's ability to efficiently metabolize—"

"Stanford, I didn't ask your opinion either."

Fred nodded sagely at Lily. "Boss ain't feeling good."

"Fred. Shut up. Now listen, 'Captain.'" He said it with the barest sneer. "We're coming in to Akan Center. They had some kind of disaster on the wheel a couple days back, and they just requisitioned the owner of this tub for the relief effort. So we're stuck here until she's done and freed up by whatever officious high-level Concord official decided to interfere with legal commercial traffic like a damned—" He halted in a fit of coughing and reached into his shirt pocket. Pulling out a small flask, he took a sip of its contents. "Anyway. We're stuck here until we can get off. It might be two or three days. I'm not sure what happened, some kind of explosion, or a breach. But one of the boys is going to be on you all of the time, armed. Both when they're both awake, and they don't need much sleep. So do me a favor—"

"—and just be nice," said Lily sweetly.

The contents of the flask had obviously fortified him because he ignored the comment. "Save it for Concord. I don't know what they want you for. You can argue it out with them." He turned to go.

"I don't believe you," she said.

He turned back. "You don't believe what?"

"That you don't know what they want me for. Even if you don't know, say, specific charges, you must know generally."

He shrugged, but his lips quirked, up and down, and she wondered if some memory was making him uncomfortable.

Strike for the weak spots, Heredes had taught her. "I still can't believe they even know that I exist," she continued. "I've never been in League space before. They can't have any record of me here, and if I had done anything criminal in the Reft—which I hadn't—how could it apply here to a bounty? I'd have a hearing first. Except it just isn't possible. No one in League space"—she stopped abruptly, seeing some emotion flicker and fade in his face—"Why did you ask me about

Gwyn? How do you know him? Why did you help Hawk get off Diomede?"

He turned and left the room. The door sighed shut with finality behind him.

And the door, closing, somehow triggered her memory again: Nevermore Station. She *had* met other people besides Heredes and Wingtuck and Hawk, from League space. She had met the people Hawk had crossed to Reft space with.

"What were their names?" she whispered to herself, into her fist. The tall, fair-skinned man who kept flushing and the dark woman with the strange dress—a swathe of gorgeous fabric, wrapping her from chest to feet—and the small red circle painted on her forehead. "An . . . An . . ."

"Bless you," said Fred.

Lily laughed. "That's it. Anjahar and Maria. The only other people who could possibly know who I am. Besides La Belle Dame and Yi."

"What would La Belle Dame and Yi want with you?" Fred asked, surprised.

"Nothing, I expect. What do you know about them?"

"Nothing, 'cept they want nothing to do with me, neither, which is the best way to have it with pirates. No interest, either side. You think us bounty boys got a bad repu— reputable . . ."

"Reputation?"

"That's it. Repu—tation."

"Do you know why Concord wants me?"

Fred grinned. "I'm not *that* stupid."

Lily grinned back. "Just thought I'd ask. May I use the washroom now?"

By the time she finished, Stanford had replaced Fred on duty.

"We will be berthing in an hour," he informed her, and immediately returned to his examination of his slate. "Fascinating," he mumbled. "The capillary shafts burst, causing the Wazhezhe converter to overload at five parts per—"

"Excuse me—" said Lily.

"I'm just surveying the information I received off of Akan transmission concerning the disaster. Would you be interested in the electrical and mechanical specifications?" He sounded doubtful.

Doubtful enough that she decided to be quite interested in

them, and she had the pleasure of his peevish explanations
for the rest of the hour.

They berthed, and Fred arrived to join the escort. Windsor
met them at the link bubble. An embarrassed-looking woman
hurried them away past them, back into the ship, at their approach.

After the civilized harmony of Diomede Center, Akan was
chaos. As they emerged from the berth tunnel the reek of
burning chemicals hit them. Fred and Stanford staggered
under the stench. Stanford even let go of Lily's arm, but
because she was still manacled, tight at her wrists and loosely
at her ankles, she did not attempt to flee.

It would have been impossible in any case. To lose herself
in the chaos, perhaps, but not to run: they had to press back
against the closed berth hatch as two large motorized carts
drove past at high speed, carrying—

Lily thought they might be bodies, covered by tarpaulins.

People swarmed the concourse, loading and unloading at
berths, a hive of activity frantic but, beneath it, ordered. A
man, face streaked with sweat and grease, rushed up to
them.

"You the owner of this sloop?" he asked Windsor, then took
in Stanford and Fred, and Lily's bound wrists. "Oh," he said,
dismissing them with reflexive disgust. "You're the bounty
hunter." He turned away and, tapping into the berth com,
began a fast-paced discussion with the captain about a food
shipment from Zeya Depot that she was being requisitioned
to go pick up.

"Come on," said Windsor. "Let's find a hostel and put up
for now. Damn. I didn't need this."

They wended their way through carts and larger flat vans
and people so engrossed in their salvage that they took no
notice of this strange party at all. Two spin locks brought
them into the commercial concourse. Unlike Diomede, whose
decorations had been almost colorless but busy with human
activity, Akan's walls and ceilings had no depiction of people
at all. A thick grass hatched door, the lintels and window
frames, and a wild motif of diamonds and woven stripes in
red and black and gold and ivory patterned the walls like a
reflection of the chaos roiling around them. Windsor quickly
identified a hostel, and he led them inside.

Refugees crowded the lobby. A man sat weeping in a chair,
clutching a small child to his chest. Others sat silent, stunned
or still in shock, on the rest of the chairs and on the grass

mats that covered the floor. A screen above showed a man talking, pointing to a chart, but the sound was turned down and all Lily could hear, even above the quiet grief that permeated the room, was the incomprehensible murmur of his words. His hair was as tightly braided as Paisley's, but his face, at least, bore no tattoos.

Windsor got to the desk and waited. A woman appeared, looking harried. Her hands were wet. Wiping them on her dirty apron, she blinked and examined the party without much interest.

"What do you need?" she asked, not hostile, just preoccupied.

"A room," said Windsor. "We got bumped off the sloop we were on when they requisitioned it for relief."

She shrugged. "Sorry. All my beds are taken. In case you didn't know, a residential concourse got breached. Every hostel here is full with those that got out." Her gaze moved past them to encompass the people in her lobby. "I've got 'em sleeping in chairs. The other residential concourses are doubled or tripled up with the survivors. Worst disaster—" She paused to wipe at one eye. "Sorry."

Windsor sighed. "Can you suggest an alternative?"

She began to shake her head, and lifted a finger to tap her lips instead. "If you give time at Hospital they'll give you a mat to sleep on in the hall. They're evacuating the worst injured to Turfan Link as fast as they can, but with all the machinery cobbled out to the repair effort, they need folks just to scrub the floors, if nothing else."

"Thanks," said Windsor. His tone was so gentle that he seemed to Lily almost a different person. "We'll try that. May as well help out while we're here."

This time the woman met his eye with the first real interest she'd shown. "Bless you," she said, and turned and went back to whatever she'd been doing.

"When did it happen? The explosion?" Lily asked as they left the hostel.

Stanford checked his slate. "Local or Standard time? The initial malfunction occurred two Standard days ago, leading within six Standard hours to the main explosion. I can convert that to Local if you wish."

Windsor interrupted Lily's reply brusquely. "How do we get to Hospital, Stan?"

"We really going there?" Fred asked.

"Why not? It won't hurt us to help them out. And anyway,

our best chance to get out of here is probably to get a space
on one of the ships taking casualties to Turfan Link. They'll
need hands to watch the wounded, if nothing else."

"Really, Korrigan," replied Stanford, "do you actually expect Frederick and myself to endure such close company with
humans in their worst state of—"

"Don't smell any worse sick than they do well," Fred
pointed out. "You just don't want to scrub floors." He grinned.

Stanford did not deign to reply. Lily supposed the expression on his face, muscled rather differently than a human
face, to be disgust. She smiled.

But whatever hopeful prognosis for travel Windsor hoped
to find at Hospital, he was doomed to disappointment. The
activity in the concourses they passed through could not and
did not prepare them for the sheer numbers of casualties that
had overwhelmed Akan Hospital's space and resources. Injured people waited patiently in hallways. Some of the children cried. The wards they looked into were wall-to-wall
beds with just enough pathways for the uniformed and unofficial caretakers.

The stoic fortitude with which the injured awaited treatment reminded Lily painfully of the riot in Roanoak District
on Arcadia, when she had waded through the mob of wounded
Ridanis who had descended on the clinic where Kyosti worked,
escaping the wrath of the Immortals.

Like a dream, she saw a swatch of blue hair down one
corridor. She jerked to a halt, took a step—was jerked back
herself by Fred's strong pull. And the person with blue hair,
clothed in white, turned—

Alien. Even at twenty meters the pattern of his—her—face
was foreign. So close, in height and build, even to some
extent in the planes of the face, to Kyosti, but utterly alien:
je'jiri. Lily shuddered, and then realized that it was looking
at her. She let Fred draw her back and followed almost
meekly as Windsor led them on through the labyrinth of
calamity.

Eventually he found a medical tech, who directed them to
another medical tech who directed them to an adolescent in
stained overalls who led them to a tiny cubbyhole of a room
where a petite woman seemed to be talking on three terminals at once.

She glanced up, waved at them to wait while she finished.
"—yes, thank the Mother for that physician. So they got

out past vector all right? Good. There's a passenger liner due
in tonight that we'll requisition for another casualty ferry. I'll
need a list by oh-seven-eight of eight hundred injured to put
on it. Thanks. Torqua, are you still there? Yes, we need more
penicillin. We've already had twelve reactions in people of
Ridani ancestry to the Lifracin. No, she was killed, but that
Concord official traveling through toward The Pale has agreed
to stay at least another week, and he has not only done the
bulk of the requisitioning work, but he's put a fast yacht out
to ask for code-one disaster aid from Concord. So it's just a
matter of time. He's coming to see me within the hour so I'll
have more information then. Good. Now, who are—*No*, min.
Your spouse is not injured badly enough to be put on the next
ship to Turfan. No, absolutely not. I don't *care* how much
credit you have, and frankly, you're wasting *my* time." She
flipped the terminal off completely, exasperated, and switched
channels on one of the others. "Bishea, how many times do I
have to tell you to screen those calls out? Yes, yes, I know."
She sighed and cut the connection. Looked up. "You can go,
Rio." The adolescent left. Turned tired eyes on Windsor,
taking in the two Ardakians and Lily's bound hands and feet.
"Now. I'm Iasi, the administrator here. What can I do for
you?"

Windsor placed his slate on the surface in front of her. "I'm
a licensed bounty hunter. I got stranded here when some
Concord official requisitioned the sloop that I'd hired for the
relief effort. We're happy to help out, so long as I can keep
my prisoner secure, until we can get passage off."

"A generous offer, min"—she clicked the slate—"Windsor.
Considering you're stuck here in any case." But she smiled.
Lost the smile when she looked up at Lily. Lily felt as if she
were being examined for some obvious flaw she was not
aware of. "Do any of you have first-aid training?"

"I've got a little," Windsor admitted reluctantly. "Fred and
Stanford here don't care to be working so closely with humans."

"Ah." Iasi's measuring gaze took them in. "Ardakians. I
understand. But certainly we have need for a pair of arms for
cleaning and hauling."

"*Really*, Korrigan," Stanford protested. "Madame, while
my cousin Frederick might be well suited to such menial
chores, you would certainly be wasting my talents on them. I
have sufficient expertise in—"

"Stanford," cut in Windsor. "Let's stick with the menial chores."

Surprisingly, Stanford took this rebuke docilely.

"And you, min"—Iasi glanced at the slate again—"min Heredes?"

"Under the circumstances, I'm happy doing anything," Lily answered. "But you'll have to ask my keeper."

"Limited menial," Windsor offered. "As long as she stays with the Ardakians and keeps her manacles on."

Iasi eyed Lily with interest. Lily felt sure that she wanted to ask what Lily had done but was too polite to do so. "I'll ask Yavari to detail you. Hold on." After some tracing, she got Yavari on a terminal. "At loading? That's fine." She switched off, but two more incoming calls lit up the terminals, one face haggard with worry, another tight with impatient concentration. "You'll have to make your own way down to loading," she said, already distracted. "Ask for Yavari. He knows to keep you together."

"Thanks," said Windsor, but she was already talking to the worried face. He retrieved his slate and led them out of the room.

They almost collided with another party, this one consisting of the adolescent Rio, a white-haired man leaning heavily on a cane, and—

"Adam!" Lily exclaimed.

Adam stopped and frowned and looked closely at her, easily taking in her captors and the manacles. There could be no doubt that this was La Belle and Heredes's son: she had only met him twice but was not likely to forget him. And in any case, he had Heredes's dusky cast of skin and green eyes, as well as his mother's blue-black hair.

When he did not answer immediately, she went on. "Adam, you've got to help me. You know *father* would want you to. I'm being taken in on charges that they won't even tell me what they are, and I've got a ship out there that I brought over from Reft space that I *must* get back to."

By this time Windsor had recovered from his surprise. "Excuse her, min. She's unbalanced. Come on, Fred," he growled. "Get her out of here."

"Hold on." Adam raised his right hand and even Fred hesitated. "*Father* would want me to?"

It was his voice. She understood instantly what her mistake

had been. It was not Adam at all. "You're his twin, the one who went bad," she said. "You must be Deucalion."

He laughed. "That's true enough. But who are you?"

"My name is Ransome, Lily Ransome. Sometimes known as Heredes."

"And?" Obviously, neither name meant anything to him.

"And I'm taking her to Concord for bounty," broke in Windsor, impatient now. "It's all legal." He fished out his slate, beginning to sound bored with this procedure. "Signed by Yevgeny Basham, Concord Intelligence. Isn't that an Intelligence crest on your jacket?"

Deucalion studied the slate. "Signed by Yevgeny." He looked up at Lily. "This is all quite legal, min Ransome. Aiding and abetting . . ." He trailed off. "There's nothing I can do. This warrant has been issued by the head of my own bureau."

"You work for Concord Intelligence?" Despite everything, Lily could not help but chuckle, a little. "Now I understand why Adam said you were no longer received in polite society."

"Adam," said his twin brother, "believes in irony. But that still doesn't explain your relationship to him. Or to our father."

Lily looked at Windsor's angry, set face, gauging what to reply, but Deucalion's expression suddenly became remote, as if he was listening to someone else.

"Yes, I hear you. Another ship is coming in? Good. A *what*?" He seemed to be talking to himself, with appropriate pauses, but no one else thought it strange. "An open letter of credit? And they call themselves—the *Forlorn Hope*? The hard-luck fleet? Damn right I'll want those specs checked."

Lily got such a kick of adrenaline that she thought her heart was going to drop straight out of her. She could scarcely breathe. She did not dare speak.

"Well, it doesn't matter right now," Deucalion went on, dismissing whatever his unheard correspondent had just said. "Find out how much space they have on board. I'll tell Administrator Iasi that we have a new casualty carrier for Turfan Link. Good. Put them in a berth convenient to Hospital and let me see their Captain when they've berthed. Out."

His gaze returned to rest briefly on Lily. "I'd like to discuss this, min, but as you see we've got a disaster on our hands. Over eight thousand casualties, and we're not equipped to handle them here. I'm sorry." He turned toward the door to Iasi's office.

"But *I'm* the captain of the *Forlorn Hope!*" Lily cried.

"Some people will say any damn thing," said Windsor roughly. "Sorry, min," he said to Deucalion. "For the interruption. We'll get her out of here. Fred."

Fred jerked her forward.

She resisted. "But it's true. I *am* the captain. And Deucalion, he's *my* father, too. You've got to—"

But Deucalion had already disappeared into Iasi's office, and did not hear her. The adolescent Rio stared at her, curious in a half-repulsed way.

Fred picked her up bodily.

"Who's your father?" Windsor asked.

"None of your damn business," Lily snapped, but delivered from such an undignified position, her anger lacked any real force. Fred hauled her into the elevator with the others, and they started down to docking. "Aiding and abetting what?" she demanded. "I have a right to know those charges."

Windsor sighed. "Aiding and abetting a dangerous fugitive. Now will you shut up?"

"Oh, hells," she muttered. Felt the prick of tears, willed them gone. Hawk, of course. Hawk, who was now on the loose in the very region where he was accounted a dangerous fugitive. Slung over Fred's shoulder, she felt it was impossible that she could find him before Concord Intelligence did.

And yet somehow, against all hope, the *Forlorn Hope* was coming in to Akan. That was something to start with.

8 A Pack of Hounds

****

Once found, Yavari had numerous tasks for them, none of which accommodated a manacled worker.

"I tell you what," Yavari said finally, having sized up the situation without Windsor having to do much explaining. "We've got a security room up in Admitting for the occasional crazy—anyway, since I hear we'll be shipping out over a thousand injured by tonight, maybe I can clear it for you. It's small, but secure. If you'll come with me, min Windsor, I'll need you to show your license. And I don't suppose"—he paused to look at the two Ardakians and at Lily standing between them—"Could you spare one of your companions to help? We just got a shipment of beds in over there."

Windsor took in loading with a comprehensive glance. Fred, go on and help. Stanford, take min Heredes over to the corner there and stay there until I get back." He tossed a spare measure of manacle tubing to Stanford. "Use this if you think you need it."

Stanford led Lily over to the only quiet corner. He tightened the cords on her wrists and ankles and then trussed up her knees as well, and left her propped up in the corner while he settled a comfortable distance away onto his haunches. Getting out his slate, he was soon absorbed in some calculations. Except for the occasional glance he ignored her, although Lily suspected his other senses helped him keep track of her as well. She began to whistle Bach's music, as much to practice her breathing as to remind herself of it. Next time she would not make the mistake of leaving Bach on the *Forlorn Hope*. It might even be that he knew what weaknesses the Ardakians had as physical opponents. Windsor she rated as dangerous by virtue of experience, but also out of shape and badly dissipated. The question with him was whether being on the edge made him more, or less, dangerous. She suspected the former.

She saw Fred now and then, out on the loading dock. The

pace of activity was hurried, but orderly. It proved a soothing
sight: the navy blue coveralls worn by the workers bore a
passing resemblance to similar garments worn in Reft space.
At least some things did not change much.

A flash of blue hair. Lily tensed. It resolved into a je'jiri
half the warehouse away. The alien had stopped to speak to a
man in coveralls. The man nodded, and the creature turned—
but *away* from Lily—and walked out of sight.

She relaxed, letting a sigh escape. And, glancing back at
Stanford, saw another je'jiri headed straight for her.

Stanford, startled by some instinct out of his concentration
on his slate, looked up also. He did not so much stand as lift
his chest, giving him the illusion of greater height.

"Hey. Honorable. This is a bounty prisoner. No parley.
Comprend?"

The je'jiri stopped about five paces from Stanford. He had
settled himself about four meters from Lily, but she could
easily see that the alien's proximity caused him considerable
uneasiness.

"I beg pardon," replied the je'jiri in clipped but precise
Standard. "Honorable. I serve temporarily the administrator
here. We are seeking blood"—it paused; Lily shuddered—
"blood compatibility. Some human blood types are at low
stock. If I may test your—" It paused again and looked at
Lily, but in that same instant she recognized from Kyosti the
slight tilt of the head and brief shuttering of eyes: it was
taking in her scent.

"Why are they sending you around?" Stanford demanded.

The je'jiri curled back its lips. It had a ferocious smile. "We
are faster than the lab."

Stanford sniffed audibly and shifted yet another meter away
from Lily. "Go ahead. But I request, honorable, that you be
quick about it."

"Certainly, honorable." But its attention had already focused past Stanford onto Lily.

Lily consciously restrained herself from shrinking back as
the je'jiri approached her. A certain loose, loping quality
about its walk reminded her of Kyosti. Its hands, cradling a
round basket of tubes and needles, had the same long-
fingered, slender grace as his had. But its posture had a
completely different set, as if each movement stemmed from
an utterly dissimilar kinetic foundation

It halted beside and, bending its knees, crouched. Their

eyes met on the level. The je'jiri's were an overwhelming green.

"You will pretend, I hope," said the alien in a soft voice, "that we are not discussing anything but this operation." It drew a tube and needle from the basket.

Lily said nothing. She was waiting for it to touch her. Preparing herself not to recoil when it did. Barely managed it. The alien's fingers were cool, moving lightly on her skin as it bound a strip of elastic around Lily's arm. With a quick jab, the je'jiri slid the needle into place. Blood welled slowly up into the vial.

"You cannot be afraid of us," stated the je'jiri. It was hard to make out shades of emotion in its clipped delivery. "You have a partner—a mate—who is jir'bra. Only a half-breed, but of the blood without question." It paused.

"Yes," said Lily, caught between repulsion and curiosity. "Yes, I do." She glanced past the alien toward Stanford.

The je'jiri nodded. "Do not be troubled. If you speak softly as I do, the Ardakian does not hear. The pitch of our female voices is difficult for their hearing."

Lily relaxed slightly. "You're not here only to take a blood sample," she said, careful to speak quietly.

"I seek your help. I am the Dai of my family. We were cast here on Akan by our previous employer. Soon this calamity struck. Now we are truly stranded, with none to hear our plea. But you are bound to the greater family. We scented you when you entered the hospital. Now we seek your aid. We must get off this center."

"But I'm a prisoner."

"*That* we can help you with. If you can help us."

"But in another week or two, traffic will have returned to normal. Then you can get a ship—"

The Dai cocked her head to one side, a curiously predatory, but unthreatening gesture. "You do not know of our custom? We do not serve for credit. We have none. We serve an employer, who thus provides all we need. Our world is not so impersonal as yours."

"I see," said Lily slowly, trying to remember what little she had heard about je'jiri on the decks of Yi's and La Belle's ships. She was not sure how Yi's taking on a hunt related to this. "You want me to hire you."

"Yes." Some unfathomable expression crossed the je'jiri's face. "We have a child. She will come into adolescence within the week. Already the signs begin to show. She *must* be isolated. In such chaos as this"—the briefest wave toward the loading dock—"We have one adolescent already, and it is difficult enough to manage him in such close proximity to humans. We have no wish to be forced into a hunt. Please, help us."

The sheer unexpected appeal of the Dai's words decided Lily—if the prospect of averting a hunt was not alone sufficient grounds. "You can free me?"

"Yes. Not immediately. We will be indebted to you, honorable mate, for this offer."

Lily stared into those alien, green eyes, and felt suddenly that this creature, whatever other impulses it might harbor within it, as violent and horrible as those she had seen, was indeed a creature of honor. La Belle Dame had said as much.

"Hey," called Stanford peevishly. "Are you done yet, honorable."

"A ship will be docking," said Lily, quickly and quietly. "The *Forlorn Hope*. I am that ship's captain. Alert the crew. Free me. If no other way, then get me aboard as one of the casualties. And I will give you a berth on the crew."

The je'jiri slipped the needle out of Lily's arm with a delicate tug, and then lifted the vial to her lips. Tipping it, she touched her tongue to the red, fresh blood. Trapped against the wall, Lily could not run. She saw the murdered man on La Belle's bridge with horrible clarity, and each je'jiri touching bloody fingers to thin lips. The same gesture their presence had forced out of Kyosti.

Stoppering the vial, the Dai rose.

Lily's fear of the alien receded as her link to freedom began to move away. "They're moving me," she added hurriedly, before the Dai could go beyond earshot.

"We will find you." Behind her, Stanford shifted as well, eyeing them suspiciously. "In any case," she continued, just loud enough for Stanford's benefit, "the hospital *does* need your blood type." She turned, precise and elegant, grinned her ferocious grin at Stanford, and strode off.

Stanford let out a great sigh of relief. "I *hate* those blue-hairs," he said, confiding in Lily as if they were suddenly best of friends. "They give me the willies. And they smell—not smelly like you humans. It's more subtle, but it makes me dizzy." He looked over at her and slid one meter closer, as if her presence made him feel better. "I don't suppose you notice it."

Lily smiled, deciding that perhaps she did not dislike Stanford as much as she thought she did. "No, I'm afraid I don't. They are—unnerving, though. What kind of groups do they travel in? We never saw them in Reft space."

"A felicitous place, this Reft space," replied Stanford. "I believe they travel in groups we would call families, or packs, ranging from ten to thirty people. Each family belongs to a larger unit, a clan, and each clan to a tribe. Tribes are autonomous. These are human terms, of course. I don't know what the je'jiri call them in their own language." He hesitated, looking doubtful. "I could look it up."

"That's all right. I don't mind if you go back to what you were doing before." Even on his alien face, she could read his relief. He turned back to his slate.

Lily considered her new family: ten to—thirty! She hoped it was a small group. Whatever else came of this, the *Hope*'s crew would know she was here. However they had followed her, they would know they had succeeded in finding her.

She was so heartened by this turn of events that she even greeted Windsor cordially when he returned. He had Stanford loosen her restraints, allowing her to shuffle to the elevator and then through Admitting into a small room with one transparent plastine wall: the secure room. It had room for a narrow bench and a single chair that swiveled down from the wall.

Lily sat on the bench. Stanford swiveled the chair back up and settled back in the space the chair had occupied. Windsor left, keying the door to lock behind him. Stanford got out his slate. Seeing his absorption, Lily lay down and willed herself to relax. Eventually she slept.

A certain amount of sound bled through the plastine wall. She was unsure what woke her, but she was alert instantly. She did not move or open her eyes, but listened. Heard it again. Faint, smothered by plastine and the low hum of bustle and movement, but distinctly there: Yehoshua's voice.

Lily opened her eyes and yawned and stretched, as well as she could, then rolled up to sit. Out in Admitting a steady stream of stretchers flowed from the hospital wards out toward the concourse beyond. Most of the injured had some kind of tubing attached to their persons.

"What's going on out there?" she asked casually, abruptly

recognizing three sets of paired Ridanis carrying stretchers: Rainbow and Paisley, and four others of her *Forlorn Hope* crew.

Stanford glanced up from his slate. "Evidently they got a ship in to transfer more casualties to Turfan Link. They must be loading." He looked out as well, surveying the scene. "A primitive method of transference, certainly, but doubtless their usual system is so overloaded that they have to resort to such measures to expedite the process."

Yehoshua walked through Admitting, speaking with—to her great surprise—Deucalion. Deucalion did not even glance at the secure room, but Yehoshua did. His eyes met hers for a measureless moment and traveled on, seeming uninterested in her presence. Behind, several more pairs of the *Hope*'s crew went past, bearing stretchers. None looked her way.

Rainbow and Paisley appeared, carrying a stretcher. A sheet rested on it, covering a large, spherical object. At that same moment, from one of the wards, a je'jiri emerged. Lily thought it might have been the Dai, but immediately after, a second je'jiri appeared, and it was hard to tell which was the Dai—or even if either of them were.

Yehoshua stopped just beyond the door of the secure room, consulting a slate. Rainbow and Paisley, as if waiting for him, paused at the door itself, the stretcher lifted a little high, up against the lock panel.

A few moments passed. The two je'jiri approached the door, one carrying a basket of needles and tubing, the other a thin slate. They spoke briefly to Rainbow. Looking apologetic, she and Paisley moved away from the door.

Stanford sat up forward on his haunches. "What do they want?" he growled. He tucked his slate into his front pocket and shrugged his shoulders. It looked like a gesture of readying for battle.

The door slid open.

"What do you want?" He growled again, lower and not a little threatening. "I've got a prisoner in here. We have authority to hold her here without being disturbed."

The je'jiri regarded him with an expression Lily could only call dispassionate. "I believe we have encountered before, honorable," she replied, her formality contrasting with his belligerence. "I have authorization from the Administrator of this complex to draw blood from this human. Her blood type is relatively rare, and there is urgent need for transfusion."

"How'd you get in here?" Stanford did not relax his aggressive posture. Lily sat still on the bench, drawing her feet up so that she could stand quickly if necessary.

"The Administrator gave us the key, honorable," answered the Dai smoothly. "You'll find it all in there. Now, min." She turned to regard Lily with those large, fathomless eyes. "If you'll lie down. My companion, who is also female, will draw the blood."

Lily lay down. The other je'jiri knelt, close in against the bed and began to assemble a needle and several vials. Stanford wrinkled up his nose and studied the slate. He held it gingerly between forefinger and thumb, as if it smelled bad.

Yehoshua walked in the door. "Is this the other casualty we're supposed to bring along?" he asked. After several days with Windsor and the boys, his voice sounded oddly unaccented to Lily's ear.

"No." Stanford shrugged his shoulders twice and took one shuffling step forward. "Get out."

"Sorry," Yehoshua replied meekly and turned away.

Stanford looked beyond Yehoshua. "Orthodox tattoos," he muttered. "I don't like this." Yehoshua was in the door, back to him. At that moment Jenny entered, obviously having missed her cue, from the concourse. Stanford clicked his teeth together. "Windsor," he said to the air. "Trouble." He launched himself at Yehoshua, pushing past the two je'jiri.

Someone cried a warning. Lily thought she might have. Yehoshua whirled and instinctively threw a back hand to Stanford's chest—it connected with his face instead.

The force of the blow slammed Stanford backward. He hit the wall hard and collapsed on the floor, his eyes open but dazed.

For an instant, everyone just stared, including Yehoshua—who transferred his attention to the arm that had done the damage.

"It is fortunate," said the Dai in a matter-of-fact voice, "that Ardakians have thick skulls."

"Get me out of here," snapped Lily, recovering from her shock.

The je'jiri retreated. Rainbow and Paisley entered, rolled her onto the stretcher without ceremony, and covered her to the top of her hair with the sheet. At her feet, Lily felt a cool, humming curve. Bach began to sing softly, but his words were muted by the sheet and by the sudden rush of noise as they hustled her out through Admitting.

"We be putting you in a van, min," Paisley whispered.

The stretcher was lifted and rocked as they set it on a level surface. Lily could only see the pale sheet. A motor, already humming, rose in volume and the van moved. Lily began to lift her manacled wrists, to pull the sheet down. A hand stayed her.

"Best to keep it up, Captain," said Rainbow in a low voice. "We still mun get you onto ya ship. It be ya best as well not to talk, I reckon."

Lily nodded and kept silent. The van motored along. She could hear the sounds of other people, shifting, asking a question; one moaned. A child's voice asked plaintively for its mother. Bach had stopped singing.

After a bit, the van came to a halt. Shoes scraped as a few people—presumably Rainbow and Paisley and the other mobile ones—climbed out around her. Then her stretcher was lifted and she was carried again.

They paused.

"Chaim Sovvanna. Ten forty-eight. Severe trauma to the head," said Yehoshua as if reading off a list.

"Check," said a second male voice. It sounded familiar.

They carried her on. She felt the subtle change of pressure as they went through the link bubble.

"Engineering," she said quietly.

A few minutes later they set her on the floor and pulled back the sheet. Jenny, Paisley, and Rainbow stared at her, their faces ecstatic.

Lily rolled up to sit. "Thank the Void," she said. "Good work. Bach, get these things off me."

Bach snaked out an appendage and began at her ankles, singing all the while:

> *Fallt mit Danken, fallt mit Loben*
> *Vor des Höchsten Gnadenthron!*

> "Fall down with thanks, fall down with praise
> before the mercy seat of the Most High"

"Bach got the dock unlocked back in Hospital, didn't he?" Lily asked. "And you coordinated it with the je'jiri."

"The *who*?" Jenny asked. "Oh, them. Yes. I guess all this

time Hawk was trying to look like them. I can't imagine why. They give me the creeps."

The last of the manacles fell away. Lily stood up, carefully, rubbing her arms and stretching her legs. "What's Yehoshua doing?"

"Checking off the manifest. You were in the last group. Then he'll close the berth and we leave."

"Did the je'jiri family get on board yet?"

"Get on board!" Jenny paused. Her puzzlement faded abruptly as enlightenment dawned. "*That's* what she meant. You're taking them on board as *crew*?"

"We'll discuss it later. Come on. If Windsor was alerted to my escape, we'll need to get secured and locked down quickly." She turned to find Blue gaping at her from where he stood by the main engineering console. "We'll want engines within the hour."

"Yes, Captain." His reply was brisk. "Paisley, get over here and run the checkout."

Paisley cast a last, elated glance at her captain and then returned to her duties. Bach and Jenny and Rainbow followed Lily out of Engineering and down the blessedly familiar corridor of the *Forlorn Hope* to the main berth access.

It was empty. They passed through the link bubble, Jenny and Rainbow in front now, and paused to stare down the short tunnel. Yehoshua stood talking, or arguing, with Deucalion. He looked impatient. Beyond him, the van had gone, already returned to the hospital for its next task. But clustered just beyond the two men stood a group of je'jiri. The very alienness of their presence was disconcerting. All of them wore packs of varying sizes of their backs, even the small children.

Yehoshua glanced down the tunnel. Saw Lily. And moved so that Deucalion had to step back, and in the space that created, the entire je'jiri family quickly filed past him into the tunnel.

As they approached, Lily gave a sharp nod to Rainbow. "Show them to Engineering for now," she ordered. "Once we're clear, we can decide about their living quarters." She met the Dai's bow as that female halted and inclined her head, acknowledging Lily's presence.

"Captain." Her tone was respectful.

"Min Rainbow will show you to a place. Wait there, and then we will find you quarters."

The Dai nodded and spoke a few words in a smooth, alien language to her people.

Lily counted while she spoke. Ten adults—after what she had seen on the *Sans Merci*, and learned from La Belle herself, she guessed five of each sex: mated pairs. And five younger ones: one a babe in arms, three older, and one who was almost of adult height yet who had an indefinable air of incompleteness.

It was staring at Jenny, an uncomfortable intensity in its gaze. As Lily watched, it abruptly transferred its gaze to her.

His gaze. The way he stared at her, it was obvious it was a male—young, not quite an adult, but quite male. Interested in her. *Desiring* her. She felt it like a wave of heat. He had a high-boned face, light blue hair that shaded the startling green of his eyes—and he suddenly reminded her of Kyosti. She could see a resemblance, felt herself respond, felt the same passion in her for him that she felt for Kyosti—

She blushed and consciously, with effort, broke off his gaze. That was when she realized that two of the adult je'jiri were restraining him bodily, one holding onto each arm. Was *this* an adolescent je'jiri?

"You *can't* take them on board without proper clearance," said a voice, close—too close.

"Get on board," said Lily. The Dai, heeding the urgency in her tone, herded her family past. Rainbow led them into the link bubble.

Yehoshua hurried up, trying to ignore a righteous Deucalion, who dogged his trail.

"It is imperative with a family of je'jiri that all obligations are being met in full. Given the nature of the risks involved in hiring them, it would be irresponsible for any Concord representative not to insist that you"—Deucalion halted in surprise, seeing Lily, and narrowed his eyes as he tried to remember her—"Didn't we just meet?" he asked.

"Stop them!"

Out on the concourse, Windsor appeared with Fred and Stanford at his back, flanked by two confused-looking civilians in hospital jackets.

Deucalion turned.

"Retreat," said Lily. She and Jenny and Yehoshua quickly moved back into the link bubble. "Bach, commence sealing."

Bach began to code into the link panel. Deucalion turned back.

"Wait one minute," he said, and came forward.

"Don't come in," snapped Lily. "Once we lock I'm not unsealing."

Deucalion, either oblivious to this statement or else disbelieving it, walked into the link bubble.

The seal slid shut behind him.

"That man has a license for you as bounty," Deucalion said, looking at Lily as if he could not possibly comprehend her. "It's illegal to flee a bounty. What are you doing?"

"I'm taking the casualties on this ship to Turfan Link," Lily replied. "Yehoshua, get up to the bridge and start detach procedures. Jenny, put the je'jiri in one of those empty labs. We need them isolated."

"But Lily—Captain—all of the labs are filled with casualties."

"Double up the casualties somewhere else. Believe me, we're safer if they're isolated. I'll explain later."

"All right." Jenny sounded skeptical but she left with Yehoshua. Lily followed them out of the link bubble, Bach trailing after her.

Deucalion kept at her heels. "But you don't understand," he continued. "Do I have to list how many laws you've just broken?"

Behind him, the second seal slipped shut, cutting them off completely from Akan Center.

"Feel free," said Lily, turning to head for the bridge. "You'll have plenty of time to give me the details because you're not getting off until Turfan Link."

"You're really prepared to go through with this?" He *still* sounded disbelieving. "It's kidnapping."

"So be it," sighed Lily.

"And furthermore, as a member in good standing of the Intelligence Bureau, I have the authority to arrest you. Perhaps you don't understand how serious—Wait one minute. How *do* you know Adam and my father?"

Now Lily did stop. "Adam is my half-brother. So are you. I'm Taliesin's daughter."

This news so confounded Deucalion that he followed her quite meekly all the way to the bridge.

9 Deucalion

****

Yehoshua and Jenny trailed discreetly behind the captain as she conducted min Belsonn—whom she continued to call Deucalion—on a tour of the casualties crowded aboard the *Forlorn Hope*.

"The Mule can't be serious," said Jenny in a low voice to Yehoshua as they paused, not wanting to seem too much like a bodyguard, three meters behind Lily as she stopped to discuss the state of the injured with the physician detailed from Akan to supervise this shipload.

"Quite serious," replied Yehoshua. He looked at her: her doubt was beginning to dissolve in the face of the Mule's, and his, adamancy. "I heard from the captain myself that he was only half-human. The Mule had already guessed it. How could he look so much like them if he wasn't half one of them?"

"He did always say," Jenny mused, "that blue was the natural color of his hair. I thought it was just his peculiar sense of humor."

"Peculiar, all right," muttered Yehoshua.

"I *still* find it hard to believe," protested Jenny stubbornly. "They're so"—she hesitated, opening and closing her hands to make up for her lack of verbal description—"so weird. I can't imagine sleeping with one."

"I don't know. From what I saw, they might have a certain—fascination. They're so—so visceral." He grinned.

Jenny shuddered. "You would consider—" She broke off. Yehoshua could not tell if she was disgusted or—was it too much to hope, so soon?—unconsciously jealous.

"They are handsome, in a completely extraordinary way."

"In a completely *queer* way. Although I must say," she gave Yehoshua a quick, conspiratorial grin, "Hawk had his own unique charm. I might have—ah—tried him myself if it wasn't for Lily."

For some reason this confession soured the entire conver-

sation for Yehoshua. He managed to return her smile, but
only because his urge to scowl would certainly cast him in an
unfavorable light.

"Yehoshua." To his relief, the captain had turned and was
beckoning to him. He walked over to her. "What happened
to the six patients we had in Medical who were still in coma?
Dr. Bisayan says that Medical has only Akan casualties in it,
and that Flower said she was completely free to help him."

"Ah," said Yehoshua, feeling uncomfortable under the scrutiny of the captain, the doctor, and the suspicious gaze of
Deucalion, who had already made a bad impression on him
by being overly officious. "I took the liberty of transferring
those patients to Diomede's hospital. Stationmaster—Diomede
Coordinator Scallop assured me that they would be well
cared for."

"And we currently have no physician on board," agreed
Lily. She nodded. "Good. They'll get better care there, and
if any of them do recover, both Scallop and Thaelisha can
explain their situation to them. At least they're as close to
Reft space as they can be."

"And alive," said Yehoshua.

Deucalion shook his head. "Medical care is that backward
in this Reft space? I can see a full report at Concord will be
necessary. There is no reason that a thorough educational
program and exchange can't be worked out to upgrade the
current state of medicine there. People shouldn't have to live
that way."

Dr. Bisayan was shaking his head and clicking his tongue in
agreement.

Lily looked at Yehoshua and pursed her lips slightly, hiding
a smile. Yehoshua kept his face carefully neutral. "Well,
Deucalion," said Lily heartily. "We'll have to ask that you
lead the expedition. I'd love to go myself, just to introduce
you personally to the current head of the government."

"You have a *single* person heading your government?"
Deucalion asked, looking shocked.

"In any case, Dr. Bisayan," said Lily, neatly sidestepping
this outraged question by returning her attention to the
physician, "there should be no problem with min Flower
assisting you as much as you need."

"Thank the Mother. No Center is staffed to handle a
disaster of this magnitude. And we have to send *one* physician on each ship. As you know, most of the other people I

have are volunteers who had little more than the usual
first-aid training. If that physician hadn't turned up fortuitously,
not more than four hours after the main explosion—but he
did. He pitched right in without even an invitation, and we
were able to send him off with the first casualty ship to
Turfan."

"Yes, but you have such a fine medical system here," said
Yehoshua, unable to resist throwing this barb in Deucalion's
direction, "that surely it wouldn't be *that* unlikely that a
doctor might happen by, on a trip, or on a passing ship."

"Of course not," answered the doctor. "But one whose
specialty is emergency medicine? Trained at *Columbia*, of all
places." He spoke the name with respect, even awe. "Yes, he
was a little strange—his manner, and that old-fashioned style
of dyeing the hair blue—and Iasi wasn't sure we ought to put
him in charge, but he was clearly competent at medicine
whatever his other peculiarities, so what choice did we
have?"

"*Blue hair?*" Lily demanded.

Bisayan shrugged apologetically. "It was really a Terran
style that died a natural death. Those of us bred in the outer
reaches, who see je'jiri more frequently, are less likely to
think it a lark to imitate them."

"A lark?" Yehoshua asked under his breath.

"But you say that he went on the first casualty ship sent to
Turfan Link?" Lily asked, hounding this point tenaciously.

Bisayan nodded.

"How long ago did that ship leave? Before us, that is?"

Bisayan waved a hand, unsure. "You must understand that
standing here talking to you is probably the longest break I've
had since the explosion. I simply don't know."

"About a day and a half before us," said Deucalion to Lily.
"Why are you so interested, Captain?"

"And we're halfway to Turfan now, is that right, Yehoshua?"
she asked, ignoring Deucalion.

"Three windows out from Akan, three in to Turfan Link, by
our charts."

"Except we're going rather slower because you only have
one pilot and one nav officer," Deucalion pointed out, forcibly
reentering himself in the discussion.

Lily regarded him for a long moment with a measuring
frown.

"Captain," said Bisayan tentatively. "If I may get back to my duties?"

"Of course." She said it absently, but the doctor nodded and hurried off. "Deucalion." She said his name as if she had just at that moment come to some conclusion about him. "As your half-sister, I feel I can trust to blood ties to ensure your support. You know what business our father was in."

Deucalion looked torn between pride and shame. "Yes. He was one of the saboteurs."

"Have you ever heard of a saboteur named Hawk?"

"*The* Hawk?" Deucalion's eyes widened, giving him a surprisingly childlike look of wonder. "The one who saved Father's life after they'd blown Ogasawara Crossroads? He operated on him with only a laser pistol, a Swiss army knife, and a—"

"—six-year-old Kapellan girl to help him. Yes. That Hawk."

"Can't be." His eyes narrowed, considering new information. "He's in Concord prison. He was arrested twenty, thirty years ago."

"He's not there anymore," said Lily.

"How would you know?"

"He was traveling with us."

Deucalion regarded her thoughtfully "Oh, he was, was he? I'm going to tell you a little classified information. He wasn't actually in Concord prison. He was in the maximum security psychiatric ward. What are you trying to tell me?"

"Void help us," Yehoshua breathed. "The psychiatric ward."

"That I think he may be the physician who showed up at Akan," said Lily. "We need to find him and get him back on board this ship."

"How did he get out?" Deucalion demanded.

"He took our recce boat at Diomede—"

"I mean, from Concord prison. There's never been an escape from that prison. And it was built sixty years ago."

"I don't know."

"I suggest you find out. I'll have to check the records. *If* I am given permission to disembark at Turfan Link, Captain."

"Oh, let's not stand on ceremony, brother," said Lily, not a little caustically. "Call me Lily. Adam does."

For an instant Deucalion looked taken aback at this reference to his twin. "Lily," he said. To Yehoshua's amusement, the informality seemed to make him uncomfortable. "From what I remember—and I may be mistaken—"

"Surely not," murmured Yehoshua under his breath.

"—and he may have been rehabilitated since he was institutionalized, but Hawk—*the* Hawk—was labeled dangerously unstable, and I believe that he had actually committed several murders when he was an adolescent. Some social psychiatrist got him off—they always do—and he was rather pushed into the saboteur network once his aptitude for medicine had shown up. They needed a certain kind of people, you understand."

"You seem to know a lot about him." Lily looked displeased, and not a little angry, but Deucalion clearly did not know her well enough to attempt to soothe her.

"Understandably, with my background," said Deucalion primly, "and raised in the thick of it, as I'm afraid I must admit I was—neither Mother nor Father seeing anything wrong with such an irregular life for a child, and Adam certainly never minded it—I've had to arm myself with knowledge to protect myself from—" He halted, looking abashed. "I even slip into primitive military terms, as you see." Recovering himself, he assumed a more comfortable stance; that of someone about to give a lecture. "Once the Akan relief is settled, you must let me handle this business. You don't want someone like that aboard this ship."

Lily sighed. "Deucalion, has anyone ever told you that you're sanctimonious?"

He stiffened. "That's unkind, Lily. That's the same word Adam used to use. But I refuse to be labeled a hypocrite."

Lily chuckled, laying a hand on his arm in a gesture meant to be sisterly. "I'm sorry. I don't think you're a hypocrite. But you have to trust me, Deucalion. Hawk belongs on this ship. When we reach Turfan Link, will you help me?"

"I can't promise that unconditionally. You must understand that. I have certain duties as a member of the bureau. I'll have to look into his records. And interview him. What was the charge on your bounty?"

She hesitated, but it would be impossible to hide the truth from him when he could discover it himself easily enough. "Aiding and abetting—"

"—a dangerous fugitive." He shook his head. "I will give you the benefit of the doubt and assume that you didn't know what you were doing at the time."

"Thank you."

Deucalion was clearly oblivious to irony once he got going.

"That will give you some immunity. Once I've seen Hawk, if
at that time I can make a case for it, and I promise to review
the data with as much impartiality as I'm capable of, then I'll
plead your side once we reach Concord."

"Once *we* reach Concord?"

"Of course." Deucalion looked surprised. "As soon as Akan
is past critical disaster response, we must get your news of
Reft space, and the recovery of this vessel—as amazing as
that is—to Concord. Didn't you tell me that is where you
were headed in any case?"

"Deucalion, why would you plead my case if you believe
Hawk to be dangerously unstable?"

He blinked, looking surprised. "Because you're my sister."
The "of course," although unspoken, was too loud to be
unheard.

"I should tell you, then, that it was Yehoshua, not me, who
said we were headed to Concord. To settle salvage rights for
this ship. If it's Concord that put the bounty hunter after me,
I'm not sure I *want*, or ought, to go there."

"But where else will you go?"

"How about The Pale?"

"I wouldn't advise it. Not with a ship whose frame is good
but whose software is one hundred years out of date. You
can't afford that kind of disadvantage there."

"That is a good point." Lily paused. It was amazing how
much like Adam he looked. Only when he spoke did he
betray himself. "We'll see," she temporized finally, to satisfy
him. "But whatever happens, I'm—glad to have your company. I never had much chance to get to know Adam."

"Adam was a rather wild youth, I'm afraid," replied Deucalion,
but a smile tugged up his lips as he said it, and a certain
gleam of nostalgia lit his eye.

"He took after Father, I suppose," said Lily, but before
Deucalion could agree she realized with a sudden weight of
dread that he did not know about Heredes's—Taliesin's—death.

"What's wrong?" Deucalion asked.

"Nothing," said Lily. "Let's finish the tour and then we'll
have something to drink in my cabin."

Deucalion looked at Yehoshua, as if asking him to explain
her sudden change of tone. But Yehoshua only shrugged.

It took them over an hour to walk through the makeshift
wards, but Deucalion seemed satisfied with the disposition of
the casualties, and Dr. Bisayan, seen again briefly, was quite

pleased with the addition of Flower to his severely short-handed staff. Afterward, Lily suggested that they break at the captain's cabin. Jenny offered to fetch drinks. While she was gone, Lily checked in with Bach, on the bridge, about their countdown to the next window.

"We have over two hours," Lily said as Jenny returned with a tray of drinks and set them down on the small table by the couch.

Deucalion sighed and slid gratefully into the one chair. "They made these exploratory ships to be both utilitarian and yet luxurious enough so that the crew wouldn't go crazy on the long trips out. Those were the days. How did you get a hold of her?"

"We found her." Lily picked up a cup, but turned it round and round in her hands rather than drinking. "Quite by accident. The *Forlorn Hope* was the ghost ship of Reft space for generations: other ships would pick up her distress beacon and then lose it. We stumbled across her. We still don't know how she got where we found her."

"Her original crew?"

"Gone. Without a trace. As if they'd all simply vanished."

"But there must have been some record on her log."

"It was gone as well."

Deucalion smiled. "It makes a good mystery. Most of that first major exploratory fleet never returned. The return of the *Forlorn Hope* will just add to the hard-luck fleet's legend."

"Deucalion," Lily began, determined to break the news of his father's death to him before she lost her resolve.

"Which reminds me," he replied, as if she had just said something else. "Based on what little I've had a chance to look at, your records and log confirm that you have indeed come from Reft space. Therefore, I have to assume you are unfamiliar with League convenants. This matter of your bringing a je'jiri family on board, for instance. Besides the usual respect for foreign cultures and habits and needs, there is a very serious aspect of je'jiri human relations that you aren't aware of. *Very* serious. Which is why I recommend that you *not* take them on."

Lily set down her drink. "I already gave my word. And I know what the prohibition is." She had no trouble recalling La Belle's words. It was impossible to forget that scene, the terrified man begging for mercy at her feet—mercy that was so utterly denied him. " 'No human will mate or have intercourse in any sexual or sensual fashion with je'jiri,'" Lily quoted. Deucalion's obvious surprise at her knowledge did not gratify her at all: it was too hard won. "I intend to keep them isolated, and to warn my crew of the full consequences of such—relations with them."

"What consequences?" asked Yehoshua, but already, exchanging a look with Jenny, he was beginning to form some conclusions.

"How does Finch work into this?" Jenny asked.

"Finch? The comm operator?" Deucalion looked from Jenny to Lily.

"We'll leave him out of this for the moment," said Lily. "I'll hold a general assembly of crew once we've off-loaded the casualties at Turfan Link and have a moment to breathe."

"Let me give you a piece of advice," began Deucalion.

"Please," murmured Lily, but she could not refrain from grinning a little and, seeing Yehoshua's expression, she had to look away.

"Evidently, you have five paired adults in this family of je'jiri. But the *adults* aren't the ones you need to worry about. They have their own methods of staying isolated from members of the opposite sex, especially nonje'jiri, those who might be foolish enough to attempt sexual relations. It's the adolescents who are dangerous."

"They're violent?" asked Yehoshua, glancing at Lily but thinking of Hawk.

"Violent?" Deucalion mused over the word. "I've never thought of the je'jiri as particularly violent. Certainly not as violent as humans."

"You've never seen the end of a hunt," said Lily grimly.

"Yes, I have," he replied smoothly. "But je'jiri don't have a history filled with wholesale murder justified by personal greed, national security, and religious intolerance."

"You sound like you admire them," said Lily with a shudder, unable to reconcile his calm tone with her recollection of their brutal murder of the man on La Belle's bridge or of Kyosti standing over the bloody corpses of Vanov and his soldiers.

"Why shouldn't I admire them? Like any wild predator on Terra or Sirra, they might have their territorial quarrels, but they don't murder their own kind and they don't kill indiscriminately. They roam in small, equalitarian packs and live by a few straightforward customs that govern them all equally."

"I thought you weren't a xenologist," said Yehoshua, sounding suspicious.

Surprisingly, Deucalion grinned. "I'm not, and I admit to being prejudiced in their favor. I saw a lot of them when I was young, and I came to respect them. They can be vicious fighters, and they have customs—or behaviors—that seem savage to us." He nodded at Lily. "The hunt being one of them. You'll find other people who think them little better than beasts, and some who've even repeatedly tried to have them barred from League space entirely. Frankly, most people are indifferent to the whole subject."

"They give me the creeps," muttered Jenny.

Deucalion chuckled. Somehow in the last few minutes he had lost something of the officiousness that otherwise marred his personality. "It's funny," he mused. "I never saw my father flustered by *anything*, under the worst circumstances, not even the time I sabotaged his operation at—well, never mind that. But I'd swear that je'jiri made him uncomfortable. Not to show it—he was an actor before and skilled at hiding his true feelings—but still . . ." He trailed off, paused, and then looked directly at Lily. "When did you see him last? How was he?"

Lily bowed her head. She was no actor. She could not disguise her sorrow. Her silence itself was statement enough.

"Are you trying to tell me he's *dead*?" demanded Deucalion. He sounded suddenly furious. "I don't believe it."

"I'm sorry," murmured Lily, willing herself to look up so that he could read the truth on her face.

He stood up. He had trouble setting down his drink because his hands were shaking. "Excuse me," he said in a tight voice, and moved to the door. Once there, he paused, reluctant but dutiful. "If you need anything, I'll be in the quarters you assigned me." And left.

The door sighed shut behind him on the same breath as Lily muttered, "Damn. I could have managed that better."

"I don't understand," said Yehoshua. "I met your father, the Sar, at Ransome House, and he was just fine. And he would never have been in League space anyway."

Jenny laid a stilling hand on his arm, but Lily shook her head slowly—not at either of them—and sighed, echoing the door. "I have two fathers, Yehoshua. One is blood, the other is spiritual, but in a way he is—was—closer to me than the one who fathered me biologically."

"I see," replied Yehoshua, not sure that he did. He was terribly distracted by the fact that Jenny was still touching him, her strong hand cool on his upper arm.

"Lily." Jenny, as if on an after thought, removed her hand and took up her cup with it instead. "What is so serious about this prohibition with the je'jiri?"

"In one sentence? If you sleep with a je'jiri, their mate will—*must*—kill you."

"*Must* kill you?" Yehoshua looked doubtful. "That sounds barbaric."

"But what if they're not mated when you sleep with them?" Jenny asked, ever practical.

"They mate for life, monogamous. Once they do mate, the mate will track you down and kill you. That's what we meant by a hunt."

"But how can they possibly know?"

Lily shrugged. "Their sense of smell is—developed in a different way than ours. I'm not sure how."

"But years might have gone by," Yehoshua protested.

"It doesn't matter."

"And Finch was your lover before—" He hesitated, not sure this was acceptable ground.

But Jenny, always quick to see the absurd, laughed suddenly. "Hawk *smelled* Finch on you? That's disgusting, Lily-hae. How bizarre. That must be why these je'jiri singled you out back at Akan Center."

"What do you mean?" asked Yehoshua, feeling more and more strongly that this was *not* a conversation he wanted to be participating in. Jenny had a certain bluntness about her that sometimes made him uncomfortable, and he was afraid that they were veering onto subjects he did not feel intimate enough with either woman—and certainly not with both together—to be discussing. The realization made him wonder if he was not perhaps, as well as being dull, a prude.

Jenny laughed again. "They must have *smelled* Hawk on her. If their sense of smell is that subtle, and you've been someone's lover for long enough, it must be pretty obvious." She grinned. "I'm liking them more and more. And if Hawk really is half je'jiri, it would make sense to approach Lily." She turned to Lily. "Isn't that right?"

"If you add in that honor compels a relative, which I

vaguely qualify as, to help those in need, then yes," she nodded, "it is. Or at least, it was my impression at the time that the Dai, the female who approached me, expected that as the—the mate of a je'jiri—"

"Even if he is only a half-breed?"

"Even so, that I would without question help them. What could I do?"

Jenny smiled. "Combined with your unfortunate habit of taking in strays, I don't suppose there *was* anything else you could do."

"I suppose," said Yehoshua, eager to change the subject, "that you ought to get a full set of the—what did he call them?—obligations regarding je'jiri-human relations from min Belsonn. If we're really going to take them on. What do they do, anyway? Once they're crew?"

"I'm not sure," Lily admitted. "Which reminds me, how did you end up at Akan Center in the first place?"

"We had a bit of surreptitious help from min Thaelisha at Diomede." Yehoshua smiled in his turn. "I think she felt sorry for us, ignorant and rude barbarians from the outer lands."

"Isn't it funny how everyone here uses the Ridani 'min' as an honorific?" Jenny said. "I never, ever heard anyone but tattoos use it in the Reft. No one would ever consider using a tattoo word, especially not as a courtesy. I think *that* more than anything else has made me realize how different it is here. That, and that you see so very few old people."

Lily was silent for a moment. Finally, she looked up, at each in turn. "Are you happy you came?" she asked quietly.

"Yes," said Yehoshua, surprising even himself at how easily the answer came to his lips. "Yes, I am."

Jenny did not answer for a long, long time. Lily simply regarded her without expression, intent and concerned. But Yehoshua felt nervous; he knew she was thinking of Lia, and he was afraid at what her answer might be.

But when she moved, she reached to take first Lily's hand, and then his. The simple ease with which she included him took his breath away.

"Yes," she said. "I'm glad that Gregori and I are here, with you."

10   Turfan Link

****

They arrived at Turfan Link at almost the same time as the casualty ship—the requisitioned passenger liner—that had by Deucalion's calculations left Akan Center half a day *behind* them. The ship Hawk had presumably been on had already left, having discharged its cargo and, according to Link traffic control, returned to Akan to render further assistance.

Gregori sat drumming his toes up onto the underside of the tac table while the captain discussed these facts with Pinto and the Mule. Except for the Ridanis left guarding the link bubble, everyone else had been detailed to help unload the casualties, under the joint direction of Yehoshua and, of course, Deucalion.

"Anyone from the crew is capable of spotting Hawk," the captain was saying. "And they know not to approach him. But if the bounty hunter got here on the liner, I have to be cautious."

"If they find him?" the Mule asked. It did not look up from the three-dimensional chart displayed in the table: the vector routes available from Turfan Link to Concord.

"Jenny will notify me and shadow him until I can get there. Deucalion did promise to see if Windsor had checked into Link traffic control. Evidently bounty hunters are required to do so at each station or planet they come to."

"Do you trust him?" asked the Mule.

"What? Windsor to check in or Deucalion to tell me the truth if he did?" The Mule hissed appreciative laughter. "No to the first, a fairly hopeful yes to the second. We don't have much choice but to trust him."

Pinto yawned. Gregori watched the tattoos around his mouth stretch and collapse at the movements. "He asked me what orthodox sect I belong to," Pinto said. *"Orthodox sect? He's* the fourth person to ask me that. Do you have any idea what it means?"

The captain shrugged. "None."

Pinto shook his head. The beaded braids of his hair clacked quietly and stilled. "I've looked over this chart five times," he said, a little grumpily. "I'm tired. Can I go?"

The captain smiled. The Mule continued to peruse the display, ignoring this complaint. "Go ahead," she said, and Pinto sighed ostentatiously and got up and left. She followed him out with her eyes, as if something about the way he walked interested her, and then with a start and perhaps the finest blush of pink in her cheeks, she turned her attention to Gregori.

"Dr. Bisayan mentioned to me that you had been a great help to him, running errands and guiding his staff when they got lost. Thank you."

Gregori smiled, pleased to be the object of her praise. But her attention quickly shifted away. She studied the table in silence, but Gregori sensed her thoughts were elsewhere. He felt, like a fourth presence in the quiet room, one of the ghosts of the *Forlorn Hope*'s previous crew enter and settle into the seat beside him to study with equal intensity but an overpowering emotion of grave alarm some unseen manifestation on the tac table.

"Mule," said the captain. Her voice sounded uncharacteristically tentative to Gregori. "While I'm waiting for news of Hawk, I need to go down and interview the je'jiri. You were there this morning when I spoke with the *Hope*'s crew about their—background. I want to see if you might in fact be the ideal person to serve as—I hope this won't offend you—general liaison to them."

Now the Mule looked up at her. Its crest raised slightly in an expression Gregori could not interpret. The stillness in the room seemed charged with some emotion. The ghost at the table evaporated under its force.

"You feel," hissed the Mule, fluid but neutral, "that because I am sterile I am also asexual, and therefore safe with these aliens."

"Partly," the captain admitted, but she did not look ashamed to be saying it, merely straightforward. She regarded the Mule frankly. "You are also only half-human and *therefore* presumably only half as susceptible, and perhaps your sta ancestry makes you less attractive to their adolescents. I understand that the girl—the young female—has finally crossed into the first stages of adolescence, and they have had to isolate her from the other adolescent, who is a boy."

The Mule hissed, long and slow. "Because you respect me
enough to be frank, Captain, I am not offended." It gave a
little, swift slip of sound, a sta-ish chuckle. "And it may be
that you are more correct than you know in thinking that I,
and they, will be safe together."

"Thank you." The captain turned to examine Gregori. "I
think it might be safe for you to come along as well. You're
young enough."

"Oh, they like me," Gregori confessed. "The Dai said I
could come play as often as I wanted to. One of the little kids
is just younger than me. But she knows math and the
computer a lot better, though. She's smart."

"How often have you gone down there?" the captain
demanded, and Gregori realized that he had just made a
tactical error in speaking so freely.

"You won't tell me not to?" he pleaded, feeling desperate.
"I *like* them."

"We'll see," replied the captain with an adult's usual and
deplorable ambiguity. "I'll have to speak with your mother."

Gregori protested no further, knowing quite well that it
would prove fruitless. Instead, he trailed along behind them
as they went down to bronze deck to the three-room lab in
which the je'jiri had made their quarters.

Surprisingly, the Dai met them outside the door. She
looked disturbed by something, and as soon as she saw the
captain she inclined her head and waited for the party to halt
before her.

"I was just to come in search of you," she explained in her
precise Standard. As she spoke she moved her head from side
to side, a subtle movement nothing like a shake of the head.
Rather, she seemed to be taking in information about the
three people standing before her. All the je'jiri had this habit;
Gregori was almost used to it. "The male who calls himself
Pinto must be removed from our rooms."

"*Pinto* is here?"

The Dai shaded her mouth briefly with one slender hand.
Gregori caught the impression of suppressed revulsion from
her, but she hid it quickly. "My sister's child has just passed
into adolescence. Already we have isolated her from my son,
for in this early stage the young ones have no self-control. I
think that is the word." She paused, polite, for the captain's
assent.

The captain's mouth drew taut with anger. "Pinto has

always been lacking in self-control. Especially with regard to—attractive females."

The Dai regarded her with an expression too alien to interpret. "Human males are singularly lacking in this trait. It lends them a rather barbaric quality."

The captain laughed, began to reply, and then sobered, as if a different, less-amusing thought had occurred to her. "I came to speak with you, but let me deal with Pinto first." The Dai inclined her head again and preceded the little group into the lab.

It was quite stark. In the intervening days the lab furniture had either been moved out or to the walls, so that the main room gave the impression of a wide expanse of floor and air, big enough to move easily far and fast. The room was empty except for the two young children building circuitlike patterns with clip-in blocks on a flat, nubbed board, a single adult seated cross-legged on one of the high lab counters with a slim computer on her—his?—lap, and Pinto.

Pinto did not even notice the captain's entrance. His attention remained riveted to the door on the right side of the lab. It stood half-slid open, and a young face of remarkable, exotic beauty and a fierce intensity of expression peered around the opening at him. The sexual tension in the air was palpable.

The adult seated on the counter glanced up, taking in the captain and Gregori and the Mule with the same slight side to side shake of her head, and then spoke a few words in their alien tongue to the Dai. The Dai replied not with words but with a brisk series of gestures with one hand.

After a diplomatic pause, the captain addressed the Dai. "If I may," she said, and together they looked at Pinto.

At the sound of her voice, Pinto glanced around. It was a little hard to see because of the tattoos, but he flushed and took a step both away from the captain and away from the door in which the je'jiri girl stared hungrily at him.

"What are you doing here?" the captain snapped.

"I—" He hesitated.

"Against my express orders. I thought I explained the situation so that any *thinking* person could understand it."

Pinto glanced back at the je'jiri girl. She watched the altercation avidly as if any strong emotion excited her interest. "I just thought I'd come get acquainted—" he began.

"Pinto. She is *off-limits*."

"She's no younger than Paisley," Pinto retorted, hot.

"Pinto. You are confined to quarters until such time as we need your services on the bridge, or I have time to drill into your stubborn brain that you *will not* and *cannot* bring your Ridani promiscuity into this particular community. It would be lethal."

"You can't order me around like that—or make your damned prejudiced comments about—"

The Mule stepped forward unexpectedly. "Pinto," it hissed softly but without sympathy. "I am physically stronger than you are. I suggest you do as the captain says, if you cannot understand any reason short of force."

Pinto stiffened with fury. Gregori braced himself for an outburst, but instead the pilot kept silent and merely stalked out, throwing one glance back at the girl still staring out at him before he left.

As soon as the door slipped shut behind him, the seated je'jiri slid smoothly off the counter and directed a string of harsh words to the girl in the outer doorway. The adolescent's face reflected a stream of emotions—from anger to mocking humor to brief contriteness—and then she vanished back into the room behind her.

"I thank you," said the Dai.

"He is still young," said the captain. This explanation evidently satisfied the Dai, because she turned her attention to the Mule.

"This one," she said, "I have scented. She has ancestry of a civilized race, I think."

The Mule's fluid laughter hissed quietly.

"I was hoping," the captain began, "that the Mule might serve as a more appropriate—more acceptable—liaison between your family and this ship's crew."

As the Dai considered this, Gregori edged away from the adults over to the two children. Without speaking, or even looking up, they moved so that he had a place to sit with them. The eldest handed him a delicately traced black block to add to the growing pattern.

Because they talked as they played and he could not understand them, it was easy for Gregori to observe both the game and the adults. With the expulsion of Pinto, the main room gained sudden life. The je'jiri adults came out of the room the adolescent girl had been banished into. They had a brief conference with the Dai and then two of them shoved a lab counter into the center of the room. The Dai invited the captain to sit on it, and the captain, without even hesitating, followed her example in climbing up on it—albeit slightly less gracefully—and seating herself cross-legged in careful imitation. Then the four other adults pulled a second counter close to it and seated themselves there, watchful. A moment later five more adults came from the other room and sat on a counter set against the far wall, separated from the captain and the Dai by the counter on which the other four adults sat. Gregori had spent just enough time with them that he was beginning to be able to distinguish male from female. The five set back from the central counter were the males. The children continued their game, oblivious to the meeting. The Mule, after refusing a seat next to the four females, remained standing.

"As you know, I am Eldest Sister," said the Dai. "These are my sisters: Hand Sister, Middle Sister, Fleet Sister, and Youngest Sister." The captain nodded at each in turn. They inclined their heads, each acknowledging. "These," she motioned to the silent males. In a row, their blue hair was startling and almost garish. The female hair was a less brilliant shade of blue. "These are my brothers: Eldest Brother, my mate, Hand Brother, Middle Brother, Fleet Brother, and Youngest Brother." The same courtesies, the same incline of the head, were exchanged, although at this greater distance they seemed less personal.

"If I may ask," began the captain.

The Dai nodded.

"Is it a custom among your people, that the males sit farther back?"

The Dai showed her teeth, a feral grin. "I take no offense at this question," she replied. "It is not so in our family that there is any separation. Your presence is disturbing to them because you are"—her hesitation was almost human itself—"You will take no offense in your turn, I hope, that I mention a condition peculiar to your species—like all human females, you are always receptive."

"Receptive? Oh." The tone of her voice made Gregori actually look up from the game to examine her. To his surprise, she blushed. "I see. Yes. Well." Her gaze strayed to survey the five males and then she looked down again abruptly, still flushed. Several of the adults shaded their mouths with their hands, hiding some reaction. "I came," she began again, more brusquely, "to discuss the terms of your employment. I agreed to take you on because of the obligation I feel toward the man I—" She hesitated.

"Your mate," answered the Dai, not allowing for there to be any question.

To Gregori's confusion the emotion on the captain's face seemed if anything a little like anger, and it puzzled him how she could be angry with Hawk. He got a quick, confused memory of blood and bodies lying prone on the floor, but it was too unclear for him to sort out.

"Yes," said the captain in a cold voice. "My mate."

"As well," said the Dai, either ignoring or not hearing the coolness of her inflection, "as the proper honor obliged to a mate's kin, we were able to assist you in escaping."

"Yes. Which puts me under a second obligation. But I don't know what terms are usual for such a relationship—with you and your family signing on as crew. And I am concerned, of course, to keep the—human members of the crew safe."

"You have not a familiarity with the treaty laws established between my people and your League?"

"We didn't come from the League. We come from a place where there are no je'jiri."

"That is curious." The Dai swept a comprehensive glance around the large room; her gaze lingered on the Mule before it returned to the captain. "It is better you locate such terms in your human libraries, so that you understand them completely, but I will attempt to outline the main points."

The captain nodded.

"First, on your part, you will provide nourishment and care and quarters of sufficient size, enough to hold the family and permit the isolation necessary to our living. This suite is small but it will suffice, as there are separate rooms for the two lodges and a common room. Second, on your part, you will instruct your human crew in matters of protocol. Such as you and I, being both female, can easily work together, and males as well, although there may be some strife still, but controllable. But such as the young male who entered into here must be kept separated from the adolescent girl, and any females of little continence from my adolescent son. For our part, we will keep our two adolescents isolated from the main population, just as we must keep them isolated from each other. In this matter, the one you introduced as the Mule might safely act as liaison, as she currently exhibits no characteristics that might disrupt either our people or yours."

"*She?*" asked the captain softly, but she went on before the Dai or the Mule could respond. "What other terms?"

"Our obligation to you then continues in the services we can provide."

"Ah. And those include?"

"Any work that we are capable of that does not violate the prohibitions on contact with those other of your crew who might be dangerous to us or to whom we might be dangerous. We have discovered as well that we je'jiri function well within human computer systems. Fleet Sister and Fleet Brother have special capabilities in these matters and have familiarized themselves with ship functions in particular. I believe that settles all major terms."

"How long does such employment last?"

The Dai blinked. It seemed a deliberate gesture, not a reflex. "Until it has ended," she replied, as if the answer was self-evident.

"I see." The captain's voice stayed carefully neutral. "I will consult our library for any further information on our agreement, but I do have one more question. Why did your last employer abandon you?"

The silence in the room held abruptly a palpable tension. A few of the je'jiri males shifted uneasily.

"Your kin," said the Dai, the clipped precision of her speech even more pronounced, "possess what you call laws, but we have cause to notice how often you break them. Our last employers found a lucrative cargo at Akan Center and preferred to evict us from our rooms to use such space to transport it. We were thus cast out into what soon became the disaster. A terrible event for your kin, and the force of the strong scents it created precipitated one of our children into adolescence before her time, before my son had passed into adulthood, and we had been able to find a family with a suitable female to mate him to. That cousins should mate is—" she might have shuddered, but to Gregori it was more a sense of her powerful revulsion at such a prospect than any actual movement that conveyed the emotion to him—"impossible. But it is difficult to keep two adolescents apart under such chaos as Akan Center must endure at a time of disaster. Your arrival was of great bounty to us."

"Then I am glad," said the captain quietly, "that we were

able to help each other. I think then, if there is nothing else, that I will leave you to get settled while I check on the rest of the crew."

The Dai inclined her head. "I have only one question," she said. "But it is of little importance, merely a curiosity." At the captain's expectant look, she continued. "Who are the other presences on this ship? Why have they not left?"

"What other presences?" asked the captain.

Gregori stood up. Nodding politely, but quickly, at the eldest child, he hurried over to stand beside the Mule.

The Dai did not answer right away. Instead, she cast her head about, that slight side to side shake, taking in some other sensory information. For a moment her keen gaze rested on Gregori. He shrank a little closer to the Mule, sure that she knew that he knew about the ghosts, too. It was clear to him that she had guessed some secret about him. She showed her teeth, as if they were accomplices, and returned her gaze to the captain.

"The other presences," repeated the Dai. "You have a word in your tongue—Ah, that is it. The ghosts of the crew that lived aboard this ship before you. All scents linger on after one has passed on to the next place, but theirs is strong, as if they are somehow still here."

It took a long time for the captain to reply. She looked caught between disbelief and curiosity. "You can *smell* the original crew?"

"You cannot?" the Dai began, and then made a swift gesture of apology. "Forgive me, I forget that you are deficient in this sense. You would not be aware of them, unless they appear to you through some other sense. I thought perhaps you had seen them."

"No," said the captain, still too amazed by this revelation to be anything but honest. "I had no idea. We wondered what had happened to them. We found the ship abandoned."

The Dai shook her head slightly. "They do not speak to us to tell us how they came to both leave this ship and not leave it."

"I don't know." The captain shook her head, an echo of the Dai. "I don't know."

By the door to the corridor, the com clicked and chimed. "Captain." It was Finch's voice. "Jenny and Yehoshua are back aboard. They're looking for you."

The captain uncurled herself quickly. Recalled her surroundings and waited for the Dai to get down off the counter first. All the je'jiri slipped down to stand, respectfully.

"I must go." The Dai inclined her head, and Lily returned the gesture. "I will send the Mule later with any specific assignments."

"It is well," agreed the Dai, and she escorted her to the door. The Mule and Gregori trailed behind.

Outside, left alone in the corridor, the captain fingered the nearest com. "Finch, where are they?"

"Still at the link bubble."

"All right. I'll meet them there." She glanced at her two companions. "You may as well come with me." Her gaze paused meaningfully on the Mule. "I may need you."

It—she?—nodded but did not speak as they made their way quickly to the link bubble. Jenny and Yehoshua had waited there, but the captain slowed as she neared them. The expression on their faces was message enough.

"He's gone," Jenny said without preamble. "No trace. I'm sorry."

"He *was* here," added Yehoshua, speaking almost on top of her words, as if he was aware that the captain found this news distressing. "He worked in Hospital here for a number of hours and then he just vanished. No one really noticed when he left."

"What kind of station security is here? They have no record of him being seen? Void knows he's noticeable enough." The edge on her voice was as much anger as fear.

"We checked through—what do they call it?—both the traffic manager and the Link coordinator. They said that at a place this big it might be impossible to trace him. He could have gone downside—there are three planets in this system that take traffic. One's inhabited. Shuttles leave all the time. But they offered to keep an eye out for this station itself."

"There is one strange thing," said Jenny as he paused for breath. "About a third of the people in this hospital that we talked to thought he was je'jiri. They didn't know about any human male with blue hair."

"I don't know what to make of that," said the captain, sounding impatient. "What about the bounty hunter?"

"Hasn't registered here," Yehoshua replied. He shrugged. "For what it's worth."

"Hells," muttered the captain.

The link seal peeled aside to reveal Deucalion. He held a

slim com-slate in one hand and glanced up from reading it
and saw the captain.

"Lily. Good. I was just coming to get you."

"Yes?" The captain's voice sounded ominously unwelcoming.

Deucalion seemed oblivious to her mood. "All casualties
have been transferred to the Link's main hospital. According
to the reports from the liner that left Akan after us, there are
enough injuries left that two carriers can accommodate them.
The first ship has already gone back. The liner will return to
pick up its passengers and continue its cruise and we'll get
the second load."

"Deucalion." The captain's anger gave her voice a clipped
tone. "Hawk is loose somewhere in this system, and for all we
know he's lost his memory entirely. We have to find him first.
And whatever your respect for the legalities in League space,
I am *not* turning myself back in to that bounty hunter, who is
still doubtless stuck at Akan."

Deucalion frowned and sighed. "Lily. You are upset."

"Damn right I'm upset!"

"Wait a minute. I'm not saying that your concern is not
legitimate. Quite the contrary. I agree that finding Hawk is
our highest priority"— she began to relax—"*after* Akan's disaster is relieved. There are people on that center who will die
if they aren't transferred to available medical care. That *must*
come first with me, and unfortunately I have authority as an
employee of the bureau to requisition this ship over your
protests. That doesn't mean I'm not sensitive to your feeling
responsible for a member of your crew—"

Jenny laughed curtly.

"Did I say something wrong?" Deucalion asked.

"Never mind," Jenny murmured.

"What if I refuse?" Lily demanded. "To take the ship back
to Akan."

"Refuse? How can you refuse?"

"Can you force me to go?"

"*Force* you? People's *lives* are at stake. Do you seriously
believe that Hawk's life might be in danger?"

"It might be."

"Do you believe that?"

"Perhaps not in danger immediately, but he's—he *needs*
us."

"The fabled Hawk? Somehow I think he'll land on his feet."

"That's all very well, Deucalion, but what if we lose his

trail? By the time we get there and back he could be anywhere—in this system, or taken ship for somewhere else. How are we supposed to find him if we lose him here?"

Deucalion blinked, looking surprised. "You have a family of je'jiri on this ship. Tracking him down will be the least of your problems. I worry more about what you'll be able to do with him once you find him again."

"The je'jiri—" She shivered. "Just like calling out a hunt."

"Not quite," he replied with a wry grin. "But just as efficient. Lily." Now he sounded conciliatory. "Help me with this. I'll investigate the charges brought against you and take it upon myself to escort you personally to Concord."

"I still haven't agreed to go to Concord with you."

"*Lily*—"

"*After* we find Hawk, we'll discuss it."

He sighed. "*After* we find Hawk."

"Agreed," she said, but she neither sounded nor looked pleased with the decision. "Yehoshua, get all crew back on board. I want us out of here as fast as possible. I've got two je'jiri to put on shift at com-tac. That ought to help our speed. The Mule will act as liaison to them."

"Wait. Wait." Deucalion raised a hand. "I've got a medical team coming on board, and a full complement of equipment and supplies for the relief effort."

"Then get them on fast," the captain snapped. "Yehoshua. Mule. Get moving. Jenny. I'll need a guard on Pinto's quarters until such time as I personally lift it." Jenny's eyes widened. She opened her mouth to speak, shut it, and saluted. "Put everyone else on loading detail. Well?"

They disappeared quickly, leaving only Gregori and Deucalion.

Deucalion grinned. "Remind me not to cross you, sister."

"You already have." She gave him what was clearly meant to be a debilitating glare and then, waving Gregori along in front of her, headed for the bridge.

11   Die Kunst der Fuge

****

Paisley sat vigilant on the couch that graced the outer room of the captain's suite. When the outer door shunted aside to admit Yehoshua, she greeted him with a look that was respectful but adamant. "Captain be sleeping. Be it ya important news you bring?"

Yehoshua smiled. "Have you appointed yourself guardian?"

"You may laugh," said Paisley darkly, "but someone mun do it. Min Bach could do it, but he be ya busy and sure none of us can understand him in any round, not less he wants us to."

Yehoshua came across the room and laid a hand on Paisley's head, his fingers tangling in her dark mass of tight braids. "I'm not laughing at you, Paisley," he said gently. "I think you're the kindest person on this ship."

"That may be. But I reckon it be min Seria you wish were ya kinder toward you."

He removed his hand hastily. "What do you mean?" he asked, not a little stiffly.

Her grin gave her an impish look. "I reckon you know right well what I mean."

"It's none of your business, Paisley. I'll thank you to keep your opinions and meddling to yourself."

"Sure," she agreed. "But min Seria be like everybody. She be mourning over Aliasing now, but she mun have ya"—she smiled again, seeing that she had embarrased him—"ya *kindness* soon enough. You just got to be there when she be ready."

"I thank you for the advice," he said with a reserve quite at odds with the warmth with which he had originally greeted her. "Now I'm afraid that I have to wake the captain."

"What be ya news?" she asked, returning immediately to her pose of the watchful guardian.

He shook his head. "We've got a problem with the bounty hunter. I can't decide whether min Belsonn is completely evenhanded and compassionate or just totally gullible. He let them on the ship."

"Let them on ya ship!" Paisley jumped up and ran over to the inner door, pressing the com.

After a moment a sleepy voice said, "Ransome here."

"Lily," said Yehoshua, not waiting for Paisley to reply, "you'd better get out here. Your brother—"

But the door slipped aside and Lily, looking rumpled, her hair still tousled from bed, appeared. She straightened her tunic as she spoke. "What's wrong?"

"The bounty hunter got on board."

Her sleepy expression vanished. "How?"

He sighed. "One of his companions got injured welding and somehow got on the list of casualties to be transferred to Turfan Link. Alien physiology, something like that. They aren't equipped to handle it here at Akan." He paused, expecting that she might reply, but she did not. "There was some argument over letting the other one go with him, but they are cousins or something, and when Administrator Iasi brought the matter to Deucalion he said it would be cruel to separate them under the circumstances. And we're the last casualty ship to go to Turfan Link. So they got the clearance to come on."

"What about Windsor?"

"He's got first-aid skills. The medical team we brought is for Akan Hospital—they're still running over capacity, but not so much that they can't handle it for the short term, *with* the extra help. So he—Windsor—volunteered his first-aid skills for this trip."

"And Deucalion, of course, wouldn't refuse the help. Is the Ardakian's injury serious?"

"I don't know."

"Get that information for me. Windsor could very well have faked the entire thing."

"How could he have done that?"

"You said yourself they don't have anyone qualified to medic alien physiology."

"But wouldn't Deucalion be suspicious? Wouldn't he check?"

Lily combed her fingers through her hair with impatient disregard for the tangles catching in them. "Deucalion's respect for other beings is clearly the model on which all civilized behavior ought to be based. But he's forgotten that people like Windsor lie as easily as they breathe. Damn. Let me wash up and change first."

As she turned, the outer door slipped open and Finch charged in.

"Lily!" Seeing Yehoshua and Paisley, he halted. "Ah, Captain. Some man has appeared on the bridge claiming he has right of access to monitor all your movements until you turn yourself in under his escort at Concord."

"What the Hells does he think he's doing?" Lily demanded. "He's on our ship. We outnumber him thirty-five to—No. With the je'jiri, forty-five adults to three."

The lights went out. Someone in the room gasped, but it was not clear who. Emergency power banked up, and lights glowed again at their lowest level: maintaining life support. The com clicked, clicked again, and a familiar voice came on.

"Captain," Windsor sounded tired. "Stanford has just gone into your operating system and rearranged a few files to which only he has the key. In essence, captain, at the first vector you try to run without the proper override codes, the engines will blow, stranding you here or in vector space— wherever that is. Stanford has these codes. Therefore, this ship is now under my control. As long as you cooperate, there'll be no problem. I'll return control of the ship with all systems intact to your first officer once we've turned you in at Concord. All life support to any areas with casualties is unimpaired. Unfortunately, the rest of you are on minimum."

"Thus keeping Deucalion pacified," muttered Yehoshua.

"Do you copy?" His voice, over com, did not sound particularly triumphant.

Unexpectedly, Lily grinned. "So he's going to play that game, is he? I don't know how good Stanford is, but Windsor doesn't know that I've got Bach. Yehoshua, back to the bridge—No, wait. Finch, who's on the bridge now?"

"I was. Bach, Trey, the Mule, and Pinto, and one of Jenny's mercenaries who seems to be following Pinto around." He made the question implicit in the cadence with which he ended the phrase.

"Never mind that. Finch, return to the bridge. I don't care how you do it, but get Bach out of there and back to me. Yehoshua, find Jenny. I want her, and everyone she can spare, armed and up in this room. Paisley, find Gregori and tell him to go to the Dai and ask her to send—" She had to pause, to think of their names. "Fleet Sister and Fleet Brother to me. I want to see if they can dig past whatever

Stanford did. On no account are *you* to go into the je'jiri's quarters. Absolutely. Then go to Medical and ask Flower to personally check on the other Ardakian's injuries. Fred— Frederick—is one of his names."

"Wouldn't this all be faster to do on com?" Finch asked.

"If Windsor's not bluffing, if Stanford really has gotten in to operating systems, then we can't trust com to work for us. Yehoshua, you'll be running the first window from the bridge. Give Windsor your full cooperation."

"But min Ransome," protested Paisley, "if we got so many, why can't we just overpower them? They only be three."

"Because I don't think Windsor *is* bluffing. I'll see what the je'jiri and Bach can make of the problem first."

"Then what are you going to do?" asked Yehoshua.

She grinned as she went to the door into the inner room. "Make sure he's sorry he ever tried it. Though I'll give him credit for audacity."

"But what are you going to *do?*"

"I'm not sure yet," she admitted. "But remember, I got my training from *Master* Heredes. Just get Bach to me."

In the dim light that was all that was left to her in the inner room, Lily stood motionless at the foot of her bed watching Deucalion pace and lecture. Bach, having come in with him, floated a handsbreadth above the bed.

"Weapons!" exclaimed Deucalion for the fourth time. "You have crew sitting out there with weapons!"

"Is there a law against it?" she asked quietly.

"Why would anyone need a *law* against it? Why would any civilized person want to carry a weapon anyway? Unless you're a disciple of the martial arts and need it for a demonstration or for practice, I suppose. I'm disappointed in you, Lily."

"I'm a practicing martial artist. I can't resist sparring with my opponent."

"There's no need to be sarcastic."

"Deucalion, considering how short a time we've known each other, there's no need for you to come elder brother so strongly. I got enough of that growing up. This is *our* ship, after all. I'd like to know what gave you the right to authorize admitting three known hostiles aboard it?"

Deucalion stopped pacing. He settled into his most characteristic lecturing position: arms crossed on his chest, chin up, mouth turned down. It was, Lily reflected, almost a parody of his father's gentle but stern teaching style. "They are not hostiles," he began.

"Before you and Bach got here," Lily interrupted, "I received a report from Paisley that the Ardakian who was admitted as a casualty was in fact faking it and has now barricaded himself and his cousin into our com-tac room, while Windsor sits up gloating on the bridge. I can't even get any own personnel in to com to run the highroad—"

"You forget that we are already running out-system with one of the Ardakians on com and will reach the first window in one hour."

"—or to find out if Windsor has actually damaged our operating system in some way."

Deucalion uncrossed his arms to shake his hand at her. "Now let's take these accusations one by one. First, they are not hostiles. They are citizens of League space."

"Which I am not."

"That's not the point here. Second, they are not carrying weapons."

"Hells, Deucalion, they don't *need* to carry weapons. Those two Ardakians *are* weapons. They're twice as strong"—she hesitated here, thinking of Yehoshua's accidental blow with his artificial arm that had thrown Stanford across a small room—"as any human. It's no wonder Windsor has kept them on as partners."

"Did it ever occur to you that loyalty and a feeling of kinship might be a more powerful motivating force than expediency?" Deucalion asked primly.

Lily chose to ignore the comment. "What if I tell you now that I will go freely to Concord? As a free citizen of Reft space? But I'm *not* letting some bounty hunter bring me in. You have yet to explain to me how Concord Intelligence can have brought charges against a person who was *never* in League space until—what?—two months ago?"

"And third," Deucalion went on, "there's no guarantee that this ship belongs to you and your people in any case. That all has to be resolved at Concord."

"You're not answering my question."

Deucalion looked uncomfortable. He glanced away from her, sweeping his gaze around the room as if its decoration suddenly interested him.

"You can't tell me, can you?"

There was a long silence. He sighed abruptly and moved without asking permission to sit down on the bed. "I have no authority to countermand the bounty. I don't work in that division."

"Ah," said Lily, sitting down next to him. "Now we're getting somewhere."

The silence following this remark seemed almost companionable compared to the argument beforehand.

"It's hard for me to believe he's dead," said Deucalion at random, but she knew he was speaking of his father. He smoothed out the bedcovers with one hand, as if the action soothed him, and then looked up at her, thoughtful. "How was it you met Hawk?"

"A League ship somehow got into Reft space. He was on board."

"Supposedly rehabilitated. Isn't that what you said? I don't understand why a trip like that could have been kept secret, but it must have been, or I certainly would have heard about it."

"Exactly what division *do* you work in?"

"Human Services. My specialty is Disaster Relief. I got a lot of practice in my youth. But Lily, did you meet anyone else from that expedition? Do you remember names?"

"Yes. A woman called Maria and a man, Anjahar."

"Anjahar—that's such a common name these days. Can you describe either of them?"

"He was tall, well-built, quite light in complexion though he flushed a lot. And he had blond hair, which is unusual in the Reft. She was more common looking: dark skin, black hair." She paused, trying to picture that long-ago scene in her mind. "I know what I remember best about her. The clothing she wore. It was sort of a—" She could not find words for it and turned to Bach. *Bach*, she whistled. *Is there a term for it, do you remember?*

Assuredly, patroness, he sang, ecstatic to be of service. *The woman designated Maria wore the costume usually called a* sari, *which is the ancient indigenous dress of a people called* Hindu, *who in prespace times lived in a nation state designated as India in the common tongue.*

"Thank you. I'm quite impressed, Bach-o." And she smiled.

Bach acknowledged the compliment with a quiet but rather florid trill.

"Mother bless me," breathed Deucalion, staring at this exchange. "You've bonded him. I just thought he was some old relic that you'd cobbled together to perform calculating functions on the bridge. Do you know how rare those are now? It's a Bach, isn't it?"

"Yes—"

"It has to be a Bach." Deucalion continued to stare, rapt, at Bach's gleaming surface. "They tried about six models on that AI program. The Meleps never achieved full function. The Mozarts all burned out quickly. The Beethovens proved too unstable to be reliable—they would always lose their input function but continue to output. The Annanas couldn't interact with humans. Only the Hildegards and the Bachs had stability at all, and the Catholic Church eventually combined with the Church of Three Faiths to get a court order impounding what Hildegards were left for any but religious purposes. That 'bot is an invaluable relic."

"Well," replied Lily, a little overwhelmed by this recital, "I know he's invaluable. Hindu India. Sari. Do these words mean anything to you? She also had a red dot in the middle of her forehead. I remember that."

For a moment Deucalion looked taken aback. "Red dot? Wait a minute. The woman Maria. There is a woman—Maria Lashmi Leung. I only know her in passing. By repute, she's a bit of a reactionary. That's why she adopted the old style native costume. I don't know why *she* would have been on an expedition like that. But she is in Yevgeny's division."

"Who's Yevgeny?"

"The man who signed your order."

"What division is he in?"

Deucalion hesitated visibly before he answered. "He's head of Rehabilitation. But he's also on the council," he added, as if that mitigated the other duty, "and he served a term in Parliament. But if Maria Leung was in Reft space, then you must have done something there—"

"Deucalion. As far as I could tell in the brief interview I had with her and her companions, the only crime I was being accused of was that of association. Which as far as I know has never been a crime in *Reft* space. First with our father. And then with Hawk, when he left them to come with us."

"*Left* them? That must be it. Even if he had been rehabilitated, he would have been on some kind of parole. Which he then violated, and you abetted. Why did he go with you anyway?"

Lily looked away from him, glad that the dim light hid her flush. "Did it ever occur to you that the League's justice might not have seemed so merciful to someone like him? They had him in solitary confinement. In sensory deprivation."

"Surely not—" He looked righteously shocked.

"Surely, yes. And to Hawk—"

"But Lily," Deucalion said, angry now, "if it's true that he's—well, it was never spoken about aloud, but certainly I heard Mother mention it once—that he was one of those rare, rare fluke half-breeds—half je'jiri." He halted, looking stricken. "But perhaps you didn't know."

"I knew," she replied, grim.

"Well, then, it would have been not just cruel but inhuman to subject him to sensory deprivation. Not that it isn't in any case, but with his peculiar melding of characteristics ..." He shook his head. "Who could have ordered such a thing?" Subsiding into silence, he mulled over this question until a new thought came abruptly to him, altering his very posture. "Lily! Since you've now reviewed the obligations attendant on human-je'jiri relations, you must understand the complications inherent in dealing with someone of Hawk's background. If we do find him—"

"When."

"—when we do find him, you might want to reconsider keeping him on board this ship."

Lily sighed. "It's too late. Like Bach, he's already bonded."

"Already bonded! In Reft space, where no one had an inkling what they were dealing with?"

She nodded.

"With whom—" he halted. Read her posture and what he could make out of her expression. Jumped to his feet. "Why didn't you tell me? This changes everything! Of course, there can be no question about separating him from you once he's found."

"Then help me get Windsor off this ship."

"I can't."

"Let me rephrase the question. If I take steps to remove him and his companions without violence, will you attempt to stop me?"

Frowning, Deucalion paced to the far wall and back again,

•efore he answered. "It is my duty as a member of the
Bureau—as a citizen of the League—to abide by the law."

"Yes," Lily interrupted, "but will you actively try to hinder
ne? I won't have that man on this ship."

"You wouldn't go with him on to Concord and trust myself
nd your crew to search for—No, I suppose not."

"It's not a matter of trust, although I certainly have no
eason to trust Windsor. But I have to be there when we find
Iawk."

"I still don't understand what happened to him. If he had
1ated you, he would never have left. They don't do that."

Now it was Lily's silence that damped the exchange. The
ir itself, in the room, seemed expectant and hushed. "Sit
.own," she said softly, at last. "Let me tell you."

When she had finished her abbreviated recital, he regarded
er not, to her surprise, with horror, but with compassion.
In other words, he thinks you're dead and has suffered a
1ental breakdown as a result."

She did not reply.

Finally, he rose. "I trust," he said slowly, "that you under
:and that for the rest of the trip to Turfan Link I will be
ompletely taken up with the casualties and the medical
:am. Doubtless I won't see you at all until we reach there."

"I understand," she replied.

"Very well. Can you let me out?"

She palmed the com-console and asked Jenny to give her
1e all clear. Once given, she punched in her code and, the
oor slipping aside, Deucalion left. Lily caught a glimpse of
:nny and six Ridanis, all armed and stationed at strategic
•cations around the outer room. It was as dimly lit as the
.ner suite, fading the Ridani's colorful tattoos to indiscrimi-
ate shades of gray. Then the door slipped shut again, leaving
er alone.

She laid down flat on the bed, cradling her head in her
1pped hands, her ankles crossed, and stared at the ceiling.
. was almost lost in gloom. She brooded over the minute
:xtures that gave shading to its contours, almost like a faint
:ho of a topographical map. The dimness of the room
1adowed her thoughts. How long she lay, brooding, she did
ot know. Bach sang softly at the foot of her bed:

> *Zwar ist solche Herzensstube*
> *Wohl kein schöner Fürstensall,*

Sondern eine finstre Grube;
Doch, sobald dein Gnadenstrahl
In denselben nur wird blinken
Wird es voller Sonnen dünken.

"A heart's chamber such as this
is certainly no finely appointed hall of princes
a dark pit, rather;
yet, no sooner shall Thy favor's beam
but gleam within there,
than it will be seen to be filled with light."

They went through.

She saw musical notation, weaving in and out on itself
now reversing itself, now symmetrical—quaerendo invenieti.

And came out.
Bach was still singing, but it was music that she did no
recognize. She continued to stare at the ceiling, but althoug
no seeming time had elapsed the ceiling's textures nov
seemed to have become a puzzle reflecting Bach's music.
"Bach," she said. "What *is* inside a window?"
He incorporated his answer into his music with extraordinar
felicity, so that there was no lapse in its flow. *An infinite stream*
"But how do you get there?"
You will find it by seeking.
"You will find it by seeking," she echoed, the rhythm c
her words slipping unconsciously into the same cadence a
Bach, and then she whistled it several times, careful to blen
it with the robot's music. She gave up when he bega
elaborating impossibily complex variations on the theme. Bu
while he continued, she stood up and in the space betwee
the bed and the wall—vast enough by the usual standards c
cramped merchantmen in Reft space—did kata.
Started with the first one she had ever learned, "First
Cause," going through it again and again, meditating on eac
variation the slightest reangling of her fingers made in th
form as an entirety. Went on to "Peaceful Mind" until sh
had exhausted it as well—except that there was an infinity c
variations within each move, each gesture, that could neve
be exhausted.

After a while, she had to conserve her energy by going more slowly again, but this added a new element, an echoing whole-note counterpoint to the quicker and strong pace of full-speed. When she began to get tired, her fatigue added still another level of contrast. She stepped up the pace again, moving on to a higher kata, and a yet higher one. She had long since lost track of the time.

They went through.

The fortress. It is bounded on four sides, each side only as strong as your own strength, but always as weak as your own weakness.

She held to the image.

She twisted her left hand.

And came out.

The few centimeters she had shifted her left hand was virtually insignificant—unmeasurable—by objective standards, but for a long moment she simply stared at her hand, astonished. She was damp with sweat; a salty bead of liquid coalesced on her lips, so that she became aware that she was thirsty. But Bach was singing again, so she went on.

"To Penetrate a Fortress." "To Look at the Sky." "Flying Swallow." "Half Moon." "Ten Hands."

Hours could well have gone by. Thirst burned the back of her throat; fatigue pulled against each muscle, each strike, each block, each slow elaboration that transformed into a quick thrust. Bach's ceaseless accompaniment seemed so integral to what she was doing, balancing each sequence, that without thinking it consciously she knew she could not be so deeply focused if he was not with her.

"Crane on a Rock." Balanced with perfect stability on one leg; poised as on the axis of the universe.

They went through.

Something about the walls had changed. They held texture not just in space but in time. She could see a pattern, a long fugue of melody out of the past, across to the present, into the future.

Experimentally, holding that vision of the walls, she lowered her right leg. It was possible to stand, although the floor had no complete material substance as she knew it.

And then she realized there was someone else in the room.

First, briefly, she knew it was Kyosti, but his presence was an echo, a faint trace—like a scrap of phrase of an earlier melody bound into a new theme. She turned, and saw the other woman.

She seemed somehow familiar to Lily: copper haired but with a reddish-toned complexion and high, square cheekbones— proud and courageous and cynical. The woman turned her head, a movement both impossibly slow and fast, without being measurable as either. And saw Lily.

Green eyes. The recollection of Master Heredes's eyes, with that same unusual and unusually vital shade of iris—Heredes, Gwyn, Taliesin: his names began to tumble and weave back in among themselves, like Bach's counterpoint, until they formed a seamless whole—the recollection jolted her. Just as the woman stepped forward and seemed to speak—

They came out.

Lily collapsed onto her knees at the foot of the bed, her breath ragged. Her hands were dry. She got caught in a fit of trembling, just sat there and shook, exhausted and exhilarated and terrified all at the same time. Bach abandoned his music and drifted over to nudge against her, singing a soft aria.

> *Schlafe, mein Liebster, geniesse der Ruh*
> *Wache nach diesem vor aller Gadeihen!*
> *Labe die Brust,*
> *Empfinde die Lust,*
> *Wo wir unser Herz erfreun!*

"Sleep, my Dearest, enjoy Thy rest,
    from henceforth watch over the wellbeing of all.
Refresh Thy breast,
    experience the joy,
    there where we gladden our hearts."

She curled up on the floor and fell asleep.

The chime of the com woke her.

"Captain Ransome," said Windsor, his voice a little fuzzy over the com. "Three windows to Turfan. Please don't be stubborn. Fred and Stanford have things well in hand at com-tac, so don't bother to try to storm them there. Your bridge crew is remaining polite, but still—numbers aren't everything. Just surrender into my custody and we won't have any trouble." The com clicked over, crackling expectantly.

Lily did not bother to answer. "Persistent bastard," she muttered to herself as she went into the cubicle to wash up and drink. She changed into a fresh tunic, the stiffest, heaviest one she possessed. Then she went back to the space between the bed and the door, whistled a few instructions to Bach, and started kata again.

Now she could focus her mind quickly and sharply on her center, could bring herself back with the accompaniment of Bach to the clean detachment of her previous meditation. Hunger and a low edge of thirst worked for her as well.

"To Penetrate a Fortress." "Jion." "Ten No Kata." "Crane on a Rock."

They went through.

Time unfolds along an infinite stream, layered back in on itself. Her left hand twisted; she lowered her right leg—but she had not moved at all. What she had done before was still present. The copper-haired woman turned to speak, but Lily lost track of her as she caught—not a glimpse, but the presence, of Kyosti in the room with her. She felt for a moment that he registered her, took her in, but any other communication vanished as swiftly as the echoing shadow of her previous movements.

She took one step forward. A second. The door receded, as if space, too, had become infinite and she could never reach it, only see its unfolded textures.

Bach, she said.

And that was the strangest thing of all. The contrapuntal music he sang, a continuous interweaving of voices, was the only thing that seemed to her to possess stability, as if it so perfectly reflected the stream itself.

We follow you, Bach replied.

Out of the infinity of textures of the door, she chose the one that seemed most solid to her, concentrated on it without losing the shadings of the rest. Walked to it and pressing her hand to the panel, found that it still acted to open: the clearest gesture she had seen, as if it had few reflections or echoing voices from other windows.

In the outer room Jenny and the Ridani guards had an almost gossamer quality, as if they scarcely existed. The copper-haired woman stared up at Lily from the couch. She seemed unaware of any presence but her own.

Lily wove her way through the crowd, careful not to touch them, afraid of what they might feel like or what dream her touch might give them. They faded out and yet again gained solidity even as she passed. Their stillness seemed ominous to her, not even for their sake, but for her own, because the texture of their being, seeming so light and transitory, made her begin to fear returning to their state.

Each step she took, through the room, out into the corridor and along to the bridge, trailed repercussions in time behind her, as if her presence here inside a window was now imprinted forever, another countermelody weaving in to the whole, necessary, unique, and yet utterly bound into the others.

Came out onto the bridge.

Someone else sat in the captain's chair. More than one occupant sat in each chair at each console, but their substance altered as she gazed: the wispy figures of her crew and the textured, multifaceted forms of unfamiliar faces. The captain turned.

It was the copper-haired woman, and that she was the captain was without question. She began to speak, but Lily had already discerned the shade of Windsor, seated with a strange man—coexistent and yet separate—at the com-console.

Bach, she said, when we come out, stun him.

In triple canon, in six parts, he replied, and drifted across the vast and tiny space of the bridge to hover at Windsor's back, never ceasing from his music.

And she waited.

But the stream stretched on. The countersubject did not end. The copper-haired woman rose and walked to each station in turn. The walls held their texture of infinite layers. The longer Lily stared the deeper her comprehension of their layers, until she caught herself lost in contemplation of their infinite variety, as if they represented in another form the infinite variety of kata, each one done again and again, always the same and yet never the same.

There was no end to it—no way to escape. She could no longer conceive of the wall as a single entity, flat, without any dimension but that of gross matter. The copper-haired woman returned to the captain's chair and spoke, but to her crew— and Lily knew finally who they were:

The Forlorn Hope's previous crew, caught somehow like

her inside a window. Caught forever, and yet for no time at all. As she was. Trapped, and unable to get out.

Bach, *she cried.* Stop singing.

Bach ceased in the middle of the fugue.

12 The Hounds Catch the Scent

****

And came out.

There was a flash of light. Windsor slumped in his chair. The gun looped at his shoulder clattered to the floor.

"Lily!"

"Captain!"

The exclamations came all at once. She slumped down against the back of the captain's chair, unable to sustain her own weight. Someone took hold of her and pulled her up.

"Captain!" His voice sounded flat, one-dimensional. "How the Hells did you get here?"

"I'm never doing that again," she said. "Never." She tried to balance on her feet, but let the man continue to hold her up. "Get Windsor to my cabin." Each word was an effort. "Fleet Brother to comp on bridge. Lock yourselves in here. No females. Now." And laughed a little, wondering if "now" meant anything.

"Trey, call Nguyen up to replace you. Then get the captain back to her cabin. Mule, call the je'jiri quarters. I'll carry Windsor. Move it."

Somehow Lily was transferred to another set of strong arms and helped back to her cabin. A dark woman came forward immediately. After a moment Lily recognized her as Jenny.

"Lily!" Jenny exclaimed.

The door opened again. "Yehoshua, what in Hells—"

"Don't ask me," he said brusquely.

"Inner room," Lily gasped, pulling herself that way as well. "Put him in—" She began to find a form and content for words. "Put him in the inner room, with me. Search him. Tie him up, Jenny." Looking up, she met Jenny's gaze and found that she could actually register her expression. "Keep guards set up in here." But the outpouring of words confused her, and she let Trey help her into the inner room and sit her on the bed. Watched as Yehoshua dumped Windsor on the floor and Jenny tied him up as securely as only a former Immortal could. Bach floated in and hovered protectively beside her.

"Yehoshua," Lily said as Jenny finished, finding that she could recall his name now. "Back to the bridge. Lock yourselves in. Get the je'jiri male to start unraveling what Stanford did—send his mate down to iron deck comp—to Main Computer—to start from that end. Bach, you start at my terminal. Now move. I don't know if the Ardakians expect some signal from Windsor. They're too close to us as it is."

"But will you be all right?" Jenny asked, at the same time as Yehoshua said, "But Captain, you need medical attention."

"Trey can stay here," Lily conceded, aware that to argue would be to waste time. "Go."

They went. And anyway, how could she explain to them that she was terrified of having to go through the next window? And not because the engines might blow—or precisely that, if it meant stranding them inside the window, like the *Hope*'s original crew.

For a long while she just sat. Eventually she gathered up enough courage to look at her hands, but they seemed normal and boringly solid, like hands always were and were meant to be. Finally convinced of this fact, she looked up. Bach had already plugged himself in to the terminal and he sang softly to himself as he investigated Stanford's sabotage.

"Bach," she said sharply. "Stop singing."

With a brief, but unmistakably flat, cadence, he stopped.

Trey sat cross-legged in front of the door, relaxed but alert, carefully examining a thin com-slate rather than looking at Lily.

"What is that?" Lily asked. The room stayed so reassuringly monotone in texture that she felt she could afford to relax as well.

Trey looked up. "Ship's manifest of the Akan casualties. Handed over to First Officer Yehoshua by min Belsonn. I took it from there. I'm trying to figure out how the bounty hunter"—she nodded toward Windsor's still form—"how Windsor falsified the alien's record to get it about. That's how it all started."

"Yes. The Ardakians." Lily rose carefully to her feet, testing her balance but keeping one hand on the bed. The floor seemed stable enough, and her legs strong enough. She let go of the bed. It wasn't so hard to stand. "I'd better talk to them before they get worried. Carry on with what you're doing. It might be worthwhile to know." She took a tentative step, a second, and then walked with new confidence over to the com-panel beside the door. Touching it, she coded in to com-tac.

"Hey, boss," answered a low voice that she recognized as Fred's more by vocabulary than by any ability on her part to distinguish his voice from Stanford's. "Stan's got the change-over keyed in but he says he can't—"

"Frederick," a second voice cut in. "Have you ascertained that you are indeed speaking with Korrigan?"

"Uh, boss," said Fred. "Is that you?"

"No," replied Lily. "It's Captain Ransome, Fred. I've got your boss under my wing. I suggest that you and Stanford change the codes and then prepare to disembark quietly at Turfan Link, at which time I will deliver min Windsor to you."

"You realize," replied Stanford, "that the vector drive will explode without my override?"

"Yes, but do you realize that if the engines go, you go with us?"

There was a short silence.

"Stan," said Fred. "I *told* you and the boss that you don't set explosives if you can't get outta the blast zone."

"Even if I correct the engines," said Stanford, ignoring this sally, "I've also reconfigured components in this operating system that will make it dangerous for you to operate this ship without my cooperation."

"That may also be, and while in the interests of goodwill and fair play it would be polite of you to restore normal operations, I have my experts working on it in any event."

"They won't find anything."

"That may be, but it won't stop them working. And I don't suggest you try a direct assault. Even if you did succeed, the attempt would be bloody and violent and a large number of people would get hurt or killed."

"How do we know you got the boss, anyway?" Fred demanded. "You could be bluffing."

"I could," Lily began, but the question was answered for her by a groan and a muffled expletive from the corner.

"My fucking head," Windsor said, his voice raspy. "What'd I get hit with?"

"How'd you get the jump on him?" Fred asked, sounding amazed.

Lily cut the connection.

"Can I get a drink?" Windsor asked. She turned in time to see him carefully testing his bonds. His face looked pale against the dull gold sheen of the wall against which he lay. As she watched, he pulled himself up to a sitting position and tilted his head back to rest against the wall. The dark stubble on his jaw and chin set off his pallor even more.

"Trey, can you get him some water?"

"Water!" Windsor looked aghast. "Don't you have anything stronger?"

"Something alcoholic or addictive? I suppose we must, but I don't think it will make you feel better."

Windsor squinted at her as if the dim light in the room was nevertheless too bright. "How would you know?" he growled.

Lily laughed. "I probably wouldn't. I never did drink much. I always figured it would interfere with my training."

Trey returned from the washing cubicle bearing a glass of water. Windsor favored it with a look of deep suspicion, but he lot her lift it to his lips and he drained it, making a face as if it tasted of some unpalatable substance. "Yeah," he said when he'd finished. "How *did* you get the jump on me?"

"You wouldn't believe me," said Lily. Trey had stopped and was looking at Lily as if she, too, would like this question answered.

"You'd be surprised what I'd believe," said Windsor, sounding tired. "Could I have some more—water?"

Lily nodded to Trey. "One more glass. Then go down to Medical and have Flower prescribe something mild to put him to sleep for the duration. You look like you need it," she added for Windsor's benefit.

"Thank you. Your concern touches me deeply. How did you get the jump on me?"

"Trade secret," she replied, although the thought of what she had done promoted an involuntary shiver. "How did Fred get on the casualty list?"

Windsor grinned. He waited until Trey had helped him to a second glass of water. "Common trade knowledge. I found someone who could be bribed. Don't bother to try to trace them."

"I won't. I was just curious." She coded in to the door and Trey left. "But I'll bet Deucalion would be shocked."

"Deucalion—?" Unexpectedly, he sighed. "Gwyn had a boy named Deucalion," he added, his voice uncharacteristically subdued. "Nice kid, but a little wild." Then, abruptly, he tested his bonds again and frowned over at Bach. "Don't see many of those around these days."

"How did you know Gwyn?" Lily asked.

"None of your damn business. How did you know him? And how come you're wearing that medallion?"

"More trade secrets." Lily leaned against the wall beside the com-panel and surveyed him dispiritedly. "That leaves us at a stalemate."

"For now." Windsor grinned again. "You're not bad, for being so young, but you'll find out that experience counts."

"How did you know Gwyn?" she repeated.

His grin vanished. "We'll leave it at a stalemate for now, Captain. I'm patient."

He lapsed into silence punctuated only by his efforts to disengage his bonds. Lily kept her arms relaxed at her side, confident of Jenny's ability to tie a lasting bond, but she remained carefully watchful and whistled a brief instruction to Bach to monitor him as well. When Trey returned, Windsor did not bother to struggle as Trey gave him an injection. It took effect moments later, and Lily, holding onto his shoulders, lowered him to the floor and arranged him in what she guessed was a comfortable position.

Then she waited. Had Jenny put a complement of four crew in the corridor around the com-tac door. Got a progress report from Bach and the two je'jiri: they had identified two anomalies and were now investigating them. Sometime later Bach reported that one of the anomalies had vanished, and soon afterward, Stanford came over com and curtly told her that the vector engines were now safe.

Yehoshua immediately began the countdown to the next window. Lily called Rainbow in, armed, to guard while she slept.

She had strange, elongated dreams. Waking abruptly, she sat bolt upright, startling Rainbow.

"When's the window?" she asked, gasping. She put a hand to her forehead and discovered that it was damp.

"You be all right, min?" Rainbow's obvious concern did not move her to relax her attentive guard on the still unconscious Windsor. "We went through ya window ya time past. Ya two hours or more. I reckon it be ya good fourteen hours before ya next one. Be you wanting me to check with Yehoshua on ya bridge?"

"No. Thank you. I'll check myself."

Rainbow's estimate proved close enough. Lily devised a careful strategy with Jenny and Yehoshua for making sure the two Ardakians got off ship without incident. Bach and the two je'jiri isolated the remaining anomaly but could not discover Stanford's point of entry. Fred and Stanford made no further attempt to communicate.

As the last window to Turfan Link approached, Lily tried to sleep, hoping to avoid it as she had the one before. But Windsor had begun to mutter and toss, and she had to send Rainbow to get a second injection for him. The warning chime sang across com. Her muscles tensed, however she tried to relax them. Rainbow had not yet returned.

They went through.

Kyosti's essence left a trail across time, across the textures still, and eternally, impressed by his passage. If she could only move fast enough on his path, she could catch him—

And came out.

She was shaking. A moment later, she had to get up to let Rainbow in.

"Captain!" Slipping inside, Rainbow stared at her. "Mayhap you should go to Medical."

"No. Help me with this injection."

"I kin get it, min. You sit down."

"Captain." Yehoshua, over com. "Nine hours to preliminary orbit, twelve to docking."

"Let Trey take over, Yehoshua." Lily turned gratefully to this distraction. "You and Jenny start cordoning off all routes from com-tac to docking. Send Paisley and the Mule to my cabin. Ransome out." She turned back and watched as Rainbow efficiently applied a second dose to the restless Windsor.

"Rainbow, when the others get here, you're relieved until we dock."

"Yes, min. And ya one?"

"We'll carry him off, once the two Ardakians have disembarked."

But once they came in to Turfan Link it proved easy enough to shepherd Fred and Stanford off the ship. Lily refused to move Windsor until the casualties were all off, and once Deucalion was relieved of that responsibility he surprisingly insisted on reminding Stanford—who with his cousin had refused to venture farther than fifty yards from the link bubble—that it was a crime in League space to tamper with the operating system of a vessel no matter what the circumstances, unless, Deucalion added with grim officiousness, it was to save lives.

Jenny reported this conversation with great glee back to Lily. With it came a thin slate containing Stanford's calculations, and as Bach put them through the system they corresponded with one of the two solutions the je'jiri had suggested. It took less than an hour to clean out Stanford's tampering. Meanwhile, Yehoshua reported, the two Ardakians waited patiently in the broad expanse of the docking corridor for the return of their employer.

"Send out the je'jiri," said Lily, now on the bridge. "When we've got a trail to follow and are ready to leave, I'll hand him over. Not until then."

She did not go below to watch the Dai marshaling her forces, preferring to let the Mule act as her liaison. The presence of a je'jiri female on comp on the bridge—one of the pair who had cracked Stanford's code—was unsettling enough. She kept glancing at her, catching her blue hair in the corner of her eye and beginning to turn, thinking that it must be Kyosti. The female's slender frame was just androgynous enough that for that spare instant one could mistake them—

"Finch." Her voice came out sharper than she intended. "Patch me a line through to Administration. I want to see what Deucalion is up to."

"Yes, Captain." His voice was flatly neutral, and he busied himself with his controls. Examining his back, she thought he seemed out of sorts, less and less the cheerful, easygoing Finch she had once known on Unruli, and she wondered if it was her fault for bringing him so far, to change him so much. "I have Hospital Administration," he said, breaking into her thoughts. "They say that min Belsonn has gone into a meeting with the local Concord representative and a visiting Intelligence official. They expect him back in two hours. Do you want to leave a message?"

"No." It was impossible not to speculate about the content of his meeting. Lily took advantage of the lull to personally inspect the com-tac room on gold deck with Bach to make sure that Fred and Stanford had left no surprises. By the time she finished, the Dai had returned.

Flanked by Jenny and one of the females, the Dai was waiting for her in her cabin. She inclined her head respectfully as Lily entered.

"We have traced your mate to his last point of contact with this station. With this information taken to the registry, we have ascertained that he must have gotten on the freighter *Helvise* destined for Karkara Link. Is this acceptable?"

This swift resolution to Kyosti's disappearance from Turfan Hospital took Lily a moment to assimilate. If they could actually catch him—but she forced herself not to fan the flames of hope too high. "How did you pinpoint that freighter?" she asked instead.

The two je'jiri females looked at each other as if the question was inexplicable to them. Jenny spoke up instead.

"The whole pack of them roamed around Hospital, and pretty soon one of the males—" She hesitated.

"It was Middle Brother whose scent proved keenest on this trail," interposed the Dai.

"Middle Brother—came up with something. I just followed after, and eventually they ended up in front of a berth. They knew to the day and the hour, and the *minute*, when he was there. So we just went to Portmaster's—they call it Registry here—and found out what ship had been berthed there at the right time. It was pretty damn fast." She looked as if she wanted to add something else but found it politic, in the presence of the two je'jiri, to refrain.

"Excellent," said Lily. "Get everyone back on board. We'll leave as soon as we're ready. Jenny. You're in charge of the prisoner. Hand him over *just* before we close the link bubble and break docking."

Jenny saluted and left.

Lily regarded the two je'jiri. However much they resembled Kyosti, there was always about them that essence of foreignness, of utter difference from herself and all things human. They regarded her in turn without any expression she knew how to read. "Thank you," she said.

"We have not found him yet," replied the Dai, "only established his trail. Now, if we may go to prepare our quarters?"

"Of course."

After they left, she checked in her inner room, but Rainbow and the two other Ridanis assigned there had nothing to report: Windsor was still unconscious. Lily returned to the bridge.

"Message from Deucalion," Finch reported as she entered. "He'll be back on board in twenty minutes, and he wants to talk with you." He swiveled in his chair to face Lily. "Why's he coming with us, anyway?"

"Because I can't stop him, short of physical force. And I think he can help us."

"You *think*—?"

"I hope."

Finch turned back to his console. "Hope is a terrible thing," he muttered, but the comment, however uncomfortable, did not seem to warrant a reply, and only Trey, sitting at scan, seemed to have heard it as well. She glanced at Lily, surprised, but went back to her work. The two techs, at weapons and life support, remained engrossed in their work. Pinto and the Mule were still off duty.

From iron deck, Yehoshua reported all crew on board. A few minutes later, Deucalion reported in. Lily met Jenny in the captain's suite and watched as a large contingent of armed crew escorted the two Ridanis carrying Windsor out. Then she sat and waited.

"Captain." It was Yehoshua. "Windsor is safely on Turfan Link grounds and we have sealed the link bubble."

Lily stood up. "Good. Commence detach. Then meet me on the bridge. We're setting a course for Karkara Link."

The hunt was on.

The bartender had the same youthfully mature face that most residents of League space seemed to have, but his was marred by a look about the eyes of one too many forays into mind-altering substances. In the half-gloom of the bar, he peered at Lily with the disinterest of a man who has grown apathetic through mental inactivity.

"Nay," he said, handing the thin slate on which Kyosti's photo was superimposed back to Lily, "I've never seen this man, nor any human with blue hair, not since it was fashionable twenty years back. But I did see—it was strange enough—" He paused and looked up and down the dark counter. The murmur of conversation from the customers in the cramped space accompanied his searching, though most were hidden by huge growths of a dull, thick-leafed plant that spread from

a line of pots set along one wall. Jenny, stationed a careful
four paces to one side of Lily, shifted position. At the door,
the Mule nodded briefly. In a far corner, Rainbow had lost
herself in the shadow of leaves. The bartender glanced for
perhaps the fifth time at the two je'jiri flanking Lily and then
turned to call into the dark room behind the bar.

"Kam! How long ago was it that rogue come in here?"

There was a moment of silence. Finally, a woman, unseen
in the gloom, replied. "Five days ago."

"That'll be it." He turned back to Lily. "We don't see them
often, je'jiri, that is." His gaze shifted involuntarily to the two
je'jiri again, before he forced it back to Lily. "But sometimes
they come through in packs, which isn't so bad, begging your
pardon, honorables." This time, addressing them, he did not
look at the two je'jiri. "But no one trusts a rogue."

"A rogue?" Lily glanced at the Dai for elucidation.

"A je'jiri adult, male or female, who travels without benefit
of family, is considered with sufficient reason to be of aberrant
status," replied the Dai softly.

"It were a rogue male, all right," repeated the bartender,
either not hearing or ignoring this exchange.

"You're *sure* it wasn't this man?" Lily asked.

He shook his head. "He weren't human. Sure, and maybe
there were some resemblance of face and such. I got a good
look, since they're rare to see, and dangerous enough. Begging pardon again, honorables."

"No offense taken," replied the Dai smoothly.

For some reason the clear, crisp sound of her voice startled
him. "It were no offense because he was je'jiri," he said
quickly, "but just because he was solo, and acting strangely."

"What did he do?"

He hesitated.

Lily waited, sure that this was the clue they were lacking.
Kyosti's trail had led them to Karkara Link and on to Nagy
Depot and Batoen Center and then here, to Nineveh Gate, a
small station orbiting a dead planet that circled a white dwarf.
And into this bar. Only now, somehow, it seemed it was no
human they were following, but a rogue je'jiri male. It
seemed impossible but all too probable to her that the je'jiri
had lost his scent, or mixed it up with another's.

"It gave me the jeebies," he said at last. "He come in here
and begun laying hands on people like he was one of them
reform preachers of the Church of Three Faiths. And then

he'd lean down and speak to them in a low voice like it were a bit of the Mother's word he was imparting. And what made it so weird is that he did it to both men and women alike. And you know how they are—je'jiri, begging your pardon—about touching you if you isn't the same sex. It was weird."

"What did he say to people?"

He grinned for a second, looking embarrassed. "Nothing people wanted to repeat."

"Did he say anything to you?"

"Well," he temporized. "He went the rounds of the entire place, and no one trying to stop him because it was queer enough to be unsettling and anyway no one wants to rile a rogue."

"You have to understand," said Lily, "that this could be important. Did he say anything to you?"

He grabbed two glasses from the rack under the bar and temporized further by pulling two drafts of a dark foamy liquid.

A small woman appeared in the door that led into the dark room. "You might as well tell them."

"Kam—" he began.

"It's no secret you drink too much," she continued mercilessly.

"He told me my liver was going bad," said the bartender sullenly, setting the full glasses on the bar and sliding them down to a couple who had managed to signal for them without words.

"And he told me I was pregnant," said Kam, "which was a surprise to me since I hadn't gone long enough to miss my cycle yet. Not that it wasn't welcome news, since we'd gone off the implants six months ago and were waiting—but it usually takes one year. But I went in yesterday, and sure enough—and the doctor was amazed I'd caught it so early."

Lily looked at the Dai and then at Jenny. "It was Kyosti. I'm sure of it."

"In any event, an unlikely je'jiri, solo or not," replied the Dai evenly.

"Then what happened?" Lily asked.

The bartender shrugged. "He left. With old Ramshackle Joes, who runs a scratch ferry between here and Zeya Depot. She's rattled enough to take any paying cargo."

"She's a dream crystal addict," Kam added helpfully. "She has to take any credit she can get. Even a rogue."

Lily sighed and rubbed her hands over her eyes. "Thank

you," she said, although this new development seemed yet
another, and greater, discouragement. "We'll check Registry."

"Ferry's name is *Better Red*," Kam offered. She looked
directly at the je'jiri, not at all discomposed by their presence. "This a family matter?"

"Yes," said Lily, feeling hopelessly tired. "A family matter. I
appreciate your help."

"Best luck," Kam said. The bartender mumbled something
unintelligible. Lily nodded to the Dai, and the two je'jiri
preceded her out of the bar, the customers quieting and
staring as they passed.

Jenny fell into step beside her. "Maybe you ought to sleep,
Lily-hae," she said. "You're on the same cycle as most of the
crew. You shouldn't have stayed up. We could have traced
this without you."

"Void knows you have enough practice," Lily replied,
bitter. "It's taken us one month to get this far, and I think he's
getting farther ahead of us. How can we possibly catch him?
What happens to him if we don't?"

"You *are* tired," Jenny laid a hand on Lily's back, between
her shoulder blades, a light pressure as they walked along the
corridors of Nineveh Gate. "Even the scruffy little stations
here look rich," she continued, as if this comment might
distract Lily from her despondency. "At least compared to the
Reft. This place is crawling with plants. Can you imagine
what it costs to maintain them? Maybe Deucalion is right,
that it would be a crime for the League's government not to
open relations with the Reft, bring them in to the Concord.
And give them the benefit of all this." She waved a hand to
encompass the spacious lines of the station, half obscured by
vines and trestles of flowering plants.

Lily did not respond. Her expression remained detached;
she might not even have heard.

"Come on," said Jenny, half-cajoling, half-scolding. "Go to
bed. I'll go with the Dai to trace down this Joes person."

"Maybe you're right," said Lily reluctantly.

"Of course I'm right. Rainbow. Mule." The two called split
back from their positions in front of the je'jiri. "Escort the
captain back to the *Hope*."

Lily allowed herself to be escorted. She *was* tired, and
discouraged. She had such hopes, starting from Turfan Link,
that they would catch up with Kyosti at the next station, then
the next, then the next. Now she wondered if it was possible

that they could catch him at all. Or if they would catch him too late. At this station and the last the people she had interviewed—people familiar with je'jiri—had stuck by their conviction that the solo male passing through was pure and simply je'jiri. *Alien.* What was he turning into? Could she ever get *Kyosti* back again? Hope is a terrible thing, Finch had said, and right now she agreed with him.

At the link bubble a message waited: Deucalion wanted to see her. She quickly ascertained that he was in the mess. Leaving the Mule and Rainbow, she went there.

He sat alone in the room. In deference to night cycle, the lights had been dimmed, but he looked up as she entered and lifted a hand in greeting.

"Something to drink?" he asked as she approached.

"No. Thank you."

"Are you sure? You look tired." He cradled a mug between his hands, lifting it occasionally to sip, but when she sat down with only a shake of her head he shrugged. "We're being resupplied. We should be ready to go in four hours. Any luck with the hounds?"

"We think he's gone on to Zeya Depot. They're out confirming that now."

"I didn't think it would take this long. I'm sorry, Lily."

"Maybe I will have a drink."

Taking her cue, he got up and fetched a mug of the hot, bitter drink called *café* that, together with *beer,* seemed endemic to League space. "Well, then," he said, looking at a loss for what to say next. "I was going to mention—but perhaps this isn't the right time."

She looked up at him, too weary to postpone what looked to be, by his expression, bad news. "Go ahead."

"While I was in arranging the resupply with Nineveh Coordinator, the Concord representative came in expressly to see me. It seems that a rogue je'jiri male had caused several public disturbances, but vanished before they finally decided to call out the constables on him. Mostly incidents that were more troubling than dangerous, but one woman claimed he tried to carry off her child and two men who came on him unexpectedly in one of the warehouse corridors said they narrowly averted an attack by freezing and speaking very softly and slowly. As one would," he added thoughtfully, "to a startled and cornered animal. That's how one of the men described it."

Lily stood up. "I think I'm going to get some rest, if there's nothing further."

"No, I—Lily—I'm sorry."

She felt the prick of tears and turned away so that he could not see her face. "There's nothing you could have done," she said brusquely, and left, unwilling to face his sympathy. She took a slightly longer route to the elevator, passing by crew cabins along corridors that at this cycle would likely be deserted. The possibility of speaking normally to anyone seemed too great a trial. So, following the trend of this thought to its logical conclusion, it was with no surprise that she crossed the path of an altercation very much in progress.

A door shot open and Paisley backed out through it with as much force as if she had been pushed.

"I *told* you not to bother me," said Finch from inside, his voice edged not so much with anger as with desperation. "I don't know what makes you think I want something that everyone else on this ship has already sampled."

"It were offered in kindness," Paisley replied with stubborn dignity, but there were tears on her face. "There be no reason for you to insult me. And it bain't true, no matter what you think about me, that I slept with ya everyone. Even if it were, there be nothing shameful about being kind."

"Especially if they pay you."

Paisley gasped, choking on a sob, and put a hand to her cheek as if he had slapped her. Then she turned and fled away down the corridor.

"Paisley!" Lily called, but Paisley disappeared around a corner, heedless of the call.

"Lily?" Finch sounded surprised, now, and abruptly he appeared in the doorway. His face had a flushed look, as if he were embarrassed, or furious, or fighting back tears.

"I'm ashamed of you. How could you say that to her, after everything she's been through?"

"What about everything I've been through?" he retorted. "What do people care for that? Why does everybody cosset her so much? And anyway, everyone knows tattoos are all whores."

"Everyone knows you're a Hells-forsaken bigot, Finch." Her own depression fueled her anger. "I wasn't aware that you ever advocated the Byssinist line of strict monogamy. Even my mother didn't, and she never missed Temple. Just because the Ridanis have a different way of expressing sexual relations—"

"Tupping everything that walks."

"Spite is one of the ugliest emotions I know. What happened to you, Finch? You never used to be like this."

His expression twisted in pain. "I used to have a home, and people who cared for me."

"Maybe that's why Paisley came to you."

"I don't want her pity."

"If you abuse her like that, you're not going to get anyone else's either."

"I don't want *anyone's* pity," Finch said, his voice flat. "Just leave me alone." He stepped back into his cabin and the door, blank and unrevealing, hissed shut behind him, cutting him off from her.

She hesitated, wondering if she should try to talk to him again. As angry as his treatment of Paisley made her, she could still sympathize with his pain. And yet would her sympathy seem any better than pity to him?

"Oh, Hells," she sighed, and walked on, preferring, like him, to be alone with her unhappiness. Mercifully, she met no one else, and the quiet emptiness of her cabin was a relief to her. She went directly into the inner room, to lie down, and stopped. Her instincts told her immediately that something was different. An impression left on the bed, a subtle air of habitation. . . . The door to the washing cubicle brushed aside, and he stepped out. Quite naked.

"Pinto!"

He held a towel in one hand but he did not immediately move to wrap it around himself, whether out of vanity, or surprise on his part, or simple invitation—she could not help but stare. He was certainly attractive enough. The tattoos lent his body a beauty made more seductive by the way each pattern drew the eye in and then on to the next. The stark geometric patterns of his face and arms continued around the planes of his slender body, accenting it with color and line. Every inch of him was covered, that was quite apparent.

She flushed. "What are you doing here?" she asked, and was appalled at how young and ingenuous she sounded.

He wrapped the towel neatly about his waist so that it draped artfully to his knees. "You've seemed—lonely, and a little sad." He walked over to sit on the bed. It made a pleasant picture, to see him sitting there, so at home. "When

I saved your life on Arcadia, I got my kinnas back, from when you saved mine. So it wouldn't be presumptuous to approach you. It was never the right time, before. But I think," and his gaze was unfortunately acute, looking at her face, and at the way she stood, "that it is, now."

What Paisley meant by "kindness" became painfully clear to her. Not the act of sex, but the free offering of love and companionship, of intimate contact when the soul most craves it. Perhaps, all along, it was Paisley's understanding of his pain that Finch hated, not her tattoos.

Pinto simply sat, patient in the way all Ridanis had learned to be in the Reft, and waited for her response.

It was too tempting. She did not move from the door. "You have to go," she said, low, a little hoarse. She looked away from him.

She felt him stiffen. "Can't lower yourself to touch a cursed tattoo, is it?" he taunted, his voice tight. She could not reply. There was a sudden silence. Then he said, softer: "Lily, look at me. Please."

She kept her gaze resolutely fixed away from him. "I can't."

"You want to." He sounded pleased with this discovery. "I thought you did. Then why not?"

"Pinto. Kyosti tried to murder Finch."

"He's not here. And he didn't murder Finch in the end, did he? Showing a Hells lot of restraint, if you ask me."

Now she did look up. "Pinto. I'm going to tell you something no one else knows." He sat, attentive and still bitterly attractive, and listened. "I had two lovers before I met Hawk. One was Finch. The other is dead. Hawk murdered him."

The quiet brutality of her statement seemed to hit him the most. "Murdered him? Like Vanov?"

"I don't know. I didn't see the body."

"He wasn't arrested?"

"They never caught him. I couldn't bring myself to turn him in." She forced herself to look at Pinto as she spoke, although she was afraid of the disgust she might see now that he knew what she was capable of. "I keep telling myself that there was nothing else I could have done. You know what he is."

"I guess he's half-alien," said Pinto. He looked neither judgmental or revolted, merely thoughtful, which was, in its own way, worse. "So the je'jiri really do mate for life, exclusively. I feel sorry for them." But unspoken, as he stood up, was his pity for her as well.

"I do want to, Pinto," she said, because she felt he deserved the truth. "But I can't."

He smiled, stopping directly in front of her. "They haven't found him yet, have they?" he asked.

"No."

"I hope we do. Hawk always treated a person for themselves, not what they looked like. Vanov deserved what he got."

"I'm not so sure," Lily murmured, "but I'm hardly in a position to argue, since it was my life he saved."

"I wonder if the je'jiri have kinnas," he mused.

He had not moved any farther away from her. His presence, so close, was if anything worse than the sight of him seated on the bed. Perhaps he could read her as easily as Kyosti could. He bent, slowly, nearer, and kissed her. Long enough, lingering enough, invitation enough—she sighed and leaned into him. Her hands crept up to touch his back.

And jerked away again. "Pinto," she snapped, "would you *leave*?"

He laughed, understanding her perfectly. "*You* have to let me out."

"Wait a minute. How did you get *in*?"

"Bach let me in."

"*Bach!*" She keyed in the code automatically and the door slid open. "*Bach* let you in"—He passed through the doorway and walked on to the far door. "Pinto! You can't go out in the halls half-naked like that!"

He paused at the far door as it slipped aside to reveal gold deck corridor. "Why not?" He grinned. "It's nothing that most of the women on this ship haven't already seen." The outer door sighed shut behind this provocative remark before Lily could reply, but she could not help but chuckle a little as she turned back to face the bed. It looked long and empty and lonely.

The com chimed. "Captain." Trey's voice. "Off-ship communication."

"Put it through." Lily felt abruptly tired again. "This is Ransome."

"Seria here. We've got the lead. The ferry left four days ago for Zeya Depot."

"Thank you, Jenny. Come back aboard." She keyed the

bridge. "Trey. Set a course for Zeya Depot. We'll leave as soon as all crew are back on board and the resupply is finished. Check with min Belsonn for that schedule."

"Yes, Captain."

"Wake me up in six hours. Ransome out." She sat down on the bed. And felt it again, that worst of emotions: hope. Maybe on Zeya Depot... "Maybe you should sleep," she muttered, and went to wash up.

13   The Good Doctor

****

Zeya Depot's coordinator was adamant. "No doubt whatsoever. A rogue je'jiri male. There was some trouble. A fight. A man thought he was trying to pick up on his woman friend, putting a hand on her, or something. The testimony is still being sorted out. In any case, the rogue was arrested—had to be restrained." The coordinator paused, sharing a look of distaste with her assistant. "Next thing I knew the Concord representative showed up and took him off my hands."

"Under what authority?" Deucalion asked.

The coordinator skipped her attention across Lily and centered it on Deucalion. "You're with the bureau. You know how it is. Once they decide to cite 'security reasons,' you're free to get records if you have time to wade through the bureaucracy. I did find out that it was an order standing from Rehabilitation, if that helps. In fairness to min Giorgas—our rep—I don't think he knew anymore than he told me, but the identifiers came back flagged as 'violent offender,' so he took him into custody and sent him off on a secure yacht."

"Sent him where?" Lily asked.

"Concord," said the coordinator and Deucalion at the same time. After a brief pause, Deucalion went on. "Rehabilitation is based at Concord. It's the only place they would send him."

"I don't suppose you could enlighten me." The coordinator looked from Lily to Deucalion. "I interviewed the rogue briefly, because of the incident, and while I thought him disturbed I didn't feel he was dangerous. I studied xeno in college," she added, as if this were explanation enough, "although I never went on to get an advanced degree."

Deucalion shrugged, glancing at Lily as if to say that it was her choice what to divulge. And because the coordinator had been both efficient and helpful, Lily felt she deserved something.

"He's a half-breed."

"Ah," replied the coordinator, trying not to look gratified.

"That explains it. That must be an interesting story, Captain, how you got a half-breed on as a member of your crew."

Lily could not help but smile at the careful politeness with which the coordinator framed her curiosity. "It is. But unfortunately, if they're three and an half days ahead of us, I don't have time to relate it to you now."

"Ah, well." The coordinator rose, undaunted by this evasion, and offered both Lily and Deucalion her hand to shake. "I had to try. Best luck to you."

"How long will it take us to get to Concord?" Lily asked Deucalion as they returned to the ship. Her usual escort—Jenny, Rainbow, and two je'jiri—followed them.

"We'll lose time to a yacht. Especially since you still don't have a full-shifted bridge complement. On a straight route we can get there in about three weeks. Let's see. If they left three and one half days ago, we can expect to get in a little under a week after they do. And once we get there we'll have the charges against you to deal with. Concord's system is such that even with my presence it could take weeks to find out where they've put him. And *then* we still have to get permission to see him."

"I'm glad you're so optimistic."

"Realistic. Bureaucracy is one thing that never changes. Not to mention the final hearing on the disposition of the *Forlorn Hope* itself. I can't predict what kind of ruling will be handed down, given its history."

"Deucalion." The history of the *Forlorn Hope* made her think, not of her own hope to keep the ship for herself and her crew, but of the fate of the *Hope*'s original crew. "What if Intelligence incarcerates me? I have to be there, in person, when we find Hawk."

Deucalion considered. "You have to face those charges, Lily."

"Charges that essentially boil down to fraternizing with a couple of saboteurs, who I didn't know were saboteurs at the time. I didn't realize that was a crime. And if it is, it makes you a criminal as well. More so, since you knew."

"Let me rephrase," he replied coolly. "If you intend to stay in League space you have no choice but to face the charges. I assure you, we assume innocence here, not guilt."

"That's reassuring."

"When you're sarcastic you sound like Adam. In any case, where would you go? Back to the Reft?"

Back to the Reft. An unlikely prospect, she thought, given the circumstances under which they had left. And that was supposing any of them even wanted to return. "We could turn privateer," she said, thoughtful. "Like La Belle. The Pale isn't under League jurisdiction. Or anywhere else outside that."

He looked shocked. "You'd *like* to be a privateer?"

"Not particularly. But if I'm given no choice—" She let the sentence hang, letting her silence speak.

"Lily." He looked as if he was about to stop right there in the middle of the corridor. Jenny, reading his body language, even faltered in her step. Then, glancing around at the foot traffic through which they made no appreciable ripple, he decided against drawing any more attention to themselves than the two je'jiri already brought them. His stride broke, but he picked it up quickly. "All right." He frowned. "You have no idea how it galls me to bend regulations in this way—"

Lily grinned. "Oh, I think I can guess."

"Now you sound like Adam again. But in this case I will. *Only* if you promise that once we have taken the first steps to resolve the problem of Hawk, you will voluntarily present yourself to Intelligence for a hearing."

"If Hawk is at Concord, how am I to manage to find him without revealing my presence there and as such being arrested?"

"You're the captain. You ought to be used to delegating by now."

She puffed out her cheeks and then released the breath stored through her closed lips. "I think it was easier when I was the leader of a small strike force. None of this waiting around on the bridge. It's much more wearing."

"Oh, yes." Deucalion cast her a grateful look. "Thank you for reminding me. We also need to bring this matter of the Reft and its civil war to the attention of the council. They'll have to decide what kind of embassy to send."

Lily could not help but smile, thinking of Alexander Jehane's reaction to the arrival of a League embassy of any sort. "Whatever kind they send," she said, "I'm sure they'll find the experience interesting." Thinking of Jehane made her think of Lia. Was she even alive? Glancing at Jenny, she wondered if the mercenary's thoughts had made the same leap as her own, but she could read nothing but trained

alertness on Jenny's face as the woman kept an eye out for
the possible, if unlikely, reappearance of Korrigan Windsor
and his boys. "Very well," Lily finished. "I accept. Let me
see Hawk first, and then I'll appear for a hearing."

"Trust me," said Deucalion. "I don't know what experience
you've had—clearly not a good one—but League justice is
fair, and as impartial as any human justice can be. You won't
be betrayed."

"I hope not," muttered Lily, but she said it too softly for
Deucalion to hear.

Concord was not so much a large station as a number of
large stations sewn together in complementary orbits. Yehoshua
stared in awe at what was to him the most marvelous feat of
engineering he had ever seen. He could not imagine how any
human ingenuity could have woven such a complex web of
interlinked stations and dry docks and arrays and more
stations—all in a bewildering variety of sizes and shapes—and
at the same time made it so utterly beautiful against the stark
background of space and distant sun. And yet, he considered,
it was always a mistake to underestimate human ingenuity.

"Gregori," he said for the fourth time. "Not only are you
not supposed to be on this shuttle, but you absolutely will not
be allowed off of it once we arrive."

"Look!" Gregori pointed away from the rather crude repre-
sentation of Concord's pattern that he was attempting to
model on his com-screen to a disk suspended off to one side
of the vast network of human life. "Is that a planet?"

"I don't know," Yehoshua replied, feeling surly and trying
to conceal it. "It must be. Gregori, will you promise me that
you won't try to sneak off this shuttle the same way you tried
to sneak on?"

"Sure," replied Gregori cheerfully.

Yehoshua thought over the entire statement. "Will you
promise me that you won't leave the shuttle at all once we
reach Concord?"

Now Gregori hesitated. He made the kind of face that only
a very clever child thwarted of his utmost ambition can make.
He shrugged his shoulders and pounded his toes into the
back of the seat in front of him.

"Cut that out," snapped the occupant of the seat.

Yehoshua sighed. "Gregori."

"I promise." Gregori subsided sulkily into the comforts of

his three-dimensional modeling of Concord's intricate maze, pausing only once to dart a glance of searing disgust at Yehoshua. Yehoshua sighed again.

"We have you clear, *Hope One*." The voice of Concord traffic control pierced the small cabin's hush easily. "You'll find a berth available at Amity five plus seven. Use the eleven forty nexus for approach."

"Great," muttered Pinto. "That makes perfect sense to me."

"Received and accepted," Deucalion said into the com. He leaned over to bring up a display on Pinto's console. Concord appeared, diagrammed in colors and patterns for flight approach. "Here. The flight paths work as—"

"I see," said Pinto, taking in the angles and lines quickly. "That's very efficient." He sounded surprised.

"It has to be," said Deucalion. "Do you know how much traffic moves in and out of here, as a daily average?"

"No. Let me see. There's the opening, and then you go round through—oh—and this grid intersects there and—that's very good."

"I'll tell you some other time," Deucalion murmured, returning his attention to com. "*Forlorn Hope*, this is *Hope One*. We will berth in thirty-five Standard minutes."

"Acknowledged. We have no further on-board relays for you, except that Gregori is to promise *not* to leave the shuttle until you return to the ship."

"Gregori?" Deucalion turned in his seat. "How did Gregori get on board?"

"You don't want to know," said Yehoshua.

Deucalion turned back to the console. "You can be *sure* that Gregori will not leave the shuttle. *Hope One,* out." He unstrapped himself from the seat and used the handholds on the other seats to get back to Yehoshua's row. "Now see here, young man," he began sternly. Gregori regarded him with astonishment. "You may think stowing away is a fun game, but I assure you that it is nothing of the kind. We are on a very delicate mission here and your presence makes it far more difficult for us to succeed. Were you to get lost on Concord—which I assure you that you would—we can just as well forget finding Hawk at all. So you will not leave this shuttle until we return to the *Forlorn Hope*. Do you understand?"

Gregori's astonishment had turned by degrees into chagrin. "Yes," he replied in a very small voice. He hung his head. His chin trembled.

"Good," said Deucalion without the least sign of remorse for upsetting the boy. He returned to the com-chair next to Pinto.

Yehoshua followed him forward. "Don't you think you were a little harsh on him?"

"No. Sometimes scaring a child that age is the only way to make them understand consequences before those same consequences overwhelm them and everyone else."

"I wasn't aware that you had so much experience with child rearing," Yehoshua replied, unable to keep an edge of sarcasm from his voice.

"I don't. But my brother and I unwittingly contributed to several near-disasters by just that kind of behavior. Almost got our mother killed, once. We were only nine years old. I have never seen my father as furious as he was on that day. And with good reason."

Yehoshua could find no reply for this explanation, so he returned to his seat. When they berthed at Concord, Gregori turned to him and said, in a low voice, "I'm sorry. I never thought that it might mean we couldn't get min Hawk back."

Yehoshua patted him on the shoulder with awkward sympathy, but it was with relief that he left Gregori to Pinto's ministrations and followed Deucalion and Paisley off the shuttle. Yehoshua was not quite sure why the captain had sent Paisley along on this expedition, except that the young Ridani woman had been remarkably subdued lately and perhaps Lily thought a glimpse of Concord might cheer her up.

And indeed, as Deucalion led them through the bewildering maze of halls and corridors and concourses that made up Concord—that made up this one small section of Concord, he had to remind himself—Paisley's face brightened and she stared about herself with infectious awe at the huge murals that ornamented each concourse.

"It be not just ya big," she informed Deucalion ingenuously, "but ya pretty as well. All ya pictures, and so bright, and so—so many."

"Concord's murals *are* famous," Deucalion conceded. "It was the Temu Assembly that suggested commissioning artists to depict human history and culture on Concord's walls. A fitting tribute, and a reminder."

"Ah," said Paisley wisely. "I reckon you all must be ya rich, as live here."

"Rich?" Deucalion chuckled. "It's a rich life, certainly."

"No. I mean ya credit rich. Like ya Senators on Central. They could have all or everything they wanted."

"Couldn't everyone?" He shook his head. "No, I suppose you lived under a primitive economy there."

"We have free trade," protested Yehoshua, disliking Deucalion's tone of voice. "Central's abuse of trade regulations was one of the factors that caused the revolution. But perhaps you've moved beyond free trade here."

"Certainly not. Where would people find their incentives? But we no longer have the vast inequities in the distribution of wealth that used to characterize that system."

"Do you mean anyone could live here?" Paisley asked, disbelieving. "Even ya Ridanis?" As she spoke, they passed a pair of people, one of whom was, like the administrator Scallop from Diomede Center, a half-tattooed Ridani.

"Ridanis?" Deucalion looked puzzled, clearly not understanding the thrust of her question. "Of course anyone can live here, given the population constraints on a closed system."

"Sure," Paisley breathed. "And glory." Her eyes shone with the wonder of it.

"Here we are." Deucalion directed them past a mural of men and women harvesting a field of grain and then off into a corridor on the left that led into a warren of offices. He halted by a wall panel next to a door and keyed in. A moment later the door shunted aside silently to reveal a small room with an elaborately contoured desk and an exceedingly tall, black woman sitting behind it.

Seeing her visitors, she smiled broadly. "Deucalion! Come in. Come in." She stood up and came forward to give him a hug, then shook hands with Yehoshua and Paisley. Under her loose, calf-length tunic, her belly swelled out in the universal proportions of a pregnant woman. "Please, sit down. I'm Kaeshima." As she turned back to the desk, Deucalion showed them how to lever out and open chairs from the wall. They unfolded into constructions of delicacy and beauty and remarkable comfort.

"You're well?" Deucalion asked once they were seated.

"Quite well. Now." Kaeshima sat down and tilted a slender screen so that Deucalion could view it as well. "I've done some investigation and on any general channel there is no

ecord of a secure yacht from Zeya Depot or any record of
his person arriving at Concord—not on the regular manifests
r even on the reports of traffic into Rehabilitation. I'm
ligging down farther now. We'll see if he turns up in classified."

"You think he won't?" asked Deucalion.

Kaeshima smiled, her very full lips mocking. "He ought to
f he hadn't shown up here before. But it could be that
hey're going to cover his arrival up entirely."

"How can that possibly be done?"

"Deucalion, I do love you for your naïveté. They leave no
rail at all. They just never enter him."

"But that's—"

"Not very sociable, I know."

"Sociable!" Deucalion stood up, as if that action were the
nly outlet for his emotions.

Yehoshua braced himself for the lecture he saw coming,
nd was surprised, glancing at Kaeshima, to see that she was
till smiling. Her eyes met his and she exchanged a complicitous
lance with him.

"That kind of secrecy goes against every principle on which
ve've built our society. It subverts democracy itself. How can
hey possibly justify—"

"Deucalion." The gentleness with which Kaeshima interrupted
im brought his tirade to an abrupt halt. "Most people can
nd a way to justify even the most unreasonable actions. I'm
ıst warning you that it might not be as easy as we'd hoped to
rack down this Hawk. Especially if he's who I suspect he
s—one of the old saboteur network. But if anyone can find
im . . ." She trailed off.

"You can. I know." Deucalion sat down, not quite meekly.
That's why I came to you, Kae."

"Flatterer. And here I thought it was for sentimental
easons." When Deucalion did not reply to this sally, she
eturned to the keyboard built into her desk. "In case no
eference to min Hawk shows up, which I suspect will be the
ase, I'm also running a cocurrent cross-check of Rehabilita-
ion, Psych, and Xenology for unusual activity or unexpected
ransfer of personnel."

"Can *anyone* access all of this information?" Yehoshua
sked.

Kaeshima glanced up, curious. "It's public." She looked
ver at Deucalion.

"They really aren't from League space," he replied.

"Ah." It was comment enough.

"Even classified material?" Yehoshua persisted.

Kaeshima continued to type as she spoke. "Define classi
fied. It's not as if it's a private organization with qualifin
standards and memberships fees. This is government. Ther
are, of course, privacy restrictions to protect the individual.
can't nose into your health records, for instance, or find ou
how you voted. But when a government starts keeping se
crets from the people—you and I—who are in fact th
ultimate authority"—she shrugged—"Certainly there is clas
sified information. But if one can prove necessity to know an
fair intent of use, that kind of information remains accessible.

"Is that what you've done here?"

"No." She grinned. "I'm circumventing the system. I snuc
in the back door. After all, I helped design the curren
software."

"But min Belsonn," exclaimed Paisley. "That be *wrong*."

Deucalion blushed. "We're in a hurry," he said, but th
excuse sounded lame. Paisley stared at him. Yehoshua chos
not to press him, seeing how embarrassed he already was
They sat for a time in silence, until Kaeshima made a brie
exclamation.

"I think we've got it." As if it was a good luck charm, sh
rubbed her rounded belly. "This may not mean anything, bu
I have a transfer of Dr. Vespa Tuan Farhad from her post i
Xenopsychology to Rehabilitation. Seven days ago."

Deucalion leaned forward. "Not *the* Dr. Farhad? The on
who worked with Soerensen on the psycholingual xenographi
correspondence—"

"I don't know, but there can't be many Dr. Farhads fittin
these specifications. And it is an unusual transfer."

"Follow that up. I wonder..." He trailed off.

"What be ya psycholingual xenographic correspondence?"
Paisley asked.

Deucalion chuckled. "I haven't a clue. Breakthrough re
search into language and alien psychology. The kind of wor
that wins Nobel Prizes. And Farhad was young, especially
be working with someone of Soerensen's stature."

"Who be—?"

"Paisley," Yehoshua said softly. "We have library files o
League history on the *Hope*. You ought to avail yourself
those."

"Yes, min," she replied meekly.

"This is strange," said Kaeshima from the desk. "She accepted a transfer to Concord prison, secure level six." Deucalion whistled. "Temporary assignment, no fixed time limit, her former post pending for her return."

"Secure level six." Deucalion shook his head. "Now, Kaeshima, tell me how we can get a message to her without alerting anyone in Rehabilitation."

Kaeshima smiled, not without sympathy. "Scarred forever by your childhood, my dear. Don't bridle up at me, Deucalion. You're the one who suggested it. Well, an old-fashioned, hand-carried note."

"And how do you suggest I get to secure level six without attracting attention?"

"You could agree to be my baby's crèche uncle and I might find an untraceable transitory message coded private to Dr. Farhad and ask her to meet you here."

"Kaeshima," he answered with some exasperation. "I've already agreed to be its crèche uncle."

"Then there you are. I should have been a saboteur."

"Please." He shuddered. "You have no idea what you are talking about."

"Probably not. How do you suggest I lure the good doctor up here?" This query brought silence from her audience. "It has to be good," she added, "to move her."

"It be only right," said Paisley pugnaciously, "that she help min Ransome, seeing as she be lovers with min Hawk."

"Lovers? I admit, sentiment is a nice touch, but I'm not sure it will be a strong enough bait."

"No." Deucalion nodded. "That's exactly the right suggestion, Paisley." Paisley beamed. He stood up and went over to lean on Kaeshima's desk. "If Hawk is pretending to be a je'jiri, and Dr. Farhad was called in for that reason—if she was even transferred to Concord prison because of his arrival—"

"It's the only lead we have so far."

"Then telling her that his mate has arrived—his *human* mate."

"Je'jiri? *Human* mate?"

"I'll fill you in later. That she has arrived and needs an urgent and private conference with the doctor. . . . Try that."

"*Human* mate," Kaeshima muttered, but already her fingers tapped rapidly into the keyboard. "You'd *better* fill me in on the rest of the story, my boy, or I'll make you join up for a season at my soccer club again."

"I'll tell you," he assured her.

She finished and tilted back in her chair, stroking her belly again. Her gaze caught on Paisley. "We don't see many orthodox here. What sect do you adhere to?"

Paisley looked first at Yehoshua, then at Deucalion, for illumination. "What be orthodox?"

"Your tattoos. And the locks."

"Bain't all ya Ridanis got ya tattoos and ya locks?" Paisley considered her own question and shook her head. "Sure, but I seen ya Ridanis here that be only half-tattooed, or scarce tattooed at all. I reckon ya pattern be sore troubled here." She hesitated, as if at some troubling thought. "Or ya different."

"Do you mean that *all* the Ridanis where you come from are uniformly orthodox?"

"Sure, if you mean they all have ya tattoos as I do. I never reckoned there be any other pattern but ours." Her expression grew unexpectedly fierce. "Even if I might have hoped it be ya true, that there be another way for ya Ridanis to live."

"You mean it was strict there?" Kaeshima's interest seemed genuine enough.

Paisley drew in her breath. "*I* think min Hawk treated us Ridanis no different than he treated any other soul because he didn't know no other way." For a moment her gaze focused on Yehoshua, and he looked away, ashamed to know that he had harbored his own share of prejudices against Ridanis in his life, like most every other citizen of the Reft, unthinking and reflexive. "*I* think," and here she turned her forceful gaze on Deucalion, "that you would be sore surprised and sore angry at the way us Ridanis be treated in ya Reft, unless you got ya special people you set aside here, as we have never seen."

"Set aside?" Kaeshima asked. "How do you mean?" And then she interrupted herself. "I've got a reply. Goodness, that was fast."

Deucalion hurried around the desk to stare over her shoulder. "Thank the Mother," he muttered. "Yehoshua," he added, "You and Paisley get back to the shuttle and return to the *Forlorn Hope*. Dr. Farhad has agreed to meet with Lily here in this office in two hours."

Lily was already seated in Kaeshima's tidy office when Dr. Farhad arrived. She had ruthlessly banished everyone except Yehoshua and Jenny from the office, including Kaeshima and a protesting Deucalion. "I want you as my witnesses," she had said. "And I'll need your support." Jenny, squeezing her hand, said nothing. Yehoshua murmured something incomprehensible, feeling embarrassed but pleased.

The door shunted silently aside and a woman entered. She paused as the door shut behind her to examine the three occupants of the office with a lively, intelligent gaze. Her hands, clasped in front of her, had a smooth, ageless cast to them, relaxed in each other's grasp.

"You must be Captain Ransome," she said with a professional's curt politeness, coming forward to extend a hand toward Lily.

Lily stood, recognizing an authority that, in their current situation, outweighed her own. "Yes. Dr. Farhad?"

"Yes. Your associates?" Still polite, her voice now questioned the necessity of their presence.

"My chief officers: Jenny Seria. Yehoshua Akio Filistia. I think it is important that they hear what we have to say."

"As you wish." The doctor shook their hands. She did not avail herself of Kaeshima's desk but took a fourth chair and sat down with Lily on one side and Jenny on the other, making their group into a tight circle. "Under the circumstances, Captain, I could not ignore this unusual and rather secretive request for a meeting. Right now, I won't question your motives for secrecy."

"If you'll excuse me, doctor, information leads us to believe that your prisoner has been brought into Concord under equal secrecy."

Dr. Farhad smiled coolly. "He is not my prisoner, as I am not a jailer. I don't know his status at Concord prison. I only know that he has suffered some kind of traumatic breakdown, and that I have been called in as a consultant. He is now my patient, and it is as his doctor that I am speaking to you now. I'm not interested in any other considerations but his health. That is the sole reason that I agreed to talk with you." She paused, but it was not to let Lily reply, only to marshal her thoughts. "You claim to be his mate."

This dispassionate attack took Lily off guard. She could not stop herself from a brief, wry chuckle. "I don't claim it. I am."

"I hope we are speaking about the same person."

"Kyosti Bitterleaf Hakoni. Also known as Hawk. I don't

know if he went by any other names. At one time part of the
saboteur network that fought in your war with the Empire."

"*My* war?"

"We're not from League space, doctor. Until a year ago, I
didn't even know it existed. But that's another story. Here is
an image of how he looked when he was my ship's chief
physician." She handed a thin com-slate to the doctor.

Dr. Farhad took it without comment and examined it in
silence, her lips pursed in concentration. The dusky skin on
her face was as smooth as that on her hands, but something in
her manner gave away, as it had in Master Heredes, her great
age and greater wisdom. The slightly flat features of her eyes
and broad cheekbones bore a similarity to Lily's, suggesting
some long-distant common ancestry. "Yes, it is Kyosti," she
said, handing the slate back to Lily. Her use of the name
surprised Lily: everyone else she knew, even those who had
known him before, called him Hawk. Dr. Farhad sat back in
her chair, hands reclasped in her lap, and regarded Lily
shrewdly. "Why are you here? What do you want?"

"I want him back."

The doctor's composure remained unruffled by this outburst. "Let me ask you a few questions, Captain. How long
have you known Kyosti?"

Lily shook her head. "Let me see. About two and a half
years."

"How long have you been lovers?"

"As long. Within a week, about."

"It is unlikely, to say the least, that he would have acted so
quickly, or given in to your interest so soon."

Lily smiled, wry again. "He wasn't conquered by my vast
charm, I'm afraid. He did it to get the protection of the man I
was traveling with at the time."

Jenny gasped. "Damn my eyes. The squirrelly bastard."
Yehoshua refrained from comment.

"He was trying to get away from Concord Intelligence,"
Lily added.

"Concord Intelligence? I don't understand. A moment ago
you said you weren't *from* League space."

"This wasn't in League space. Surely you know he was in
Concord prison for over twenty years, had just gotten out and
was taken with an expedition to—" Lily halted. Something
she had said had finally gotten a reaction from the doctor.

"Twenty years in Concord prison!" Dr. Farhad's agitation

took the form of unclasping her hands and lifting them to
straighten the already immaculate coil of black hair pinned up
at the nape of her neck. "I was never informed of this. It is
not noted in the files I was given last week—" This time,
when her lips pursed, her disapproval was evident. "I can
assure you, I will be speaking to Rehabilitation about this.
That is unconscionable. Now." The matter was dismissed but
clearly not forgotten. She fixed her severe stare on Lily once
more. "In the time he has been your lover, have you noticed
any—strange behavior?"

Yehoshua coughed behind his hand. Jenny sighed and
looked somber.

"He killed one of my former lovers," Lily said in a flat
voice. "And attempted to murder the second. Luckily I only
had two. And I believe I know what precipitated—whatever
condition he's in now. He thought I had been killed. In
response—" Coming so calmly, the words took on a surreal
aspect to her. She could still see the blood. "—he killed—
how many?"

"Fifteen," said Yehoshua.

"Fifteen people. It was—ugly. He ripped their throats out,
just like a je'jiri would."

"Ah." The doctor's expression lightened. "Now I begin to
understand. First you must understand, Captain, that you
mistake the agency. Je'jiri do not go berserk. Only humans
are berserkers. Mix them, and you get a volatile brew, one
that, like oil and water, is never soluble. His attachment to
you—if you are his mate, as you say—is of necessity bound
by his je'jiri ancestry. But such furious violence is all too
human. That is why he has retreated into this je'jiri guise."

"What do you mean?"

Dr. Farhad nodded, making a decision. "I think you will
need to see him for yourself. If you will come with me." She
rose. "I can admit only you, Captain. Your associates will
have to stay here."

"Lily—" Jenny began.

"No, Jenny. I'll go. Go back to the shuttle. I'll meet you
there. I do have one more question. Doctor, you call him
Kyosti. Somehow I get the impression that you've known
him, or of him, before now."

Dr. Farhad smiled for the first time, but it was a sad smile,
touched with irony. "Some fifty years ago, Captain, I was an
ordinary social worker in the city of Helsinki, on Prokiya

Four. I was called in on the case of an adolescent boy of seventeen who had committed a horrifying series of murders. Father dead, mother unknown, family indifferent. The old story. Until I discovered that he had only been living with his aunt and uncle for six years, and that they had concealed—out of shame—the fact that he was that rarest of things, a half-breed. Instantly I changed my entire treatment of him. My original area of interest was in xenopsychology, but I had never been able to get even an entry-level post in either the public or private sphere. Thus, social work. And now, everything changed. I made a brilliant reputation working with that poor, troubled child. I won a university post, and later graciously accepted a position in Xenopsychology Research here at Concord. Yes, I know Kyosti quite well." She went to the door, and it opened before her. "Why do you suppose I was called in now?"

14   Ghost

****

They took elevators, one long pneumatic tube ride, and finally walked down the only drab corridors Lily had seen in League space to reach secure level 6 of Concord prison. A second tube ride and four seemingly casual checkpoints punctuated the trip. The security here was unobtrusive but thorough. Lily wondered if unseen security scanned and probed them as well. Dr. Farhad remained unconcerned and led her through it all with impressive aloofness. Whatever her origins as an ordinary social worker, she had clearly grown accustomed to the privileges that attend one who gains status as a great mind. It occurred to Lily that the security leading to level 6 was organized solely to keep prisoners in, not—as it would have been in Reft space—to keep visitors out as well.

"You're quiet," said Dr. Farhad as they passed through two keyed doors into a large observation room. A single technician turned from the main console and acknowledged their entrance.

"I'm nervous," Lily admitted, following the doctor forward to a long wall of clear plastine that overlooked a series of small, sparsely furnished rooms.

The first room was empty, the second contained an unfamiliar je'jiri male, and the third.... Her eyes skipped back to the second room.

"It can't be," she whispered.

"Oh, it is," replied Dr. Farhad, cool and composed at her side. "Blood, retina, fingerprints all confirm it."

Lily knew it with the immediacy of primeval instinct: she was looking at an alien, not a human. He sat, not in a chair or couch, but on a high counter, legs crossed, back straight: just as the je'jiri clan had sat at her conference with the Dai. The set of his shoulders, the tilt of his head, the way his hands held the thin com-slate balanced on one knee, all bore the stamp of an alien musculature. The unruly mop of his hair stood out startlingly blue against his pallor: He was as pale as a ghost, too pale to have human skin. He was no one she knew.

Lily stared. Slowly, painstakingly, she constructed bone and muscle to find an echo of *her* Kyosti, but it was a difficult match. There were certain physical resemblances, purely structural. Any likeness ended there. He sat with the perfect stillness of the hunter, studying the screen.

"It has been difficult to communicate with him," said Dr. Farhad, jarring Lily out of her scrutiny, "because he only speaks and responds to the je'jiri tongue now. I speak a few phrases, not well—it is a difficult tongue conceptually for us. Of the two specialists who live on Concord, one is currently on assignment and the other has only been available twice for short periods. He was not, in any case, very communicative."

Lily tore her gaze away from Kyosti—it was too painful to look at him. Dr. Farhad's curt professionalism was easier to deal with. "Have you tried je'jiri?"

"Yes." The doctor moved away from the overlook. The technician moved swiftly to let her sit in the chair that, poised in front of a long console, allowing her to observe all three rooms and access an impressive bank of screens and keyboards at the same time. "There is a clan currently in residence here. They agreed to send one male. He arrived and spoke with Kyosti for some time, but when he returned he informed me that there was nothing the je'jiri could do. When Kyosti's mother sent him to his father's kin, just before puberty, evidently she severed all clan ties, so that he has in fact no kinship within the je'jiri kin system at all. He was considered by their lights too dangerous—too primitive and violent, if you will—to be allowed into je'jiri society."

"*They* call *us* violent? After what I've seen them do?" And yet, looking out at him, there was a surface edge of serenity to him now that had never existed before, a veneer of calm. She doubted somehow that it ran very deep. "Perhaps I'm beginning to understand why he is trying, however unconsciously, to protect himself by becoming je'jiri."

"Perhaps you do, at that," replied the doctor. "However, it is no protection. I thought I had helped him, when he was a boy, to find a balance, to integrate both halves, but it was a makeshift cure, I fear, and one that has clearly disintegrated."

"When I met him, I think he was trying very hard to be human. To not be je'jiri at all."

"No better solution. Concord has record of two other cases

f half-breeds. One committed suicide at age eighteen. The
ther died recently after eighty years in a catatonic state.
.yosti has done very well."

"Very well," Lily echoed. The statement seemed incongru-
us to her, seeing this person—this creature—that had some-
ow inhabited Kyosti's body. "What happened to him as a
oy? Why did his mother send him away? Surely it was a
ruel thing to do."

"Cruel enough. When he spoke of that time, it was with
reat pain. I think he was well loved there—I could guess
hat from what he said and how he said it. I can guess—or
ope—that it was as painful a parting for his mother as for
im. But imagine a human adolescent in je'jiri society. The
lan member who visited us here said it bluntly: it would not
e tolerated. Thus he was sent to his human kin."

"To become human," Lily said bitterly.

"I interviewed them extensively, the aunt and uncle, and
randparents. They meant well. But he was a strange child.
lis father had died under strange circumstances and had
een the black sheep of the family as well. And they had had
o inkling that the child even existed—simply had him
umped in their laps. They should have called Social Services
t once, of course. But they didn't."

She turned back to find refuge in Dr. Farhad's even
xpression. "What did he do, at seventeen?"

Dr. Farhad's smile was sad. "What do you suppose he did?
le had sex. No one had prepared him for the consequences.
he young woman was three years older than him and
ealthy enough in her self-esteem to have had two previous
overs. They both died. Evidently she was disturbed enough
y his behavior—not knowing, I think, that he had committed
he murders—that she stopped seeing him and began a
elationship with a new partner. As we reconstructed it
fterward, it was the new partner who figured out the con-
ection. This young man was not a pleasant character. Kyosti
racked them down and the young man killed the woman,
hinking it would save his life. Of course it didn't. Originally it
vas thought that Kyosti had murdered the woman as well—"

"He would never have!"

"No, so we discovered." Dr. Farhad's eyes gleamed as she
xamined Lily in the subdued light of the observation room.
I'm beginning to think you are indeed what you claim to
e."

"So you were called in."

"Yes. He did try to kill himself twice afterward. I worked with him for several years. Eventually he was deemed stable enough to begin to attempt to live in the world again. I encouraged him to study medicine."

"*You* encouraged him—?"

"It fitted his—particular talents. It gave him a sense of purpose, a mission. I was disappointed when he joined the saboteur's network. I never thought it a job conducive to mental health. But his parole board approved, and it was his choice."

"He had another lover there," said Lily, and then lapsed into quiet, remembering the story Kyosti had told her—it seemed so long ago—at Bleak House Station. How his lover had slept with his best friend to see if it was true that he would have to kill any man she slept with. "But I think she abused him, abused the relationship. She died, at Betaos."

"At Betaos? The famous engagement? They used to say that the blue-hair physician killed an entire chameleon—excuse me, Kapellan—battalion single-handed. One of those exaggerated legends that grow up."

"I'm not so sure," Lily replied, slow. "She died there. He could have done it, if he'd gone berserk. I've seen what he can do, under similar circumstances. I don't like to remember it."

Dr Farhad tapped a message into one of the keyboards and a file came up on a screen. "I see I have a great deal to fill in. Which reminds me, what more do you know about his term in Concord prison? I am deeply disturbed to hear of it. It should never have happened, not with his psychological profile."

"Other than that it was about twenty years—No. He told me once he'd been in something called sensory."

"Sensory deprivation!" Dr. Farhad lifted her hands to pull at the tight coil of her hair, lowered them once again to tap furiously into the keyboard. "That's the worst possible treatment they could have subjected him to!" She seemed to be talking more to herself than to Lily. "It would be *torture*. Nothing better than torture." She checked the screen, but whatever she wanted evidently did not come up. She resumed typing. "I'll have their heads for this. Absolutely against procedure. Unforgivable." She subsided into incomprehensible muttering.

Lily drifted back to the plass wall. The je'jiri male who sat on a high counter in the middle of the room continued his tranquil contemplation of the slate balanced on one knee. He moved a hand, brushed one pallid cheek with the back of the hand. An alien gesture, precise and exotic, like a ritual whose movements make no sense to the audience.

"I have to talk to him," Lily said. How else will I know if he exists anymore? She left that thought unspoken.

"I'm sorry?" Dr. Farhad glanced up from the bank before her.

"I have to talk to him."

"Do you speak any je'jiri?"

"None."

The doctor stopped typing. "How will you communicate?"

Lily was silent, staring down at Kyosti. There was one way they could communicate without words—and she shuddered. How would it be to make love to an alien, a foreign creature who lacked the least trace of the safe familiarity of humanity? Who could hunt its prey across years and uncounted distance, driven on by forces as strong as those, the same as those, that drag the tides in tune to the movements of the planets, all for the simple pleasure of ripping out the prey's throat with its bare teeth. If he grinned now—that remote, unreadable je'jiri grin—would he show canines? How did they make love, if they made such a thing at all, bonded for life without choice?

"I have to try," she said, her voice so shuttered as to be almost choked.

At first Dr. Farhad did not reply. Her silence seemed considering, not disapproving. "The room to the left," she said at last, "is a close observation room, separated from the one he's now in by plass. He can see you from there. I want you first to go stand in that room so we can observe his reaction. After that, I'll consider letting you into the room with him. I should add, I control access completely to his suite. It's coded both to my voice and my retina."

"All right," said Lily, short, because if she said any more she would begin to talk herself out of this. She turned away from the wall and let Dr. Farhad lead her below. The doctor motioned her to enter the close observation room alone and then disappeared upstairs. Lily entered slowly, hesitant but determined.

He noticed her movement immediately. He looked up.

Saw her. His eyes—deep blue, with a far hint of green—met hers, and they stared at each other. There was no sign of recognition whatsoever on his face. His gaze dropped away, and, disinterested, he returned to his slate.

Lily felt like she had been slugged in the abdomen. Her breath didn't feel right, taut and uneven. She wanted to cry.

Dr. Farhad's voice, disembodied, carried out from the speaker in the panel next to the outer door. "You'd better come back up."

"No. Let me in with him."

"I can't do that. Surely you understand, Captain. The risk—"

"He won't hurt me." Her palms felt damp and hot. Unconsciously, she had clenched her hands; she forced them open. "You have to let me in. Don't you understand? There's only one way I can possibly reach him."

Silence from the panel. Some minutes later Dr. Farhad appeared personally in the room. Her movement attracted Kyosti's notice. He looked up, examined her, and with equal disinterest looked down again. Her face, as she searched Lily's expression, was somber. "Are you sure?"

"No," Lily snapped. "I'm not sure at all. I'm terrified at having to touch that—that alien out there, but if Kyosti is in there, if there's any hope of getting him out again, I have to try."

Dr. Farhad sighed, heartfelt and, strangely enough, compassionate. "Let me call two more fellows, in case there is any—problem. In case we have to intervene."

Lily flushed. "You're not going to—*watch*?"

"No, my dear. Through that curtained door there are private sleeping quarters. But the initial encounter—we must be cautious."

"Agreed," Lily conceded, not without relief.

"I'll be right back."

The assistants took less time to arrange than Lily had feared. It gave her less time for second thoughts. Quickly enough, Dr. Farhad returned and placed her hand on the panel next to the inner door, stood quite still, staring at nothing, and then turned back to Lily. Unexpectedly, she reached out and touched Lily's hand with her own, a smooth cool meeting. She said nothing, just stepped back. The door slipped aside. Lily stepped through. It shut behind her, sealing her in.

Kyosti looked up. So close, with nothing between them, the inaccessible alienness of his entire being struck her with double force. This was not Kyosti. She was alone in the room with an unknown, unpredictable je'jiri male.

Then he tilted his head from side to side, and scented her. His eyes were half-shuttered as he concentrated on smell. He uncrossed his legs. She took an instinctive step back, away, but he only slid off the counter with precise grace and stood there, examining her less with his gaze than with—

She shivered but held her ground. The sense of being thoroughly inspected without sight unnerved her. She felt the prickle of sweat at the back of her neck. Realized that he would know of it as well.

He moved. She held. In a slow, broad arc he circled her. Once around, he circled again, closer this time. And a third, bearing in, so close now that she could with one step reach out and touch him.

"Kyosti."

He halted, hearing her voice, and cocked his head to one side as if trying to make sense of her word. Then he spoke, just a few words, but the language meant nothing to her.

"Kyosti," she repeated. "Can you understand me at all? Do you know who I am?"

He circled her again, keeping a static distance. Stopped in front of her. There was something in his eyes—not, she thought, any recognition of her as *Lily*, but a recognition of *what* she was to him. He looked up at the blank wall above that concealed the one-way glass. Clearly, he was aware that Dr. Farhad and her observers existed on some unseen plane.

He turned deliberately and walked with a predator's easy grace across to the curtained door. Pushing the fabric aside so that it gathered in his hand, he stepped into the gap and paused, half in one room, half in the other. Behind him, she could make out a pallet arranged neatly on the floor of a small room. He waited, expectant but not impatient. The unearthly pallor of his skin gave him a weird and inhuman attractiveness, set off by the unexpected brilliance of his hair. He was startlingly and beautifully exotic. And she understood truly for the first time how a human, despite full knowledge of the consequences, might succumb to the lure of such forbidden fruit.

Her footsteps, on the carpeted floor, made scarcely any sound at all, however heavy and deliberate they felt to her.

As she approached him, he moved aside to let her pass into
the private room. She felt the heat, the presence of him, so
near to her as she slid through the arch, but he did not touch
her. She restrained herself from glancing back toward the
one-way plass wall.

The room she entered was small: a single pallet and a shut
door that led, she expected, to the washing cubicle. She felt
him approach behind her, felt him half a hairbreadth away.
His breath stirred her hair. She shivered again, but this time
not out of fear. She turned.

He dipped his head, brushing her cheek with one side of
his face, like a scenting ritual. His skin felt cool and dry.
Pausing, he waited again, as if in this ritual it was now her
turn to respond.

She hesitated. The heightened pull of her body toward his,
so close as they stood, seemed absurdly strong, as if at any
moment, kept apart, her muscles would start to tremble.
However alien he now was, the intensity of her attraction to
him was both bitter and sweet to her. She lifted one hand and
pulled it through his hair, savoring the soft, thick texture. His
breath caught. Catching, it caught hers as well.

After that, even if she had thought of talking, she would
have had neither the time nor the breath.

And he spoke finally, a word she knew, long after events
had progressed to their conclusion, lying on the pallet, when
he held her as closely as it is possible to hold someone and
still be two separate people. His eyes shut, he said something
that she did not understand at first, until he shifted so that
his lips brushed her ear, and he spoke again, a murmur:
"Lily."

15 "tears seven times salt"

****

he woke, abrupt, disoriented. Began to move, but someone
ad pinned her. That damn Windsor: she began to twist away.
Stopped herself, because it was *not* Windsor. She was
aked. And next to her—her heart raced, making her dizzy.
.n alien. Void help her, a cursed je'jiri. How in the Seven
Iells—

She caught herself in a series of gasps as she remembered.
ven in the way he slept, he looked not human. He stirred,
isturbed by her movement, stretched while still caught in
hat unmeasurable zone between sleep and waking, and
pened his eyes to look directly at her.

A je'jiri's gaze, feral but calm. The green tint to his blue
yes seemed especially pronounced, brought out somehow
y the blue tips of his hair that lay in disarray about his face.
hen he smiled.

If she had felt disoriented before, she felt it doubly now. It
vas a human smile. It was *Kyosti's* smile, set off against his
'jiri looks.

"I had the worst nightmare," he said, so smoothly that at
rst she did not understand him because she expected not to.
Jehanists were about to kill you. They *shot* you"—his voice
hook—"Mother's curse on them, and I went crazy—" He
aoved suddenly to press his face against the curve of her
eck and shoulder. "Thank the Mother, it was just a dream."

He held her a moment longer. She could not find a voice to
peak with. Lifting his head back from her, he raised a hand to
troke her hair. Caught sight of the hand, of his skin—and
topped dead, staring. His eyes widened. *Human* surprise.
)n his je'jiri face, the human mannerisms looked incongru-
us, unbelievable. His gaze traveled down his arm, down his
ody, to where his legs tangled in with hers.

The silence stretched out until it was like a tight string
trung out in the air, ready to snap. He disentangled himself

from her and got up, stiffly, and went into the washin
cubicle. Lily sat up. Pulled on her tunic, and followed him

He was standing in front of the mirror, hands on either sid
of it, palms flat on the wall, staring at himself. Confusio
compounded his shock. His eyes flicked, a brief movemen
seeing her reflection appear.

"What happened to me?" he asked, hoarse.

"Kyosti," she began, tentative, not knowing what to say.

He turned abruptly away from the mirror and stalked ou
of the washing cubicle back to the pallet, settling himself wit
instinctive ease into a je'jiri cross-legged seat on the paddin
That fast, she thought, he reverts. Without thinking he walk
and moves as if he were still one of them. Corrected herse
because he still *is* one of them.

Eyes shut, he concentrated on something far removed fro
her and this room, as if listening for a sound that ha
heretofore eluded him. He scented again, that side-to-sid
tilt of the head so natural to je'jiri that it defined them. Whe
he opened his eyes, he addressed her in a foreign tongu
easily, fluently, with no awareness that she might not unde
stand him.

"I can't understand you, Kyosti," she said quietly. "Yo
have to speak Standard."

He gazed, unblinking, blank, at her. She waited, frozer
suddenly convinced that she had lost him again, and the
something sifted through his consciousness and his expressio
changed.

"Lily," he said. It was like touching an object to be su
that it was no hallucination. He hesitated, tried the wor
again. "Lily." His accent had changed. Now her name sounde
on his tongue, as if the syllables did not come naturally to h
lips.

"Yes," she replied. The pain of watching him struggle wa
so acute that it seemed physical. "Kyosti, you've been ill."

"You've-been-ill," he echoed, enunciating each word, mim
icking her pronunciation. He shook his head, trying to fre
something. "Today is three Terce. Today should be thre
Terce. Today *is* Seven Sextant." He hesitated again, the
asked her a question in the foreign language.

She moved to sit down beside him. "Kyosti. I can't unde
stand that language. You have to speak to me in Standard
Reaching out, she put her arms around him. He relaxed int

her embrace, stilled, head resting between the curve of her shoulder and jaw.

Jerked away abruptly. "Pinto!" he cried. He scrambled to stand so quickly that he stumbled, catching himself, and headed for the curtained arch, tense and oblivious. Lily pushed up and tackled him. He kept trying to go forward. She got a leg under him and flipped him onto his back, pinning him. Sat down on his abdomen, pressing his arms down on either side of him.

"Kyosti! I didn't sleep with him! I didn't sleep with him! One kiss does not constitute—" She broke off, realizing that she was yelling, as if he was deaf. He stared at her. She could not tell if he comprehended her words or not. It suddenly made her furious, that she had searched this long, diverting so many resources, and that she had not simply gotten Kyosti back without any additional cost. It didn't seem fair. "What kind of person do you think I am?" she demanded. "Do you think I would threaten him like that, by sleeping with him?"

He was no longer tense under her. He looked, if anything, bewildered. It was not an expression that reassured her. "I've been ill," he said quietly, as if the concept was new to him. "I'm missing days. Weeks. What happened to them?"

His confusion was so unlike the Kyosti she knew that it hurt her, to see the uncertainty in his face, to hear the clipped, measured way he spoke Standard, as if it were a foreign tongue that he spoke only for her benefit. She did not know how to answer him for fear that what she said might shatter the tentative control he had found.

"I think you ought to speak with Dr. Farhad," she said.

"Dr. Farhad," he echoed. "I know her." He sounded unsure.

"Yes. You know her."

"Can she tell me what happened, to the weeks that are missing?"

"Yes." Lily hoped her voice sounded more confident than she felt. "We'll get properly dressed and then we'll go call her."

He remained silent. She continued to hold him, not sure he understood her. But then he shook his head, as if he was clearing something, and he looked directly at her, for that instant, at least, perfectly sane. "Do you know how many people I've killed? No matter how many I heal, I can never atone for those who died." And then, as if that exhausted

what humanity remained in him, he shifted his gaze away
again and asked another question in the foreign tongue.

Lily eased the pressure on his arms, slowly, and as he
seemed content to remain calm, she stood up, freeing him.
Dressing, she kept a careful watch on him, but he merely put
on his clothes and straightened them with an attention to
detail that almost reminded her of Kyosti. He allowed her to
lead him out of the small room, but once out in the larger
room he let go of her and paced across to the high counter
that was, besides a single table and chair, the only furniture
in the room. He climbed up onto it and composed himself,
cross-legged, to wait. But as she moved to the door, she felt
that his entire awareness was centered on her—not just his
sight, but every other sense as well.

The door wafted aside as Lily got to it. Dr. Farhad stood
just across the threshold. Whatever she had felt on seeing
Lily emerge intact from the privacy room with her patient
was no longer apparent from her expression. She looked, as
usual, cool.

"Will you come in?" Lily asked. "I think you can begin to
talk to him now."

Dr. Farhad stepped inside and the door shut behind her.
"What will you do?" she asked.

"I have to go try to arrange for his release. And to
discharge an obligation."

"His release. It is rather early for that." The doctor looked
past Lily to the still, blue-haired figure seated on the counter.
"He's not going to recover here."

"No," Dr. Farhad agreed. "Prison is not a healthy place for
je'jiri, half-blood or otherwise. Insist that Rehabilitation consult me before they make a decision."

"I will." Lily turned and walked back to stand in front of
Kyosti. She reached out to lay a hand over one of his. His
gaze did not waver from her face. "Kyosti. This is Dr.
Farhad."

He glanced at the doctor, blinked. "I remember you," he
said, but immediately he looked back at Lily.

"Kyosti. I have to leave for a short time. Dr. Farhad will
stay and talk with you. But I will be back soon."

"Of course you will." He regarded her solemnly but with a
depth of trust that unnerved her.

Despite her audience, Lily leaned forward and kissed him.
A chaste kiss, but somehow it sealed her promise. Then she

turned and left him with Dr. Farhad. She chose not to look back, but as she stepped through the door, she heard the doctor's calm voice.

"I'm glad you remember me, Kyosti. It's been many years, hasn't it?"

The door slid to, cutting off his reply. Above, she found three assistants monitoring at the large bank. One agreed to lead her out and then, in that excess of goodwill that she had found to be a common trait shared by most of the people she had met in League space, to show her personally back through the confusing vastness of Concord's interlinked building blocks and unbroken flow of murals to concourse Amity and *Hope One*'s berth.

Everyone on board—Pinto, Paisley, Jenny, Yehoshua and Deucalion—turned at her entrance. No one spoke. Their politeness seemed charged more with tension than courtesy, as if everyone expected the worst but did not want it confirmed. A brief pique of annoyance caused Lily to walk all the way forward in silence to strap herself in to the chair beside Pinto before she turned. They still waited, eyes following her least movement, her faintest change of expression. The feeling of being on stage made her uncomfortable, and she wondered—quite at odds with the situation—what hidden trait in Master Heredes had made him choose acting as a career, before, and even during, his saboteur days.

"I saw him," she said. They let out their breaths in a collective sigh, but still no one spoke. "He's definitely not well." She hesitated, but looking at her audience she realized that of all people, these deserved to know the truth. "He can't decide whether he wants to be human or je'jiri—not consciously, I mean. It's like he's struggling back and forth inside himself. He's got no recollection at all of what happened at Forsaken except as the vaguest dream."

"Nightmare," murmured Yehoshua.

"I don't even know if he would remember any of you. Or Reft space. Most of the time he spoke in the je'jiri language."

"Oh, Lily," Jenny began.

It sounded too much like pity to Lily's ears. "I don't think it's hopeless," she cut in sharply. "He remembered my name. And I'm satisfied that he's in the hands of a competent doctor. Quite competent."

"I should think so," broke in Deucalion. "*The* Dr. Farhad, after all."

"But what do we do now?" asked Yehoshua.

Lily looked at Pinto. "Get traffic control. We detach and return to the *Hope*."

"Lily!" Deucalion stood up. "You *promised* me that if I arranged for you to see Hawk, then you would in good faith turn yourself in on the charges—"

"Deucalion. I will not wait on their convenience in Void knows what kind of a restraining area they provide. I'm not a citizen of League space. I've got no guarantees they'll treat me fairly, not after I arrive here to find a bounty hunter stalking me. I expect to be treated with the respect given any refugee. And I do have responsibilities to my ship. Therefore, we return to the *Hope*. Once there, you can arrange whatever kind of hearing is appropriate for my circumstances with the department that issued these charges—in front of some kind of impartial panel as well, I hope—and I will come over to Concord for that hearing, with you, at the stated time. Not sooner."

"We have clearance for detach," announced Pinto, and then, perhaps accidentally, perhaps not, he undocked the shuttle just roughly enough that Deucalion lost his footing and barely caught the edge of his seat to save himself from falling. He sat down heavily and turned an accusing gaze on Lily. The rest of the shuttle's occupants braced themselves for the lecture.

"Very well," he replied in a constrained voice, and to everyone's surprise he simply removed his slate from his belt and began to key into it.

Someone, possibly Jenny, stifled a chuckle.

Back on board the *Forlorn Hope*, Lily sent Trey to review what files they had on the League's legal system. Then she announced an all-hands inspection of ship and crew. Deucalion interrupted her before she could start.

"Two days from today. Ten hundred hours, in Rehabilitation Main Concourse, Sanger Block, Hearing Room Laefina Zed. Does that satisfy you?"

Lily laughed. "You sound so disappointed, Deucalion. Did you want me hanging by my thumbs?"

"You know very well I don't want—Oh, never mind." With the barest sketch of an excuse, he left, looking irritable.

Jenny, party to this interchange, laughed in her turn. "He can't complain that you reneged on your promise. But I think it irks him that you're dictating the proceedings, not him."

"Who knows? But it gives us time for this inspection, which we sorely need. This boat hasn't had a thorough shakedown since before we left Reft space. Are you ready, Officer Seria?"

Jenny grinned. "Aye, aye, Captain."

"Bach?"

A glorious assent in full orchestration.

Yehoshua waited with a full shift and crew on the bridge. He acknowledged Lily but his gaze lingered longer on Jenny. When the mercenary smiled back at him, he seemed abruptly embarrassed and hastened to Lily's side as she made the rounds of each console. The Mule gave the longest interview, evidently not having lost its—her?—initial enthusiasm for the unadulterated pleasure of being a full-fledged navigator. Finch gave the shortest. He did not seem sullen, merely withdrawn, and he ran comm through its paces so efficiently that it took scarcely any time at all, compared to the other stations. For some reason, Pinto watched him with a quizzical look on his face, but he made no comment. Yehoshua went with them from the bridge.

They got through silver deck before Lily decided to call a halt for the day. Conveniently enough, the last place they visited was the galley and mess. Deucalion sat alone at one of the tables, a cup of café at his right hand, busy keying in to his slate.

"Do you mind if we sit here?" Lily asked, coming up to him.

"It's your ship," he said, then caught himself and managed a smile. "That wasn't very gracious. Of course I don't mind."

"I'll get drinks," said Yehoshua.

Lily and Jenny settled in chairs across from Deucalion. Bach hovered at Lily's back.

"Does the 'bot always shadow you like that?" Deucalion asked.

"Sometimes. If it's necessary."

Bach began to sing a muted aria.

> *Ich folge dir gleichfalls mit freudigen Schritten*
> *und lasse dich nicht,*
> *Mein Leben, mein Licht.*
> *Beförde den Lauf un höre nicht auf,*
> *Selbst an mir zu ziehen, zu schieben, zu bitten.*

I follow you with eager steps
and will not forsake you,
my light, my life.
Show me the way, urge me on,
ask me to go with you always.

Lily went on over Bach's singing. "You seem busy. What are you working on? My arrest warrant?"

"That's hardly fair—" He stopped himself. She grinned. "Somehow, I suspect you and Adam got along just fine. No, I'm writing up a proposal for a three-ship ambassadorial expedition to Reft space to present first to the Intelligence Council and then to Parliament, for approval."

"To Reft space?"

"You must admit, Lily, that from what information I've gleaned from talking to you and your crew and researched in your library, it is a union consummately to be wished or something like that. Isn't that from Shakespeare? I never was any good at quoting."

"What's Shakespeare?" Yehoshua asked as he set down a tray of drinks. He hesitated at the chair beside Jenny, and then, evidently thinking it impolitic to leave Deucalion alone on the other side, circled the table to sit beside the other man.

Deucalion sighed. "Which only goes to prove my point. It's a meeting that is long overdue. Is it really true that Ridanis are segregated there? Paisley made some comments, which I thought I simply misunderstood until I came across some references . . ." He trailed off. "It just seemed too—bizarre—to believe."

"Yes," Lily agreed. "I think it's long overdue for Reft space to join up with the home worlds again. Although you'll meet resistance from Jehane."

"Jehane? Oh, yes, one of the leaders of this civil disturbance you've had. It still seems impossible to me that in this day and age humans could behave with such—" He broke off, seeing how Jenny's and Yehoshua's expressions changed.

"Well," Lily put in apologetically. "You do have a tendency to lecture, Deucalion."

The pause that followed this remark was stiff. Finally, Deucalion keyed off his slate and stood up. "If I may, Captain, I beg leave to return to my quarters." But he did not, after all, wait for her permission before walking with deliberate ease out of the mess.

Jenny was polite enough to wait until the door had shut behind him before she laughed. "Oh, Lily, I'm sorry, but if I had to endure one more lecture about us primitive barbarians I think I'd vent myself. It's a good thing he's never seen my complete arsenal of weapons. Or has any inkling of the kind of training an Immortal gets. I know I ought to be more sympathetic, but I think he's just never been used to being laughed at."

Yehoshua, too, was smiling, but now he shook his head. "I'm not so sure. I think maybe he is used to being laughed at—or at least, had it happen a lot and never really got used to it. It's the sore spots that hurt the most, after all. With your permission, Captain, maybe I'll catch him up and ask him more about this proposal."

"That's a generous offer. I didn't realize you liked him."

"I don't dislike him. But I wonder if he doesn't have a hard time making friends."

"I think it's a good idea."

"Here." Yehoshua picked up the cup of café Deucalion had abandoned. "I'll say he forgot it." He picked up his own drink as well and left them.

Jenny watched him go. "What do you think of him?" she asked suddenly.

Lily shrugged. "I think he means well, but that his tendency to lecture gets in the way of—"

"Yehoshua?"

"Yehoshua? I thought you meant Deucalion. You must know what I think of Yehoshua. He's absolutely dependable, levelheaded, competent, and capable of taking over command if necessary. Exactly the kind of person who makes a good First Officer."

"Do you suppose he's any good in bed?"

"Jenny!"

"Just a thought. I never was cut out for celibacy, you know. That's how I got into the whole mess in the first place."

"Jenny—"

"Save your sympathy, Lily. I don't think I need it anymore. Really. Like Yehoshua said, it's the sore spots that hurt the most and *that* one will always hurt. But life goes on, sooner or later, with or without you. That's the choice we always have to make, whether to go with it. So what do you think?"

"Well." Lily could not help but chuckle. "He'd be dependable."

Jenny laughed. "Kiss of death, Lily-hae. You would get the only man on board who it seems to me is capable of sustained, interesting—although Pinto might well—"

"Doubtless Pinto would."

There was a brief silence while both women contemplated Pinto.

"I hate men who are beautiful," said Jenny with, perhaps, more heat than she was conscious of. "You can't trust them."

"Pinto is straightforward," Lily countered, and she blushed a little, remembering how straightforward he was, indeed.

"He *is* a Ridani. They're all straightforward, Lily." Her voice dropped suddenly, taking on a more solemn, intimate tone. "How is it really, with Hawk? How bad is he?"

Lily could only shake her head. "I don't know. I just don't know."

The call came in the next day while the captain and her entourage were inspecting Engineering.

"An urgent request to speak with you, Captain," said Finch over com. "From a Dr. Farhad."

Lily glanced at her audience: Blue and Paisley, Jenny and Yehoshua and Bach, two technicians. At her gaze, as if with one thought, they all retreated to give her privacy. Bach stayed. "Put her through. Dr. Farhad? This is Captain Ransome."

"I am deeply disappointed, Captain." Even through the com-link, Lily could hear the uncharacteristic edge on Dr. Farhad's otherwise calm voice. "You assured me—" She broke off, evidently too overcome by emotion for a moment to continue. "I scarcely expected an action of this kind. And with a patient so manifestly fragile. I thought you had a real concern for him."

"An action of *what* kind, doctor?"

"It has not been my experience," continued Dr. Farhad, as if Lily's relay had not reached her, "that kidnapping is any kind of solution toward finding a cure with a deeply disturbed patient. It is most likely to exacerbate the disturbance, not soothe it, which, I assure you—too late now, unfortunately—is my *only* goal in this matter, whatever Central Intelligence may have done to him in the past. I thought I made it clear to

you that I disapproved of their previous incarceration of him
and meant to make a report to that effect." She paused for
breath.

For an instant, the only thought Lily could muster was that
she was relieved that she was not having to face Dr. Farhad's
disappointment in person. "Dr. Farhad. If you'll let me speak
a moment." Lily took in Dr. Farhad's silence on the comnet
as assent. "*What* kidnapping?"

The silence extended. "I trust," said the doctor finally, but
more slowly, and with a touch of uncertainty, "that this is not
some ploy on your part to attempt to lead me off the scent. I
understand that he is your mate, and that bond runs very
deep, and the obligations—as you put it when you left—are
both strict and all-consuming. But that does not excuse—"
She was getting her breath back.

"Doctor. One moment please." Lily glanced up to see
Yehoshua signaling to her. She waved him over.

As he approached, she could see the frown furrowing his
temple. "Captain." He looked puzzled. "Finch says there's
another urgent incoming. From our old friend. The bounty
hunter. Windsor. He says he wants to speak with you about
Hawk."

The report left her speechless. Doctor Farhad chose this
silence to start again. "Let me repeat, Captain, that does not
excuse your strong-arm kidnapping of your mate from my
care. I shudder to contemplate the damage this may have
done him. I can only thank you"—here her voice grew
plainly sarcastic—"for minimizing the damage done the suite
and our equipment and for so gracefully handling whatever
gas you used to render myself and my assistant unconscious.
At least you have some scruples. The door will have to be
completely replaced. And Kyosti—I haven't reported this yet,
Captain. Please, if you will only let me come over to your
ship and continue seeing to his care." She hesitated.

Lily felt numb, like all her nerves had blunted to nothing.
"Yes," she said tonelessly. "You'd better come over to my
ship. I'll send someone for you."

"I prefer to arrange my own transportation. Thank you. I'm
sure, under the circumstances, that you understand."

"Certainly," Lily agreed absently. "Ransome out." She turned
to Yehoshua. He took a step back, as if something in her
expression or demeanor startled him. "That bastard."

The com startled to life again. "Captain? We've got *another*
incoming."

"Is it about Hawk?"

"No, but—"

"Then it can wait. I'm coming up and I want no interruptions.
Understood?"

"Yes, but it's from that pirate La Belle—"

"*And* a full-alert code two. Ransome out." She turned and
left. Behind her, Bach sang:

> *Nun mögt ihr stolzen Feinde schrecken:*
> *Was könnt ihr mir für Furcht erwecken?*
> *Mein Schatz, mein Hort ist hier bei mir.*
> *Ihr mögt euch noch so grimmig stellen,*
> *Droht nur, mich ganz und gar zu fällen,*
> *Doch seht! mein Heiland wohnet hier.*

> "Now may you proud foes be affrighted,
> What fear could you awake in me?
> My precious, my treasure is beside me here!
> You may appear as grim as may be,
> threaten to lay me low completely,
> but lo! my Saviour dwells here."

16 Bounty

****

"This is Ransome."

Static snapped over comm.

"Captain. This is Windsor." Background noise muffled his voice. "I have Hawk. I'll trade him for you. Land a shuttle on Discord by twenty-one hundred hours at these coordinates." A pause, and then he spoke the numbers slowly, as if he were reading from a list. "Disembark alone. A one-for-one trade, Ransome. Don't try anything."

"Listen, Windsor. Hawk is seriously ill. You're jeopardizing—"

"Captain, the link has been cut from their end. I got a quick trace, but it won't be very accurate."

"Thank you, Finch." Even meaning the words, she could not keep the hard edge of anger out of her voice. She had not sat down in the captain's chair, but stood, two fingers still pressing down the "comm" button. Realizing, finally, the futility of this action, she lifted her hand. "What's Discord?"

The Mule answered. "The planet which shares the same orbital path as Concord. According to what files I've accessed, it is designated wilderness and recreation zone."

"The whole planet?"

"Evidently."

"Finch, do you have a trace on that link yet?"

"Yes. This is approximate, but it reads to the same coordinates as we were given."

"Thereby giving him plenty of time to move by the time we can get there. Yehoshua." He had followed her up from Engineering and now he waited. "Prepare a shuttle. I'll need you and Pinto, and Jenny. Choose another six for backup. No je'jiri. Armed. Trey on the bridge. Finch, stay on comm as much as you can. Take a break when you need to, but we need your expertise."

"Yes, Captain." The substance of her praise, even in the clipped tone with which she delivered it, seemed to satisfy him.

"Mule. When Dr. Farhad arrives, I'd like you to act as liaison. I trust to your judgment to explain the situation to her."

"As you wish, Captain," the Mule hissed. Its crest lifted slightly, but subsided again. Pinto unstrapped himself from his chair.

"But Captain, what if it's a bluff?" Yehoshua began. "I'm not sure the wisest course is to—" Lily turned her gaze on him, scarcely aware of him except as an object which she had to move in order to reach her goal. He faltered, shook his head. "I'll meet you at the shuttle." He inclined his head, acknowledging her unspoken order, and left the bridge.

"Now." Having dismissed this obstacle, she shifted her attention to Trey. "You'll be in charge of the bridge. Dr. Farhad is to be allowed on board. No one else. Not even if we're delayed and an inquiry comes from Concord or Intelligence. I leave you the unenviable task of explaining this to Deucalion—to min Belsonn."

The Mule hissed its fluid laugh, and even Finch smiled, but Trey merely assented without any visible emotion. Lily whistled to Bach and left the bridge with the robot drifting at her back. She stopped in her suite.

Bach. Access all information on the planet Discord. What you can get in, say, twenty minutes. Then meet me at the shuttle bay.

Affirmative, patroness. If I may suggest?

A two-note assent.

Thou mayest well be served to take two shuttles, that which delivers thee to the appointed rendezvous, and a second that can serve as a second voice to thy plans, one unexpected by thine opponent.

"Surely he'll expect something like that." The thought of Windsor made her cold with fury. She felt as if all her emotions had frozen, leaving her only a narrow beam of cognition from which to draw her choice of actions. "But I think you're right."

Bach accepted this encomium with a muted trill, understanding, perhaps, the intensity of Lily's passion. He plugged in to the wall terminal while she changed and fitted a pistol and rifle onto a light harness.

Her stride, taking her through the ship down to iron deck, was deliberate and swift. Passing crew members, she had enough perception to know that they did not speak to her because of the entire expression of her face and body.

But even her expression was not enough to deter some. Of course, Deucalion was waiting at the shuttle. Jenny had blocked the hatchway ramp with her own person. She was fitted out in full mercenary rig, looking dangerous and not a little fierce.

"Guns?" Deucalion demanded as soon as he caught sight of Lily. "You can't simply use—"

Lily ignored him. "Jenny, tell Yehoshua I want the second shuttle as well. Put your people on it. You're our backup."

"Backup!" Deucalion went on as Jenny, responding with a salute, disappeared down the hatchway. "Lily. May I remind you that you have a hearing tomorrow. You gave me your word that you would attend."

Now she turned on him, and in the face of her anger, even he stopped speaking. "So I will. But perhaps under slightly different circumstances."

"I thought you were adamant that you would not let the bounty hunter bring you in. I think your case in that matter was legitimate. You don't want to appear as a criminal—"

"The circumstances have changed. He just put a price on my bounty that I can't refuse. He says he has Hawk. I'm turning myself in to him, in exchange."

"You're not making sense. How can he have Hawk?"

"He broke him out of Concord prison."

"Impossible."

"It may be. That's why we're going armed, and I'm taking a backup force with me. If it's a bluff, he'll pay for it." She waited, expecting his reply and ready to deflect it off the shield she had constructed around herself, to protect herself from any stimulus that might tug at the edge of her focus. Then she realized that Deucalion was speechless. He merely gazed at her. The absurdity of his being unable to find words made her smile, a little.

Finally, as her silence wound away into the throbbing hum of the shuttle's engines at lowest power, he spoke. "You've been around je'jiri too long. I think you've absorbed a trace element of them into your blood. I wouldn't want you on *my* trail, unless you were coming to help me."

The comment left *her* speechless.

"Have you always been this way?"

The truth of the statement hung like a physical presence in

front of her. Her pursuit of the martial arts Heredes had
taught her; her pursuit of Heredes himself, that had led,
ultimately, to his death. Paisley on Harsh. Each expedition
led for Jehane, even at the end, as she tried to save Robbie—
Pero—from death. And the choice to leave the Reft and find
League space.

"Yes," she said slowly, considering it. "I suppose I have."

Deucalion smiled slightly, shaking his head with a weak
chuckle. "So Father finally did get a child who took after him.
Once he took up on something, he wouldn't let it go until he
had finished. I'll go with you."

"You don't need to."

"Certainly I do, sister. You need a Concord representative
to protect your interests and to make sure that this bounty
hunter turns over his hostage. He'll be prosecuted for that,
you know—I can't imagine why he did it, unless he hopes
that no one will *believe* that Concord prison's security could
be breached. And anyway, the only way you can stop me from
going is to use force."

"I don't have time." But she had to grin at the sound of her
own annoyance. "You're a damn sight stubborner than I am,
Deucalion."

"*That's* a trait I got from my mother." He walked down
onto the hatchway.

"Aren't you going to take anything? Or change your clothes,
even?"

"Oh, no, dear sister. I'm not taking the chance that you'll
just leave me."

She laughed and let him precede her onto the shuttle.

By the time Bach arrived, the second shuttle was staffed
and ready to go. With Pinto at the controls and Lily at comm,
it left only Yehoshua and Deucalion and Bach to the rest of
the shuttle. Lily regarded Pinto with misgivings, unsure of
how Kyosti might react to him and yet wondering if Pinto and
Yehoshua would seem familiar enough to Kyosti to garner any
recognition at all.

"Once I'm gone, if he panics, you might have to restrain
him until you can get him to secure rooms on the *Hope*," she
said, and no one had to ask her who she was talking about.

The detach from the *Hope* went smoothly. The second
shuttle followed them, and then curved off on a new course to
come in toward the rendezvous point from an opposite, and
presumably less conspicuous, direction. Lily's sporadic and

perfunctory replies on comm left the cabin swathed in uncomfortable silence.

"Why Discord?" Yehoshua asked finally, wanting any distraction. "It seems a strange name for a planet next to a construct like Concord."

Deucalion smiled. "Heraclitus, I think. Opposites attract. Originally, when this system was chosen as Concord's home, they meant to build it on the planet. It's a class-A habitat. But they realized that disrupting its ecology to that extent would be a negation of all that Concord stands for. There was a lot of argument over it. Hence, Discord. Eventually it became a designated wilderness and park. The only permanent habitations are for the park rangers and the zoned resorts."

"So people can visit it?" Yehoshua shook his head. "There were never enough class-A planets in Reft space not to use them all for agriculture."

"No, Discord has been left as it is, but it serves a good recreational purpose as well. In the zoned areas people can holiday, do sports, hike, swim, observe, some even war game."

"They do *what*?"

Deucalion shrugged. "It's a kind of sport. It's very safe. I've never done it myself, having had enough of the real thing in my youth."

"People play at"—Yehoshua coughed, deliberately obscuring his amazement—"Never mind. Are we landing in a—ah—zoned area or a—what did you call it?—wilderness area?"

"As far as I can tell, a wilderness area. It makes sense, although it's against the law. One is supposed to have a permit. But if this bounty hunter actually broke into Concord prison, I doubt if he's concerned with as minor a breach of law as *that*."

Yehoshua, who could not help but agree, did not answer. In time, they came down through a bank of clouds to see a carpet of trees laid out in topographic detail beneath them. A lake broke the monotone of green along one horizon, but otherwise, aside from the occasional bald strip of meadow and several watercourses cutting their silvered way through the forest, the ranks of trees stretched unbroken out along all sides.

"That's it," said Pinto. "That escarpment along that ridge—

that clearing. I see no sign of another ship." He looked at Lily
as if expecting her to change her mind.

"Land." Lily tapped in a tight beam to the other shuttle
but did not call on it. Bach winked blue lights in the sea
behind her. Pinto shook his head slightly, but he brought the
shuttle in smoothly, landing on a fairly level patch of ground
as close to the center of the clearing as he could manage. The
engine volume cut substantially as he lowered the engines to
standby. There was silence in the cabin as the three men
waited. Lily unstrapped herself, unstrapped Bach, and headed
for the hatch.

"Lower the ramp. Deucalion, don't try to follow me. I'm
going out alone."

"But—" All three men spoke at once. Lily paused at the
hatch lock and stared each one down in turn. Deucalion took
the longest, but he, too, did not attempt any further objection.

Lily paused at the top of the ramp, Bach hovering behind
her. The brush of air against her face, the high fence of trees
about fifty meters from the shuttle, reminded her of her
landing on Arcadia. She tried to remember how many planetfalls
she had made in the intervening time; it had not been many.
And she smiled, thinking how ironic it seemed that she had
gone to so much trouble to escape the confines of Ransom
House only to confine herself in the thin, constraining walls
of a spaceship.

Movement caught at her peripheral vision, and she turned
her head in time to see one of the Ardakians fade back into
the screen of forest. She walked down to the bottom of the
ramp and waited.

Wind brushed a stray lock of her hair across her eyes,
obscuring her vision, and as she reached up to brush it away,
two figures appeared at the edge of the trees. One was
stocky, not much taller than her; she recognized Kore
Windsor immediately. The other figure—tall, slender—stood
with a posture unfamiliar to her. A moment later she realized
that with that pale blue hair, faded out in the bright sunlight,
it could only be Kyosti, who at any other time she would have
recognized at a glance from twice the distance. With
sudden wrench of fear, she wondered if he still remembered
her, or if the break from Concord's prison had broken the
tenuous link she had reforged with him. Without thinking
she took ten steps out away from the ship, caught herself,
stopped, and waited again.

Windsor moved, and Kyosti walked forward, Windsor a steady two paces behind him. They walked halfway into the gap between trees and shuttle, and halted. In the forest behind Lily could discern no sign of either Fred or Stanford.

Bach, at her shoulder, sang softly.

Herzliebster, was hast du verbrochen, Dass man ein solch scharf Urteil hat gesprochen?

"Beloved, what has thou done wrong that they have pronounced so hard a sentence?"

Lily reached up to lay a hand gently on his gleaming surface. "Don't worry," she replied quietly. "He doesn't have me yet. Why do you think I brought you along?"

Hast thou a plan, patroness?

"No," she admitted. "First, to get Kyosti back. If I'm the price for that, so be it." She began to walk, to meet Windsor. Floating behind her Bach sang in muted tones, as if he were speaking to himself, or musing over some problem.

Was wollt ihr mir geben? Ich will ihn euch verraten.

"What will ye give me, and I will deliver him unto you?"

Nearing them, Lily saw Kyosti tilt his head from side to side, scenting. Then, abruptly, she knew he had caught her scent by the way his attention—even if signaled only by the turn of his head—fastened onto her. Windsor stood beside him in the deceptively casual stance of a well-honed fighter. Lily forced herself not to look at Kyosti, to look only at Windsor. Closing, she was surprised to see that whatever signs of dissipation and weariness she had discerned before in him were completely gone now: it was not just his Ardakian companions who made him dangerous and effective. Seeing him now, she could not help for a moment but be reminded of Master Heredes. She halted three meters from him and allowed herself a glance at Kyosti.

Kyosti's gaze did not waver from her face. She could feel it remain on her even as she turned to regard Windsor.

"I'm unarmed," he said. He grinned. It made his face come alive. "I haven't had this kind of challenge in a long, long time."

"Boredom can take its toll," she replied. "How the Hells did you get him out of there?"

"Trade secret. It helps to have a computer expert and an explosives expert to hand as well. Just like the old days." He was still grinning, but no longer at her. "They've forgotten that there wasn't a security line that we couldn't breach."

"Who's forgotten?"

His expression sobered instantly. "It's not important. Are you turning yourself in to me? No tricks?"

"I'm unarmed. That's the only guarantee I'll give you. Until Hawk is free."

"And then—?"

"Then I'll go with you."

For a moment he merely gazed at her, trying to read something, but he merely shook his head and took one step back from Kyosti. Spoke several sentences in the language of the je'jiri.

Kyosti swiveled his head smoothly to regard Windsor with the characteristic unblinking and disconcerting je'jiri stare. His reply, clipped and precise, was short.

Windsor shook his head again and answered, still in the alien language. His delivery did not have the precision of Kyosti's, but it sounded fluent to Lily's ears.

"What are you saying?" she demanded.

His reply was brusque. "Telling him he can go free."

"My shuttle—"

"Not into your hands. Not into anyone's hands. *Free.*"

"You said you would trade him for me."

"Trade you for his freedom. There's a difference." The brilliant light of Discord's sun illuminated harsh lines—not of age, but of old dissipation—on his face. "I won't allow him to be forced back into that prison. I agree to let him go. Not to you."

"Not to anyone?" she echoed, sardonic now. "You have no honor at all, have you? You can't even be trusted to hold a simple agreement."

"No honor among thieves." His voice was bitter. "But there is loyalty. People forget that."

"I'd like to know what makes you think *I'd* let him go back to prison."

He shook his head. "Even if you meant not to, how could you stop it? Stop Concord from taking him in again?"

"Once you let him go 'free,' how can you stop them?"

"At least he'll have a chance to get to The Pale."

Lily deliberately looked away from Windsor and directly at Kyosti. He returned her gaze intently, but neutrally.

"Kyosti." She spoke slowly and with careful enunciation, so that he would have no trouble understanding her. "The shuttle behind me carries three men. I trust them to take care of you. Will you go with them until such time as I can return to you?"

"Yes," he replied without hesitation.

For a moment, she allowed herself to be diverted by Windsor's expression: he look dumbfounded. Then, catching himself, he spoke swiftly and passionately to Hawk. Hawk's reply was brief, punctuated by a shrug made alien by the set and movement of his shoulders, and he moved away from Windsor to align himself instead with Lily.

"Now," said Lily. The relief she felt—the simple joy—at Kyosti's complete trust was abruptly overshadowed by the knowledge that she was about to lose him again.

"You're his *mate*?" Windsor stared, astonished, at her. "Mother's tits. No *wonder* you were willing to trade yourself for him. I had a hunch you'd do it, but I didn't know why." He lifted a hand, and at the signal the two Ardakians appeared at the edge of the forest. Both were armed. Both used the cover of the trees to effectively shield themselves from any fire the shuttle might produce. "Sorry," Windsor continued, apologetic. "But I can't take the chance that you'll try to escape again. Fred's got enough firepower to blow the shuttle, and it is rather a sitting target. You might have positioned it better."

"I always meant to keep my end of the exchange. Hawk for me. I trust"—she let her voice grow skeptical—"you'll let both Hawk and the shuttle go."

Windsor laughed, brief and bitter. "I've got a damned poor reputation, don't I?" He sobered abruptly. "Tell him to go. I want to get this over with."

"Kyosti."

Instead of replying, he dipped his head, brushing her cheek with one side of his face, and then walked away across the meadow, toward the shuttle. In the silence of the vast landscape, unpopulated by any humanity but themselves, a high buzzy whine sounded in the distance, steady and growing.

"I'll be damned," Windsor breathed. "How in hell did you end up with Hawk?"

But finally, several discrete bits of information clicked into place in Lily's mind. "You were a saboteur. That's how you know him. *That's* where your loyalty lies."

"You pissing well didn't think it lay with Concord Intelligence, did you?" He sounded offended, and taken by surprise.

Lily laughed. "Damn my eyes!"

His surprise turned to suspicion. "What's so damn funny? I know you weren't one of us." The harsh lines on his face furrowed, giving him a look of great pain. "Bastards. Those pissing bastards."

Lily reached inside her tunic and drew out the medallion. Seeing it, Windsor lost his color—the pasty white of his face made him look sick and hopeless. "What does this mean anyway?" she asked. "Do you know?"

"How did you get that?" His voice was so tight that she could barely hear it. "How did you meet Hawk?" He paused, and she waited, aware that he was about to say something else, but was reluctant to. "How—how do you know Gwyn?"

"I got this from him. He's my father."

Windsor blanched. He looked beyond Lily, and she glanced over her shoulder to see that Kyosti had reached the shuttle but had halted at the ramp, watching them. Looking back at Windsor, Lily suddenly and inexplicably felt guilty, because it was obvious that this new knowledge was causing the bounty hunter inner anguish. The distant whine had grown to a low rumble.

"You're Gwyn's *daughter?*" It was as much as he could do to get those three words out.

"Not by blood," she said quickly.

"No, you mean in the craft." He looked abruptly and terribly sad. "It comes to the same thing. Oh God, they betrayed us both."

It took her a blink to register his words. "What are you talking about?"

"Go," he said brusquely. "Take Hawk and go. They just said you'd been traveling with Gwyn. I didn't ask for specifics. I didn't want to know. I damned well spent the whole hunt pretending it was just a coincidence, that and the mark."

"What mark?"

"The medallion. Just go. I can't take you in now."

"Wait a minute—"

The rumble arced up to a scream, and a ship buzzed low

and fast over the meadow. It was a sleek, modern vessel of a type she had never seen before. As she stared, it overshot the meadow, banked and turned, and returned, lower now.

Windsor swore, reached out, and yanked Lily roughly to the ground. She fell flat on her stomach beside him.

Fire streaked out from the ship—laser fire. Streaks of flame lit and died in the grass. There was a sudden, horrifying snap, followed by a low explosion, and a gout of fire and smoke erupted from the shuttle's far window—Lily rolled to her feet.

"Get down!" Windsor shouted.

Kyosti still stood by the ramp, staring up as the ship banked and turned again for its return. He showed no indication that he was aware that he was in any danger.

Deucalion appeared, stumbling down the shuttle's ramp. Smoke billowed out behind him.

"Fred. Stanford." Windsor spoke to himself, and yet obviously to the two Ardakians who were clearly too far away to hear him. "Can you get a shot?"

Already the ship was firing again. Seams of light peppered the metal of the Hope's shuttle. Lily began to run, but someone—Windsor—tackled her from behind and threw her headlong into the grass. Laser fire singed grass and dirt one meter in front of her face. Behind, from the cover of the trees, two guns sounded.

"Let me go," she cried, and struggled, but Windsor, whatever his other faults, was as trained a fighter as she was—and he had far more experience on his side.

At the grounded shuttle, smoke and fire streaming from every opening and several ragged holes, Deucalion yelled something at Hawk and then turned to go back inside. Hawk did not move, oblivious to everything but the arc and turn of the ship in the sky above as it banked for its next pass.

"We're the targets," Windsor shouted. "Break for the trees." He tugged at her, and did not let go as she rose with him. "You can't help them by going to them. Break!" They ran for the trees.

Fire seared the meadow around them as they sprinted. She felt its hot breath sting her cheek and singe her hair. They flung themselves into the cover of the nearest tree, not five meters from Fred.

Seeing them, he lowered his large gun. It looked archaic, but effective. "Sorry, boss. No range at their speed."

Lily turned.

In time to see Deucalion reel, alone, out of the *Hope*'s shuttle. Hawk still watched the sky. The other ship banked again.

A beat, and then Yehoshua appeared dragging a limp Pinto with one arm and carrying the shuttle's hand-pack radio in the other. Deucalion helped him maneuver Pinto down the ramp.

Hawk, finally, turned, registering the men's presence with sudden interest. Words were exchanged. Deucalion hoisted Pinto across his back. The men jogged as well as they could away from the shuttle.

The other ship dipped low, firing.

This time the shuttle vanished in an explosion that threw the three men and the unconscious Pinto on to the ground. Lily felt it, a wave of heat and pressure, even as far as the trees.

The ship pulled a tight circle, altering its course to streak low across the prostrate men and begin firing at the trees. Behind it, coming in low over the hills, appeared a second vessel of the same type. It did not fire at all, but came to an impossible halt in midair and sank, engines screaming, to land beside the charred, smoking hulk of the ruined shuttle.

17   Sans Merci

****

As soon as the ship in the air had overshot their position, Fred hoisted his gun nimbly over one broad shoulder and moved quickly over to where Windsor and Lily huddled between two tree trunks.

"Armored, boss." He made a movement with his head, indicating the ship that had just landed. "We got nothing that'll crack it."

Windsor swore, a string of oaths that Lily did not recognize. "The bastards must have brought those in from The Pale." He looked at Lily, and she was surprised to see that he was grinning. "They must want you pretty badly. He hoisted himself up, a smooth, trained movement at odds with the stubble on his unshaven face and the shabbiness of his clothing. "Let's go. This cover isn't good enough. And we've got company."

She turned as he turned. Above, she could hear the arc of sound as the ship pulled around over the trees. But the other ship, the one that had landed, had lowered a ramp and now armed figures—two, four, eight—emerged out of the ship.

"My crew—" She could see no sign of them in the grass. Before she could move, Fred grabbed her.

"Ransome. The odds aren't with us right now. *Let's go.*"

"I won't leave them to be killed!"

Windsor looked sincerely perplexed. "Why would they kill them?"

"I have no idea. But someone just tried."

"Not for them, Ransome. For us. They're safe enough."

She tugged against Fred but his hold was ridiculously strong. "Do you expect me to take that chance?" she demanded.

Windsor sighed and made a sign with one hand to Fred. "No. You'll just have to trust me."

Lily did not bother to dignify the comment with a reply.

Fred's grip shifted, and she twisted her arm, spun, and broke for freedom.

Only to find herself hoisted up next to Fred's gun, as helpless in his grasp as it was. Her view was of the farther depths of the forest, and of Stanford, appearing as if by magic some five meters away from behind a tree that should not have been broad enough to conceal his stocky form.

"Korrigan," he said primly, "there are twelve armed humans headed this way. No. Six have broken off to retrieve min Ransome's companions. I suggest we make haste."

"He's right, boss." Fred turned and now Lily could see the meadow and the small figures fanned out in order. Six had surrounded her party. She could not see Hawk or Pinto, but Yehoshua had risen to his knees, hands clasped behind his head, and Deucalion rose as she watched and set his hands on his hips. The armed men, approaching, hesitated and lowered their guns, evidently cowed by Deucalion's posture or by one of his lectures.

"Go on ahead," said Windsor. "Stanford, you got any gas?"

She could not see them, only heard a soft *thump* as something thrown was caught, and then Fred began to move quickly away. His gait, a remarkably smooth jog, covered distance more quickly than a man could run, and he was nimble enough to weave through the dense wood without faltering. Bach followed smoothly behind them.

After about ten minutes Fred stopped and set Lily down. "Boss is right," he said gruffly, swinging down his gun as well. He did not appear to be winded. "They won't kill them. You saw it yourself."

"They just blew up our shuttle. Why should I believe you?"

Fred tugged on one ear with a thick hand. "Seems to me you got no one else to believe."

She pulled her tunic straight, to give herself time to think. Those men had, after all, lowered their guns on seeing Deucalion. Perhaps his Intelligence badge gave him and his companions immunity. "It seems I'm with you whether I want to be or not. All right." Bach floated watchfully at her back. "I'm still with you then. Who are they? Why do they want to kill me? Or your boss?"

A branch snapped behind her. She whirled. Fred did not move. Windsor and Stanford appeared, Windsor looking pale and out of breath.

He paused, leaning against a tree. "Call me Korey," he said. "Gwyn always used to. It must be the saboteur connection. It's the only link between us. Someone must finally have decided to be rid of us once and for all."

Lily went white, and she felt sick with sudden fear. "Then, even if the others are safe, we just abandoned Hawk to them. I've got to go back."

Simultaneously, both Fred and Stanford wrinkled their noses and looked to the left. Stanford made a face and took two sidesteps right.

"Company, boss," said Fred.

He came out of the trees, a tall, slender figure, hair muted in the shadows made by the forest's canopy.

"Kyosti!"

His gaze flicked over her, but she knew him well enough, even as changed as he was—especially as changed as he was—to understand that he marked her more by scent than by vision now. He moved to stand close to her and turned to speak a quick sentence in the language of the je'jiri to Windsor.

Windsor replied and then looked at Lily. "He says that they took the other three men captive and that all twelve of those from the shuttle are on our trail."

"And Pinto—he's alive?"

Kyosti shuttered his eyes and appeared to take in a breath, or the smell of the air. "Alive," he said. Strangely, his hands twitched, as if some reflex had taken hold of them, and he hesitated and finally spoke in slow, struggling Standard. "Not so badly hurt. He will live." It was, clearly, a diagnosis, however general.

"Thank the Void," Lily breathed. "Well—Korey. Now what? Who do you think is hunting us?"

"As far as I know the only people who knew I was hunting you were the ones as hired me—Concord Intelligence. But I can't believe Yevgeny Basham would turn coat like this. He's fair, however hard he might be."

"I suggest we try to find out once we're safely on my ship. I have a shuttle at—Bach, what are the coordinates?"

In Paisley's voice, Bach reeled them off.

"Mine's closer." Windsor made a hand sign to Fred and Stanford. "We'll go ahead. They'll cover the back."

"Doesn't that put them in more danger?"

"Diplomatic immunity, of a fashion." He grinned. "Even

for two outlaws like Fred and Stanford. Can't risk damaging trade agreements by offending the honorables who govern in the Ardakian system."

"Which way?" He pointed, and she let him set the pace. He took it at a slow run. Lily did not find it hard to keep up, and she wondered how badly he had ruined his health in the last few years. Kyosti loped effortlessly along beside her. The effect was uncanny: he had never shown such obvious fitness before, or such preternatural alertness. At every three steps he took in a quick breath, scenting, and he never once faltered on the uneven footing of the forest floor. How had he gotten away from the meadow? She did not think the Kyosti she had once known could have done it.

They came to a ravine hidden in a wrinkle of the low hills, and Windsor turned down it. Of Fred and Stanford's passage behind them she heard nothing. Wind stirred the trees above, and then the low, hard sound of a ship passing close above grew and thundered and ebbed about them. A moment later, an explosion—not too far, not too close.

"Shit!" swore Windsor. "Fucking sons of bitches and their whores of fathers with them—" He broke off. "Come on."

They scrambled down a steep slope and followed a rushing stream until it curved around a high bank and emptied into a pond at one end of a tiny, circular meadow. The burning remains of a small ship lay strewn across the high grass. Smoke spiraled up to mark its resting place. As they paused at the edge of the clearing to stare, the whine of an engine built in volume behind them.

Lily faded back into the trees, but Windsor continued to stare, in disgust, or fury. "Come on," Lily hissed, as if the ship approaching above might hear her if she spoke above a whisper. "We'll have to double back and try to reach our other shuttle."

For a beat, she thought he had not heard her. Finally he turned and gave her a wry, twisted smile, bitter as he usually was, as if life had long since treated him to a cruel joke. "The bastards ruined my credit line for certain now, with that. How the hell do they expect me to pay for it?"

Meeting his eyes, Lily felt suddenly—not sorry for him but a sense of compassion, of comradeship, a strange enough thing to feel, after her first acquaintance with him. "Don't you get a substantial bounty for turning me in? I thought I was worth quite a bit to you."

"Looks like you're worth my life, Ransome." He slipped into the shadow of a broad-trunked tree as the ship streaked past overhead and dropped another explosive onto the hulk of the stranded ship for good measure, reducing it to an unrecognizable bulk of metal and smoke and spitting fire. "No. My death. Which I guess is worth more to Concord Intelligence."

"You don't have any enemies? From someplace else? Who might have wanted you killed?"

"Kapellans might want me dead, but they'd never act on it. It's not their way. Gwyn's the only one of us they hated enough to ever try to kill outright. No, these are human ships. And human agents. Only someone from Concord Intelligence would have known my movements, known about you. And only someone who really hated us would have gone this far." He paused, listening. "Yeah," he said, but not to her. "We'll circle back." His gaze shifted back to Lily. "All right, Ransome. What were those coordinates again?"

Lily did not like moving in forest. She was used to clean, clear lines of sight, used to gauging for corners and set widths of corridor or tunnel and hard surfaces for leaning and pushing off from. Nothing here seemed solid enough to rely on—too much wind, too much extraneous noise, too many curves and gaps and inconstant backdrops. Windsor seemed right at home. Bach sang to himself—*Am Abend da es kühle war* "In the evening, when it was cool"—at such low volume that she could only hear him because he hovered not two hand's-breadths from her right ear. Even Hawk appeared unfazed by the way the shadows shifted without warning. And Fred, to her vast surprise, sniffed about several broad tree trunks and then with more speed than grace scrambled up one and vanished from her view. Stanford hoisted the heavy gun Fred had been carrying onto his back and strapped it there, oblivious to its extra weight.

They had not walked more than ten minutes when Windsor halted her with a raised hand and, pausing, she heard a brief snatch of conversation from ahead.

Hawk, beside her, said, "Four."

Windsor glanced at her. "We're six," she said.

"Send the 'bot up. Each take one."

They fanned out. It proved easy enough: a distraction from above, provided by Bach, a quick, controlled move in to get

inside their guns, and all four of the soldiers—if that was
what they were—were out flat on the ground. It had been a
long time since Lily had felt herself to be the least experi-
enced fighter in any group, however small. Even Hawk had
dispatched his target with uncharacteristic precision. A je'jiri's
precision.

Lily paused, standing over the unconscious figure beneath
her, and stared at Windsor, suddenly at a loss. Did he mean
to kill them? And a wash of memory hit her—of the first
person she had killed, in the raid into the 30s dig on Harsh.
She forced herself to look down. Through the thin plastine
helmet she recognized the face of a man—young enough,
with pale skin and thin lips gaping open. Nausea hit her. She
was no longer sure she could kill someone this helpless.

"They've got trank guns," said Windsor in disgust. "Look
at where the levels are locked on. This would kill an ele-
phant. I wonder if these poor sods knew, or if it was meant to
be an accident?"

"Korrigan," said Stanford as he took his victim's gun and
reconfigured the level of tranquilizer. "We have another
group of four closing at northwest."

"Ransome." Windsor was also setting a new level in the
gun he held. "You know how to work these guns?"

"No."

"Stan, shoot them all. Here." He tossed the gun he had
just reset to Lily. "Let's go."

"You're just going to kill them?"

He stopped, staring at her. "*Kill* them? Why the pissing
hell would I want to kill them? They're just hirelings, and if
I'm any bet by this gear, they're probably from some pumped-
up detective firm and don't even know what they're doing, or
what they're up against. It's them as hired them as *I* want."

To his left, Stanford shot—once, twice, three times—and
came over to Lily where she still stood above the unconscious
man. "Might I request that you stand aside, please?" he
asked, more sarcastic than polite.

"Oh," said Windsor, looking at her. "We're just tranking
them. Acceptable levels. Not the ones that were meant for
us."

Relief flooded her, wiping away the weight that had settled
on her. She stepped back. "Oh." Hawk was already fading
back into the trees, attention on the distant approach of the
next four.

"Where do you come from, Ransome?" Windsor asked.
You've got some pretty strange notions. It ain't war any-
nore. We did our job. Haven't you had enough killing?"

"More than enough."

"Korrigan. Two hundred meters, northwest."

"Split and fan out. Same tactics."

They took out the next four and made a wide swing around
he meadow where they had originally met. Encountered no
ne else. It took just over an hour across the rough terrain,
eeping a careful watch, halting frequently to listen, to come
vithin wrist-com short-line hailing distance of the *Hope's*
econd shuttle. They could not risk any other communication
or fear it would be picked up. The ship hunting them passed
verhead at least six times, and they continued to hear it
unning a slow sweep pattern over the area as they walked.
Lily did not see Fred at all, but once a branch came crashing
own from above and almost hit Windsor in the head. He
wore good-naturedly into the air, talking to Fred through
heir invisible com-system.

Lily attempted com, got no answer. "I don't want to try it
gain. In case they can pick it up. I'll send Bach ahead."
Windsor shrugged his assent and she spoke her commands to
Bach, rather than whistling. Bach blinked lights and rose and
anished into the leaves. Kyosti came and crouched at her
eet, still but alert, like some kind of hunting animal. It made
er nervous, the uncanny quietness with which he regarded
er and their surroundings in turn.

"Aren't many of those left," said Windsor.

The comment startled her. "Je'jiri?"

He grinned, glancing down at Hawk, then back at her.
"Those 'bots. We used them, those we could get. Motley was
ae best with'em. She'd bonded a Mozart. They say she was
ever the same after it burned out."

They waited. Bach returned and sang softly, *Patroness, I
aw the shuttle. It is undamaged. I did not venture into the
learing itself, but saw no sign of any of the shuttle's occu-
ants or of any other activity.*

Lily translated. Windsor rubbed the perpetual stubble on
is chin.

"It isn't likely they missed it," said Lily.

"They might have. Fred, take a look."

Wind—or Fred—rustled in the branches above and was
lent. They waited again. Under the trees, it grew darker as

the sun sank towards evening. Lily could hear the trail of the ship as it passed close by them and faded into the distance

Windsor shifted suddenly. "Are you sure?" he said to the air, then turned to Lily. "Fred says no sign of a fight. If we make a rush for it we can get off the ground before they strike."

Lily nodded, and they went on. The preternatural silence with which Kyosti padded beside her, following her direction without comment except for the occasional brief string of words directed at Windsor, made her uneasy. Even now, she had to keep reminding herself that this was not the same man—or man at all.

Soon enough they reached the edge of a clearing. The Hope's number two shuttle sat in the middle of the stretch of grass and flowering stalks. All was quiet. Lily lifted the wrist-com to her mouth. "Ransome here." Like an answer, a figure appeared on the ramp, staring around. It waved, not at them, but at their presence. The shuttle's engines came to life, warming up for the lift.

"That's Jenny." The sound of the shuttle's engines masked the noise of the distant ship circling the area. "It must be clear."

"Fred." Windsor's comment was a command. He looked at Lily. "We'd better break now. That ship will be back." A moment later branches cracked and a spray of sticks and leaves peppered the ground as Fred dropped nimbly out of the canopy.

They broke out of the cover of the forest in a group, spread out quickly. Jenny, seeing their numbers, raised her gun, but held it steady until Lily halted at the base of the ramp.

"Jenny. They're clear. Let's go."

Jenny nodded and turned to go inside the shuttle. Lily let the others precede her, watching the sky until all were inside. Above the far rank of trees, she saw a slim metallic shape skimming toward them. She hurried inside and closed the ramp behind her, strapping in as the pilot jogged the controls and began a steep rise from the ground. Lily could not help but reflect, thrown to one side by the hard bank, that even under such circumstances, Pinto would have made the ascent smooth. Where was Pinto now? Surely they would not have killed an injured man.

They rose, shuddering under the strain and scream of engines. A sudden blow rocked them.

"Shit!" Windsor grabbed chair arms and pulled himself
•rward to the front. "Bastards are firing on us."

A second blow.

"Lost the number three thruster," swore the pilot. "And
ve got a broken connection to the back four throttles."
•moke seeped in through the roof panels. "I can't hold it."

"Put it down." Lily reached reflexively for the gun clips on
er belt. "Jenny. Everyone armed. Windsor—Korey. What
'eapons do you have?" •

Windsor chuckled. "You've got a damn lot of nerve." A
idden, hard jerk of the shuttle sat him down in the center
isle. He grabbed and held onto an arm and stopped speaking
; the shuttle yawed crazily to one side and then bumped
•ughly to a landing back in the clearing. Out of the front
lastine window they could all see as two of the fine silver
iips landed gracefully beside them. "What kind of weapons
• you think these people have? In a firefight, we'll lose."

Lily unstrapped and retrieved a pistol and a laser rifle from
ie locker beside her. Rainbow handed out weapons to the
ther crew. "I thought you said they meant to kill us, I'm not
•ing quietly."

"Boss," Fred was looking out the front window. "We've got
•mpany out the forward ship. Concord Intelligence badge.
nd the guy who was with the Captain—he's got a CI badge,
•o."

Lily looked up. "Deucalion!" •

"Deucalion?" Windsor rose and stared. "I thought he
•oked familiar. Hell if it ain't Gwyn's boy." The statement
rought him to pause and glance wonderingly at Lily. "That
ould make him your brother."

"Half-brother. Yes." Lily moved forward to peer out as
ell, but the smoke was getting heavy and fogging the
lastine. Behind her, several people began to cough. "He
asn't under restraint?" she asked Fred.

"No, Cap'n. Not as I could see."

"I'll go out. Jenny, cover me." She went to the lock and
und both Windsor and Kyosti with her, Jenny behind them.
Kyosti, stay here," she ordered. He simply gazed at her as if
• did not understand her words. She considered, briefly,
king Jenny to restrain him, but a quick glance at Jenny's
ce as the mercenary examined Hawk with undisguised
iriosity made Lily decide against it. She was not ready to
:pose to the others how much he had changed. "Korey."

"Fred and Stan can cover me," he said in a voice tha
brooked no argument. "I'm tired of this mess. If Gwyn's be
isn't on our side, then there's no point in trusting anyone
Intelligence."

Lily shrugged and led them down to halt at the bottom
the ramp, letting Deucalion and the people with him come
them. Deucalion, walking with a stiff limp, looked furious a
he neared. A woman wearing plain gray fatigues and th
badge of Concord Intelligence walked beside him. She ha
black hair pulled tight in a bun on her head and dark oliv
skin. A single red dot—cosmetic, surely—marked the cent
of her forehead. Lily recognized her immediately.

She spoke under her breath to Windsor. "That's the woma
I met in Reft space."

Windsor's eyes narrowed as he stared at her. "I'm sure,"
muttered. "It has to be. She was with Basham when the
pulled me in. There's something about her . . ."

The party stopped some five meters from them.

"Deucalion. Where is Yehoshua? What happened to Pinto'

Deucalion glanced at the woman standing beside him. H
gaze, cold and measuring, focused on Lily, Windsor, an
Hawk, each in turn. "Yehoshua is with Pinto on board th
other ship. Pinto is hurt, but receiving care. This is Mar
Rashmi Leung. She came along just in time. I don't kno
who the hell shot at us, but when I find out . . ."

"Maria," murmured Lily, just as Maria said, "Yes, we hav
met before." And drew a pistol from her fatigues. The othe
in her party—six of them—drew pistols as well.

Deucalion stared. "What are you doing?" he demanded

"Move away, Belsonn," Maria snapped. "This doesn't co
cern you." She looked at him briefly, her lips twistin
"Although I suppose it does, given your breeding."

"This violates every covenant of the Concordance. I su
gest you—"

"Belsonn. I *said* move aside."

Lily began to lift her hand, slowly, to signal Jenny.

"We have guns trained on your ship," added Maria. "Yo
and Windsor and Hawk can come quietly with me, or yo
and all your companions can die. That's the choice."

"We'll kill you first," Lily replied, quiet.

"It won't make any difference to my plans. My people ha
their orders. Just as long as we're rid of you. Of your kind

"You're serious," said Deucalion. He had not moved awa

Now he stared, as if those two simple words had left him bereft of further speech.

"Damn." Windsor turned his head to look at Lily. "I can shoot her first, Ransome, but she's right. Those two ships will make short work of us. I should have known. I *hate* it when I miscalculate."

"I don't expect you miscalculate often, do you, Windsor?" Maria's voice was entirely unsympathetic, yet not at all gloating. "Or you wouldn't have survived as long as you have."

He gave a short, caustic laugh. "In my former line of work, there was no room for miscalculation. I've gotten sloppy lately."

"I don't understand." Lily looked from Maria to Deucalion to Windsor, seeing some relationship between the three of them—between their separate roles in the League's history— that she could not sort out from the information she had, much less comprehend. "Why do you want to kill us?"

"Kill them!" Again, the two words exhausted Deucalion's outrage for the moment. He looked utterly confused.

"You're a danger to everything we've built."

"*I* am? I'm not even from the League."

"Your kind. What you represent of human nature. Concord was too lenient after the war."

"So you've taken matters into your own hands." Windsor grinned. "I kind of like you, min Leung. You're sort of like a bounty hunter, hiring yourself. Carrying out your own justice."

Her face tightened, and she pointed the pistol at him. "I don't need your opinion, Windsor. You gave up a right to have one long ago, by the deeds you did."

"Fred," said Windsor into the air. "Lower the gun. That won't help any. I can't help it she's crazy."

Her face remained a stiff mask. She seemed not to respond at all to this dig. "Belsonn. I told you to move aside."

He found his voice again. "I won't." He walked across the gap to stand beside Lily. "I'll have you before the tribunal for this."

She sighed. "No, you won't. I'm not leaving any witnesses." She made a sign, and one of the helmeted figures moved away. A stream of armed figures emerged from the two ships she controlled, fanning out to surround the shuttle.

Lily felt a hand brush her elbow: Kyosti's touch. She glanced up at him, but his face was utterly impassive, alien, and she could read no emotion in it. "How can you possibly justify killing us?"

The mask of Maria's face did not alter, and Lily began to wonder if she was a little mad, madder, in her own way, than Kyosti was now, because she had brought it on herself. "Necessity," said Maria, cold as the vacuum of space. "And the justice denied all your victims."

Windsor smiled wryly. If he was scared, he did not show it. "Whatever happened to mercy?" he asked.

"It is my duty to save society from people like you." She lifted her head, listening, and they heard it as well. More ships approaching. "Even if you kill me, resisting now, it doesn't matter. My orders are set. Those are the reinforcements. No trace of your presence here will remain."

Out of her peripheral vision, Lily saw Windsor shade his lips and mouth the words, "play for time." She gave a little whistle, as if she was trying to act nonchalant under such pressure, and heard a faint answering call from the shadowed height of the ramp. Jenny was still standing there, hiding some thing behind her.

"But there will be traces," said Lily. "The people on my ship know I came down here. They know what coordinates I came to, who I was to meet. Are you aware that Dr. Farhad has just arrived on my ship and will be wanting to know where I am? She has a particular interest in Hawk. She was in charge of his treatment."

"That was a mistake. And anyway, accidents happen."

The roar of engines heightened.

"Pissing hell," said Windsor suddenly and loudly. "I know who you remind me of. Benizar. She looked like you."

"You killed her," said Maria with such searing hate that it was almost like heat boiling off of her. "You bastards."

"I damned well saved her life more than once. Just like she saved mine. Who the hell are you to judge? How did you know her anyway?"

Maria hesitated. Three ships skated in over them, banked with breathtaking precision and dipped the stopped, screaming in midair, and floated down to land softly on scarred grass. Looking closely at the ships, Maria slipped abruptly behind the screen of her hirelings. Deucalion lunged forward, but Lily caught him, her reflexes faster than his intent, and tripped him. He sprawled onto the grass as the six men jerked back from his movement and crouched.

The ramp of the forward ship opened.

"Kill them," said Maria calmly.

Lily whistled for Bach. Windsor spoke one gutteral, foreign word, and Fred and Stanford appeared on the ramp, heavily armed. Pistols raised. And Deucalion stepped out and sauntered down the ramp of the newly arrived ship, unconcerned by the scene playing out before him.

Except Deucalion still lay sprawled in the grass at Lily's feet.

"Hold your fire!" snapped Maria. She turned.

Deucalion scrambled to his feet. Lily and Windsor stared. Behind, Bach began to sing:

> *So recht, ihr Engel, jaunchzt und singet,*
> *Dass es uns heut so schön gelinget!*
> *Auf denn! wir stimmen mit euch ein,*
> *Uns kann es so wie euch erfreun.*

> "Then fittingly, you angels, rejoice and sing,
> that things turn out so favorably for us this day!
> Up then! We will join in with you,
> for we can rejoice just as you."

And a second figure appeared at the top of the new ship's ramp. Even at such distance, Lily would have recognized her anywhere.

Beside her, Deucalion froze. "Mother," he breathed, and then, as if everyone else had vanished, as if he were alone and not about to be murdered with the rest of his companions, he walked blindly through the ring of armed men, past Maria—not giving the slightest sign he knew she was there—and toward the woman and man waiting for him.

18 Gwyddno's Weir

****

He knelt in front of her, and she touched his head with her right hand, a benediction. Adam waited at the foot of the ramp with the patience of a man long-used to such displays. Of the scene before him, suspended in the act of playing out, he appeared indifferent. Of Maria's hirelings and ships and weapons, he and La Belle appeared entirely unimpressed. Their three ships, sleek, beautiful vessels, sat in all their quiet, deadly splendor on scorched grass.

But Maria herself simply stood and watched, as if this card, played out now, had obliterated her ability to control her own hand.

"My God," said one of the men with her. "Is that La Belle Dame? The privateer?"

"Yes," Maria answered. No one made any further comment. Whatever words passed between La Belle and her son could not be heard. They were brief. She removed her hand and Deucalion stood up and stepped back and to one side, letting her walk past him down the ramp. He followed her, but as she set out across the grass toward the group gathered at the shuttle, he paused next to his brother. The two simply looked at each other a moment. Lily, distracted by La Belle's serene stroll through the clearing, glanced back at the brothers in time to see them grin, exchange a few words, and embrace, and then, so perfectly in tune that only the practice of long years and the accident of identical genetic material could account for it, they turned together in exact time—as if the movement had been choreographed—and followed their mother, twin attendants. As they came up behind La Belle, Lily realized that, except for their clothing, she could not tell them apart.

Silence, except for the brush of wind through the low grass, hushed the two parties as they watched La Belle's progress toward them. She wore a plain white blouse with belled sleeves and black trousers, cut full, banded at each

ankle. Her feet were bare. Her black hair hung in a thick
braid to her waist, except for a few wispy strands at her
forehead that stirred in the breeze. She did not alter her
course to go around Maria and Maria's hirelings. Rather, they
moved aside to let her pass through their ranks. No one
spoke. La Belle did not even look at them, as if they were of
no interest to her. She halted in front of Lily.

"I have a message for you," she said.

The incongruence of the statement, delivered in such
circumstances and with such simplicity, took Lily aback. "You
just saved my life." She did not know what else to say. The
adrenaline of moments before had been somehow absorbed in
La Belle's slow walk across the meadow, as if La Belle herself
were a sponge that could consume any strife but that she
herself generated.

La Belle did not even glance at the group behind her. At
Deucalion's approach with Adam, Maria had begun to back
away, although her people continued to stare alternately at La
Belle and then at her three ships.

"Hold on, min Leung." Deucalion left Adam's side and
pushed through the armed men to take hold of Maria's arm.
"I'm calling you in on charges. You tried to murder us. You
went so far as to hire people to aid you. I suppose you had to
import these—*citizens*—from The Pale in order to find people willing to abet you in your crime. I'm astonished, and
disappointed, that a member in good standing of Central
Intelligence could stoop to such methods. Mother. Adam."
He included them with a glance that swept them both. "I ask
you to witness this arraignment."

"They aren't citizens," Maria said, coldly removing Deucalion's
hand from her sleeve. "They are not legal witnesses for a
citizen's arrest. Therefore, I will leave now." She motioned to
her hirelings, and they swiftly dropped back toward the two
ships they had arrived in.

Deucalion reached out and grasped Maria's arm again.
"No! I won't just stand here and let you leave."

"How can you stop me, aside from assaulting me yourself?
With your background, I wouldn't be surprised if you chose
such a method."

"You can say that after you just tried to murder us? Mother!
Surely you'll support me in this!"

"I am uninterested in min Leung's crimes. You have a
tribunal for such cases, I believe, Deucalion."

"But without witnesses other than those involved—"

"That is the choice you made. In The Pale, we choose other forms of justice."

In the pause left by La Belle's words, Maria shook off Deucalion's hand again. "I'm only sorry I failed," she said, looking first at Deucalion, but shifting her stare to encompass Lily and Windsor and Hawk as well, and perhaps with more animosity, if that were possible. "The League would be better off without you."

Deucalion stepped back, repelled by the vehemence of her hatred. Hawk simply stared impassively at her, buffered by his alienness. Windsor's mouth turned up with his characteristic bitter grin. Lily tried to match this woman with the earlier Maria she had met on Nevermore, but her competence, it seemed to Lily, had been overcome by her obsession. And looking around at the others, she saw that La Belle was smiling, a tiny ghost of a thing, chilling in its coolness.

La Belle's gaze focused for a brief moment on Maria, and now it was that woman's turn to step back, retreating. La Belle's smile vanished, and she clasped her hands together lightly as she regarded the other woman. "What you resist, you become."

Maria flushed with anger. Her hand tightened on her pistol. Lily began to move, to place herself between Maria and La Belle. She was astonished that Adam did nothing—until she saw how La Belle's gaze was weapon enough. Maria thrust her pistol into her belt and turned on her heel and strode away toward her ship. She did not look back.

"Stop!" Lily cried. "You still have two of my crew." Maria paused, half-turning back. Her lips turned up, a mockery of a smile. "I will deliver them to Concord, min Heredes. You will have to turn yourself in to recover them."

"You still hope to trap me."

"I don't hope to *trap* you," Maria replied. "But if it is all I can accomplish now, then at least the net will serve to hold you so I know where you are. In any case, for you to get them from me now you would have to fire on us, and I believe we not only outnumber you, but possess far superior weaponry and armor."

"Damned hypocrite," muttered Deucalion.

Lily began to step forward, lifting one hand as a signal to Jenny.

Windsor laid a hand on her arm to stop her. "Don't try it."

"She's got my *people*. You spoke of loyalty—do you expect me to trust her?"

"What do you think I'll do?" Maria asked scornfully. "I suppose you think I would kill them."

"You meant to kill us."

Maria looked her up and down, but Lily found it no trouble to stare her down. "*You* are different," Maria said, and she turned away and strode to her ship, her back protected by the men she had hired.

Lily watched in furious silence, Windsor's strong grip still a restraint on her arm, as Maria's people boarded and the two ships took off. As the high roar of their engines faded into the growing twilight, Deucalion turned back to look at his mother with surprise.

"Do you mean to say that you didn't come here to save us?" he demanded.

La Belle seemed unmoved by the sudden passion of his question. "That was incidental to my purpose—not that I'm sorry to save you, my son. But as I said before, I have a message for Lilyaka Ransome. From your father."

"My *father*!" Lily stared. "How could you have been to the Reft and back already? You didn't even know I came from Unruli."

La Belle blinked. It was the only time Lily had ever seen her the slightest bit nonplussed. "Ah," she said abruptly. "You mistake me. From Taliesin."

"But he's dead."

La Belle smiled, a secret, intimate expression. "Joshua Li Heredes is dead. *My* Taliesin is not dead. They have never been wise enough to catch him, hold him, and kill him all at the same time. He is the master of the art."

Lily was too stunned by this revelation to do anything but parrot the last phrase. "The art?"

"The art of transformation. Didn't you know?"

Lily simply gaped at her.

"'The second time I was bewitched I was a blue salmon.'" For a moment she did not recognize the voice. "'I was a dog, a stag, a roebuck on the mountain; I was a tree, a spade, an ax in the hand.'"

"Kyosti!" He tilted his head, and briefly, so briefly, *he* looked at her. His lips twitched up in a lazy smile, and he blinked, and turned his gaze to La Belle. "'I lay nine nights at rest in her womb.'"

La Belle smiled. "'I have been dead and have been alive,'" she finished.

Even as she said it, Jenny appeared on the ramp above, moving past Fred and Stanford. Kyosti tilted his head to one side, scenting her, and in that instant the Kyosti who could quote vanished again.

"Master Heredes—Taliesin—is *alive*?" Lily shook her head. "How can he be alive?"

"Father is alive?" Deucalion echoed, and he moved to stand next to Adam, as if he found consolation, or confidence, there.

Adam answered. "It was only four bullets. Only one lodged in his brain. When we found him he was in a coma and the senators couldn't decide whether to unplug him from the terribly primitive life-support they had him on and hope that would do him in, or to let him linger on and hope he'd eventually do them the favor of dying while they could claim they'd done everything in their power to save him. I think at least one of them was hoping he would come out of it so they could find out how he had cracked their computer net." He grinned. "Mother persuaded them to give him into our keeping."

"But then—" Lily shook her head. "Then when we met at Blessings, you must have had him with you. Why didn't you tell me? How could you not tell me?"

"Lily." One did not argue with La Belle when she used such a tone of voice. "We did not know at that time whether he would live. I would not have left you with *that* kind of hope—unresolved and painful. I did not know then that you would make the choice to seek out the League. You might never have been able to find out if he had survived."

"So you thought it was better to keep me in ignorance," Lily replied, rather bitterly. "I'm not sure I appreciate *that* choice."

"Ah—Ransome," said Windsor, sounding unexpectedly nervous. "This is La Belle Dame you're speaking to."

La Belle laughed. "Taliesin's daughter is free to speak to me in any way she sees fit. Nevertheless, that choice was mine, and I made it as I thought best at the time."

"But you came now." The shock of the news was finally wearing off, and Lily felt a sudden, wild exhilaration flood her, a new rush of adrenaline. "He's not just alive, but out of danger?"

"He is alive. He is even well, if a little changed. That is the message I came to deliver. You will find him on Terra, in the district named Cymru. I think he would be pleased to see you. Now, if you will, I have other urgent business to attend to. Adam."

La Belle turned and without a second's glance padded in her bare feet back across the meadow to her ship.

"But—" Lily began, and hesitated, seeing that it would be fruitless to attempt to stop La Belle once she had decided to go.

Adam came over to her and put his hands on her shoulders. "You're looking well, sister," he said, both mocking and sincere. It was a combination only he could pull off. For that instant, she wondered how she could ever mix the two brothers up.

"How did you find us? It was awfully damned convenient of you to show up when you did."

Adam grinned. "Mother always has liked the grand entrance. Her timing is impeccable. But in fact, when we came into Concord system, we'd been following your trail for some weeks. When we hailed your ship, you'd already gone, and Mother has an appointment in The Pale, so rather than wait, we followed you down."

"Lucky for us," Lily murmured.

Adam looked a little embarrassed. "It does rather go with the territory. I'll see you again, sister." He turned away, pausing before Deucalion. "We'll be in Siddi for the Holy Days."

Deucalion nodded. "If I can make it."

Adam grinned and left, following his mother's path across the clearing and up into the ship. They both paused, at the top of the ramp, and looked briefly back. Deucalion lifted a hand in farewell. Adam, like a mirror, returned the gesture. La Belle merely looked, but even her looking held the quality of speech. Lily thought, abruptly, that La Belle probably did not pause to look back often. And then they were gone. The ramp retracted into the ship, and the opening sealed. Engines roared and with a shudder, La Belle's ship lifted. The two beside rose at the same time, and they vanished beyond the horizon of trees.

"Oh, Hells," swore Lily suddenly. "Why do I listen to you? That woman has Yehoshua and Pinto. And how am I supposed to find this place called Cymru?"

"I know where it is," said Windsor unexpectedly. "I grew up on Terra. In the Angels sprawl."

"You can give me coordinates?"

"I can show you on a map. Finding him once you're there will be your problem."

"Isn't this a little premature?" cut in Deucalion. "We have to return to Concord immediately to report this."

"After an official of Concord Intelligence just tried to murder me and my crew? I think not. After what I've seen, I see no reason to go along with you or your guarantees any more, Deucalion. Jenny! Get on comm and tell the *Hope* to ready for departure from this system." Jenny nodded and ducked inside.

"No." The source of the objection surprised her. It was Windsor. Fred and Stanford had ambled down the ramp to stand beside him. "He's right. We have to go."

"So you can get your damned bounty?"

"No. It's fair enough you think that, but I'm giving that up."

"Convince me."

"She was after me, too, Ransome. Remember that. But if that doesn't convince you, then I give you my word in this." He reached underneath his shirt and pulled out a medallion, twin to the one she wore. "On the fellowship. Gwyn would have honored my pledge." He spoke a few words in the foreign tongue to Hawk, frowned at Hawk's reply, and looked troubled.

"What did he say?"

"He really has lost his memory," Windsor said. His voice shook a little. "I thought maybe he was faking it a little, to cover himself. He doesn't know what the medallion is."

His worry and concern was persuasive. "All right. Let's say I believe that, for now. It still won't make me turn myself in."

Windsor shook his head. "It's gone beyond whatever charge they've brought against you. *She's* the renegade, using her authority to commit assault and attempt murder, and then calling *us* throwbacks. I'm by God going to her superior. trust Yevgeny Basham to be fair."

"*You* trust him?"

"Yes."

"And anyway, Lily," added Deucalion, "what other means do you have to get Yehoshua and Pinto back? Or were you planning to leave without them?"

The gaze she turned on him was searing. "Don't even suggest it. But if Windsor can break Hawk out of the highest security prison the League has, then I by the Void can get them back from that woman."

"No!" exclaimed Deucalion and Windsor at the same moment."

"It'd be a big mistake, Cap'n," added Fred from where he stood to one side of Windsor.

"Why?"

"You would consider use of force?" Deucalion demanded.

Lily laughed. "Why shouldn't I? After this?"

Windsor shook his head. "Don't do it. Not in Concord system. You and your crew will end up in Concord prison with no one to spring you. It wouldn't be fair to them, at the least."

"Yes," agreed Deucalion mendaciously. "Think of your crew."

"I *am* thinking of my crew. And my ship, which I don't doubt Concord will find some excuse to remove from our stewardship. We're getting Yehoshua and Pinto and we're heading off to see if this Pale I've heard mentioned is more welcoming than the League."

"Lily! You can't do that. That place is lawless—every kind of troublemaker and social misfit drifts there—"

"Sounds like we'll fit right in."

"Say," put in Windsor. "Can you take the boys and me with you?"

"There's been a terrible misunderstanding," protested Deucalion. "You've seen the very worst side of—I'm sure there's an explanation. For all I know this has all been some plot devised by Maria Leung that we've been thrown into without our knowing it. Things don't normally work this way." He was beginning to look desperate. "Why do you think I choose to live in the League, chose this position?"

"Because you're the bad twin," Lily replied caustically.

Jenny stepped out onto the top of the ramp. "We've got incoming, Captain. Four ships. Some debate as to whether they're the same as any we've seen before."

"Stanford," said Windsor. "Take a look."

Stanford loped up the ramp.

"Do I let him on?" Jenny asked, blocking the entrance.

"Yes," Lily replied. "I'm coming aboard."

Jenny shrugged and let him pass, disappearing inside with him.

"Any of you coming on with me, or do you care to take your chances here?"

There was a pause. Deucalion looked at Windsor, an appeal for support, but Windsor just crossed his arms and looked up the ramp, waiting for Stanford's assessment. It came quickly enough. "Yes?" Windsor said to the air. "All right." He looked at Lily. "Stan says it's official Intelligence flyers, running under authority code, with Basham himself aboard. I think we should wait. If we don't wait, they'll just chase and bring you in anyway. That ancient tub you've got doesn't have a chance against a flyer."

"Just how are you communicating?" Lily asked.

"With the flyers? By your comm."

"No, with Stanford." She lifted her wrist reflexively and glanced down at her wrist-com.

"Implant, of course." Windsor shook his head again, sighing, and exchanged a look with Deucalion. "And as good of a ship as the *Forlorn Hope* is, the fact is, Ransome, that Stanford tells me it's two centuries out of date. You can't out-run anything in the League, not even to get out of the system."

"And Basham will see that Yehoshua and Pinto are returned immediately," added Deucalion persuasively. "I *know* him, Lily."

"Don't matter now," interposed Fred. "While you been talking, they got here." He waved his hand at the sky.

Four ships banked in. Two circled. Two landed close to the position where La Belle's ships had put down.

"This better work," muttered Lily.

"Patience," replied Deucalion.

"My best virtue."

The hatch unsealed and a ramp opened out. Several figures emerged, headed by a white-haired man of indeterminate years. They crossed briskly and halted in front of the *Hope*'s shuttle.

"Deucalion!" The white-haired man looked surprised. "What on earth are you doing here? We've gotten a flood of calls about unsanctioned landings and unauthorized fire in this area."

"Yevgeny. May I introduce Lily Ransome? I believe you know—" Deucalion gestured toward Windsor.

Yevgeny Basham smiled a gently wry smile. "Min Windsor

and I are acquainted, in a fashion. I see you delivered your bounty, min Windsor."

"No, I don't," said Windsor roughly. "I waive all rights to it. And I won't cooperate if you try to bring her in now."

"Indeed." Yevgeny raised his eyebrows, looking thoughtful. "Deucalion? You realize, of course, that as well as the original charges of aiding and abetting a fugitive who is a known threat to the lawful peace, min Ransome has accumulated charges since her arrival in League space of resisting arrest, illegal possession of historic property, reckless endangerment, and now, this afternoon, failure to appear at an arranged hearing as well as aiding and abetting escape from a maximum security facility, and now this disturbance here on the surface."

"There is an explanation," Deucalion began.

"Yes," said Lily, speaking directly at Basham. "There is an explanation, min Basham. I can give it to you now."

He turned his attention to her. His eyes were shrewd, and measuring. If he did not trust her, she thought, he did not yet distrust her either. "I think you would be better served, min Ransome, to give it before a convened hearing. I have been told that you claim salvage of what is believed to be the original *Forlorn Hope*."

"Yes."

"Incredible." He studied the shuttle behind her for a few moments in silence. "That vessel certainly lends credence to your claim. I haven't seen its like since my days in history class. Well, min Ransome—"

"*Captain* Ransome," said Jenny in a loud voice from the ramp above.

"Captain." He blinked, weighing this information, and Jenny's weapons, as well. "I think it would be best if you would travel on my ship. And let some of my people escort yours."

"If I won't?" she asked, trying to temper the belligerence she felt. "If I choose just to leave? After one of your own officers attempted to kill me, you might understand that I hesitate to trust you."

"One of my officers attempted to kill you?" His surprise did not looked feigned—or he was a very good actor. "This grows more serious. Deucalion?"

"It's quite true. She tried to kill me as well. Threatened everyone here. Maria Rashmi Leung."

Yevgeny frowned. "I would be sorry to discover that she had. In truth, Captain, I would not blame you for choosing to simply run. You wouldn't get far. Your vessel is out of date. Now. I can reconvene the hearing in two hours. Will you travel with me, Captain?"

Everyone waited, as if this decision on Lily's part was of vital importance. Even Deucalion did not intrude with his opinion. Lily realized suddenly who Yevgeny reminded her of, with his keen eye and mellow, but sharp, demeanor. He reminded her of Master Heredes. She wondered if he would be aghast at being compared to one of the infamous saboteurs—to the master of the art himself.

"I will," she replied, because she knew she really had no choice. "I would request that my robot Bach be allowed to come with me, as well as my Special Officer min Seria, and min Windsor and his two companions."

Yevgeny merely nodded. "That seems reasonable."

Windsor grinned. "Insurance," he muttered so softly that only Lily could hear him. "Wise move."

Lily reached to lay a hand on Kyosti's arm. "Hawk as well."

Now Yevgeny looked briefly startled, but he controlled it very well. "He would be coming with us in any case, as an escaped prisoner. He belongs—"

"He belongs with me."

"Lily—" began Deucalion, warning.

"You know it's true. But," and she kept her gaze focused on Yevgeny Basham, "I'll save that story for the hearing." Then because it gave her an illusion of control over a situation she knew now, and finally, controlled her, a situation that she would have to completely resolve before she could ever make a new life for herself and her crew—wherever they ended up—she removed her hand from Kyosti's arm and waved toward Yevgeny's ship. "Shall we go?"

19 Due Process

****

"You're crazy," muttered Jenny. "We should have just run for
and blasted through anyone who got in our way."

Lily tilted back her chair and stared at the clear dome
bove. Stars and the void of space and filaments of Concord's
ast superstructure showed through the clear material that
ade up the huge semicircle. When they had been shown
to this chamber, the dome above had been opaque; then
me switch had been thrown and the surface had cleared
d screens had rolled back to reveal the stars. "I don't think
e could make it. Their technology is more advanced than
nything we have. They may not choose to use weapons, but
ey've got them. Sometimes it's better to negotiate."

Bach, floating just behind her chair, sang.

> *Geduld, Geduld!*
> *Wenn mich falsche Zungen stechen.*
> *Leid' ich wider meine Schuld*
> *Schimpf und Spott,*
> *Ei! so mag der liebe Gott*
> *Meines Herzens Unschuld rächen.*

> "Patience, patience!
> even when false tongues sting me.
> Contrary to my guilt I suffer
> abuse and mockery.
> Ah, then, may dear God
> avenge my heart's innocence."

Lily chuckled. "Yes. Especially when you're outnumbered
d outgunned."

"After everything that's happened, you still trust them? It's
talk, Lily. Deucalion claims to be so shocked by our civil
ar, all of the Reft's old-fashioned—he calls them—customs,
t I don't see that they've treated you much differently."

"I don't know." As she considered, Lily let one hand drop down to rest lightly on Kyosti's hair. Its blue strands snaked around her fingers. He was reclined at her feet, perfectly still, not so much reposing as waiting with a predator's anticipation of its prey. "Think about the people we've run into. Most helped us. And Windsor was just doing his job. I think that Maria Leung is the exception."

"Yes." Jenny grinned suddenly. "We ought to introduce her to Kuan-yin. Don't you suppose they'd get along?"

But Lily simply smiled. "They already were introduced some time ago. They didn't get on well at all. As I remember, Kuan-yin called her a bitch."

Jenny laughed. In the great domed chamber, the sound was swallowed immediately. The pair of attendants who had shown them into the chamber—they did not quite have the demeanor of guards—glanced at them from their stance by one of the doors, looked away again, returning to their conversation. The acoustics in the room were exceptionally sensitive. Lily and Jenny, lapsing into a brief silence, could hear the attendants' words.

". . . and the shift manager said, 'Sure, Nazik, I'll believe that the *Sans Merci* just hailed into system. Maybe you'd like to offer to lease me some cryo berths, too.' And Nazik said, 'No, really,' and by this time about four of the other people on shift had come over to stare at her screen and someone called up the specs on the overhead, and the shift manager turned around to swear at the person who'd done it and looked up . . ."

The door opposite the attendants opened. First the low harmony of voices speaking casually together spilled into the chamber, then a number of people who quickly sorted themselves out as they took seats in the circle of chairs in which Lily and Jenny were already sitting. Arranged in such a manner—rather as if they were seated at a large table and the table had been removed—it was hard for Lily to think of the occasion as a tribunal. It seemed more like a social meeting, everyone comfortable in padded chairs with consoles embedded in each arm and no furniture or levels to set off those judging from those being judged.

Of the six people now seated in the circle, she recognized only Yevgeny Basham. The other five were strangers, three women, one a Ridani—like Diomede's coordinator Scallop she was only half-tattooed—and two men. One of the men had very pale skin and red hair; Lily could not help staring at him, and she wondered if he dyed it or if, like Kyosti, that was its natural color. Then she flushed when he smiled at her, and she looked instead at Yevgeny.

He nodded, acknowledging her gaze. "Let me introduce the board," he said, and he went around the chairs. Qaetana, from Administration; Maphuna, from Environment; Chao, Services; Chapman, from Medical—the red-haired man; and Isfa'han, from Parliament—the Ridani woman. Evidently Yevgeny was the only representative from Intelligence. He paused, after the introductions, and looked expectantly at the Ridani woman, who settled her hands in her lap and looked at each member of the circle. "I will be moderating," said Isfa'han. "I would like to begin by asking min Ransome to explain a bit about her background."

So she told them, about Reft space, about growing up on Unruli, about Heredes's academy and his kidnapping by the Kapellans and her subsequent search for him—a pause here while they all looked at Kyosti and looked away. How she had lived on Arcadia and aided Pero, and how she had joined Jehane's revolution and followed it to its end, for her at least, in Pero's death. And finally, the decision to take the *Forlorn Hope* and its crew to find the lost route back to League space.

The tale took longer to tell than she expected. As she watched her audience, she saw signs that some of what they heard shocked them—minute signs, certainly, because all six were clearly trained to listen without judging, but signs nonetheless: an averting of eyes here, a slight flush there, a hand covering a mouth. Chapman, the red-haired man, even grimaced once, when she told of Pero's murder. She did not mention Hawk's activities at all, except that he had traveled with her.

Silence followed her story. Isfa'han took notes on her console and, after an interval, coughed slightly to alert the others that she was about to proceed. "That brings us to the captain's activities in League space. I show in my records that Intelligence brought a bounty hunter in on min Ransome, on the charge of aiding and abetting a dangerous fugitive." All six looked at Kyosti. He did not look back at them, but rather beyond them, as if they did not really exist for him or were too unimportant to register. "From the record I have here of min Hakoni's arrest on Zeya Depot, it does appear that he is unstable and potentially violent."

"My division took that case," said Chapman. "I recall the recommendation that he was clearly unfit to function in society and was to be removed immediately into psychiatric isolation. Austen Chorianis even got Dr. Vespa Tuan Farhad to agree to study the case until further notice."

"He was broken out of his isolation cell from Concord Rehabilitation Center," Yevgeny said. "That's another serious charge levied against min Ransome."

"Under the circumstances, min Basham," said Chapman, "I'm surprised that he has been allowed"—now he paused, glancing almost nervously at Hawk, as if he feared the statement might precipitate some savagery—"to be present at this hearing."

"I can vouch for him," interposed Lily stiffly. "I take full responsibility for his actions."

Chapman looked at Yevgeny and then at Isfa'han, as if Lily's comment held no force for him. "I realize that this is classified information, but under the circumstances I must disclose that min—Hawk, as he has called himself at other times, is a half-blood, human and je'jiri."

Yevgeny's expression did not change. Lily doubted the information came as a surprise to him. Everyone else looked truly shocked.

"Yevgeny." Isfa'han's tone scolded. "Why wasn't this information included in my file?"

One woman—Chao—stood up. "I need better guarantees than a simple voucher to risk myself in this close proximity."

"Told you," muttered Jenny under her breath.

"Min Chao. Please."

Lily surveyed her audience, halting her gaze on Chao. "I'm his mate. That ought to be voucher enough."

Chapman flushed bright red. Even Yevgeny looked surprised, by which Lily assumed that she had caught them all off guard. Perhaps even horrified them. Chao sat down, but she drew her feet in under her chair as if she was pulling herself as far away from Lily and Hawk as possible. "That's disgusting," she murmured, not quietly enough.

"I admit myself intrigued," said Isfa'han. "But I must tell you, min Ransome, that the penalties for aiding and abetting a dangerous fugitive are severe. For good reason. You are also charged with aiding one Gwyn Himavant Simonides."

Lily tapped her fingers on the arm of her chair. "I'm still

not sure what laws they had broken that made them into fugitives."

Chao and Chapman both began to speak at once. Isfa'han waved them to silence. "As well as the following charges." She read off the same charges that Yevgeny had read to Lily in the clearing on Discord. "There are other witnesses relevant to the case. I'll bring them in now."

After a pause, the door beside which the two attendants stood opened. For a moment no one appeared, although several figures shifted and moved at the entrance, caught in some turmoil. Raised voices could be heard. A woman, looking rather harried, stepped inside. "Min Isfa'han," she pleaded, "I have tried to tell her that this is a closed hearing but—"

Dr. Farhad brushed past her without a second glance and strode across the chamber to the circle. Both Isfa'han and Yevgeny, seeing who she was, stood up, and the other four, taking a moment longer to register her identity, swiftly stood as well. She walked directly into the center of the circle, not deigning to shake hands with anyone.

"Where is my patient?" she demanded, turned, and saw him. "Kyosti!" Her face softened an instant—but only an instant. Seeing that he was safe, or safe enough for now, under Lily's hand, she turned back to face Yevgeny. "I have, to my great distress, discovered some serious abuses in the treatment of this patient, by Concord Intelligence. A patient, I might add, whose condition is precarious but at the moment stable. And who was, when I last treated him some fifty years ago, recovering from a complete breakdown. I now have reason to believe that he was lured into work for which he was not suited and that it eventually contributed to a subsequent breakdown, and that a later imprisonment in Concord prison was not recorded and that he was subjected to torture."

"Torture!" gasped Chao.

"Surely not," protested Chapman. "I've been with Medical for thirty years now—"

"Perhaps no one in Medical at that time was aware that to deprive a person of je'jiri blood—even if he is only half-blooded—of all sensory perception to—God help us, but I cannot possibly imagine what they were trying to accomplish! In order, I must presume, either to gain information he was unwilling to provide or else simply to deprive him of his sanity."

"Dr. Farhad!" Yevgeny's voice was quite cool. Lily suspected he was a poor man to cross. "Are you willing to stand by such accusations?"

"Quite willing." Dr. Farhad raked her audience with a scathing gaze, then swept a stray lock of hair into its proper place in its tight coil on her head and sat down beside Lily. Kyosti looked up at her with interest and spoke a single word in je'jiri. She replied, briefly, and returned her attention to Yevgeny. "I do not intend to let Intelligence gets its claws into him again. I will use my very substantial influence to make sure that it does not."

This pronouncement left Yevgeny speechless. Isfa'han coughed again, capturing the group's attention, but into the pause as the circle settled back to business, the figures left forgotten at the door entered quietly into the chamber.

"Yehoshua!" Lily stood up. Jenny rose as well. Hawk lifted his head and scented, and came up gracefully and swiftly to his feet. "Pinto!"

"Begging your pardon," said Lily tersely, reflexively, to Isfa'han, and she strode out of the circle of chairs and across the white, marbled floor to meet Yehoshua and Pinto halfway. Yehoshua was limping. Pinto was seated in a maglev chair.

"Thank the Void," Lily said under her breath as she came up to them and could see that they were a little battered but in one piece, and she hugged first Yehoshua and then, leaning down slightly, Pinto. The air around the edges of his chair vibrated, a soft tickle at her skin that faded as she pulled back from him, suddenly aware of Kyosti standing directly behind her.

But Jenny pushed past him and embraced Pinto as well, with her keen fighter's instinct placing herself between Kyosti and the only male in the room he had focused on. Pinto seemed oblivious to the fuss. Yehoshua had flushed a little, watching Jenny embrace the pilot, and flushed a little more when she moved away and with a great grin of relief—perhaps of something else—hugged him tightly as well.

"Kyosti," said Lily in an undertone as she moved to take Jenny's place between the two men, "go back and sit down by Dr. Farhad."

He cocked his head to one side, taking in her words. After a moment he turned crisply and paced smoothly back into the circle to sink down between Dr. Farhad's chair and the one Lily had just vacated.

Yehoshua blinked. "What was that all about?" he asked quietly. "Never mind. Are you both all right?"

Pinto winced as she laid a hand on his shoulder. "I'd be dead if it wasn't for Yehoshua. That last shot—I don't even remember it. I don't know how he got me out."

"I carried you," said Yehoshua, short. He glanced at his right—artificial—arm. "You weren't very heavy. We're all right, Captain. Or at least, not much worse for the wear. But what about you?" He looked beyond her toward the tribunal.

"Oh, we've just started. You haven't missed much. Where is—?" She stepped past Yehoshua, toward the door. "Windsor. Fred. Stanford. I'm very glad to see you." She offered her hand to the bounty hunter.

"I'll bet you are," said Windsor, shaking her hand without hesitation. She supposed he had bathed—at any rate, his clothes were clean, if rumpled, but his face still had the same stubbled, nonshaven appearance, and his dark hair was unkempt. In contrast, Fred and Stanford seemed neatly groomed, as if they had been at some pains to mat down their hair. Stanford still wore his shoulder harness, but the only instrument she saw attached to it was his thin com-slate. Stanford shook her hand with some reserve, but Fred pumped it enthusiastically.

"Don't get a chance to do this much," he growled. "Nice place, huh? Where do we get to sit?"

Lily grinned, waving toward Yevgeny. "You'd better ask our host. I think the main chairs are filling up. If you'll excuse me." She waited for the last arrivals. "Deucalion. And—" paused, and when she spoke again, her voice was many degrees cooler. "Min Leung. I'm so pleased to see you here."

Maria simply walked past her as if she did not exist, or were of too little importance to acknowledge. It seemed a poor and unconvincing imitation of La Belle.

"At least she's being made to appear," Lily said to Deucalion.

He looked grim. "I'll see that she's brought to account for her actions. I'm only sorry that Mother wouldn't witness—or even let Adam—" He shook his head. "Never mind."

"Haven't you tried to reach them again? Perhaps a recorded message?"

"They've already left the system. She only came to tell you about Father." A different look sparked in his eyes a moment. "At least we learned that he's not dead."

She had to ask, now that he had mentioned the subject
"Do you know where Cymru is?"

"Of course." But he did not elaborate, moving instead to
the chairs. She followed him and, seating herself, found that
the circle was full except for an empty chair that Windsor had
forsaken, seeing that there was not room enough for the
Ardakians to sit in as well. A rank of chairs behind held them
and Yehoshua, and Pinto in his elevated chair. Deucalion sa
beside Jenny, Maria next to Yevgeny. There was a silence in
which Maria arranged her dress and Isfa'han surveyed the
new arrivals with an expression of dry amusement on her
half-dappled face. "While you settle yourselves in and sor
yourselves out," she said, with a touch of irony, "I'll bring u
the rest of the file."

While the Ridani woman scrolled up more notes, Lil
leaned to speak softly to Dr. Farhad. "How did you get here
I thought you would have been on the *Hope* by now."

Dr. Farhad looked at her, reproving. Her lips thinned
"Once I arrived, the young woman called Paisley apprise
me of developments. I then had the skiff that brought m
turn around and bring me back here. Just in time, I see
Her disapproval fairly radiated around the circle.

"Now." Isfa'han folded her hands in her lap. "Since all th
principals are here, perhaps we can continue. Without inter
ruption. This list of charges is quite extensive. Most of ther
seem adequately substantiated. Intent, of course, we can onl
deduce from this hearing now, and it seems clear to me tha
we're dealing with a person whose customary, socialize
behavior is rather different from our own."

"If this story about"—Chao checked her console—"Re
space is true."

"Have you reason to doubt it?" asked Isfa'han.

"I have logs to prove it," said Lily without heat. "I hav
never been aware that logs could be faked."

"That's true," conceded Chao. She frowned and glance
past Lily. "But if that's a still functional, and bonded, compo
er, there's no telling what you might have accomplished."

Patroness, Bach sang, *are they questioning my honesty?*

No, Bach, she whistled. *They are praising your abilitie*
Bach finished off Lily's phrase with a gorgeous, and expressive
brief, coda. Lily turned back to face Isfa'han. "I am accuse
of aiding and abetting a fugitive. Two fugitives. I won't de
that I—as you phrase it—aided and abetted them—"

"You see," interrupted Maria vehemently. "She does *not* deny it."

"Let her finish, Maria," said Yevgeny curtly.

Lily waited a moment, but Maria did not continue. "But in so far as I was a citizen of Reft space, was not even aware of the existence of the League except as the place my ancestors came from, I don't understand how you can charge me under your laws for traveling with people whose fugitive status I could not have been cognizant of and whose government had no jurisdiction over me in the first place."

"Ignorance is always the excuse of the deviant."

"Maria," warned Yevgeny.

Deucalion stood up. "If ignorance is the captain's excuse, min Leung, then I would like to know what yours is. If the honorables here are not aware of it, I would like to state for the record what occurred on Discord."

"Deucalion," said Yevgeny softly. "Please sit down."

"I refuse to let her prejudice the tribunal!"

"How can I prejudice them?" Maria asked with false sweetness. "The facts prejudice themselves and lead to only one conclusion—that these people are unfit to function in society."

"*You're* unfit—"

"Deucalion!" Yevgeny silenced him.

"If you will excuse me again," broke in Isfa'han placidly. "I believe that this hearing was convened to focus specifically on the charges laid out here against min Ransome. A separate hearing must be convoked to deal with these other charges."

"Unsubstantiated charges," said Maria.

"Only because I couldn't get outside witnesses to—"

"Please, min Belsonn," interrupted Isfa'han more forcefully. "We *will* proceed with the matter at hand."

Deucalion sat down, mouth turned down, both fists clenched and placed on his thighs.

"Thank you," said Lily drily, and she exchanged what could only be called a complicitous smile with Isfa'han. Yevgeny Basham could be heard to sigh as he looked at the two other representatives of Intelligence, who had subsided but only to glare at each other in silence.

"So you admit to the charges," said Chapman. "I would think that makes intent pretty clear. I did read the dossier on his case before I came. My recommendation would be for the maximum penalty."

"I concur," said Chao, and Maphuna nodded as well.

"Perhaps you would enlighten me as to what the penalty is," cut in Lily.

Jenny leaned forward. "You're not going to just take this, are you?" she demanded. "They've already made up their minds before they got here." Lily lifted her hand and Jenny sat back, crossing her arms over her chest and glowering as only a dangerous mercenary can do.

"Min Basham?"

Yevgeny sighed and brought up information on his console. "A prison term, to be commuted with public works or some service to the public as agreed on by the tribunal."

"If you imprison me, you have my crew and my ship on your hands. I'm responsible for them. For that matter, they came here because of me. I hope you're taking that into account."

"There is some legal question," said Isfa'han, "about the status of the *Forlorn Hope*. There is some sentiment that your claim on it as salvage is legal, but again, it is government property, no matter how old, and that claim may not hold."

"That ship is all we have. How else are we expected to live?"

"How do you expect to make a living with an outmoded vessel?" asked Isfa'han.

"I expect," said Maria scornfully, "that as soon as they're free they'll abscond with it to The Pale and make a living as a privateer."

"We can't allow an historic vessel like that to be used in such a manner," added Chao, looking worried. "I recommend it be removed to government bond and the crew be given the same standard educational and living vouchers as any citizen to start fresh."

"No!" Lily stood up. "I refuse to give up the *Hope*. I'll fight you every step of the way if you try to take it from me. Legally, for as long as I can. Physically, if I have to. And I refuse to be a criminal just because it's more convenient for you to treat me as one. We came a long way to get here. We've brought Reft space into contact with the League. You ought to thank me, if only because you can send missionaries there now—not that they'll necessarily thank *you* for it. And appreciate that you conduct yourselves in a civilized manner. In the Reft they probably would have shot me—and my crew.

be safe—out of hand. I see that shocks some of you. Maybe
ou ought to find a way for us to utilize what skills we have,
ne that will minimize the—ah—bad habits we've brought
om where we grew up, in some employment that will be of
ervice to you."

"We can't make exceptions on sentencing," said Isfa'han.
Once guilt is found. It is one of the first principles of our
overnment—that all shall be sentenced equally."

"But imprisonment can be traded for public service," put
Yevgeny. "It has always been accepted that good works are
better rehabilitator than a cell."

Beside Lily, Dr. Farhad stirred. "By the tone of your voice,
take it you have something in mind. I would warn you
gain, I am here to look out for the interests of my patient,
nd it is my firm belief that he will only recover if he is
eleased into the custody of min Ransome, with proper
verseeing, of course."

"I hear you, Dr. Farhad," said Yevgeny. He glanced around
ne circle, seeing that he had everyone's attention. Lily
oked around as well, and once she felt assured that the
mosphere was at least not uniformly hostile to her cause,
ne sat down. "It had occurred to me before," continued
evgeny, "that your skills might well be utilized by Intelligence."

"By *Intelligence*?" exclaimed Deucalion.

Lily exchanged a glance with Jenny. Jenny shrugged, pull-
g a wry face as if to say, "I told you so." "In what fashion?"
ily asked, feeling suspicious.

It did not alleviate her suspicions when Yevgeny hesitated,
ancing once again around the circle, as if gauging their
sponse, before he went on. "It has not escaped our notice,
ere in Intelligence, that The Pale is rather outside our
rovenance."

"As it is meant to be," said Isfa'han. "Rather like a safety
lve."

"For the worst element," interposed Maria smugly. "Those
ho can't function in normal society."

"Nevertheless," continued Yevgeny, cutting her off, "we
e at a disadvantage for lack of good intelligence. Partly we
ck good information on Kapellan movements. Partly we lack
formation on the movements of the various organizations
d groups who inhabit and govern—"

"If you call that government," said Maria.

"—of those people who live there," finished Yevgeny, with

a tone that might have been exasperation. "You have broke League law, Captain, and if you want to live here, you hav to accept the consequences, as a citizen of League space. Bu it doesn't serve anyone's purpose to simply imprison you And the *Forlorn Hope*, with a little refitting, will continue t be an excellent and spaceworthy vessel."

He paused, and in the silence everyone heard Fred say, i what was doubtless meant to be a whisper, "How come the always take so long to get to the point when what they'r going to say you're not going to like?"

"It's diplomacy, Fred," said Windsor, not bothering t whisper.

But Yevgeny had himself well in hand, and if he wa annoyed by this interplay, he did not show it. "Intelligenc will second your claim to the *Forlorn Hope*, Captain, and w will recommend that one Hawk, currently under the custod of both Intelligence and Medical for psychiatric reasons, b released into *your* custody. If you agree to work for us. W need a ship, working in The Pale under the guise of privateer, to bring us intelligence of the movements of th Kapellans and of the privateers currently active there."

Beyond the circle, Windsor coughed into his hand.

"You want me to be a spy," said Lily, meeting Yevgeny' eyes, "as ransom for Hawk, and for the ship, and for freedor for myself and my crew."

"I think that is exaggerating the situation. You can serve u well there. We have not previously found anyone else wh met enough of the correct specifications for the job wh could."

Windsor coughed again.

"Or, I suppose," replied Lily, "who would. I'm curious know what the rest of the tribunal thinks of this."

"I would agree," said Chao. Maphuna and Qaetana nodded

"I disagree," said Chapman. "I think it's just throwing fu on the fire. I think it's a bad idea."

"Prison is the only safe place for these people." Mar turned her head to stare at Lily, but after a moment, whe Lily did not flinch from her hard gaze, she looked away. " would only encourage them."

Dr. Farhad lifted a hand to her hair. "I was not aware th you were a member of the tribunal, min Leung, but as yo are offering unsolicited and unofficial opinions, I will ad mine as well, in, of course, a purely professional capacity. M patient needs continuity and peace and a stable environment to recover effectively. Such a course of action would not benefit him. But then, min Basham, I suspect that this solution derives more from your needs than theirs."

"Be that as it may," said Yevgeny, "it is the solution being offered. Min Isfa'han?"

"I don't like it, but I will not, at this time, recommend against it. In any case, by four votes to one, we have a majority accepting. Captain?"

Lily looked around the circle: at the six members of the tribunal, who were, she supposed, being as objective as any person could, with a thousand prejudices and ignorances leavened by hope and some confidence in human goodness tempering each one; at Maria Leung, whose hostility was not masked at all, whose hatred aligned her more surely with those throwbacks she despised than any actions they had ever done; at Deucalion, who looked furious but was restraining himself with unusual discipline; at Jenny, whose skepticism showed as clearly as the way she unconsciously held her right hand at the belt pouch that should have held a gun; at Dr. Farhad, who simply waited with faint disdain, secure in her position as a respected scientist. Kyosti sat with alien stillness at her feet, uncannily patient, as if such human ways of doing things had nothing to do with him. Behind her, Bach sang, too quietly for her to make out words. Beyond the circle, Fred was grooming himself with a heavy hand, and Stanford was, as usual, calculating on his slate. Windsor had his head rolled back on the seat back, eyes shut, as if he was asleep. Yehoshua sat forward, elbows on his knees, listening intently, and he met her eyes and shrugged. Pinto, beside him, sighed and looked bored. Lily smiled, wondering what Paisley would make of this great domed chamber, and looked back at Isfa'han.

"I'll think about it," she said.

"You don't think they'll really just let us go," hissed Jenny, but Lily laid a hand on her sleeve and she frowned and stopped speaking.

"You'll *think* about it?" echoed Yevgeny, looking surprised.

Isfa'han chuckled. "Are you negotiating with us? I'm not sure you're in a position to."

"Maybe I'd prefer prison," said Lily. "I know some of those privateers. I'm not sure I *want* to spy on them. It might be dangerous."

Dr. Farhad chuckled.

"And I have one piece of unfinished business I'd like to complete first. I'd like to go to Terra."

"On holiday?" said Maria with a sneer.

"I'd like to visit my father, whom I thought was dead," said Lily coolly. "Which reminds me, min Isfa'han. How do I file charges for attempted murder and aggravated assault—or whatever you call it here—against Maria Rashmi Leung? I'd like to do that as well, before I go. If, of course, you let me go."

"Impossible," exclaimed Maria. "She's not even a citizen of the League."

"Maria," warned Yevgeny.

"Everyone has access to the courts," said Isfa'han. "You ought to know that."

"Even those who willfully abuse the systems we have so carefully set up to keep peace and harmony—"

"Min Leung." Without raising her voice, Isfa'han cut off Maria's tirade as effectively as if she had shouted. "I have been more than generous in letting you air your position, but you have abused the privilege once too often. I don't want to have to ask you to leave. Now. If min Ransome chooses to file charges, then they will be resolved in a separate tribunal."

"I'll file charges of my own," said Deucalion. He smiled suddenly, looking sly and very like his father. "Also, I would like to point out that min Ransome has not been allowed an advocate at this tribunal. That's grounds for a rehearing, I believe. I'm surprised you overlooked it."

The silence that followed this remark was eloquent. All six members of the tribunal looked at each other, as if expecting someone else to take responsibility for this oversight.

Yevgeny shook his head finally. "I should have refused to mentor you, Deucalion. You've gotten slippery."

Isfa'han shook her head. "Min Ransome is, indeed, due a rehearing. I did not confirm that an advocate would be present. Under the circumstances, I don't think it unreasonable for her to be allowed a specified and finite amount of time to think over this offer before a new hearing is convened. A parole to Terra, however..."

"How can we be assured you'll come back?" demanded Chapman.

"I'll go with her," said Deucalion. "I'll act as her parole officer, post myself as her bail."

"Do you trust him?" Maria demanded.

"*I* trust him," said Yevgeny. "And anyone here is welcome to reference min Belsonn's record and see that it is exemplary. In addition, I can add an escort of several other Intelligence officers as insurance."

"I'd like to take a few of my people with me," said Lily. "But perhaps you can add additional officers to cover them as well. I would leave the *Forlorn Hope* and the rest of my crew as—"

"Hostages," muttered Jenny.

"As good faith."

"As Intelligence, I see no reason not to honor min Ransome's request. It will give her time to consider our offer and to consult with a qualified advocate, who will, I am sure, apprise her of the advisability of accepting it." Yevgeny folded his hands in his lap, and Lily realized that he was feeling smug, secure that she had no choice but to do as he wished.

"I don't like it," said Chapman, but the other three all looked at Isfa'han for guidance, and Isfa'han merely nodded. "Four weeks," said Isfa'han. "Twelve days run either way on a fast yacht, and four to conduct your business. And, min Ransome, if you break this parole, and attempt to escape, your vessel and crew will be impounded and you will face a mandatory and minimum thirty-year prison sentence once we catch you again. Without your own ship, we will catch you before you can reach The Pale."

"I don't abandon my own people," said Lily. She rose.

"I do have one question," said Qaetana. It was the first time she had spoken. "Before you go. Several of the engineers in my section asked me to ask you. How did you break min Hawk out of Concord prison? It was built to be escapeproof."

"But I didn't—" Lily broke off, glancing over the tribunal's heads at Windsor and the boys. Fred pulled his lips back to expose his teeth, the Ardakian grimace that he used as a smile. Stanford was obviously not listening. Windsor had his eyes shut, and he looked very tired.

"Lily," said Deucalion. "You needn't answer any questions without an advocate present. I'm surprised they didn't inform you of that in the first place."

"Oh," she said. Jenny mouthed an "oh" as well, clearly surprised at this privilege. "Then, if you will forgive me, min

Qaetana, I will wait to answer that question. May we be excused?"

The members of the tribunal rose, one by one. Chapman was still frowning. Maria did not stand. She looked enraged, but contained.

"We will convene again in four weeks," said Isfa'han. "Captain, I would be pleased to escort you to your ship and then onto a secure yacht."

"Certainly," she acceded graciously, knowing she had no choice. But in the stir created as the other members of the tribunal left, dragging Maria in their wake, she turned to Deucalion. "Why didn't you mention the advocate earlier?" she asked in an undertone. "You could have saved me this entire hearing."

Deucalion lifted his hands, palms up, and shrugged. "Lily, you're a trained martial artist. You know that you never reveal your best move until you've found out your opponent's whole repertoire. We're one up on them now. *And* I know a good advocate who will take advantage of that."

"You would," said Lily.

"Anyway," he added, "it would be a terrible mistake to agree to spy on Mother. It's been tried. It didn't end happily. She's not very forgiving, even to family." His smile was enigmatic and rueful.

"No, I don't imagine she is," agreed Lily diplomatically. She restrained her curiosity.

"We'll have to devise some other public service," he continued.

"Hoy. Do you have any ideas?"

"Yes, in fact—" But he stopped as Isfa'han and Yevgeny came up to them.

"You were saying?" Yevgeny asked.

"In fact," Deucalion said, "it was at the original Concordance of New Era fifty eight that the position of advocate was developed as a more positive tool for conflict resolution than what was used before."

"Which was?"

Both Deucalion and Yevgeny smiled. "Lawyers."

20 Ya Green Grass Land

****

s the train clacked and rolled in its rhythmic clatter along
e track, Paisley gazed out the plastine window at the lush
reen countryside. No, Yehoshua corrected himself, it was
ot plastine, it was the far more fragile substance called glass.
le was surprised that it was still used in League space, after
e remarkable technology he had seen, but then, he was
irprised at the antiquated train in which they were riding.
urely the engineers in League space could design a more
reamlined, modern railcar rather than this model that was
early ancient, or built to look ancient and run with more
oisc along slatted tracks than he thought necessary, or
arming. But after everything he had seen, after Diomede
id Concord and Terra orbit and the brisk efficiency of
eathrow Terminal, where they had landed, he had to assume
at they wanted these trains to be exactly as they were:
uaint and old-fashioned and slow.

He looked back at Paisley. Her expression was one of
verence, as if what she saw brought back some long-
rgotten and exalted memory to her. Jenny moved on the
at beside him, and he turned his head to see that she, too,
oked at Paisley. She noticed his gaze and winked at him,
aring her amusement at the awe on Paisley's face. Next to
isley, Gregori was engrossed in making the tabletop—a
ear surface that when manipulated properly was in itself an
tire com-screen—display the interlaced threads of Terra's
ansportation web.

"Too bad Pinto isn't here," said Jenny in a low voice,
dding at the view outside the window. "It would remind
m of home."

"It be so *green*," breathed Paisley. She did not even look at
r seatmates, merely relapsed into her enraptured gaze at
e steep-sloped hills and the meager scattering of trees
imped at the edges of rock-walled pasture. A silvered

stream paralleled them, and under the lee of a hill a village
stood, dark, squat houses that looked millennia old. In a low
singsong voice, Paisley began to speak words, an old song.

> Far come they tae ya green grass land
> Morning bright-o day
> Where Dancer lead them hey come ho
> Sunlight comes in morning.

"Maybe not," added Jenny, as if she were answering her
own question. "Pinto always hated those old tattoo songs.
And anyway, there weren't many mountains in Central. Nothing as old as those buildings, or so small. Size was an
important consideration in impressing one's acquaintances.
He probably wouldn't want to be reminded of it." She
frowned suddenly, her gaze focusing not on the scene outside
but on some vision farther away.

Yehoshua sighed. Undoubtedly, the memory of Central had
brought her round to thinking of Aliasing. He lowered his
gaze to stare morosely at the multicolored network of lines on
the tabletop. From the seats on the other side of the aisle, he
could hear Deucalion haranging the advocate he had hired to
plead their cause. He glanced over to see Lily, no longer
bothering to hide her smile, watching her half-brother with
amusement clear on her features.

"There has to be some way to get out of the service
requirement."

"Deucalion. We've gone over this point ten thousand times.
To her credit, the advocate had the same look of amusement
on her face that Lily did. "Service or prison. I can't change
that. What I can do is force them to accept a change of terms
in the service. But we have to have an alternative that we can
present to the tribunal."

"It just infuriates me that that woman simply walked out of
that hearing smug as you please, simply walked away from
her misdeeds, from everything she did to us, as if she was the
holiest person present."

"Which she obviously thought she was," said Lily. "Deucalion,
we've gone over *this point*—if I may borrow a phrase—*twenty*
thousand times. Min Havel has filed the charges and we'll just
have to wait. We can't dwell on it. We have to move forward."

Next to her, Bach sang softly, but Yehoshua could not quite
make out the tune. He thought it sounded familiar.

"And she may well walk free without any charges sticking," added min Havel. Deucalion groaned and grimaced, but restrained himself from a speech. "However much you may deplore it, that's the way the system works."

"Remember, Deucalion, however much I'd like to, as Jenny would say, pin her ass to the wall, that's not my first concern. I need a job for the *Hope* and the crew that we can do. We can't—don't want—to go back to Reft space. We'd be fools to take up Yevgeny's offer, and I don't want to work for Intelligence anyway. So we have to find something legal that they'll settle for."

"Good luck," muttered Deucalion, obviously still dwelling on Maria's sins.

It occurred to Yehoshua that Lily's advice was good: dwelling on things never got a person anywhere. So he coughed slightly, to gear himself up, and returned his attention to Jenny. She was still frowning, staring out the window but not seeing the landscape beyond. "Pinto wouldn't have been interested in scenery anyway," he said. "He's like me—so used to space that this is more a curiosity than anything else. And he certainly wouldn't have traded a look at Terra for being in on the *Hope*'s refitting. He and the Mule could hardly wait to get their hands on the new nav-pilot linkup."

For an instant, Jenny looked at him as if he was as alien to her as the je'jiri. Then she grinned, and her usual cheerful cynicism sparked from her expression once again. "You're right, of course. But I'm glad you came along, even if you would rather have stayed for the refitting. Those three"—she waved toward Lily and Deucalion and the advocate—"haven't stopped wrangling since we left Concord, and I've got no patience for legal matters." Yehoshua coughed to hide his smile. "It always seems more efficient just to blast the bastards. Oh well. And Paisley's been gaping like an idiot ever since we came into orbit around Terra, so she's no company. And Finch." Finch was seated several seats back, strangers in the three seats around him; he was frowning with mute sourness at the com-slate he'd been given, presumably reading something. "I don't know why Lily brought him."

"Probably thought it'd do him good to be free of the ship for a while. He's been out of sorts."

"Finch is terminally out of sorts. So why the Hells do you suppose she'd think he'd feel better traveling in close company with Hawk all this way, I ask you? Because to be frank,

Yehoshua," and she dropped the level of her voice until he had to lean closer to hear her, "every time I look at Hawk, I *still* feel spooked. He gives me the creeps."

Together, reflexively, they glanced over their shoulders to the four seats and table directly behind that at which Lily sat. Despite the train being crowded, despite the passengers in ones and twos filtering through at each stop as they looked for seats, the two aisle seats beside Hawk and Dr. Farhad remained empty. Hawk sat staring at Lily. His blue hair marked him as surely as a beacon would, but it was the entire attitude of his bearing, the cast of his shoulders, the way he tilted his head, sniffing rather than looking as anyone passed by, the inhuman way his mouth was set, that branded him and kept anyone from sitting down. Dr. Farhad seemed oblivious to her surroundings as she studied writing on her slate and occasionally glanced up to ask Hawk a question. Occasionally he replied. Not often.

The tabletop shifted color suddenly, and both of them jumped and then glanced about self-consciously. Gregori had changed the map; now he examined a grid of this island's transport web.

"King's Cross," he said carefully, trying the words on his tongue. "What's *king* mean?"

Yehoshua looked at Jenny and they both shrugged. "I don't know," replied Jenny. "What is it?"

"Terminal we left from, in that city. *London*." His face brightened and he gazed up at his mother. "I know. Old Nanny Skipsy used to sing me this song, 'London bridge is falling down.' Do you remember her? I used to think it was a thing, like a stress factor. Do you think it was that city we come through?"

"*Came* through," Jenny corrected automatically. "I don't see why not. Old songs like that must have come from somewhere."

"Nanny Skipsy?" Yehoshua asked.

"Engineer on the boat we shipped on before the *Easy Virtue*. Damn my eyes, but I'd swear that old woman was about one hundred years old. She knew the strangest things. Said she'd learnt them from her grand'mam, who learnt them from *her* grand'mam who was a crippled yeoman from the wreck of the *Bitter Tidings*, the old highroad boat that Central blew up when it tried to run Reft space."

"Did you believe her?"

"No. I thought she was crazy. Now I'm not so sure." She waved a hand to encompass the landscape, the train, and the many other occupants of the carriage, dressed in the unfamiliar fashions of the League and conversing in the unfamiliar cadences of League Standard.

"Never believed you'd be setting foot on Terra itself?" Yehoshua asked, grinning.

But before Jenny could reply, Paisley turned her head smoothly and fixed them with a gaze almost uncomfortable in its intensity. "Tirra-li. We hae found ya green grass land." Her Ridani accent, which had softened over the course of their travels, had come back doubly strong. She began to chant in a low, singsong voice. *"We'll come one day tae green grass land / Morning bright-o day / When Jehane he dance us down ya way / Sun shine bright-o morning."*

Yehoshua and Jenny regarded each other in silence. Paisley regarded them as if some great revelation had just come to her and she expected that it was as obvious to them as it was to her. A low chime heralded the conductor's voice over the carriage intercom, which was embedded in the tabletop console.

"Cerrigydrudion."

Deucalion rose abruptly. "We get off here," he said.

Lily stood as well, glancing around to mark each of her people. "Let's go."

They pulled down their carrys from the overhead racks and got off the train. Finch trailed behind, standing at the edge of the group as the train pulled away from the tiny station and Deucalion surveyed the ticket booth and turnstile that led onto a quiet street, along which ranks of two-story, drab houses stood up against one another. Two people went through the turnstile. The man sitting in the ticket booth stared at them.

"This is the town he was born in," Deucalion said to Lily. "It's my best bet as where he'd go to ground."

"But how do we find him?"

Deucalion grinned. "Obviously you're not a native. First we get a place to stay and stow our gear, and then we go down to the pub and gossip with the locals. They'll know about him, if he's here. And I can't imagine he'd go anywhere else in Cymru."

"Lead on." Lily hoisted her carry over one shoulder and waited.

The pub proved also to be the inn, and with some doubling up, and the relinquishing of their room by two of the children of the house, the innkeeper found enough room for the entire party. Yehoshua found himself in a room with Deucalion and Finch. Finch tossed his carry at the foot of his bed and lay down on his stomach, face turned to stare out the many-paned window—glass again, Yehoshua noted, whorled and so thick that it gave a slight distortion to the view outside. From their room they could see the pub's courtyard and a gate that led onto a broad circle of green lawn in whose center lay a pond. As he looked, he saw Lily and Bach come outside, followed by Dr. Farhad and Hawk. They sat down at one of the tables, and a young woman came out after them and wiped the table off and then stood talking. She looked once at Hawk, eyes widening, and after that pointedly did *not* look at him again.

"Don't see many je'jiri on Terra, do they?" said Yehoshua, and Deucalion, who had been looking outside as well, turned.

"Not any more. There were some incidents..." He declined to say more. "We'd better go down." He threw his carry down on his bed and left.

"Are you coming, Finch?" Yehoshua asked.

"No."

"Aren't you hungry?"

"No."

Yehoshua sighed and followed Deucalion out. Jenny had arrived before him, and she grinned and waved him over to the table where she sat with Gregori and the advocate. Deucalion had pulled a chair up to Lily's table. "Where's Paisley?" Yehoshua asked as he sat down.

"She pitched her carry on the top bunk and headed straight out the door. Look." She directed his gaze to the gate, and then he saw Paisley out on the green, staring alternately at the grass, the pond, the steep hills surrounding the village, and the sky.

"It's unusually good weather," said the advocate. "It usually rains this time of year. I'd suggest the ale and the ploughman's lunch."

"What's *ploughman*?" Gregori asked.

Under cover of the advocate's earnest explanation of this term, Yehoshua leaned closer to Jenny. She rested her chin on her fist and tilted closer to him as well, so close that it took his breath away for an instant and he forgot what he was going to say. She smiled, and he flushed, abruptly aware that she knew quite well what effect her proximity was having on him.

"Finch is sulking," he said, because it was the only thing that came to mind, or at least the only thing that came to mind that he could say in such a public place, at such a time.

"And Paisley is blissing. They ought to trade a little across and both come back toward center. I'm worried about her. It isn't like her to be this quiet."

"Knowing Paisley, she won't be for long." He paused as the young woman came and took their orders and retreated. Several people had gathered in the courtyard now, mostly, Yehoshua suspected, to stare at the newcomers. They politely kept their attention primarily on Bach, who floated at his usual spot just above and behind Lily's left shoulder.

Jenny got a considering look on her face. "Last night Dr. Farhad asked me a second time about Gregori's hair."

"About his hair?"

"About the color of his hair. She asked me first if anyone in my family had hair that color, and when I said no—" She chuckled and held out a dark brown hand. "As if we would, with this complexion. Then she asked about his father..." She trailed off, and for a moment Yehoshua was afraid she was thinking of Aliasing again, but she merely looked thoughtful. "Blond hair is rare enough, in Reft space. The funny thing was, this time she asked me questions about Jehane—not just what he looked like, but how he acted, what he was like. His personality."

"What did you tell her?"

"I told her he was a dangerous, manipulative, self-absorbed bastard," Jenny said with rather more heat than was typical for her. "She didn't seem surprised. I wonder why."

"Who know? I'm only glad she's here to guard Hawk when Lily can't be with him. What's going to happen when he gets let loose to wander around the *Hope* by himself?"

"If any of us get to wander around the *Hope*. Anyway, what makes you think Lily will let him?"

"It's clear to me she's bringing him along, if she gets out of the prison sentence."

"Let's concentrate on keeping her out of prison, Yehoshua, and worry about Hawk when we have to. Look at it this way, maybe the je'jiri will take an interest in him."

"Maybe they will. I hadn't thought of that." He contemplated the je'jiri for a moment, and shook his head. "Poor Finch. No wonder he's sulking."

Jenny laughed. "You're too compassionate, Yehoshua. Like Pinto, I don't have much sympathy left for Finch." She paused as the young woman returned, handing round mugs of dark ale and a smaller mug of milk for Gregori, and then waited as they all sampled it. Jenny's eyes widened, rather like the young woman's had when she had first seen Hawk. "This is good! I could get used to this."

The young woman laughed and went back to the kitchen.

"You've made yourself welcome now," said the advocate, smiling. "They make their own ale here, and you just complimented it."

"Have you been here before?" Yehoshua asked, suddenly suspicious.

Min Havel chuckled. She had a thin, sharp face, and she could hold her own with Deucalion at his worst, but in his few encounters with her away from Deucalion and Lily, Yehoshua had decided that she was not ill-natured. "No," she answered, "but there's a placard in the window that says the ale is brewed on the premises."

"No," said Lily from the other table, raising her voice in exasperation. "Deucalion, you simply refuse to understand. We *can't* go back. Even if we wanted to. And if we'd wanted to, we wouldn't have left there in the first place and risked taking a lost road to a place we weren't entirely sure existed."

Hawk straightened, taking in air in the way Yehoshua now recognized as je'jiri scenting—and he had begun to suspect that they could smell more subtle fragrances than odor.

"But it's the obvious choice," Deucalion began, and Hawk turned his predator's gaze on Deucalion as Lily began to look angry.

Jenny brushed her fingers against the back of Yehoshua's hand, and he jerked, startled. "Firefight," she said. "You'd better go back her up. He'll listen to you."

"Will he?" the advocate asked with interest. "You'd be the first one."

"Excuse me," said Yehoshua, and he got up quickly and, dragging his chair behind him, crossed to the other table. "Mind if I sit down?" he asked, pulling up his chair and sitting between Hawk and Deucalion before anyone could reply. Hawk tilted his head to one side, then the other, scenting him. Yehoshua stiffened slightly, but Hawk evidently

marked him as acceptable and at last sat back in his chair. The
tension around the table eased noticeably. Dr. Farhad tapped
on her com-slate. The action irritated Yehoshua: could she
never stop taking notes? He felt as if every moment surrounding Hawk was simply one long psychiatric observation,
and his sympathy for the man progressed in that instant from
nervous pity to a sudden urge to see that he *did* recover, so
that he might be spared this indignity.

"Yehoshua," said Lily, "could you please explain to Deucalion
once again that it would not be a good idea for us to join the
League's expedition to Reft space?"

"But it would be a perfectly acceptable service to exchange
for the one Basham proposed," Deucalion went on, ignoring
her mood in his enthusiasm for his idea. "You know the way,
or at least have run it, and you know the area and the
customs—"

"And the current government," interrupted Lily, "who
would cheerfully cut our throats at the first opportunity and
would certainly not trust any emissary claiming us as companion and guide. In any case, how can you guarantee that the
person in charge of the expedition would want us along?"

This point evidently had not occurred to Deucalion, because he looked abruptly surprised. "Oh," he said, "didn't I
tell you?" He paused expectantly.

"No."

"I asked Yevgeny for that position, and he agreed to
support my application and it's already been sent before
Diplomatic Council. He expects it will be approved without
any delays. I ought to know when we return to Concord."

Yehoshua gaped at him. Lily did as well, but recovered
sooner—which was one reason, Yehoshua supposed, why she
had through the course of their adventures taken on the role
of commander and captain. She laughed. "Why in the Seven
Hells would *you* want to go to Reft space?" she asked. "No,
you don't need to answer. I already know."

Deucalion drew himself up, looking offended. "I don't
need to sit here and be insulted."

"But I haven't said anything yet."

"You don't need to. I know what you'll say. Everyone says
it. He's going because he can't help but want to tell them the
correct way to do things. He can't help wanting to enlighten
them because he thinks he's always right."

Yehoshua had to hide his smile behind one hand, because

it was exactly what he was thinking, and he saw now that Deucalion was more sensitive—or at least more pervious—to criticism than he had thought.

But Lily simply chuckled. "But isn't that why?"

"Helping people to live better than they were," he replied stiffly, "is not an impulse that ought to be laughed at."

"But I'm not laughing at the impulse, Deucalion."

"No. You're just laughing at me." He relaxed abruptly and smiled. "You remind me of Adam in some ways."

"I guess I'll take that as a compliment."

"You shouldn't. I still think"—he paused as the young woman brought their food, and started over—"I was one of the people who encouraged Yevgeny to push for the refit of the *Forlorn Hope* to start immediately."

"I was wondering how that happened. I got the impression from min Basham that he assumed that I was going to accept the offer he made."

"I might have led him to believe you would accept—" Deucalion coughed.

"You lied to him! Deucalion, you can't imagine how fond I am of you. You're the only person I know who can bend all his own rules without seeming hypocritical."

"In any case," he continued, ignoring her comment, "*I* was hoping all along that I could use the *Hope* as the lead ship in the expedition to Reft space. It would be ready by the time the expedition can be put together."

"I said no, Deucalion."

"But Lily," Deucalion replied, so placidly that Yehoshua was immediately suspicious. "If it's the only alternative to spying in The Pale, you may not have any choice."

Lily's answer was to begin eating. Hawk watched her a moment, scenting something Yehoshua could not detect, and then favored the plate set in front of him with detached interest. He tried a bit of cheese and then settled back and closed his eyes without eating anything else. The young woman deftly brought Yehoshua's plate over from the other table, and since everyone else had started, he ate as well. Paisley wandered in from the green and sat at Jenny's table.

As they finished up, a short, black-haired man whom Yehoshua recognized as the innkeeper strolled out onto the courtyard and, after a fractional pause by the locals drinking at a nearby table, came over to stand beside Lily.

"Everything is to your liking, I hope?" he asked. Hi

Standard was particularly difficult to understand, but peculiarly
melodious for all that.

"Yes," Lily assured him. "Very much so. It's very lovely
here."

"Ah," he agreed. "It is that. What brings you to these
parts?"

She glanced at Deucalion, but he simply nodded. "My
brother and I," she indicated Deucalion, "came here looking
for our father."

"Why would your father be here, of all places?" the
innkeeper asked, but Yehoshua could see that he was intrigued.

"He grew up here. Many years back. Name of—" She
hesitated, as if she was trying to remember something long
past and almost forgotten. "Taliesin ap Branwen a Jawaharlal."
She recited it more than said it, like a lesson learned in
school. "He told us he was headed back here some time past,
but we were both far out near The Pale, and we lost touch.
We were wondering if he'd settled in here in the past six
months."

The innkeeper's face creased with a broad smile. "That
would be Taliesin Jones, would it? I went to school with him,
you know. A good lad, and a fine tenor. It was a sad thing
when his folks had to move to Lloegre, to England. Yes,
indeed. He's taken the old Davies place while they're out by
Urfan Link on a mining job. Just a crofter's cottage, you
understand, and the dog's no trouble, but it's a fair enough
place to write poetry in while he's waiting for a lease to come
up in the area."

Lily had gone a little pale, and she was breathing unsteadily.
"How would we get there?"

The innkeeper shook his head. "Oh, there's no use going
now, is there? He's down to Llangollen these three days for
the local Eisteddfod." He paused, seeing her expression.
"But don't worry, he's sure to be back tomorrow morning by
midday. I'll tell you the way then. It's just up back on Mwdwl
within two kilometers north. A light walk for a morning.
You'll see."

"Thank you," she replied with apparent calm. "We'll go
then." The innkeeper excused himself and left to tend to a
local calling for ale and, presumably, some information about
these strangers. Yehoshua watched Lily. Hawk had looked up
as well. She was slightly flushed, and she hoisted her mug of

ale with an unsteady hand. "I can't believe he's still alive," she said in a low voice. "That we'll see him. Tomorrow."

At first no one replied. Then Deucalion stood up. "I think I'll go take a walk," he said.

"You haven't finished your food," Yehoshua pointed out.

"I'm not hungry," he replied, and he left, heading out the gate onto the green and quickly disappearing from view.

Lily set down her mug and turned to stare after him. "Maybe I'd better go talk to him."

"Do you think so?" Yehoshua asked. "I get the impression he'd like to be alone. I've never met your father—or at least, *this* father—but from what I've heard, it seems to me that he might not be the easiest person to meet again after so long. Not from what Deucalion's said."

"Adam once referred to him as a tyrant." Lily shook her head. "I could never imagine how anyone could see him as a tyrant. Or be troubled about meeting him."

Dr. Farhad looked up from her food—she ate with the same efficiency as she studied Hawk—and surveyed her company with a professional's eye. "They are sons. It has long been known that with a father, a daughter is privileged."

Yehoshua chuckled. "Is that true, Lily?"

"I don't know. Deucalion and I haven't compared notes much. I think I'll look around the village this afternoon. Care to join me?"

Yehoshua shrugged. "Might as well. I don't know what else to do here. It's a lot different than anywhere else I've spent time. What do you expect to see?"

Lily grinned. "I'm not sure. But I can't get out of the habit of checking my ground, in case of"—she glanced at Dr. Farhad—"an emergency."

"Old habits die hard," said Dr. Farhad coolly, but Yehoshua got the distinct impression that Dr. Farhad knew quite well what Lily meant.

21   Night

****

In this place, the senses were overwhelmed with the strength of *je'humari* existence. It was possible to keep focus only by letting her scent alone crowd against him, like a barrier to the rest.

Hawk stood in darkness at the gate that led from the courtyard onto the green. Behind him, a few stragglers from early closing still drank, and the innkeeper stood in the door to the pub and mildly scolded them for not yet leaving. Of those he traveled with, most were still sitting outside enjoying the last fingers of ale. It was easy to distinguish them in the midst of unfamiliar smells: Jenny, sharp-scented, trustworthy, and a toughness baited with laughter; Gregori, bright as a healthy child always is; Yehoshua, mixed of dependability and a humor that matched well with Jenny's, although he seemed unaware of it, or of the strength underpinning him, one that others relied on without he or they being aware of it; Deucalion, a turbulent mixture of honor and guilt and inflexibility; and Dr. Farhad, whose scent had a dry, cutting edge that he did not much like, but which he trusted. Bach smelled of metal and machinery, but underlying it was a second scent, ancient and depthless, a trail of scent that, had he the leisure to follow it, could lead him into the heart of creation.

And *her*. He frowned. He could tell, at that moment, that she was thinking of him. It shaded her essence with doubt. He stirred and turned, and caught *his* scent. Took a step before that other part said, from a place he did not understand: *no, you may not kill him*. He looked up, staring, until he found the dark window, its shutters open, and the figure, barely outlined against a weak light, that stood there, looking down. Finch's scent was laced with anger and self-pity and shored up by a good nature buried under accumulated sourness. As Hawk watched, it arced with longing and cramped, depressed desire.

Hawk flushed with the heat of the course: he touched his

tongue to his lips, as if he was tasting the blood of his prey—and with a sharp yank of alien will, stopped himself again. It was not Lily that Finch was staring at.

For an instant, Hawk was amazed that he had missed her entrance onto the courtyard. Her fragrance was shot through with the brilliance of virtue and generosity and compassion, and rich with the perfume of idealism. It took him a moment to *see* her, but everyone else was staring as she came up to their tables.

She had unbound her hair. The myriad braids, beaded and hanging to her waist, were gone—vanished into a huge cloud of black hair. Like the void of space, it encompassed her entirely.

"Paisley!" It took him a moment to sort out the voice. It was Jenny. "What happened to your hair?"

Paisley brushed at her hair. "I took ya binding off," she stated in a preternaturally clear voice. "Be it came to me, min, as here in ya green grass land, ya Ridanis have no reason to bind their hair. I mean to keep it unbound, for ya reminder. Min Belsonn." She regarded him with her steady, sure gaze—much of what she was, he wished to be, but was too self-doubting to become. "I mean to go over ya way with you, whether or not ya *Hope* goes. If Jehane be not ya real Jehane, if he have no mind to bring ya Ridanis up where they mun go, then it be *my* trial to help, them come here. To ya League. For ya green grass land be here. And it be wrong o' me if I do not tell them that they can come. For they can come here, can't they?"

"Well, yes." Deucalion sounded, not uncertain, at least but surprised.

"But Paisley." Lily stood up. Hawk could smell the sudden flush of sorrow in her. "But that means you're leaving us."

Paisley's own regret echoed Lily's sadness. "Yes, min. Be i you know well enough it hurts me sore to leave you, but you will understand that I mun go, if I can."

"Yes," Lily replied, soft, "I understand. And I'll encourage min Belsonn to take you. You will take her, won't you Deucalion?"

Under such threat, Deucalion could only shrug. "Of course I still think, Lily, that you—" He hesitated under her glare. "Never mind. Whatever happens, I'll need a representative who knows Reft space."

"I think it's a shame," said Jenny.

"How can you say so, min Seria? I mun do my duty."

"No, not that. Of course you have to go. I just think it's a shame about the braids. I always thought they were so pretty."

Paisley hesitated. For the first time, Hawk scented something else about her, a bouquet that he hadn't ever been aware she possessed—vanity. "Sure, and mayhap after ya people have been sent home, mayhap then, it wouldna' be so wrong o' me to weave ya braids back in." She thought about this a moment. "For then it would be ya choice, not ya binding." As if this settled something within her, she sat down at the table next to Deucalion and launched into an interrogation of his intent and plans and methods in regard to the expedition to Reft space.

Up above, a shutter closed, and Hawk caught on the breeze the faint whiff of the salt of tears.

Jenny laughed and rose. "Care to go for a walk, Lily-hae? I don't think I need to endure this. Off to bed with you, Gregori."

"But—"

"That's an order, young man."

"I'll go up with him," said Yehoshua quickly.

"No, why don't you come with us," Jenny replied. "Gregori?"

The boy murmured agreement and left. Hawk slipped into the shadow of a line of hedge as Jenny and Lily and Yehoshua came out to the gate.

"Damn my eyes," swore Jenny. "But I should have guessed she'd take it upon herself to save the whole damn Ridani population."

"It's funny," Lily mused. "When I first met her, she told me an old Ridani story, about how they got out to Reft space and how they would be saved by Jehane. All the Ridanis thought that Alexander Jehane was *that* Jehane. But he just took the name because it served him to do so. Now I wonder if Paisley won't be the real Jehane."

"I wish her luck," said Yehoshua.

"Yes." Lily lifted her gaze to stare at the stars. "Because she's a lot like Robbie Pero. She'll need it." She paused and looked around, and Hawk felt her attention center to him again, doubt, fierce protectiveness, and troubled desire. "Where'd Hawk go? Do either of you see him?"

"No."

"No. But he can't have gone far, Lily-hae. I think Farhad has an electronic leash on him. She always seems to know where he is."

"I think I'll just check, though," Lily replied. Her doubt mingled with worry and the faintest hint of anger as she walked away from Jenny and Yehoshua.

"Where do you think he went?" Yehoshua asked.

"Who the Hells knows," Jenny replied. "I've never seen a person as changed as he is now. I don't think he can be cured."

The dark bulk of Yehoshua's shoulders moved in a shrug. "Maybe he doesn't want to be. Void knows he's gone through more than we can imagine. Dr. Farhad let a few things slip on the trip out here. Not much, but enough."

"I didn't know you felt so much sympathy for him."

"Don't you?"

Hawk could feel the warmth of her grin as a fragrance on the air. "Of course I do. I liked him too well before to give up on him now. I just—"

"You just?"

"I just wish it wasn't so hard on Lily. Can't you feel the edge in her, all the time, since he came back? Like she's not sure whether she's glad to have found him. He can't be what she expected. Not now. Hells, even now that I've gotten to trust that pack of je'jiri on the *Hope*, I'll never really feel completely comfortable around them. Did you see the way everyone stares at him? He's got to notice. He's not blind. And I know Lily does."

"What can she do? If she's mated to him—" But Yehoshua halted, as if the subject he was encroaching on now was fraught with complications. And the scent of his love for Jenny suddenly overwhelmed the common night smells.

"Which reminds me," said Jenny casually—but not casually at all. "There's something I've been meaning to ask you, Yehoshua."

"Yes?" He smelled hopeful, scared, nervous, and excited all at once.

Jenny laughed. She was sure of herself, without being disagreeable about it. "You know damn well, Yehoshua. I just can't decide whether your restraint does you credit or not."

There was a silence. A train whistle sounded in the far distance, calling as if to its mate. Yehoshua's breathing changed. Hawk took in a sharp breath, feeling what sparked between them. Yehoshua's reply was not spoken, but had it been shouted it would have been less jarring to Hawk. He slipped several steps back until he came up against the stone wall of the courtyard, the hard, cold stone pressing into his back

The two forms, Jenny and Yehoshua, molded together for a long, drawn-out space, and then, abruptly, separated.

"Did you hear something?" Jenny asked, sounding almost nervous, and then she chuckled. "I'm as jumpy as a novice," she murmured. "Maybe I can talk Paisley into taking Gregori into Dr. Farhad's room."

"Jenny . . ."

"You don't want to?"

"You know damn well—" Yehoshua broke off.

"I don't think I've ever heard you lose your temper before."

"I'm not losing my *temper*—damn it, Jenny." There was another silence. "Oh, all right," he said at last. "Go and ask Paisley. She of all people will understand."

"I suppose she will," replied Jenny. Her scent, as she walked away, Yehoshua fast at her heels, was quite smug.

The last stragglers from the pub filtered away into the night, singing some ancient tune in perfect four-part harmony. Paisley and Deucalion broke off their conversation and headed inside, but as the door shut behind them Hawk heard her begin to talk again. The exhalation of desire coming off of Jenny and Yehoshua faded, too, as they went inside. The innkeeper sang in a soft, gorgeous baritone as he wiped off the tables, and his song faltered, and then started up again, when Bach joined in. The light click of Dr. Farhad's fingers on her com-slate ran as an undertone to their singing.

The aroma of moisture on the grass, the perfume of closed flowers, the piercing sweetness of cool air, all caressed him. Out across the green, water lapped against the shore, clean and fresh. Even the stone against his back had a musty, pleasant smell that reminded him of the cool, rock shelters he had slept in with his mother on spring nights, when he was a child.

Where had she gone? He lifted his chin and tilted his head from one side to the other, scenting, and caught her trail on the tarrying end of a breeze. And went hunting.

In this place, she was an easy quarry. He cornered her by the pond, where she stood on the thin white shoreline, staring at the stars as they rippled on the wind-stirred surface. Her bouquet was mixed of constancy, quickness, and the quiet confidence of a master of the art, but underneath it, wearing away always at her being, the core of restlessness that led her never to be satisfied entirely with what she had, and what she was. Her head lifted to gaze upward at the night sky, not as dark as space, nor as brilliant with stars.

Breeze pulled at the strands of her hair. She was, not at peace, but for the moment content and yet still questioning, wondering, what she could do next. She was not thinking of him at all. Suddenly her scent changed again, and she turned.

"Kyosti." She regarded him with astonishment. Her fragrance mixed and altered and blended as he watched her, confusion and pity and fear, and desire the sweeter for being touched by wonder. "The moon," she said at last. "It's rising behind you."

He did not turn to look at it; he would far rather look at her. But some dim memory stirred within him. Like a voice heard through muffled layers of cloth, or from down a far distance, he heard words, and it sounded rather like his own voice, and yet not his voice at all. But he repeated some of the words, even though he was not sure what they meant. "'Now she shines among Lydian women as, into dark when the sun has set, the moon, pale-handed, at last appeareth.'" The pungent smell of garbage being turned out into a can distracted him, and he faltered.

"The wheel of the night," she said, her voice so low it almost seemed not to come from her at all. "The honor that patterns you. You once told me that you looked your best under the kinnas wheel." She hesitated, and he felt from her the unexpected perfume of tenderness. She took two steps closer to him and slipped her hand up to cradle the back of his neck. "I'd forgotten."

He leaned in to her and dipped his head, as was the honored custom, brushing her cheek with his so that she could mark his scent as he marked hers. Something, the movement perhaps, caused her to hang back a moment, uncertain, and then she breathed in sharply and embraced him without reservation.

From across the green, he felt Dr. Farhad sigh and get up and leave. Only Bach, the last presence left in the courtyard, remained, quiet, his metallic scent underwoven with the counterpoint of joy.

22   Taliesin

✳✳✳✳✳✳✳

ght woke her. Thin panels of brightness striped the bed and
e blankets and the long lines of Kyosti's body in an alternat-
g pattern of light and dark. She lay in bed, a little irritated
waking so early, and a little amused that, in retrospect, it
uld never have occurred to her to close the blinds, be-
use the idea of a sun rising above the horizon in the
orning was not one that came habitually to her. A pro-
ammed hour in which lights were turned up from low to
gh, signaling the beginning of the most active shift, per-
ps; it was the life she knew best.

Some time after she had fallen asleep Bach had come into
e room. Now he rose from the chair on which he had
ttled for the night and sang, softly,

> *Brich an, o schönes Morgenlicht,*
> *Und lass den Himmel tagen!*
> *Du Hirtenvolk, erschrecke nicht,*
> *Weil dir die Engel sagen,*
> *Dass dieses schwache Knäbelein*
> *Soll unser trost und Freudesein,*
> *Dazu den Satan zwingen*
> *Und letzlich Friede bringen!*

> "Break through, oh lovely light of morn,
> and let the heavens dawn!
> You shepherd folk, be not afeared,
> because the angel tells you:
> that this weak babe
> shall be our comfort and joy,
> thereto subdue the devil
> and bring peace at last."

Lily slipped out of bed and, pulling on her tunic, padded
the window, pushing aside the blinds. The shutters were

open, and she could see down into the courtyard and o
onto the green. Someone was awake before her: Paisle
staring at the sun's line as it rose above the low, stark hills.
rattle sounded from the kitchen—the innkeeper and his hel
stirring now to prepare for the day.

Lily smiled. Unfastening the window, she eased it ope
and leaned out over the casement. As if she had heard th
movement, Paisley turned and looked up and waved. Li
waved back. After a moment, she put on the rest of h
clothes and went downstairs to stand beside Paisley at th
gate, watching the sun rise. Bach followed her down. Th
said nothing for a long while, content in silence. Bach sang
muted hymn, solemn and proud.

"You don't blame me for it?" Paisley asked at last. "It I
you, min Ransome, that I be sorriest to leave. If it weren't f
you, I would never have come here, have seen such thing
to know what I mun do. What I *could* do."

"Then I'm glad I brought you, Paisley. It's a far cry fro
Unruli Station, though, isn't it?"

Paisley nodded, stricken to unusual reticence by the thoug
of just how far a cry it was.

"I'll make sure that Deucalion understands that you'
the official emissary. I don't want any misunderstandin
about that. Especially when you get back to Reft space. Y
have to make sure he understands that Reft space—th
Jehane—"

"I reckon I know what manner o' man Jehane be, min
will tell min Belsonn, as often as I may. It be up to him
believe me. Certain he'd believe you better. Be you ya f
sure you won't be coming?"

"No, we won't be. It's not the right direction for the rest
us to go in, I don't think."

"But ya service. Ya tribunal. You don't mean to be ya s
surely? What else can ya *Hope* do?"

Lily closed her hands about the cold iron of the gate. D
wet her palms. "I'm beginning to have an idea. I think it v
be too reasonable for the tribunal to refuse, and too valuab
I just need to do a little more research."

There was another bit of a silence. Then Paisley squirme
remembering that she was, after all, not yet seventeen. "I
min, what *be* it?" she demanded.

Lily chuckled. "What was the *Forlorn Hope* origina
meant for, Paisley?"

Paisley looked at her, mystified. "It be ya highroad ship, ain. Ya exploratory—" She broke off.

"Ya exploratory ship," Lily finished for her. "Exactly."

Behind, the innkeeper emerged from the kitchen. "Ah, ou're up betimes, are you? Will you be having something ot to drink, café perhaps, or cocoa?" While he served them, e sang as well, a simple melody that Bach harmonized.

Later, the others came down, some separately, like Gregori, ad some, Lily noted with interest, together.

"Good morning, Jenny. Yehoshua." She regarded them eculatively. Yehoshua flushed and went to sit down with *cucalion at a different table. Jenny merely grinned and ased herself into the seat next to Lily. "You look pleased ith yourself."

"Quite pleased," replied Jenny, and ordered her breakfast.

Kyosti emerged from the inn, cast about, and focused on ily. Dr. Farhad came out directly behind him, but she let m sit down at the table with Lily and Paisley and Jenny and ent herself to sit next to the others. Kyosti, sitting, looked a tle puzzled, and the edge on him, the clean, alien presence ε had possessed so strongly, seemed blurred, like a picture, audging, that is seen to conceal something else underneath. e glanced at Jenny, and at Paisley, and narrowed his eyes, oking puzzled, as if he was trying to figure something out out them.

"Good morning, Hawk," said Jenny, curious.

"Good morning," he said without a trace of accent, and osed back into perplexed silence.

"Do you want us to come up with you today?" Jenny asked ly, to cover the uneasy quiet that settled around the ole.

"No. I think just Bach and I and Deucalion." She hesitated. nd Hawk."

"And Dr. Farhad?" Jenny asked, jesting slightly.

"No." Lily examined Kyosti intently. His attention, surpris- ;ly, had wandered from her, and he was looking around the urtyard as if he was trying to remember where he was. "I n't think Dr. Farhad, this time."

After their meal, and the innkeeper's directions—he apolo- ed that there were no vehicles heading up that road this y—Lily found herself walking along a wide dirt path with ucalion beside her, Bach at her shoulder, and Kyosti iling behind. The day was fair and fine, or so she deduced

from the warmth of the air and the clear sky. Deucalion wa
too quiet—too tense—to notice. The aria Bach sang had
light, playful melody that made the long climb easy, if on
walked in step. They passed no traffic, although once in th
distance she heard the sounds of animals and saw white back
heading up another slope, a darker beast at their heels. .
slight figure, a boy, perhaps, lagged behind, stick in on
hand, a small brown carry slung over the opposite shoulde
He saw them and waved, and though she was too distant t
make out his face, she waved back, and Deucalion, too polit
to be entirely abstracted, waved as well.

This brief human contact cheered her. A few trees decorate
the slopes, but mostly it was grass and the occasional crooke
line of tumbled stone wall. The road narrowed and branche
and true to the innkeeper's directions they headed rigl
down a defile, and came around an outcropping of stone in
a tiny nook of a valley at the base of which lay a cottage
Smoke rose from its chimney. The whole scene looked s
utterly primitive to Lily that at first she did not realize that
was a dwelling. But as they neared, a small brown anim
rushed out of the building, making the most horrendou
noise, and a figure appeared in the doorway.

She would have recognized his posture anywhere, even
such a range.

"Gwennie. Gwennie, *fach*. Come, girl." His voice, witho
precisely shouting, carried the distance easily.

The beating of her heart quickened, and she felt her brea
grow shallow and fast, as if she were climbing to some gre
height far too swiftly. Deucalion became, if anything, mo
silent. Bach ceased singing.

The animal turned tail and trotted back to the cottage
stand beside the man in the doorway. He simply watched
they neared, not moving, and yet Lily knew that he wou
recognize her as easily as she recognized him. Soon she cou
see his face: he looked older, without looking aged, and the
were a few streaks of silver in his brown hair. His face w
composed—far more composed than hers, she imagine
because a grin kept trying to break out onto her lips, and s
kept forcing it back, trying to keep with the dignity of t
situation and the quiet serenity of the valley. Perhaps he h
left such ties behind, preferring, after everything, to start
life utterly anew. She felt a sudden misgiving. She should r
have come.

At two meters she halted, and he looked at each of them in turn, that steady, calm gaze that she knew and loved so well.

"Well, Lily," he said, in exactly the same tone he had always used at the academy. Then he did smile, and she let out the breath she had forgotten she was holding. "It's good to see you." He came forward, and they embraced. After a moment, he stepped back and turned to regard his son. "Well, Deucalion," he said in exactly the tone she recalled from the academy—the one he reserved for those students he thought ought to be doing better. "It's been a long time."

"Yes," said Deucalion. Neither of them moved toward each other.

Heredes—Taliesin, she corrected herself—switched his gaze to Hawk, and for what was surely the only time since she had known him, she thought he looked uncomfortable. "But, Lilyaka, who is this? I didn't know you were traveling with je'jiri—" He sounded almost disapproving, and then he faltered, and blinked. "Hawk?"

Kyosti was examining the covered pens behind the cottage, which were dank with the odor of some animal that had but recently left them. He did not respond to Heredes's question, or even appear to have heard it, or realize that it was meant for him.

"He's been—ill," said Lily.

"So I see." Heredes regarded him a moment longer, his expression unreadable, and then waved toward the door. "Will you come in?"

"I'll wait outside," said Deucalion quickly. A look passed between the two men that was to Lily unfathomable.

"As you wish," replied Heredes, quite reserved. "What about Hawk?" he asked Lily.

"Who knows? We'll just have to see." Heredes turned, and she followed him inside, Bach trailing behind her. Despite her expectations, the interior was neat and clean and well lit by its four windows. It boasted only a bed, a table and chair, and a portable cookery. A white, flat, thin substance she did not recognize littered the table, and she went across and touched it. She stared at it a moment before she realized that the markings on it were writing—words. "What is this?"

He laughed. "That's paper. I see you still have your composer."

"Oh, yes." She turned back to him and grinned. "I could scarcely do without him."

Patroness, Bach sang, in a sharp key, *I was not aware that the lack of my presence wast something thou considered*.

"It isn't, Bach. It is something I devoutly wish will never come to pass."

His cadence, in reply, was brief, but ascending.

"Tea?" Heredes asked.

"Yes." She paced the room, measuring it out as she had measured cells on that long journey to find him.

He chuckled finally, watching her from his station at the cookery. "You may sit down, if you wish."

But she didn't sit. She halted in the middle of the room and stared at him, shaking her head. "I thought you were dead."

He blinked. "Didn't I tell you once, that it's terribly—"

"—boring being dead?" she finished for him, and they both laughed. She sat down. He put a kettle on the cookery burner. "What are you doing?"

"Ah, but here, Lily, one does not make tea in any fashion but the traditional way. It would be heresy. This will take a few minutes." He crossed to sit on the bed. "Actually," he said after a pause, "it *was* rather dull. Evidently I was in a coma. I had a bullet in my brain. It's a very lowering thought, when one comes to know of it."

"When did you find out?"

"Much later. I was on Bella's ship by that time, under the very best medical care, but it was still a difficult recovery."

"You ought to have been dead."

"Yes, I suppose I ought to have been. But I've always hated doing what other people expect of me."

"Is that why you came here?"

He considered the question gravely. "No. Perhaps, in the end, this was the likeliest place for me to have gone to ground."

"Concord Intelligence is looking for you, you know."

He smiled, wry. "They're looking for all of us, all that are left. They don't know to leave well enough alone. We won't trouble them."

"They think you will. *I've* had trouble enough."

He shook his head. On the cookery, the kettle began to whistle, and Bach, not to be outdone, added a harmoni pitch. Heredes rose. "That's a feint if I've ever seen one. I'll take it. How *did* you come to be here, Lilyaka?"

So, while he poured the hot water into a pot and out again, and then filled it up over a scattering of dried leaves, and after a bit poured the contents of the pot into ceramic mugs, she told him.

"Well," he said when she had finished. He took a sip of his tea, got up, and poured them both a second mugful. "Well, Lily." Just that. Then he nodded, and Lily knew, at that moment, that she would never receive a greater compliment. They sat in mutual, easy silence while she savored it.

A dark form appeared in the open door, tall and slender, head tilting once from side to side. "Lily?" it said.

Heredes shifted on the bed.

"Come in, Kyosti," Lily said. He entered, pausing to scent again, and then moved with a predator's grace across to Lily and sank down to sit at her feet. He looked at Heredes, unblinking, and then up at Lily. Heredes gave a slight cough. For a fleeting instant, Lily had the insane thought that he was nervous, but she dismissed it. "What have you been doing here?" she asked him. "Are you going to stay? The innkeeper said you were waiting for a lease."

"For the time, yes, I think I'll stay. After I came out of the coma, I began hearing words, so like any good Welshman, I returned home to discover whether I was mad or a poet, since I wasn't dead."

The confession took her rather by surprise, and yet, she realized, he was really no different from the Heredes she had known before. "Which is it?" she asked.

The answer came from an unexpected source. "'Never was there in Gwyddno's weir, anything as good as tonight.'"

Heredes laughed. "Welcome back, Hawk. Although I will confess to you, Lily, that I'm still not sure. But I have a good deal of time to discover which it is. 'There is a fine fortress on the shore of the sea. Graciously there his desire is granted to everyone.'" He paused. "As well, I'm still struggling to remember the language. It's been a very long time since I spoke it last."

"Which language?"

"The one spoken here. And the one spoken by poets. But you've told me what has happened to you. You haven't yet told me what you intend. As much as I hesitate to give advice"—he hesitated—"I don't recommend taking up their offer. It's bad enough to have enemies, but to consciously choose a course of action that will create them for you is, to my mind, a little foolish."

"No, I don't intend to become a spy in The Pale. In fact, I just thought of something last night." She glanced down at Kyosti, flushed a little, and looked up again. "I was out on the village green, looking up at the stars. They seem different, seeing them from the surface of a world, than being surrounded by them. Less accessible and more desirable. On the ship, they're just part of you. I suppose you take them for granted, just like we took the high weather for granted on Unruli, or you take the hills and grass and clean air for granted here. But it made me think: the *Forlorn Hope* was built to be an exploratory vessel. Why not recommission it? With its current crew and whatever specialists and additional crew it needs. We've the experience of running the road from the Reft to League space—with a pilot and navigator, and Bach, able to calculate to the finest edge and run the way without beacons or stations to guide us. We're all of us more used to space—or at least to enclosed spaces—than planets. And those that aren't," she spared a glance for Kyosti here, "have other compelling reasons to take such a course. The League must need to keep pushing outward, if not in the direction of The Pale, then toward the Reft, or in some other quadrant."

"Well, it's not me you have to convince. It's this tribunal. And I doubt if they'll take my testimony as a good recommendation."

"No, I doubt if they would. Which reminds me, what do you know about Korey Windsor and his two Ardakians?"

"I'm glad to hear they're still with him, if only because he needs the companionship. He was a hell-raiser, Korey, back when I knew him. He always drank too much and ran right on the edge in all his operations. He got shot up badly twice. Barely lived. But I would trust him at my back." As he said this, he looked at Hawk, and looked, if anything, guilty.

"That's high praise, from you."

Heredes met her gaze. "Lily, for me, after what I've seen and what I've done, that is the single quality on which I judge a person. Trust them not to stab me, and trust them to hold their own in a fight. Anything else is inconsequential."

His expression was serious in a way she had never seen it before, and she realized that he was speaking to her as to a peer, judging that she was fit to receive and understand such information. "I wonder if I really knew you, before," she said softly.

"You knew me well enough. You learned enough from me, Lily, that I can safely say that you learned to find your own way. That is the greatest gift a student can give a teacher: to return at last to them as an equal."

They talked on, into the afternoon, talked about his childhood and about his life as an actor, discussed strategies for recommissioning the *Forlorn Hope*, laughed at Lily's description of the effect Pinto had on the female population of the ship. Heredes even spoke, briefly and with great reticence, of La Belle. Kyosti sat uncannily silent at Lily's feet. He scarcely moved the entire time. The dog lay panting on the hearth, watching them with dark eyes and dozing off now and then.

When she rose, finally, knowing that she had to return both to the inn and then on to Concord, she felt both regret and pleasure—regret for leaving after so short a time, and pleasure at knowing that he would be here, even if it was years before she could return. They went outside. Deucalion sat on the fence surrounding the pens, but he clambered down when he saw them and walked over. Lily embraced Heredes again, and they traded words of farewell, and then she turned to go.

"Are you coming, Deucalion?"

He hesitated, glancing at his father. "No. I'll be down in a while."

Seeing that there was other business to complete, Lily whistled to Bach and, Kyosti beside her, they left. When she looked back, from the last turning in the path where she could still see the cottage, neither of the men had yet moved.

It was night before Deucalion showed up at the inn. Lily had forsaken the tables in the courtyard to stand out at the gate, pleased to be alone in her own company, but she moved to one side to make room for him when he came up beside her. Because he said nothing, at first, she said nothing. It was another brilliant, clear night, the moon high and curved, attended by stars. In the courtyard behind, the evening crowd laughed and talked, a buzz of words in strange accents and strange languages. Hawk was content to sit with Jenny and Yehoshua and Paisley and Bach at one of the tables, Dr. Farhad watching him from an adjacent table where she sat with the advocate and Gregori. Gregori had taken a liking to the advocate, who patiently explained in painstaking detail the answers to his incessant questions. Finch had finally emerged from his room, and although he sat beside Dr. Farhad, he did not speak, but kept glancing at the other table and looking away as quickly.

"So you mean to try for the recommissioning," said Deucalion abruptly into their silence.

"Yes. Do you think it will work?"

He looked a little pale, or perhaps tired by the long walk. But he managed a smile. "Between us, and with Havel's help, I think we can pull if off. Havel is very sharp." His mouth twisted a little, as if something pained him. "She's a throwback, like we are. She's happy to twist the system to her advantage, without any scruples at all."

"Deucalion." She faltered, hearing some old pain in his tone that she did not want to enflame. "You have scruples."

"I have what scruples I choose to have," he said bitterly. "As has been clearly pointed out to me."

That he was speaking of his father was obvious to her. "I'm sorry," she replied.

He shrugged, but the effort to appear casual failed. "We made peace, of a kind." He did not speak for a long while, but finally he sighed, and it was a more hopeful sound. "We made something to build on," he finished. "Then we'll be heading back to London tomorrow? We'll need to send notice to the yacht skipper that we'll leave tomorrow night or the next morning, so he can put in for a launch schedule."

"No." Lily leaned against the gate and smiled, to herself since Deucalion had turned his head enough away that she could no longer see his expression. "I made a promise, before we landed on Terra. I have one more place to visit."

Now he turned. "But Lily, none of your people have ever been on Terra before. Where could they want to visit?"

She turned back to look into the lit courtyard, at Jenny and Yehoshua, sitting rather closer together than friends might; a Paisley, who was diligently attempting to draw intelligible speech out of Hawk; at Gregori, intent on the com-slate that the advocate was pointing to; even at Finch, who looked up at her as she stared and ventured the faintest hint of a smile.

And at the smooth, metal-bright globe hovering watchfully, faithfully, loyally, behind Kyosti.

"I promised Bach," she said. "I promised I would take him to a place called"—she had to hesitate to recall the unfamiliar sound—"Leipzig."

23 Highroad

****

Gregori twisted his glass around and around in his hands, growing bored. Six months at Concord had been long enough to wait, and now this final evening seemed interminable. He wondered if throwing the glass at min Belsonn would make him stop lecturing long enough for someone else to talk, but he supposed that it would only turn the topic of the lecture to childish misbehavior, a subject he was sure that someone of min Belsonn's personality could know little about, but have lengthy opinions on.

"And furthermore," continued Deucalion, "not only did Maria not appear for the hearing scheduled to discuss our charges, but evidently she has left Concord altogether. Evidently she has chosen not only to betray the trust invested in all of us as citizens and governors of the League, but to escape from her responsibilities as well, as if that absolves her. She's no better—she's far, far worse—than the people she wants to eliminate. Yevgeny just received information that traces her to Diomede. It is supposed that she has gone on into The Pale, from which we can all devoutly hope she will not return." He paused for breath, looking outraged, and the captain calmly handed a bowl of vegetables to him and spoke before he could continue.

"From my few encounters with her, I imagine she'll get along just fine there." She grinned. "Maybe she'll join up with La Belle."

"La Belle would never have her," he replied, sounding affronted, and lapsed into silence.

Gregori was profoundly grateful. For some reason, he could not concentrate when min Belsonn was off on one of his speeches. The conversation drifted to other, more desultory things: Blue deciding to accept an apprenticeship at Karkar: Engineering Academy rather than work with the new Chie: Engineer assigned to the *Forlorn Hope* by the council over seeing Exploratory expeditions; Paisley moving her few pos sessions to the block where the members of the Reft expedition were gathering in preparation for their journey; the medical specialist who had examined Yehoshua's artificial arm and pronounced that not only did it have augmented strength but a full range of software add-ons, like tracking and a computer linkup and enhanced tactile perception, that Yehoshua had never suspected existed, much less learned to use.

Gregori let the conversation flow past him, only partly aware of it. He was just happy to be back on the ship, sitting in the mess, eating, all the tables filled with old crew and new crew mixed together as they settled in at last. He felt like he was home again.

Six months in dry dock had not improved Gregori's impression of station life—or any life but that aboard a ship. While the *Forlorn Hope* was refitted, he had been forced to live in quarters more spacious, by the meter, than his mother's cabin on the *Hope* but made cramped by Yehoshua's constant presence and the knowledge that, just outside the door, hordes of station personnel and constant vehicle traffic surged and rumbled past at all hours.

They had introduced him to a play and education group, consisting of twelve children about his age, and he felt he tolerated this arrangement fairly well, all things considered. A few of the children were even interesting, and he was not entirely sorry to hear that five of the twelve would be boarding with their parents when the *Hope* cast off.

There was a stir around the table as Paisley came in, and a space was made for her to sit next to the captain. Gregori yawned. A few minutes later, Dr. Farhad walked up, and this time his mother moved aside to let the doctor sit down between her and Gregori. Gregori watched Dr. Farhad sit down, caught between apprehension and interest.

"Dr. Farhad!" said the captain from down the table. "What news for us?"

Dr. Farhad accepted a glass of beer from Jenny and took a sip before she answered. "The transfer has been completed. My position has been neatly divided between that of parole adviser for Hawk, and Chief of Xenopsychiatry. There were others equally qualified for the xeno position, but I fear I rather pulled strings and emphasized the illegal and unethical treatment Hawk received during his prison sentence in order to get myself appointed. There hasn't been a newly commissioned exploratory vessel for some years and a number of

people have been eager to get on. To be frank, Captain, I've
been wishing for some time to get my hands back in to
practice xeno work. And with a je'jiri family officially bonded
to you, I've got plenty of work before we even get out of
port."

"I'm glad you're aboard," said the captain, and Gregori
knew she was being sincere.

"What about you, Gregori?" Gregori fastened his hands
tight around his glass and ventured a glance up at Dr.
Farhad. The doctor's gaze was too piercing for his liking. "Are
you glad to be back on board?"

"Yes."

"Tell me," she said, and she lifted one hand so that for an
instant he had a terrible fear that she was about to touch his
hair—but she lowered it again, "in one of our talks do you
remember telling me about the other people on the ship—
the ones nobody else can see?"

"You can't *see* them," said Gregori, a little impatient that
she had not grasped this point. "At least, not really. And
anyway, the je'jiri know they're here. So does Hawk."

"Well, then," Dr. Farhad replied, switching her ground
smoothly, "the ones no other human can tell are here."

"What about them?"

"Are they still here?"

Gregori blinked. Then he sat back and concentrated, not
on the conversation and the bodies and the general atmosphere of enthusiasm and anticipation coloring the air, but on
the presences that existed farther back, a whisper, or a faint
haze, against the backdrop of life. Grumpy walked past,
headed out the door on the trail of some kind of practical
joke. Fearful left an argument to return, as ever, to the Green
Room. And the Other Captain, her presence, as he focused
on her, almost as sharp as if she actually was standing there,
paused in the doorway to survey her crew as they supped.

"Yes," he said. "They're still here. I think they'll always be,
don't you?"

Not it was Dr. Farhad's turn to blink. "I don't know the
answer to that question, Gregori. I'm still trying to find out
why you do."

"Oh. Why do I?"

"I think it has something to do with the color of your hair,
but"—she paused as a plate full of food was handed to her by

enny—"we'll have time enough to discover what we can
about that."

"My father had hair the very same color," Gregori offered.
"And I bet," he said, because the thought had just occurred to
him, "that he would have known about the other people, too."

"I'll bet he would," agreed Dr. Farhad.

"I think he knew how people felt, more than most people
do," Gregori confided. "And he could use it. It's how he got
people to do what he wanted. It's why Lia left."

"Are you still sorry about that?"

Gregori risked a glance at Yehoshua, who sat directly across
the table from him and was, as usual, trying, but failing, not
to stare stupidly at Jenny as she laughed. "I used to be," he
said, "but I'm not so sure I am any more. Anyway, she
wouldn't have wanted to be on an exploratory vessel." He
said the last two words with great relish.

Dr. Farhad smiled. "And you are?"

"Oh, yes!"

Smile still on her lips, she turned away to set to work on
her food.

—Yevgeny's still angry about being outmaneuvered,"
Deucalion was saying, "but he's good-natured about it as
well. He said he oughtn't to have tried outflanking people of
our experience."

The captain chuckled. "Is that how he phrased it? *Our
experience?* That was very tactful of him."

"Oh, Yevgeny is a master of tact. He spent some years in
the Diplomatic Corps, you know, before he went into Intelligence. Once he knew that the majority on the tribunal would
support our request, you must admit he did everything he
could to support it, and push it through."

"He likes you, Deucalion. I can't imagine why."

Deucalion grinned. "He keeps hoping he'll reform me. I
still don't know why he thinks I need reforming."

"Because," said the captain firmly, but with humor, "you
can't escape your upbringing. Just think," and she surveyed
the table at large, "I went to all that trouble to escape the
confines of Ransome House, and here I am, consigning
myself to a ship that's far smaller and far more confining."

"But min Ransome," objected Paisley, "it be far less confining. You can go ya anywhere you please. Pretty much."

"It's true," admitted the captain, "that the horizons are less
limited."

"Ransome."

The captain turned at the sound of her name. Eyes widening, she stood up. "Windsor! Fred. Stanford. How did you get on?" Then she laughed, waving them forward to seats that the others at the table moved to make free. "Never mind. I'm not sure I want to know. I'm surprised to see you here. I didn't think you would remain on Concord."

Windsor grinned. He still looked scruffy, but the color in his face was healthy and his smile, cheerfully sly.

"Got a job," Fred said. He grinned as well.

Stanford detached his slate from his shoulder harness and set it down on the table. "You can see the specifications here." He slid it forward so that the captain could examine it.

She studied the screen for a moment and then shook her head. "What is this?"

Windsor coughed. "After you left for Terra, secrets intact, that woman from Administration—the Sirin, Qaetana—hired us as consultants to reconfigure the security system at Concord prison."

"No." The captain, and then Jenny, and then Yehoshua started to laugh.

"Do you mean to say," demanded Yehoshua, "that they never found out who actually sprang Hawk?"

"Don't know," confessed Fred. "We never asked. Pay was too good."

"And it was certainly not information that we would spontaneously reveal," added Stanford primly.

Several people broke out talking at once, and Gregori, who had been dislodged from his chair by their arrival, decided to reacquaint himself with the ship instead. He wandered out of the mess, nodding at the Mule and Pinto where they sat with their new pilot and navigational compatriots, at Rainbow with the brilliant Ridani contingent, at two of the children from his play group, and finally got out the door into blessed solitude.

Only it was not quite solitude. Despite the many people crowded into the mess, as many were at duty stations, busy with the last preparations for casting off the next day. He dodged carts and crew on his way down to bronze level where he fled into the comparative quiet of the remodeled je'jiri quarters.

The Dai welcomed him with a brief nod, and he was allowed to sit in on a one-hour lesson in three-dimensional modeling with the children. After that, as he understood, he

vas no longer welcome to stay, since there were other needs
hat the je'jiri did not share with aliens, so he left and
meandered along the corridors, aimless. He skirted the Green
Room and took an elevator to silver deck, strolled the crew
abins, pausing now and again to read the unfamiliar names
ppended to the doors of each one. All were filled. Halted,
earing the captain's voice through an open door.

"You want to *what*?" She sounded incredulous.

Finch's voice, replying, was stiff, but it held an undercur-
ent of pleading in it. "I want your permission to attach
ayself to the expedition that is returning to Reft space. If
hat's possible."

"You don't need my permission, Finch. I'm just surprised
hat you want to go."

"I haven't been that happy here. You know that."

"That's true enough. I'm sorry that I haven't had more time
) spend with you . . ."

"It's nothing to do with you, Lily," he said quickly. "I know
ve been maybe a little hard to get along with, or haven't
ied to make friends like I could have."

"And you certainly have been hard on the Ridanis. Espe-
ially Paisley. You'll be the only other one of us going back,
inch. I just hope you'll be kinder to her than you have been.
's not been easy for her to leave. Will you promise me that?
lease?" Her voice was almost gentle.

His silence stretched out so long that it was a confession in
self.

"Damn my eyes," murmured the captain. "No. Finch.
he's why you're going back, isn't she?" Gregori decided he
ad been wrong in thinking her incredulous before, because
was nothing to the astonishment in her voice now.

"We all make mistakes," Finch mumbled.

Gregori felt a presence come up behind him, and he
hirled, expecting to see a shadow, or a faint haze in the air.
ut it was only Paisley. She put a hand on his hair, a liberty
e would have allowed no one else but his mother, and
aited along with him. Neither of them could see inside
inch's room.

"If that's going to be your attitude, Finch," the captain
apped, "then I think you'd better not go."

"No," he said fiercely. "You misunderstand me. I guess I
eserved as much. I *meant*—we all make mistakes when we
y to convince ourselves that we can't"—he hesitated, and

then plunged on—"that we can't love someone who we think
we ought to despise or hate, or fear, because of *what* they
are. Not *who* they are. Yes, I'm going back because of Paisley.
I thought I ought to try to make it up to her, the way I've
treated her, and the other Ridanis, by helping her now. I only
realized—when I found out she was leaving. That's when I
thought, how would I feel if I never saw her again."

There was a pause. "I do understand, Finch," said Lily
softly. "Only too well. But I think you ought to ask Paisley
first."

Paisley drew her hand down off Gregori's hand and slipped
past him, disappearing inside the room. There was a longer
silence. Then, Paisley's voice, softer even than the captain's:
"I don't want ya man, Finch, if that be what you're meaning.
I mean to bring ya Ridanis to ya green grass land, and if you
will help me—well then, you'll be beside me, won't you?"

"Yes," said Finch, so muffled that his assent was barely
audible.

A moment later the captain emerged out into the corridor
looking thoughtful. "Well, hello, Gregori," she said, seeing
him. "Looking for someone?"

"No." He waited, expectant.

"Would you like to come with me to Medical?"

He nodded eagerly and followed along with her, acknowledging the people they passed with an air of importance
secured him by the captain's company. She did not speak,
and when they entered Medical she stopped inside the door
and simply watched for a long while.

Flower was putting the scan on one of the new beds
through its paces, and she looked up and nodded, seeing the
captain. The other physician was half-hidden in one of the
isolation rooms, on her hands and knees as she fiddled with
the controls under a console. But it was Hawk that the
captain watched.

First his form standing at a counter in the lab: he opened
each drawer and took out each tool, each piece of equipment,
handled it, smelled it, and set it back in precise order. Then
he moved to the next counter and repeated the procedure.
Gregori could tell by the way his posture had changed when
they had come in that Hawk knew that the captain was there,
but what he was doing engaged his attention more surely, at
this moment, than she did.

The captain was smiling, equal parts mixed of sadness and

lief and pleasure. Finally, Hawk ventured out onto the
ain ward and he crossed slowly to them, touching each bed
 he passed, pausing at each scan and running his fingers
cross it, as if he could feel in the grain of its plass and
etal exterior the health of its mechanisms inside. To Gregori,
e still looked more je'jiri than human, so much so that
regori would have said, had he not been told by his mother
hat had happened, that this was a different person entirely.

Except when Hawk glanced up at the captain at last,
oming close enough that they could see clearly into each
her's faces. Then he was Hawk, in his eyes, at least. He
opped in front of the captain and turned his head to look at
lower, at the other physician, at Gregori, and back at Lily.

He said something in je'jirin first, then consciously stopped
mself and concentrated. He began to speak, gave up, and
ut his eyes. Lily waited, patient. Flower drifted into the
b, leaving them in peace. Hawk opened his eyes suddenly.
When I count,'" he said in the clipped-accent Standard
at was similar to the Dai's, "'there are only you and I
gether. But when I look ahead up the white road, There is
ways another one walking beside you.'"

"That's you, Kyosti," said the captain quietly. "Both of you
e still here. You just have to put them together."

Hawk's expression did not change, but he seemed to be
nsidering her words as if they might possibly have made
nse to him. The captain sighed, but she did not give up.
how me the new equipment," she said.

Now he clearly understood her, and with the muted voice
at Gregori recognized as je'jiri enthusiasm, he led them on
our of Medical's refit. He had not lost any of his facility as a
octor, whatever else he had suffered. When, after a while,
e door to Medical shunted aside and Dr. Farhad joined
em, Gregori slipped out and roamed further on and up,
ding himself at last on the bridge.

Trey and a number of unfamiliar faces were on duty,
nning the ship through her final checks. He curled up in
e one out-of-the-way corner and, lulled by the smooth flow
their voices counting off stats and measures, he fell asleep.

Woke. A little disoriented at first, groping up, because
meone had thrown a blanket over him but otherwise let
n lie. Still there were voices, almost twin to the ones he
d fallen asleep to, but more of these were familiar.

"We have clearance from traffic control," said Trey.

"Rolling back hold two," said Yehoshua. "I have a secure o
hatch one. Hatch two secured. Hatch three secured."

"I have received preliminary vector coordinates," hisse
the Mule.

"Hatch four secured. Hold one and hold three are level.

Gregori sat up. From his vantage point, he could see th
captain's profile clearly. Bach hovered at her elbow, h
surface gleaming in the hard light of the bridge.

Com crackled. "All hands secured," said Jenny over th
click and pop of the speaker.

"Hatch five secured," said Yehoshua. "All hatches and hol
are worthy, Captain."

Lily keyed in to her console. "Traffic control, this is Ca
tain Ransome of the *Forlorn Hope*. We are ready to detach.

"Detach acknowledged," responded the disembodied voi
of traffic control. "Good luck, *Hope*."

"Thank you," said the captain, and she smiled. "Pinto?"

"Detach commenced," said Pinto. He adjusted the stillstr
a final time and looked over at the Mule. The Mule looke
back, and its crest lifted as it hissed in approval.

"Did I ever tell you the story," began Yehoshua to th
bridge at large, "about how my grand-pap got caught inside
mining remote that was pulled into a window by the wake
a big military cruiser?"

"Why, no," replied the captain solemnly, "I don't thi
we've heard that one, Yehoshua."

The ship jarred slightly. "Detach accomplished," said Pi
to. "We are free."

The door to the bridge slipped aside and Hawk appeare
He took two steps onto the bridge and halted. Lily turne
saw him, and nodded. He came up to stand just behind h
hand resting on the back of her chair.

"Commence countdown to window," the captain ordere

"Three forty seven," said the Mule. "Three forty eigh
Homing at fourteen ought three two seven degrees."

"Check," said Pinto.

Bach began to sing:

> *Ich will dich mit Fleiss bewahren,*
> *Ich will dir*
> *Leben hier,*
> *Dir will ich abfahren.*

Mit dir will ich endlich schweben
Voller Freud
Ohne Zeit
Dort im andern Leben.

"I will keep Thee diligently in my mind,
I will live
for Thee here,
I will depart with Thee hence.
With Thee will I soar at last,
filled with joy
time without end,
there in the other life."

On the screen above, the vast superstructure of Concord receded and dropped out of view as they turned, appearing again on the back screen while the front filled with the measureless shore of stars.

ABOUT THE AUTHOR

Alis Rasmussen was born in Iowa and grew up in Oregon. She graduated from Mills College, in California, having spent her junior year abroad studying at the University of Wales. She is currently living in San Jose, California, with her husband, three children, and two newts. She has a brown belt in Shotokan karate and occasionally practices broadsword fighting in the Society for Creative Anachronism. In addition to the *Highroad* trilogy, she is the author of a fantasy novel, *The Labyrinth Gate*, and is at present at work on a new novel.

•

THE MUTANT SEASON

by
Karen Haber
and
Robert Silverberg

•

They have lived among us for centuries, shielding themselves from bigotry, hatred and intolerance with their extraordinary psychic abilities. Now they have emerged into the light of daily living, seeking the freedom they've been so long denied. . . .

But the first mutant senator, Eleanor Jacobsen, has been savagely murdered. Finding her assassin has become the obsession of one courageous group of mutants, all torn by the rivalries that threaten to tear the clan apart. As society faces the explosive implications of radical evolution, the mutants must find a way to protect their identities, their lovers—and their very lives.

•

•